495

THE WORLD'S CLASSICS

A JOURNEY FROM THIS WORLD TO THE NEXT

AND

THE JOURNAL OF A VOYAGE TO LISBON

HENRY FIELDING, best known for his novels *Joseph Andrews* (1742), *Tom Jones* (1749), and *Amelia* (1751), was born at Sharpham Park in Somerset in 1707. He was educated at Eton, and, after studying classics at Leyden, came to London, where he supported himself by writing comedies and political satires for the stage. These attacks on the government helped to bring about the Licensing Act of 1737, which put an end to his dramatic career; he promptly took up the study of law, and was called to the Bar in 1740. In 1734 he had married Charlotte Craddock, who provided the model for Sophia Western in *Tom Jones*. Charlotte died in 1744 and in 1747 Fielding married her maid, Mary Daniel. From 1739 to 1741 he ran the *Champion*, intermittently continuing his political journalism with several more papers in the 1740s. In 1748 he was made Justice of the Peace for Westminster, and in 1750 he organized the 'Bow Street Runners', London's first organized police force. He travelled to Portugal in 1754 to recover his failing health, but died near Lisbon that same year.

IAN A. BELL is Professor and Head of the Department of English Language and Literature at the University of Wales Swansea. He is the author of *Henry Fielding: Authorship and Authority* (1994), *Literature and Crime in Augustan England* (1991), *Defoe's Fiction* (1985), and numerous articles on eighteenth-century writing, crime fiction, and Scottish literature.

ANDREW VARNEY teaches English in the University of Wales Swansea. The author of articles on most major writers in the period from Milton to Johnson, he is currently preparing a study of eighteenth-century writers in their cultural context.

THE WORLD'S CLASSICS

HENRY FIELDING

A Journey from This World to the Next

AND

The Journal of a Voyage to Lisbon

Edited with an Introduction and Notes by

IAN A. BELL and ANDREW VARNEY

Oxford New York
OXFORD UNIVERSITY PRESS
1997

Oxford University Press, Great Clarendon Street, Oxford OX2 6DP

Oxford New York
Athens Auckland Bangkok Bogota Bombay Buenos Aires
Calcutta Cape Town Dar es Salaam Delhi Florence Hong Kong
Istanbul Karachi Kuala Lumpur Madras Madrid Melbourne
Mexico City Nairobi Paris Singapore Taipei Tokyo Toronto
and associated companies in
Berlin Ibadan

Oxford is a trade mark of Oxford University Press

First published as a World's Classics paperback 1997

British Library Cataloguing in Publication Data
Data available

Library of Congress Cataloging-in-Publication Data
Fielding, Henry, 1707–1754.
[Journey from this world to the next]
A journey from this world to the next; The journal of a voyage to Lisbon / Henry Fielding ; edited with an introduction and notes by Ian A. Bell and Andrew Varney.
(The World's classics)
I. Bell, Ian A. II. Varney, Andrew. III. Fielding, Henry, 1707–1754. Journal of a voyage to Lisbon. IV. Title. V. Title: Journal of a voyage to Lisbon. VI. Series.
PR3452.B45 1997 823'.5—dc20 96–32012
ISBN 0–19–282334–5 (pbk.)

1 3 5 7 9 10 8 6 4 2

Typeset by Graphicraft Typesetters Ltd., Hong Kong
Printed in Great Britain by
BPC Paperbacks Ltd.
Aylesbury, Bucks.

CONTENTS

INTRODUCTION

Thus, gentle Reader, I have given thee a faithful History of my Travels for Sixteen Years, and above Seven Months; wherein I have not been so studious of Ornament as of Truth. I could perhaps have astonished thee with strange improbable Tales; but I rather chose to relate plain Matter of Fact in the simplest Manner and Style; because my principal Design was to inform, and not to amuse thee.

This is how Swift has Gulliver begin his farewell to his reader in the last chapter of *Gulliver's Travels* (1726). The full irony of the passage is only available if we know that the early decades of the eighteenth century in Britain saw a tremendous vogue for accounts of voyages and journeys. Some were factual, like the voyage accounts of Captain William Dampier at the beginning of the century. Others were invented, and, like *Gulliver's Travels*, very often satirical. Still others, like Defoe's account of *The Life, Adventures and Piracies of the Famous Captain Singleton* (1720), blended extravagant invention with remarkable fact almost inextricably. The result is that in the first half of the eighteenth century the voyage account was a highly self-conscious literary form, and that every voyage narrative was in some degree an intertext of every other one.

The present volume brings together two voyage narratives by Fielding. Although his most famous novels, *Joseph Andrews* and *Tom Jones*, have plots that centre on journeys, they are not properly travel accounts as the interest is in the personal stories rather than in the travelling itself. By contrast, *A Journey from this World to the Next* and *The Journal of a Voyage to Lisbon* do both belong to the travel tradition, the first to that phase of it which is invented and satirical, the second to the tradition that narrates actual journeys. Both texts show Fielding standing in an ironic, or at the very least quizzical, relation to the genre in which he is practising. This is of course utterly familiar in Fielding: his fiction meticulously deconstructs the illusions on which the production and the reading of fiction rests—by making the figure of the author so provocatively salient in *Tom Jones*, for example—and Fielding's best plays travesty by parody and preposterousness all other kinds of theatrical entertainment. There may have been partly snobbish reasons for this: Fielding wrote, like almost every other author of his time, out of urgent and immediate need for money. Much of the contemporary criticism of Grub Street has a strong social thread: authors were derided for their desperation, their opportunism, their ignorance and simply their poverty. Fielding was a gentleman. His irony about his writing is in part a way of creating a social distance between his self and the world his writing belonged to.

A Journey from this World to the Next signals its distinctiveness from the very first paragraph of the *Introduction*, with its train of 'whethers' generating doubt about the nature and authenticity of the ensuing narrative, and its casting of the question back on the reader to decide. *The Journal of a Voyage to Lisbon* does it through the extended and discursive Author's Preface which offers a rather lofty account of the character of journey narratives and of whether their publication is warranted, which is by no means taken as axiomatic. Thus each work, characteristically of Fielding, approaches its own nature by indirection.

We are nowadays very hospitable to the idea of travel, and travel books, offering the experience of travel vicariously, are a publishing staple. It was not simply so in the eighteenth century. Travel could be just an idle quest for inconsequential knowledge or worthless curiosities (which is why Gulliver's souvenirs from the land of the gigantic Brobdingnagians include an apple-sized 'Corn that I had cut off with my own Hand from a Maid of Honour's Toe' that he later has made into a cup and set in silver); or if it was undertaken to make one's fortune it could be an impertinent encroachment on God's Providence. Travel, and the texts that recorded it, needed justification. In *The Journey* Fielding (like Swift) makes his narrative so extravagant that it justifies itself by being a critical parody of the plethora of foolish voyage narratives that unscrupulous authors foisted on a credulous public. In the *Journal* he vindicates his narrative by using events of the journey as the starting-points for innumerable disquisitions on topics of public interest—the importance of having grand naval ships, or the regulation of the London fish trade, for example. Both works thus show Fielding as we recognize him from his great novels: not simply as the creative imagination behind a series of entertaining literary works, but as a constantly vital intelligence so engaged with the work in hand that every strand and fibre of the work as it takes shape, and its very nature, becomes an articulation of that intelligence.

A Journey from This World to the Next

As a writer, Henry Fielding enjoyed his brightest moment of popular and critical celebrity immediately after his hugely influential comic novel *The History of the Adventures of Joseph Andrews, and of his Friend Mr Abraham Adams* was published on 22 February 1742. However, this triumph was short-lived and the period following the book's initial appearance was a particularly difficult one in the career of its author. Both personally and professionally, Fielding's life was beset by disasters. Charlotte, his eldest daughter, died suddenly just before her sixth birthday only a few weeks after the novel came out, and around the same time, the deteriorating health of Charlotte Craddock Fielding, his hitherto supportive wife, was beginning to give cause for serious concern. After a long and painful illness, she too died in November 1744. And as all this was happening, the recurrent monetary problems which had dogged Fielding's professional life for some time were intensified. Just as he was trying to deal with the deeply distressing emotional difficulties of the double bereavement, the author was also experiencing his customary financial hardships in a particularly acute form, being heavily pressed throughout the early part of the decade for immediate settlement of substantial debts by his many creditors.

As was to be the case with the extraordinary circumstances of the composition of *The Journal of a Voyage to Lisbon* twelve years later, Fielding responded to such severe and potentially debilitating adversities by throwing himself fully into his writing, trying to make sense of his life and simultaneously command the best living from his pen by exploring every literary means available to him. By building on the commercial success of *Joseph Andrews*, he hoped to establish himself as a major writer. At this time, the most urgent pressure on the author came not from his own deteriorating health, as it was to be later, but from the chronic shortage of money. Having received a mere £200 from his publisher Andrew Millar for the full rights to the manuscript of *Joseph Andrews*—a sum which initially seemed generous to the author, but which was all too quickly dispersed—Fielding spent most of the remainder of 1742 and 1743 producing occasional essays and journalism, as well as continuing to write his oppositional political pamphlets, all for only modest financial returns. In pursuit of instant commercial success, he even turned to the theatre again, and had a rather lacklustre comedy called *The Wedding-Day* performed at Drury Lane in February 1743. However, despite any lingering public awareness of the author's reputation as a highly successful playwright (in the period immediately before the 1737 Licensing Act made life difficult for him), and despite the contemporary popularity of his comic novel, this piece lasted only six nights on the stage, and seems to have brought Fielding little more than £50 in benefits.

Desperate to find a more remunerative form of writing, Fielding then announced through various advertisements in the press the imminent publication of a new work called *Miscellanies by Henry Fielding, Esq.*, which would be an anthology of poems, prose, and dramatic pieces, lavishly produced in three volumes under the author's personal supervision. By marketing some of his more ephemeral work in this particular way, Fielding was seeking to capitalize on his recent celebrity by offering an attractive compilation of both previously published and hitherto unseen (and perhaps in some cases as yet unwritten) pieces to a carefully selected affluent audience. But the books would not be cheap. As the subscription announcement in the *Daily Post* on 5 June 1742 put it:

> The Price to Subscribers is One Guinea; and Two Guineas for the Royal Paper. One Half of which is to be paid at Subscribing, the other on the Delivery of the Book in Sheets. The Subscribers Names will be printed.

Eventually appearing almost a year later on 7 April 1743 after a number of delays, these rather expensive *Miscellanies* were thus funded by advance subscriptions. In effect, Fielding made a significant amount of money (probably around £800 in all by the end—four times what he had gained from his first novel, and £200 more than he would get for *Tom Jones*) by getting his up-market sponsors to hand over half of their cash before he had produced the book. In return he had to promise his subscribers only that their generosity and patronage would be publicly acknowledged in the final text.

Probably written in some haste and put together under the pressure of deadlines during the period running up to publication, *A Journey from This World to the Next* was included in the second volume of these *Miscellanies*. To fill up the pages, two makeweight pieces were also included—the text of *The Wedding-Day*, and the script of a brief play from 1737 called *Eurydice*—perhaps indicating that the *Journey* had originally been thought of as a longer work which would fill the entire volume. However, even if it may be seen as an unfinished and fragmentary text, the *Journey* is still one of the two substantial narratives to be found in the *Miscellanies*—the other being *The Life of Mr Jonathan Wild the Great*, which alone comprised the third volume.

Although it has been largely neglected by commentators on Fielding, both then and now, and although it remains a difficult work to categorize, *A Journey from This World to the Next* is an illuminating and informative text. Its narrative provides us with a fascinating series of historical and biographical sketches, reiterating the main recurrent themes of Fielding's work and of so much of the more familiar writing of the mid-eighteenth century: namely, the nature of true greatness, and the vanity of human wishes. As Fielding tells us in the 'Introduction', the book confirms and develops the following 'Moral': 'That the greatest and truest Happiness which this World Affords, is to be found only in the Possession of Goodness and Virtue'.

The 'Moral' looks simple and clear, but as is always the case with Fielding's work, the apparent lucidity of meaning is shadowed and challenged by complexity and confusion, with the very status of the text and its authority being casually undermined from the start. In his 'Introduction', Fielding ironically disclaims all personal responsibility for the genesis of the text. Rather than being his own authorial production, this part of the *Miscellanies* is, he claims, the result of an entirely serendipitous discovery. On buying a bundle of pens from his usual supplier, a Mr Robert Powney of the Strand, Fielding notices that they have been wrapped in what looks like some old pieces of manuscript paper. On closer inspection, the author discovers that he has in his hands some fragments of a hand-written narrative, and after making enquiries he is provided with another hundred pages of the text by his stationer. We are invited to believe that this manuscript had been left behind by a fugitive tenant of Powney's, in lieu of overdue rent. The anonymous author had himself investigated all avenues of publication for his work, but meeting with no success, he had fled to the West Indies in despair. Entirely uninterested in literature, Powney the stationer then used the pages for scrap.

Fielding, however, claims to be intrigued by what he has found, and seeks verification of the value of the manuscript. Looking for an authoritative adviser, he turns to none other than the fictional character of Mr Abraham Adams, the comically pedantic and bookish hero of *Joseph Andrews*, who also pops up at the end of *Tom Jones* and makes cameo appearances throughout Fielding's later journalism. Abraham agrees to read the manuscript, and give his opinion. Detecting the influence of Plato, rather churlishly acknowledging the author's knowledge of the ancient tongues, and suspecting 'that there was more in it than at first appeared', the learned parson encourages Fielding to ensure that the entire text be published. Given Adams's belief in the commercial possibilities of his own sermons in *Joseph Andrews*, we might resist the temptation to be convinced by this recommendation. However, Fielding confirms his character's judgement, and offers the comment that the author 'discovers a philosophical Turn of Thinking, with some little knowledge of the World, and no very inadequate Value of it'.

Without offering further editorial comment, apart from sensibly advising greater caution in the disposal of waste paper in the future, Fielding then lays before us this strange narrative. For readers habituated to the narrative practices of the novel, and less familiar with the heterogeneous forms of eighteenth-century writing, the *Journey from This World to the Next* may be disorienting and hard to grasp. The book is clearly playful in its presentation, disjointed and fragmentary in its form, but none the less in a number of ways it is intellectually and thematically coherent with the better-known novels and essays by Fielding, and these points of consistency are worth identifying.

The ironic mixture of fact and fiction introduced at the very beginning—Powney is a 'real' figure, where Adams is 'imaginary'—lays the foundations for the major concerns of the subsequent narrative. In its mingling of historical characters and events with authorial invention, and in its desire to subject the sublunary world to sceptical interrogation, the *Journey* offers us a satiric enquiry into the nature of reality and illusion. Paradoxically, Fielding is here experimenting with extreme non-naturalist forms of story-telling and embellishing the truth in a great variety of ways to establish and confirm what he sees as the most basic but most regularly overlooked realities of human existence. At one point in the book, we are shown the defeated king of the African Vandals articulating sentiments voiced by so many other characters in Fielding's work: 'Vanity, Vanity, all is mere Vanity' (I. xii).

The main narrative text of the *Journey from This World to the Next* falls into three discrete parts. In Book I, Chapters I–IX, the liveliest and most engaging part of the whole book, the recently deceased narrator takes us with him on a sardonic and ironically revealing tour of the underworld. Influenced by the classical Greek satirist Lucian—a writer described by Fielding in his *Covent-Garden Journal* in 1752 as 'the Father of True Humour'—this section of the narrative stages a confrontation between the modern world and the ancient world, and anatomizes contemporary life by looking it at from an unconventional but revealing point of view.

Unfamiliar and artificial though this form of presentation may now seem, we should remember that the satiric journey into the nether regions was a conventional and widely used literary device at this time. Although perhaps best known to modern readers through the episode of the sorcerers in Book III of Swift's *Gulliver's Travels*, it also obliquely informs Fielding's depiction of London society in *Tom Jones* and his dramatization of prison life in *Amelia*. However, Fielding's variant of the 'News from Hell' motif in the *Journey* is significantly indebted to two texts by Lucian in particular. In the Greek satirist's *Dialogues of the Dead* the great names of the ancient world gather in the nether regions to discuss the persistent vanities and follies of humankind, and in *The Voyage to the Underworld* a boat filled with the spirits of the recently deceased is the appropriate stage for a discussion of the transitory nature of human life. In both cases it is perhaps mainly the mood and atmosphere of the original Lucianic texts which are echoed in Fielding's work, without specific episodes being closely imitated. However, the correspondences between the texts are still worth bearing in mind, since Fielding's deliberate affiliation to classical models gives extra credibility to his view of the recurrent and endemic nature of human folly.

In fact, Fielding exploits the convention of the narrator from beyond the grave in the *Journey* with studied casualness, opening the main part of his narrative with the direct statement, 'On the first of *December* 1741, I departed this Life, at my Lodgings in *Cheapside*' (I. i). The lower world is left behind without undue sorrow or regret on the part of the unnamed narrator. His laconic style is justified as soon as we see that the world he has departed from seems to contain little but a crowd of uncaring relatives squabbling over the will and a sozzled old woman sitting by the lifeless body. The narrator is then conveyed by Mercury to a coach in which other spirits are awaiting their transportation to Elysium, and as they talk he hears sordid tales of how they in turn left the world behind them. The cumulative effect of these dialogues, and of the ensuing encounters with the City of Diseases, the Palace of Death, the Wheel of Fortune, the Court of Minos, and with Elysium itself, is to reiterate and confirm 'the Vanity, Folly, and Misery of the lower World, from which every Passenger in the Coach expressed the highest Satisfaction in being delivered' (I. ii).

The most significant episode in this first section occurs in Book I, Chapter V, where the travellers come to a crossroads, and have to choose which one of two paths to follow. One of the roads is almost impassable, blocked with undergrowth and debris, while the other affords the most pleasing and open of prospects. Yet we are told that great crowds were attempting to negotiate the bad highway, and only a few proceeding along the good one. On enquiry, the spirits are told that the obstructed road is the path to greatness, and the clear road leads to goodness. Obviously this episode offers a set-piece illustration of one of Fielding's most important recurrent themes, developed further in both *Tom Jones* and *Jonathan Wild*, reminding us that the contemporary world has dislocated the ideas of greatness and goodness from each other, and that the false allure of the first is both absurd and reprehensible, albeit undeniable.

The topic of 'greatness', a central concern of the *Miscellanies* as a whole, appears regularly throughout the text of the *Journey*. In the preceding chapter, set in the Palace of Death, we have been introduced to the figures of Alexander the Great and Charles XII of Sweden, two characters who were conventionally thought by many at this time to represent cautionary varieties of 'greatness', their appearance here once again illustrating the inauthentic virtue of transitory military achievement. By providing such familiar points of reference for his contemporary readers, Fielding is alerting them to the main thematic consistencies of the text, underlying its haphazard formal appearance.

As the chapter at the crossroads goes on, Fielding introduces a speech by the Spirit King, which is intense and statesmanlike, putting forward the case for goodness with great clarity, and eloquently denouncing the current infatuation with greatness. Yet when he finally sets off down the road to goodness, he cannot leave the world behind him: 'He was gone a little way, when a Spirit limped after him, swearing he would fetch him back. This Spirit, I was presently informed, was one who had drawn the Lot of his Prime Minister' (I. v). Like Mr Wilson in *Joseph Andrews*, the Man on the Hill in *Tom Jones*, and perhaps even like Fielding himself in the *Journal of a Voyage to Lisbon*, the Spirit King remains beset by the encroachments of the world even as he seeks to devote himself to a more ascetic version of goodness.

The satiric representation of the limping Prime Minister trying to fetch his monarch back from the path to goodness also introduces the first of a number of explicit contemporary political references which the first readers of the *Miscellanies* would easily have recognized. By this device, Fielding aligns his narrative to the copious body of writing which was critical of the eminent public figure Robert Walpole, effectively Prime Minister of Britain from 1721 until 1742 (and, interestingly, one of the subscribers to the more expensive edition of the *Miscellanies*). As in other oppositional texts like John Gay's *Beggar's Opera* (1728) and Fielding's own *Jonathan Wild*, the figure of the 'Great Man' Walpole is here made to stand for all manner of self-aggrandizement and political impropriety, the fictionalized Prime Minister becoming an epitome of everything that is held to be wrong with the contemporary world. The *Journey* contains a number of such local references, and in this first section it bears all the marks of Fielding's attachment to what has been described as 'Patriot' Oppositional politics, a loose grouping given to expressing hostility in particular to the recently increased professionalization of political life and the simultaneous disappearance of statesmanlike high-mindedness from the public arena. Elsewhere, though, the book seems less obviously partisan and local in its references, and eventually it bespeaks and articulates a disenchantment with manipulative politicians of all parties at all times.

The second section of *A Journey from This World to the Next* comprises Book I, Chapters X–XXV, where the narrator adventitiously meets an especially loquacious spirit, and we are treated to a bizarre first-person account of the many reincarnations of Julian the Apostate between his death in AD 363 and his eventual admission to Elysium in 1555. These reincarnations bring Julian in contact with various parts of the social scale—at one point he is the King of León, at another an anonymous sausage-maker from Syria—and they offer an unusual way of providing an overview of the history of the times. Many of the details in this section remain elusive, and as a whole it may seem directionless to the modern reader.

However, Fielding's choice of narrative voice in this part of the text is especially bold and interesting. The significance and status of Julian (Flavius Claudius Julianus), emperor of Rome between 360 and 363, remained a controversial issue in eighteenth-century accounts of classical history. Famous for having renounced Christianity, Julian had encouraged a short-lived pagan revival throughout the Roman Empire, promoted religious toleration, and persistently disparaged the luxurious and thoughtless lives of his contemporaries through a series of edicts and dramatic satires. For many early ecclesiastical historians, Julian's paganism had to be most vehemently denounced, but for a number of later writers—most notably Montaigne, Shaftesbury, and Gibbon—Julian's personal austerity and judiciousness in his imperial office entirely redeemed him.

In the *Journey*, Fielding's main narrator pretends to start from the hostile position of the orthodox ecclesiastical writers—'no Man ever had a better Title to the Bottomless Pit than he' (I. x)—only coming round to the more enlightened view of Julian after he has heard of his posthumous adventures. But rather than developing another view of the historical figure of Julian, Fielding uses the many identities of his new narrator to provide a historical panorama in which betrayal, ingratitude, and selfishness are repeated throughout many different ages and cultures. Skilfully compiling material from a wealth of secondary historiographical sources, the text reappraises the recurrent theme of the *Miscellanies* and anatomizes in detail the imaginative and spiritual poverty of the quest for 'greatness'. Although there are sections where the narrative introduces satirical descriptions of persisting historical 'types', the tone and atmosphere of this long section is significantly less playful and exuberant than the opening chapters, and the diversity of scene and setting is less important than the uncomfortable moral continuities Fielding wishes to assert.

At the end of Book I, Chapter XXV, the Julian narrative breaks off abruptly and we are tersely informed that 'Part of the Manuscript is lost, and that a very considerable one'. The *Journey* then resumes at Book XIX, Chapter VII, '*Wherein* Anna Boleyn *relates the History of her Life*'. With unembarrassed sleight of hand, Fielding here seizes on the opportunities created by his prefatory description of the fate of the manuscript, and unapologetically incorporates part of an entirely different and apparently unrelated narrative into the text.

Indeed, so marked is the shift in register and substance at this point that most modern commentators see the 'Anna Boleyn' (or 'Anna Bullen') section as not even being the work of Henry Fielding at all, preferring to identify it as an unattributed early production by his younger sister and fellow-novelist Sarah Fielding. The footnote accompanying the cessation of the Julian narrative begins to suggest such a possibility:

> I have only to remark, that this Chapter is in the Original writ in a Woman's Hand: and tho' the Observations in it are, I think, as excellent as any in the whole Volume, there seems to be a Difference in Style between this and the preceding Chapters, and as it is the Character of a Woman which is related, I am inclined to fancy that it was really written by one of that Sex. (I. xxv)

We must of course remember that there is a great deal of deception going on throughout the entire book, and that Fielding is still pretending to be publishing something he found being used for wrapping-paper. However, playfully or not, he is suggesting that there might have been a change in the authorship of the text at this point, and there is clearly a serious point at issue.

It is possible to identify a degree of circumstantial evidence suggesting that there was extensive collaboration between the two literary Fieldings around this time. In *Joseph Andrews*, for instance, authorship of the epistle from 'Leonora to Horatio' is attributed to 'a young Lady' (II. iv), and most modern scholars take that to be a reference to the as yet unpublished Sarah. Later on, both Fieldings worked sequentially on a novel called *The Adventures of David Simple*, first published under Sarah's name in early 1744, then republished in a second edition, which had been substantially revised by Henry, later the same year. It seems, then, as though at this point, when Fielding may have been growing increasingly less confident of his abilities to finish the *Journey* on his own before his subscribers asked for their money back, Sarah's existing fragment of manuscript could be hurriedly pressed into service.

All the same, although it may well have been written by a different author, and although it is considerably less fluent in style, the 'Anna Boleyn' narrative is thematically coherent with the rest of the *Journey*. From the evidence of many of his other works, it can be argued that Fielding believed in the special and distinct nature of women's history. In all three of his main novels, he introduced narratives of women's experience which both parallel and challenge the experience and claims to authority of the male protagonists: Joseph and Fanny, Tom and Sophia, William and Amelia Booth. And according to the footnote quoted above, Fielding was also willing to believe in the 'gendered' nature of writing when it suited him to do so. In the *Journey*, the

Boleyn narrative becomes the female equivalent of the male quest for 'greatness' seen throughout the earlier sections of the book. Her story is replete with further confirmation of the prevalence of treachery and envy in the world, and her eventual fate is a reminder of the miseries which attend even (or especially) the most exalted.

As the narrative comes to its end, Anna is presented at the gates of Elysium, with the following words:

> *Minos* paused for a small time, and then ordered the Gate to be thrown open for *Anne Bullen's* Admittance; on the Consideration, That whoever had suffered being a Queen for four Years, and being sensible all that Time of the real Misery which attends that exalted Station, ought to be forgiven whatever she had done to obtain it. (XIX. vii)

And so the 'curious Manuscript' ends in a gesture of toleration. Fielding breaks off his *Journey from This World to the Next* with a kind of reconciliation rather than an act of defiance or a cry of outrage. For us as readers, the return journey from the next world back to this one is awaiting us as soon as we put down the book, and Fielding wants us to return both sadder and wiser.

The *Journey* remains a literary and historical curiosity, a book unlike any other, and a reminder of Fielding's literary virtuosity. It may seem to be so unlike his other work that it stands aloof from the better-known novels, but its idiosyncratic reconfiguration of many of Fielding's recurrent ideas and themes, its reiteration of the motif of 'greatness', and its formal exuberance, make it required reading for anyone interested in both the diversity and the continuity of eighteenth-century writing.

The Journal of a Voyage to Lisbon

In the early summer of 1754 Henry Fielding, though only 47, was in a deplorable physical state. He was dying of his life-style: unremitting hard work, heavy eating, and heavier drinking. His medical advisers diagnosed dropsy: it was a symptom of cirrhosis of the liver. *The Journal of a Voyage to Lisbon* is an account of a voyage he made with his wife and other members of his family and household in the vain hope that life in a warmer climate would restore his health.

If one aspect of the truism about 'the death of the author' is that texts generate meanings independently of their author, then the volume published as *The Journal of a Voyage to Lisbon* in 1755 gives a grim edge to it. Fielding never saw the volume. He had died in Lisbon four months before it first appeared; and he had never read quite what we read. The title-page tells us that the work is 'By the late HENRY FIELDING, Esq:', and the title-page is followed by a 'Dedication to the Public', not written by Fielding but probably by his first biographer Arthur Murphy. The dedication emphasizes the character of the work as the product of a dying man, and it seeks to enlist pathos in its cause: 'let your own imaginations place before your eyes a true picture, in that of a hand trembling in almost its latest hour, of a body emaciated with pains, yet struggling for your entertainment'. The cause is at least in part to raise some money for Fielding's nearly destitute family, 'some convenience to those innocents he hath left behind'.

The author's death, his dying, the severity of his last illness, his appalling incapacity, the symptoms and treatment of his disease, are prominent in the reader's experience throughout the volume. In the very first journal entry Fielding describes his feelings on saying goodbye to those of his children who were not coming with him and his wife on the voyage. He thought he would never see them again, and all the philosophical stoicism he had acquired in his forty-seven years of life was useless to him:

> On this day, the most melancholy sun I had ever beheld arose, and found me awake at my house at Fordhook. By the light of this sun, I was, in my own opinion, last to behold and take leave of some of those creatures on whom I doated with a mother-like fondness, guided by nature and passion, and uncured and unhardened by all the doctrine of that philosophical school where I had learnt to bear pains and to despise death.

In Fielding's great novels he alone knows how the story ends; the reader can only guess. In this posthumously published autobiographical narrative the reader knows how the story ended; as the narrative goes on the author can only guess. Exactly how and when all the *Journal* was composed is beyond determination now. There was certainly an element of rounding-off and polishing, but the bulk of it was evidently a journal written at the time of the experiences it describes, or with a day or two's retrospect at most. This will not disconcert any reader at all familiar with the mixed and often inconsistent form of many eighteenth-century narratives. *Robinson Crusoe*, to take a conspicuous instance, in the early stages of Crusoe's island narrative offers a journal account of some of its character's experiences, and then revisits them in retrospective first-person narration. However Fielding's *Journal* was composed, it is inevitably an intertext of the story of his life and death. Something similar happens in Sterne's *Tristram Shandy* (1760–7), where there are repeated references to the state of the narrator's health and the successive publication of the volumes of the narrative. Volume IV, for instance, ends:

> And so . . . I take my leave of you till this time twelvemonth, when (unless this vile cough kills me in the meantime) I'll have another pluck at your beards, and lay open a story to the world you little dream of.

Sterne may be talking about his own health and the progress of his own publication, but *Tristram Shandy* is none the less a comic fiction and the reader receives the ending of Volume IV in that context. No such context screens Fielding's mortality from us; indeed it is particularly stark to the reader approaching the *Journal* from the fiction, where the figure of the author is robust, worldly, superior to the chances of human life, invulnerable and, as the presiding deity of the narrative, outside time.

The focus of the attention we give to death is not a cultural constant, as is confirmed in the variety of funerary practice in different cultures and different times. The lachrymose narrative of the death of Little Nell had a social and cultural aptness in the nineteenth century that many twentieth-century readers have found grotesque. In Milton's century the overwhelmingly important aspect of death was that it was the gateway to absolute Judgement. In the eighteenth century in Britain, in a culture which had in a manner of speaking restored value and legitimacy to life, the near approach to death was often felt to be the period of a human life when that life attained and revealed its epitome, its characteristic essence. This reading of dying arrives at sublimity in the protracted narrative of the death of Richardson's long-suffering and invincibly virtuous heroine Clarissa Harlowe, whose dying process is one of a progressively manifested sanctification in which she becomes almost entirely spiritualized. In a crisper form it is seen in the sequence of vignettes which ends Pope's first *Moral Essay* (1734): representative figures are seen dying true to the Ruling Passions that had animated them through life. Narcissa dies vain, vainly trying to retain her beauty:

> 'Odious! in woollen! 'twould a saint provoke',
> (Were the last words that poor Narcissa spoke)
> 'No, let a charming chintz, and Brussels lace /
> Wrap my cold limbs, and shade my lifeless face:
> One would not, sure, be frightful when one's dead—
> And—Betty—give this cheek a little red.' (246–51)

The author of the Dedication to the *Journal* discovers the same principle in Fielding's last complete work. Developing the metaphor of a fading lamp that will even as it approaches extinction flare up with its original brightness, he goes on:

> In like manner, a strong and lively genius will, in its last struggles, sometimes mount aloft, and throw forth the most striking marks of its original lustre.

This observation has set the tone for one of the ways in which the *Journal* has been most commonly read, and indeed for the nature of the claims that are made for its literary merit. It is read against the great fiction. Martin Battestin finds it notable for a change in mood: he says the *Journal* is remarkable for passages 'in which the once genial creator of Parson Adams and Tom Jones reflects irritably on the characters of men'.[1] Pat Rogers, who is much more taken with the work, has the same comparisons in mind:

> It is one of his most appealing books, moving in its courage and unabated power of observation, and as rich in humanity as the best of his novels.[2]

Using the kind of language we commonly apply to works of the imagination, he speaks of the Ryde episode as affording 'some brilliant sketches of boarding-house existence' (p. 216), and comments very favourably on the account of the visit of Captain

[1] *Henry Fielding: A Life* (London, 1989), 588.
[2] *Henry Fielding: A Biography* (Cambridge, 1979), 214.

Veal's dreadful nephew to the ship lying at anchor off the Isle of Wight:

> The contrast between the uncle—crafty, self-important and aloof—and the easy-going young coxcomb of a nephew is drawn with the utmost economy. Some of the writing in the *Journal* belies its tragic occasion. Fielding's pen moves with all the old vivacity and comic insight. In particular, Captain Veal emerges as a rich and complex character. (p. 216)

There is nothing wrong with sympathetic and responsive commentary of this kind, but there is something more that needs to be said. The nightmarish landlady at Ryde and the bizarre captain are not characters in a novel. Parson Adams, Square, Thwackum, the horrible Blifil, are all subject to the controlling ideologies of Fielding's fiction. They play their part in, and are accommodated within, a scheme of understanding. The representations of Mrs Francis and Captain Veal are without doubt refracted through Fielding's skills and habits as an author of imaginative fiction, but they come to us in the context of what Fielding, using a phrase of his age, calls in his Author's Preface 'true history'. They are representations of people he had to cope with and they are as intractable, wilful, and unaccountable as people can be. The engagement of the incapacitated and terminally ill but still spirited Henry Fielding with these difficult people is something quite different from apparitional occurrences in a fiction.

It is of course inevitable that we should make comparisons with the fiction, but we need also to be wary of finding quality or interest in the *Journal* only when it is most like the novels. It is perhaps particularly unwise to do so in the light of the fact that there is right in the middle of Fielding's Preface a passage in which he deprecates 'romance' as against 'true history'. This passage is especially startling as the writer who is at the forefront of his consciousness in this passage is Homer, and particularly as the author of the *Odyssey*, the work which above all others seems to lie at the imaginative heart of *Tom Jones*. 'I must confess,' says Fielding in making the comparison, 'I should have honoured and loved Homer more had he written a true history of his own times in humble prose, than those noble poems that have so justly collected the praise of all ages.' In what seems like its flat-footed insensitivity this might almost be a sentence Gulliver could write, and it is a natural instinct in a Fielding reader to fly from what is literally said and to look for irony. The tone of the Preface is in some parts ironic, but it is not so here. The passage introduces a consideration of the relation of reality and fiction where the discourse is sober to the point of starchiness.

The Preface as a whole identifies what is to be valued and what deplored in travel narratives as a 'species of writing', and it is abundantly clear that the travel narrative Fielding would commend—genuinely informative, sparing of inconsequential detail, truthful—is nothing like a novel—nothing like his own, certainly. It is also not entirely like the journal that follows, despite some fairly bald claims Fielding makes for it. He says, for instance, that 'if any merely common incident' is presented in the journal it is there for the sake of the 'observations and reflections resulting', which will tend 'to the instruction of the reader or to the information of the public'. Exactly how the reader is instructed or the public informed by the story of the progress of Mrs Fielding's terrible toothache, or the story of where Fielding's servant William found the missing tea canister, might be hard to say. But the point is not important. As all readers of eighteenth-century narratives know, prefaces are one species of writing and stories are another.

What is important is the kind of interest Fielding identifies as significant in travel narratives: that is the human interest. He is quite of his time in having no curiosity about the natural world except as it bears on human life. People and how they live and organize themselves are what it is worth writing about:

> If the customs and manners of men were everywhere the same, there would be no office so dull as that of a traveller: for the difference of hills, valleys, rivers: in short, the various views in which we may see the face of the earth, would scarce afford him a pleasure worthy of his labour; and surely it would give him very little opportunity of communicating any kind of entertainment or improvement to others.

When in the *Journal* he compares the attractions of river and sea views he prefers the latter, because there he can see more, larger, and nobler ships.

The most extended topographical description in the book comes towards the end of the entry for Thursday, 23 July. This concludes the longest coherent episode in the *Journal*, the vivid and entertaining account of the Fieldings' enforced sojourn windbound at Ryde. It describes the village, the landscape in which it is set, and the situation and history of the house belonging to the thoughtful gentlewoman who was so hospitable to the family during their stay. It begins:

> This pleasant village is situated on a gentle ascent from the water, whence it affords that charming prospect I have above described.

That prospect was the Solent full of ships. Then the soil is mentioned, as being a gravel draining so well that even after violent rain 'a fine lady may walk without wetting her silken shoes'. The greenness and abundant vegetation are mentioned as testimony to the fertility of the soil. Religion forms part of the landscape: 'in a field in the ascent of this hill, . . . stands a neat little chapel . . . adequate to the number of inhabitants'. The house of the 'polite and good' gentlewoman is then mentioned:

> It is placed on a hill, whose bottom is washed by the sea, and, which, from its eminence at top, commands a view of great part of the island, as well as it does that of the opposite shore.

There follows a history of the house and how it came into the lady's possession.

The details, the phrasing, the rhythms, combine in generating a sense of *déjà vu*. As readers we have been here before. It was six years before, to be exact, and we were reading the description of Squire Allworthy's house, Paradise Hall, in *Tom Jones*, I. iv. The echo is heard even in the functional parts of the description: when Mr Allworthy walks onto his terrace the dawn opens to his eye 'that lovely prospect we have before described'. Mr Allworthy inhabits a perfectly symbolic, idealized, balanced, eighteenth-century English landscape: hill and valley, lawns and woodland, running water and a lake, pasture and agriculture, land and sea; in sum, art and nature. It is the same vision of the landscape Pope had discovered in Windsor Forest in 1713:

> Here hills and vales, the woodland and the plain,
> Here earth and water seem to strive again,
> Not chaos-like together crushed and bruised,

> But, as the world, harmoniously confused:
> Where order in variety we see,
> And where, though all things differ, all agree.
>
> *Windsor-Forest*, 11–16

That we are hearing a real echo of the account of Paradise Hall is confirmed when Fielding describes how the lady has improved the estate, and particularly the gardens,

> with so elegant a taste, that the painter who would assist his imagination in the composition of a most exquisite landscape, or the poet who would describe an earthly paradise, could nowhere furnish themselves with a richer pattern.

What we are dealing with is not a conscious recension of the passage in *Tom Jones*, though it may well be that the linguistic and cultural rhythms Fielding established there were unconsciously emerging as he contemplated the Ryde landscape. Neither is, of course, more real than the other: each is an imaginative vision made up with the elements of a real topography, much like the idealized landscapes in the background of Italian Renaissance paintings. What is interesting is the light the parallel casts on how Fielding saw and interpreted the world, and it bears as much on his fictional as on his non-fictional writing.

Fielding is in some ways like the eighteenth-century writer he might be thought least to resemble, Defoe. Like Defoe, he sees the world typologically and symbolically, and always in terms of its implied meanings for men and women in society. The *Journal* demonstrates this clearly and repeatedly. It is apparent, for instance, in the couple of paragraphs that immediately precede the description of Ryde. In them Fielding compares the value of seeing either an encamped army or a fleet of ships. His mode of reading the sight of an encamped army is essentially typological as it relates the image to pre-existing notions:

> what, indeed, is the best idea which the prospect of a number of huts can furnish to the mind? but of a number of men forming themselves into a society, before the art of building more substantial houses was known . . . [alternatively] there is a much worse idea ready to step in before it, and that is of a body of cut-throats, the supporters of tyranny, the invaders of the just liberties and properties of mankind . . . plunderers . . . murderers . . . destroyers . . .

So the encamped army is the type either of primitive man or of a Gothic horde. In the next paragraph Fielding concedes that a fleet of naval vessels might be open to similar criticism, and goes on to say how he would prefer the sight of 'the honest merchant-man'. This would excite in him a happier symbolic vision:

I am more pleased with the superior excellence of the idea, which I can raise in my mind . . . while I reflect on the art and industry of mankind, engaged in the daily improvements of commerce, to the mutual benefit of all countries, and to the establishment and happiness of social life.

Wherever we read in Fielding, his consciousness is continually and restlessly engaged in lively contemplation of the way men and women live as individuals in society, and the vision which he communicates is essentially satirical, sometimes in the spirit of relatively genial social commentary we call Horatian (and find in, say, *The Rape of the Lock*), and sometimes with the more acerbic moralism associated with the Latin satirist Juvenal, of whom Swift and Dr Johnson are the most characteristic eighteenth-century avatars.

This is as true in the *Journal* as it is anywhere else, and any sequence of pages reveals a full and energetic mind beginning from the detail of the voyage and then branching out into more and more topics, not with the associative whimsy of a Tristram Shandy, but with the intellectual vigour of a man who always searches out how one thing is related to another. The entry for Monday, 1 July (which I take virtually at random), begins with a farewell, proceeds to an account of the behaviour and manners of a couple of uncouth customs officers, develops into an account of hierarchy (reinforced with a long quotation from Plato), extends that into a reflection on the Acts of Parliament that establish the authority of those who regulate trade, dilates into a rhapsody on trade itself, and concludes with a little paragraph describing the delightful evening passage down to the Nore once the ship finally weighed anchor.

In this entry there are three main components: vividly detailed presentation of idiosyncratic human individuals, broad contemplation of social organization, and foregrounding of the authorial consciousness. These components are universally present in Fielding's writing and they mark what is a highly characteristic eighteenth-century imagination: Fielding's is a constitutional imagination. The establishing of a working polity, a constitution, was the great cultural achievement of Britain in the eighteenth century, and of course it was widely admired by Enlightenment Europe. Fielding is everlastingly thinking about the management of our social life, our constitution, whether it is about the arrogance of coachmen, the need to have large ships in the Navy, or the stranglehold London fishmongers have on the trade. In the last case he has a simple remedy to propose: 'I humbly submit the absolute necessity of immediately hanging all the fishmongers within the bills of mortality.' (Monday [27 July])

It is of a piece with this constitutional imagination that the publication does not begin at the beginning of the voyage. It starts with Fielding's account of how he set about putting right an evil that was besetting the constitution. In the summer of 1753 street gangs were infesting the capital and had been responsible for a series of serious robberies and murders. The Secretary of State called Fielding in, as principal Justice of the Peace for Westminster, to suggest what might be done. Fielding rapidly devised a cheap and effective system of informants and thief-takers. By the winter the streets were free of this set of crimes at least.

Having dealt with this evil in the public constitution it was now time, more than time, for Fielding to turn to his own and to set in train the sequence of attempted cures of his ravaged body, undermined by overwork and disease, that he describes in his Author's Preface and which conclude with the attempt to sail south into a more genial climate. And it is here that we come to what is perhaps the most arresting and engaging feature of the whole of the *Journal*.

By the time he leaves home in late June 1754 Fielding is almost entirely incapacitated. He cannot walk; he has to be transported everywhere. Even the carriage ride from Ealing to Rotherhithe is a serious test for him. He has to be carried across the mud to be put into the little boat that will take him to the ship, and once against the ship's side he has to hauled aboard with a system of pulleys. Even before he is aboard ship his body is steadily distending with horrific accumulations of fluid that have to be drained out of his abdomen with a tube at regular intervals. When this is first done fourteen quarts (three and a half gallons) are taken out of him. For much of the time he is on board the ship he stays immured in the tiny cabin with no company but his seasick wife and daughter and the deaf, irascible, uneducated captain. Thus we have the paradox of the account of a voyage written by one who is almost totally immobile, transporting the little family for which he is responsible to a new world, while he himself cannot move at all and is locked into the old world of his moribund body.

And yet what the book conveys above all is a sense of vitality and activity. There is no self-pity in it, and as a journal it is an account of what does happen rather than what does not. There is an energy, a mobility, as Fielding chases characters, books, ideas, suggestions, reflections, and jokes, that transmits the keenness of his living rather than the imminence of his dying. What comes alive is of course the text; this *Journal* becomes the embodiment of the vitality; the decrepitude of the man feeds the spirit of the author. They are in a very severe storm (Saturday, 25 July) and the others fear for their lives. Fielding explains why he does not, but then goes on:

> Can I say then I had no fear; indeed I cannot, reader, I was afraid for thee, lest thou shouldst have been deprived of that pleasure thou art now enjoying; and that I should not live to draw out on paper, that military character [the captain's nephew] which thou didst peruse in the journal of yesterday.

What Fielding does as he dies is to turn himself into text, and it is as that of course that he survives.

NOTE ON THE TEXTS

A Journey from This World to the Next

The text of this edition follows the first publication of the narrative in volume ii of *Miscellanies by Henry Fielding, Esq.* (1743). Minor corrections to spelling and syntax have been made where necessary, and the text has been checked against the Wesleyan edition edited by Hugh Amory. The paragraphing in the final chapter is editorial, and follows Amory.

The Journal of a Voyage to Lisbon

The story of the publication of *The Journal of a Voyage to Lisbon* is complex and uncertain. The work exists in two versions, called the 'Francis' and the 'Humphrys' versions after the name given in the texts to the landlady with whom the Fieldings stayed on the Isle of Wight. Both versions were printed in January 1755, and 'Humphrys' was issued in February. It differs significantly from 'Francis', which probably more nearly represents the work as Fielding left it. Along with some other emendments, 'Humphrys' truncates and modifies very caustic accounts of Captain Veal and of the landlady as they appear in 'Francis'.

The likelihood is that 'Francis' was given to the printer in January with a view to quick publication in order to raise some money for Fielding's widow and children. As it was printing, however, Fielding's brother John, who was blind, discovered that the text was likely to give offence and accordingly prepared a tamer version, which was given to the printer and put on sale on 25 February. It seems that 'Francis' was held back and not issued until December 1755, perhaps to capitalize on news of the devastating Lisbon earthquake, which reached England in late November.

The present edition follows 'Francis' and reproduces the original capitalization, spelling, and punctuation, although full points after abbreviations have been omitted, and obvious typographical errors have been silently emended. Major differences between 'Humphrys' and 'Francis' are given in the notes. Details of all variants may be found in the text and annotation in *The Complete Works of Henry Fielding, Esq.*, ed. W. E. Henley, vol. iii (repr. New York and London: Barnes & Noble and Frank Cass, 1967), which reproduces 'Humphrys'. *Henry Fielding: a Life* by Martin C. Battestin and Ruthe R. Battestin (pp. 610–12) summarizes all that is known of the publishing history.

SELECT BIBLIOGRAPHY

Place of publication is London except where otherwise specified.

Editions Consulted

A Journey from This World to the Next, in *Miscellanies by Henry Fielding, Esq.*, ii, The Wesleyan Edition, with introduction and commentary by Bertrand A. Goldgar and text edited by Hugh Amory (Oxford: Clarendon Press, 1993).

The Journal of a Voyage to Lisbon, in Henry Fielding, *Complete Works*, ed. W. E. Henley, iii (repr. New York and London: Barnes and Noble, and Frank Cass, 1967).

Fielding, Henry, *The Journal of a Voyage to Lisbon*, ed. Tom Keymer (Harmondsworth: Penguin, 1966).

Secondary Reading

1. Biography

Battestin, Martin C. (with Ruthe R. Battestin), *Henry Fielding: A Life* (1989).

Hume, Robert D., *Henry Fielding and the London Theatre 1728–1737* (Oxford, 1988).

Rogers, Pat, *Henry Fielding: A Biography* (1979).

2. General Criticism

Alter, Robert, *Fielding and the Nature of the Novel* (1968).

Battestin, Martin C., *The Moral Basis of Fielding's Art* (Middletown, Conn., 1959).

Bell, Ian A., *Literature and Crime in Augustan England* (1991).

—— *Henry Fielding: Authorship and Authority* (1994).

Harrison, Bernard, *Fielding's* Tom Jones*: The Novelist as Moral Philosopher* (1975).

Hatfield, Glenn W., *Henry Fielding and the Language of Irony* (Chicago, 1968).

Hunter, J. Paul, *Occasional Form: Henry Fielding and the Chains of Circumstance* (Baltimore, 1975).

Paulson, Ronald, *Satire and the Novel in Eighteenth-Century England* (1967).

—— and Lockwood, T. F., *Henry Fielding: The Critical Heritage* (1969).

Preston, John, *The Created Self: The Reader's Role in Eighteenth-Century Fiction* (1970).

Rawson, C. J., *Henry Fielding and the Augustan Ideal Under Stress* (1972).

Smallwood, Angela, *Henry Fielding and the Woman Question* (Hemel Hempstead, 1985).

Varey, Simon, *Henry Fielding* (Cambridge, 1986).

3. A Journey from This World to the Next

This text has attracted little separate attention. The most useful general accounts will be found in Goldgar's introduction to the Wesleyan edition, and in Bell's *Henry Fielding: Authorship and Authority*, 123–44. More specialized accounts are:

Burrows, J. F., and Hassall, A. J., '*Anna Boleyn* and the Authenticity of Fielding's Feminine Narratives', *Eighteenth-Century Studies*, 21 (1988), 427–54.

Goldgar, B. A., 'Myth and History in Fielding's *Journey from This World to the Next*', *Modern Language Quarterly*, 47 (1986), 241–5.

4. The Journal of a Voyage to Lisbon

There is little separate critical commentary on *The Journal of a Voyage to Lisbon*, other than of highly specialized interest. Some helpful material can, however, be found in the following:

Bowers, Terence, 'Tropes of Nationhood: Body, Body Politic, and Nation-State in Fielding's *Journal of a Voyage to Lisbon*', *ELH* 62 (Fall 1995).

McCrea, Brian, *Henry Fielding and the Politics of Mid-Eighteenth-Century England* (Athens, Ga.: University of Georgia Press, 1981) 187–96. On political ideas and attitudes in the work.

Pollard, Alfred W., 'The Two Editions of Fielding's *Journal of a Voyage to Lisbon*', *The Library*, 3rd ser., 8 (1917), 75–7 and 160–2.

Rawson, C. J., *Henry Fielding and the Augustan Ideal Under Stress*. Interesting incidental remarks, mainly on manner and mood; see index.

Rivero, Albert J., 'Figurations of the Dying: Reading Fielding's *The Journal of a Voyage to Lisbon*', *Journal of English and Germanic Philology*, 93 (1994), 520–33.

Varey, Simon, *Henry Fielding* (Cambridge, 1986). Chapter 6 is devoted to the *Journal*.

A CHRONOLOGY OF HENRY FIELDING

1707 22 April: HF born at Sharpham Park, near Glastonbury, Somerset. His mother, Sarah Gould Fielding, comes from an old and wealthy West Country family; his father, Edmund Fielding, has aristocratic connections, but is a career army officer, ultimately rising to the rank of General.

1709–19 Boyhood spent on farm at East Stour, Dorset.

1710 8 November: Sarah Fielding born. She became a prominent novelist herself, occasionally contributing to her brother's novels and including his contributions in her own works.

1715 Failed Jacobite rebellion ('The Fifteen') in Scotland.

1718 14 April: death of his mother. Within a year, Edmund Fielding marries a Roman Catholic widow, and quickly finds himself involved in an acrimonious legal battle with HF's maternal grandmother over the children's custody and inheritance rights.

1719–24 Education at Eton. Among the students is George Lyttelton, a future patron.

1720 12 April: Ralph Allen, HF's future patron, signs his first contract to improve the postal service.

1721 16 September: birth of his half-brother John, who ultimately joins in HF's efforts at criminal reform and becomes a magistrate himself.

1722 Robert Walpole comes to power as head of government.

1728 29 January: publication of his first work, *The Masquerade*, a satirical poem.

16 February: production of his first play, *Love in Several Masques*.

16 March: registers as a student of letters at the University of Leyden, where he studies intermittently for nearly a year.

1729 Autumn: takes up residence in London.

1730 Founding of the Methodists by John and Charles Wesley, whose beliefs HF mocks frequently in his works.

1730–7 Writes over twenty comedies and burlesques, including *The Author's Farce* (1730), *The Tragedy of Tragedies; or the Life and Death of Tom Thumb the Great* (1731), *Don Quixote in England* (1734), *Pasquin* (1736), and *The Historical Register* (1737).

1734 28 November: elopement and marriage with Charlotte Craddock.

1737 June: passage of the Theatrical Licensing Act, partly in response to HF's political satires. The law closes his theatre and ends his career as a dramatist.

1 November: begins studying law at Middle Temple.

1739 15 November–June 1741: edits the *Champion*, a paper aligned with the Whig Opposition to Walpole.

1740 Probable time of his first meeting with David Garrick, who quickly becomes the leading actor of his day. HF praises him repeatedly in *Tom Jones* and elsewhere.

20 June: called to the Bar.

6 November: Samuel Richardson's *Pamela*.

16 December: beginning of the War of the Austrian Succession, which lasted until 1748.

1741 4 April: *Shamela*.

1742 January: Walpole retires from politics.

22 February: *Joseph Andrews*.

1743 Birth of Henrietta (Eleanor Harriet), his first child to survive to adulthood.

February: William Hogarth's *Characters and Caricaturas*, inspired by the preface to *Joseph Andrews*, includes profiles of himself and HF.

12 April: *Miscellanies*, including poems, plays, essays, and two works of fiction: *Jonathan Wild* and *A Journey from This World to the Next*.

1744 4 May: Sarah Fielding's *David Simple*. HF makes revisions and contributes an introduction for the second edition, published 13 July.

November: death of his wife Charlotte.

December: several of his patrons receive appointments in the newly formed Pelham administration, including Russell and Lyttelton.

1745 February: advertises *An Institute of the Pleas of the Crown*, a legal treatise he never actually completes.

5 November–17 June 1746: edits the *True Patriot*, a pro-Hanoverian paper defending the country against the threat of invasion by Prince Charles Edward Stuart and his Jacobite followers. The rebellion, popularly known as 'The Forty-Five',

becomes especially threatening in early November, when the Jacobites move into England from the North; by December, however, they begin their retreat back to Scotland, and the following April, they are defeated at Culloden.

1746 12 November: *The Female Husband.*

1747 25 February: *Ovid's Art of Love Paraphrased, and Adapted to the Present Time.*

27 November: marries his housekeeper, Mary Daniel, formerly his first wife's maid.

5 December–5 November 1748: edits the *Jacobite's Journal*, another pro-Hanoverian paper. Richardson's *Clarissa* published in three parts (1 December 1747, 28 April 1748, 6 December 1748); HF enthusiastically reviews it in the *Jacobite's Journal* in January 1748, and writes to Richardson in October to express his admiration for the book.

1748 25 February: 'premature' birth of his son William.

Late summer–early autumn: reads parts of *Tom Jones* to friends and privately circulates printed copies of the first two volumes (Books I–VI).

25 October: final writ empowering him to act as magistrate for district of Westminster, London.

1749 12 January: commissioned magistrate for County of Middlesex. This appointment resulted, in part, from the political influence of George, first Baron Lyttelton—the dedicatee of *Tom Jones*—and the financial generosity of John Russell, Duke of Bedford, also mentioned in the novel's dedication.

10 February: official date of publication of *Tom Jones*; Fielding's bookseller, Andrew Millar, actually began distributing the books a week earlier, and the first edition was already exhausted by this date. The second edition was published on 28 February; the third edition on 12 April; and the fourth edition (with HF's revisions) on 11 December.

1750 January: embarks on a concerted attack against criminal gangs, beginning the formation of London's first organized police force, the 'Bow Street Runners'; John Fielding soon joins in the project, and continues it after HF's death.

21 January: birth of his daughter Sophia.

19 February: opening of the Universal Register Office, a clearing-house for employment, merchandise, and real estate, devised by HF and managed by John Fielding.

1751 19 January: *An Enquiry into the Causes of the Late Increase of Robbers.*

19 December: *Amelia.*

1752 4 January–25 November: edits the *Covent-Garden Journal*, his last periodical.

13 April: *Examples of the Interposition of Providence in the Detection and Punishment of Murder.*

1753 29 January: *A Proposal for Making an Effectual Provision for the Poor, for Amending Their Morals, and for Rendering Them Useful Members of the Society.*

1754 6 April: birth of his son Allen. At around the same time, illness causes him to resign from the magistracy.

26 June–7 August: his voyage to Lisbon, the *Journal* of which was published posthumously in 1755.

8 October: his death at Junqueira, near Lisbon.

A JOURNEY FROM THIS WORLD TO THE NEXT

THE INTRODUCTION

WHETHER the ensuing Pages were really the Dream or Vision of some very pious and holy Person; or whether they were really written in the other World and sent back to this, which is the Opinion of many, (tho' I think, too much inclining to Superstition;) or lastly, whether, as infinitely the greatest Part imagine, they were really the Production of some choice Inhabitant of *New Bethlehem** is not necessary nor easy to determine. It will be abundantly sufficient, if I give the Reader an Account by what means they came into my possession.

Mr *Robert Powney*, Stationer, who dwells opposite to *Catharine-Street* in the *Strand** a very honest Man, and of great Gravity of Countenance; who, among other excellent Stationary Commodities, is particularly eminent for his Pens, which I am abundantly bound to acknowledge, as I owe to their peculiar Goodness that my Manuscripts have by any means been legible: this Gentleman, I say, furnished me some time since with a Bundle of those Pens, wrapt up with great Care and Caution, in a very large Sheet of Paper full of Characters, written as it seemed in a very bad Hand. Now, I have a surprizing Curiosity to read every thing which is almost illegible; partly, perhaps, from the sweet Remembrance of the dear *Scrawls*, *Skrawls*, or *Skrales*, (for the Word is variously spelt) which I have in my youth received from that lovely part of the Creation for which I have the tenderest Regard; and partly from that Temper of Mind which makes Men set an immense Value on old Manuscripts so effaced, Bustos* so maimed, and Pictures so black that no one can tell what to make of them. I therefore perused this Sheet with wonderful Application, and in about a Day's time discovered that I could not understand it. I immediately repaired to Mr *Powney*, and inquired very eagerly, whether he had not more of the same Manuscript. He produced about one Hundred Pages, acquainting me that he had saved no more: but that the Book was originally a huge Folio, had been left in his Garret by a Gentleman who lodged there, and who had left him no other Satisfaction for nine

Months Lodging. He proceeded to inform me, that the Manuscript had been hawked about (as he phrased it) among all the Booksellers, who refused to meddle; some alledged that they could not read, others that they could not understand it. Some would have it to be an atheistical Book, and some that it was a Libel on the Government; for one or other of which Reasons, they all refused to print it. That it had been likewise shewn to the R—— Society, but they shook their Heads, saying, there was nothing in it wonderful enough for them. That hearing the Gentleman was gone to the *West-Indies*, and believing it to be good for nothing else, he had used it as waste Paper. He said, I was welcome to what remained, and he was heartily sorry for what was missing, as I seemed to set some value on it.

I desired him much to name a Price: but he would receive no consideration farther than the Payment of a small Bill I owed him, which at that time he said he looked on as so much Money given him.

I presently communicated this Manuscript to my Friend Parson *Abraham Adams** who after a long and careful Perusal, returned it me with his Opinion, that there was more in it than at first appeared, that the Author seemed not entirely unacquainted with the Writings of *Plato*: but he wished he had quoted him sometimes in his Margin, that I might be sure (said he) he had read him in the Original: 'for nothing,' continued the Parson, 'is commoner than for Men now-a-days to pretend to have read *Greek* Authors, who have met with them only in Translations, and cannot conjugate a Verb in *mi*.'*

To deliver my own Sentiments on the Occasion, I think the Author discovers a philosophical Turn of Thinking, with some little knowledge of the World, and no very inadequate Value of it. There are some indeed, who from the Vivacity of their Temper, and the Happiness of their Station, are willing to consider its Blessings as more substantial, and the whole to be a Scene of more consequence than it is here represented: but without controverting their Opinions at present, the Number of wise and good Men, who have thought with our Author, are sufficient to keep him in countenance; nor can this be attended with any ill

Inference, since he every where teaches this Moral, That the greatest and truest Happiness which this World affords, is to be found only in the possession of Goodness and Virtue; a Doctrine, which as it is undoubtedly true, so hath it so noble and practical a Tendency, that it can never be too often or too strongly inculcated on the Minds of Men.

BOOK I

CHAPTER I

The Author dies, meets with Mercury, *and is by him conducted to the Stage which sets out for the other World.*

ON the first of *December* 1741[1], I departed this Life, at my Lodgings in *Cheapside*. My Body had been some time dead before I was at liberty to quit it, lest it should by any accident return to Life: this is an Injunction imposed on all Souls by the eternal Law of Fate, to prevent the Inconveniencies which would follow. As soon as the destined Period was expired (being no longer than till the Body is become perfectly cold and stiff) I began to move; but found my self under a Difficulty of making my escape, for the Mouth, or Door, was shut; so that it was impossible for me to go out at it, and the Windows, vulgarly called the Eyes, were so closely pulled down by the Fingers of a Nurse, that I could by no means open them. At last, I perceived a Beam of Light glimmering at the top of the House, (for such I may call the Body I had been inclosed in) whither ascending, I gently let my self down through a kind of Chimney, and issued out at the Nostrils.

No Prisoner discharged from a long Confinement, ever tasted the Sweets of Liberty with a more exquisite Relish, than I enjoyed in this delivery from a Dungeon wherein I had been detained upwards of forty Years, and with much the same kind of Regard I cast[2] my Eyes backwards upon it.

[1] Some doubt whether this should not be rather 1641, which is a Date more agreeable to the Account given of it in the Introduction: but then there are some Passages which seem to relate to Transactions infinitely later, even within this year or two.—To say the truth, there are Difficulties attend either Conjecture; so the Reader may take which he pleases.

[2] Eyes are not perhaps so properly adapted to a spiritual Substance: but we are here, as in many other places, obliged to use corporeal Terms to make our selves the better understood.

My Friends and Relations had all quitted the Room, being all (as I plainly overheard) very loudly quarrelling below-stairs about my Will; there was only an old Woman left above, to guard the Body, as I apprehend. She was in a fast Sleep, occasioned, as from her Savour it seemed, by a comfortable Dose of Gin. I had no pleasure in this Company, and therefore as the Window was wide open, I sallied forth into the open Air: but to my great astonishment found my self unable to fly, which I had always during my habitation in the Body conceived of Spirits; however, I came so lightly to the Ground, that I did not hurt my self; and though I had not the Gift of flying (owing probably to my having neither Feathers nor Wings) I was capable of hopping such a prodigious way at once, that it served my turn almost as well.

I had not hopped far, before I perceived a tall young Gentleman in a Silk Waistcoat, with a Wing on his left Heel, a Garland on his Head, and a Caduceus in his right Hand[3]. I thought I had seen this Person before, but had not time to recollect where, when he called out to me, and asked me how long I had been departed. I answered, I was just come forth. You must not stay here, replied he, unless you had been murthered; in which case, indeed, you might have been suffered to walk some time: but if you died a natural Death, you must set out for the other World immediately. I desired to know the Way. 'O,' cried the Gentleman, 'I will shew you to the Inn whence the Stage proceeds: For I am the Porter. Perhaps you never heard of me, my Name is *Mercury*.' 'Sure, Sir,' said I, 'I have seen you at the Play-House.' Upon which he smiled, and without satisfying me, as to that Point, walked directly forward, bidding me hop after him. I obeyed him, and soon found myself in *Warwick-Lane*;* where *Mercury* making a full Stop, pointed at a particular House, where he bad me enquire for the Stage, and wishing me a good Journey, took his Leave, saying, he must go seek after other Customers.

I arrived just as the Coach was setting out, and found I had

[3] This is the Dress in which the God appears to Mortals at the Theatres. One of the Offices attributed to this God by the Ancients, was to collect the Ghosts as a Shepherd doth a Flock of Sheep, and drive them with his Wand into the other World.

no occasion for Enquiry: for every Person seemed to know my Business, the Moment I appeared at the Door: The Coachman told me, his Horses were to, but that he had no Place left; however, tho' there were already six, the Passengers offered to make room for me. I thanked them, and ascended without much Ceremony. We immediately began our Journey, being seven in Number; for as the Women wore no Hoops, three of them were but equal to two Men.

Perhaps, Reader, thou may'st be pleased with an Account of this whole Equipage, as peradvanture thou wilt not, while alive, see any such. The Coach was made by an eminent Toyman, who is well known to deal in immaterial Substance, that being the Matter of which it was compounded. The Work was so extremely fine, that it was entirely invisible to the human Eye. The Horses which drew this extraordinary Vehicle were all Spiritual, as well as the Passengers. They had, indeed, all died in the Service of a certain Post-Master; and as for the Coachman, who was a very thin Piece of immaterial Substance, he had the Honour, while alive, of driving the *Great Peter*, or *Peter*, the *Great*,* in whose Service his Soul, as well as Body, was almost starved to death.

Such was the Vehicle in which I set out, and now those who are not willing to travel on with me, may, if they please, stop here; those who are, must proceed to the subsequent Chapters, in which this Journey is continued.

CHAPTER II

In which the Author first refutes some idle Opinions concerning Spirits, and then the Passengers relate their several Deaths.

It is the common Opinion, that Spirits like Owls can see in the dark; nay, and can then most easily be perceived by others. For which Reason, many Persons of good Understanding, to prevent being terrified with such Objects, usually keep a Candle burning by them, that the Light may prevent their seeing. Mr *Locke*, in direct opposition to this, hath not doubted to assert that you may see a Spirit in open Day-light full as well as in the darkest Night.*

It was very dark when we sat out from the Inn, nor could we see any more than if every Soul of us had been alive. We had travelled a good way, before any one offered to open his Mouth: Indeed, most of the Company were fast asleep[1]: But as I could not close my own Eyes, and perceived the Spirit, who sat opposite me, to be likewise awake, I began to make Overtures of Conversation, by complaining *how dark it was.* 'And extremely cold too,' answered my Fellow-Traveller, 'tho' I thank God, as I have no Body, I feel no Inconvenience from it: But you will believe, Sir, that this frosty Air must seem very sharp to one just issued forth out of an Oven: for such was the inflamed Habitation I am lately departed from.' 'How did you come to your End, Sir?' said I. 'I was murdered, Sir,' answered the Gentleman. 'I am surprized then,' replied I, 'that you did not divert yourself by walking up and down, and playing some merry Tricks with the Murderer.' 'Oh, Sir,' returned he, 'I had not that Privilege, I was lawfully put to death. In short, a Physician set me on fire, by giving me Medicines to throw out my Distemper. I died of a hot Regimen,* as they call it, in the Small Pox.'

One of the Spirits at that Word started up, and cried out, 'The Small-Pox! bless me! I hope I am not in Company with that Distemper, which I have all my Life with such Caution avoided, and have so happily escaped hitherto!' This Fright set all the Passengers who were awake into a loud Laughter; and the Gentleman recollecting himself with some Confusion, and not without blushing, asked Pardon, crying, 'I protest I dreamt that I was alive.' 'Perhaps, Sir,' said I, 'you died of that Distemper, which therefore made so strong an Impression on you.' 'No, Sir,' answered he, 'I never had it in my Life; but the continual and dreadful Apprehension it kept me so long under, cannot I see be so immediately eradicated. You must know, Sir, I avoided coming to *London* for thirty Years together, for fear of the Small-Pox, till the most urgent Business brought me thither about five Days ago. I was so dreadfully afraid of this Disease, that I refused

[1] Those who have read of the Gods sleeping in *Homer*, will not be surprized at this happening to Spirits.

the second Night of my Arrival to sup with a Friend, whose Wife had recovered of it several Months before, and the same Evening got a Surfeit by eating too many Mussels which brought me into this good Company.'

'I will lay a Wager,' cried the Spirit, who sat next him, 'there is not one in the Coach able to guess my Distemper.' I desired the Favour of him, to acquaint us with it, if it was so uncommon. 'Why, Sir, (said he) I died of Honour.'—'Of Honour, Sir!' repeated I, with some surprize. 'Yes, Sir,' answered the Spirit, 'of Honour, for I was killed in a Duel.'

'For my Part,' said a fair Spirit, 'I was inoculated last Summer, and had the good fortune to escape with a very few Marks in my Face. I esteemed myself now perfectly happy, as I imagined I had no Restraint to a full Enjoyment of the Diversions of the Town; but within a few days after my coming up, I caught cold by over-dancing myself at a Ball, and last night died of a violent Fever.'

After a short Silence, which now ensued, the fair Spirit who spoke last, it being now Day-light, addressed herself to a Female, who sat next her, and asked her to what Chance they owed the Happiness of her Company. She answered, she apprehended to a Consumption: But the Physicians were not agreed concerning her Distemper, for she left two of them in a very hot Dispute about it, when she came out of her Body. 'And pray, Madam,' said the same Spirit, to the sixth Passenger, 'How came you to leave the other World?' But that female Spirit screwing up her Mouth, answered, she wondered at the Curiosity of some People; that perhaps Persons had already heard some Reports of her Death, which were far from being true: That whatever was the Occasion of it, she was glad at being delivered from a World, in which she had no Pleasure, and where there was nothing but Nonsense and Impertinence; particularly among her own Sex, whose loose Conduct she had long been entirely ashamed of.

The beauteous Spirit perceiving her Question gave offence, pursued it no farther. She had indeed all the Sweetness and Good-humour, which are so extremely amiable (when found) in that Sex, which Tenderness most exquisitely becomes. Her Countenance displayed all the Cheerfulness, the Good-nature, and the Modesty, which diffuse such Brightness round the Beauty of

Seraphina[2], awing every Beholder with Respect, and at the same time ravishing him with Admiration. Had it not been indeed for our Conversation on the Small-Pox, I should have imagined we had been honoured with her identical Presence. This Opinion might have been heightened by the good Sense she uttered, whenever she spoke; by the Delicacy of her Sentiments, and the Complacence of her Behaviour, together with a certain Dignity, which attended every Look, Word and Gesture; Qualities, which could not fail making an Impression on a Heart[3] so capable of receiving it as mine, nor was she long in raising in me a very violent Degree of seraphic Love. I do not intend by this, that sort of Love which Men are very properly said to *make* to Women in the lower World, and which seldom lasts any longer than while it is *making*. I mean by seraphic Love, an extreme Delicacy and Tenderness of Friendship, of which my worthy Reader, if thou hast no Conception, as it is probable thou may'st not, my endeavour to instruct thee would be as fruitless, as it would be to explain the most difficult Problems of Sir *Isaac Newton*, to one ignorant of vulgar Arithmetic.

To return therefore to Matters comprehensible by all Understandings: The Discourse now turned on the Vanity, Folly, and Misery of the lower World, from which every Passenger in the Coach expressed the highest Satisfaction in being delivered: Tho' it was very remarkable, that notwithstanding the Joy we declared at our death, there was not one of us who did not mention the Accident which occasioned it as a Thing we would have avoided if we could. Nay, the very grave Lady herself, who was the forwardest in testifying her Delight, confest inadvertently, that she left a Physician by her Bed-side. And the Gentleman, who died of Honour, very liberally cursed both his Folly, and his Fencing. While we were entertaining ourselves with these Matters, on a sudden a most offensive Smell began to invade our Nostrils. This very much resembled the Savour, which Travellers,

[2] A particular Lady of Quality is meant here; but every Lady of Quality, or no Quality, are welcome to apply the Character to themselves.

[3] We have before made an Apology for this Language, which we here repeat for the last time: Tho' the Heart may, we hope, be metaphorically used here with more Propriety, than when we apply those Passions to the Body, which belong to the Soul.

in Summer, perceive at their Approach to that beautiful Village of the *Hague*, arising from those delicious Canals, which, as they consist of standing Water, do at that time emit Odours greatly agreeable to a *Dutch* Taste, but not so pleasant to any other. Those Perfumes, with the Assistance of a fair Wind, begin to affect Persons of quick olfactory Nerves at a League's distance, and increase gradually as you approach. In the same manner, did the Smell I have just mentioned, more and more invade us, till one of the Spirits looking out of the Coach-Window, declared we were just arrived at a very large City; and indeed he had scarce said so, before we found ourselves in the Suburbs, and at the same time, the Coachman being asked by another, informed us, that the Name of this Place was *the City of Diseases*. The Road to it was extremely smooth, and excepting the abovementioned Savour, delightfully pleasant. The Streets of the Suburbs were lined with Bagnio's, Taverns, and Cooks Shops; in the first we saw several beautiful Women, but in tawdry Dresses, looking out at the Windows; and in the latter, were visibly exposed all kinds of the richest Dainties: but on our entering the City, we found, contrary to all we had seen in the other World, that the Suburbs were infinitely pleasanter than the City itself. It was, indeed, a very dull, dark, and melancholy Place. Few People appeared in the Streets, and these, for the most part, were old Women, and here and there a formal grave Gentleman, who seemed to be thinking, with large Tie-wigs on, and amber-headed Canes in their Hands.* We were all in hopes, that our Vehicle would not stop here; but to our sorrow, the Coach soon drove into an Inn, and we were obliged to alight.

CHAPTER III

The Adventures we met with in the City of Diseases.

WE had not been long arrived in our Inn, where it seems we were to spend the Remainder of the Day, before our Host acquainted us, that it was customary for all Spirits, in their Passage through that City, to pay their Respects to that Lady

Disease, to whose Assistance they had owed their Deliverance from the lower World. We answered, we should not fail in any Complacence, which was usual to others; upon which our Host replied, he would immediately send Porters to conduct us. He had not long quitted the Room, before we were attended by some of those grave Persons, whom I have before described in large Tie-Wigs, with amber-headed Canes. These Gentlemen are the Ticket-Porters in this City, and their Canes are the *Insignia*, or Tickets denoting their Office. We informed them of the several Ladies, to whom we were obliged, and were preparing to follow them, when on a sudden they all stared at one another, and left us in a Hurry, with a Frown on every Countenance. We were surprized at this Behaviour, and presently summoned the Host, who was no sooner acquainted with it, than he burst into a hearty Laugh, and told us the Reason was, because we did not fee the Gentlemen the moment they came in, according to the Custom of the Place. We answered with some Confusion, we had brought nothing with us from the other World, which we had been all our Lives informed was not lawful to do. 'No, no, master,' replied the Host, 'I am apprized of that, and indeed it was my Fault, I should have first sent you to my Lord *Scrape*;[1] who would have supplied you with what you want.' 'My Lord *Scrape* supply us!' said I, with Astonishment: 'Sure you must know we cannot give him Security; and I am convinced he never lent a Shilling without it in his Life.' 'No, Sir,' answered the Host, 'and for that Reason he is obliged to do it here, where he is sentenced to keep a Bank, and to distribute Money *gratis* to all Passengers. This Bank originally consisted of just that Sum, which he had miserably hoarded up in the other World, and he is to perceive it decrease visibly one Shilling a day, 'till it is totally exhausted; after which, he is to return to the other World, and perform the Part of a Miser for seventy Years; then being purified in the Body of a Hog, he is to enter the human Species again, and take a second Trial.' 'Sir,' said I, 'you tell me Wonders: But, if his Bank be to decrease only a Shilling a day, how can he furnish all Passengers?' 'The rest,' answered the Host, 'is

[1] That we may mention it once and for all, in the panegyrical Part of this Work, some particular Person is always meant, but in the satyrical no body.

supplied again; but in a manner, which I cannot easily explain to you.' 'I apprehend,' said I, 'this Distribution of his Money is inflicted on him as a Punishment; but I do not see how it can answer that end, when he knows it is to be restored him again. Would it not serve the Purpose as well, if he parted only with the single Shilling, which it seems is all he is really to lose?' 'Sir,' cries the Host, 'when you observe the Agonies with which he parts with every Guinea, you will be of another opinion. No Prisoner condemned to Death ever begged so heartily for Transportation, as he, when he received his Sentence, did to go to Hell, provided he might carry his Money with him. But you will know more of these Things, when you arrive at the upper World; and now, if you please, I will attend you to my Lord's, who is obliged to supply you with whatever you desire.'

We found his Lordship sitting at the upper End of a Table, on which was an immense Sum of Money, disposed in several Heaps, every one of which would have purchased the Honour of some Patriots,* and the Chastity of some Prudes. The moment he saw us, he turned pale, and sighed, as well apprehending our Business. Mine Host accosted him with a familiar Air, which at first surprized me, who so well remembred the Respect I had formerly seen paid this Lord, by Men infinitely superiour in Quality to the Person who now saluted him in the following manner: 'Here you, Lord, and be dam——d to your little sneaking Soul, tell out your Money, and supply your Betters with what they want. Be quick, Sirrah, or I'll fetch the Beadle to you. Don't fancy yourself in the lower World again, with your Privilege at your A——.'* He then shook a Cane at his Lordship, who immediately began to tell out his Money with the same miserable Air and Face, which the Miser on our Stage wears, while he delivers his Bank-bills. This affected some of us so much, that we had certainly returned with no more than what would have been sufficient to fee the Porters, had not our Host, perceiving our Compassion, begged us not to spare a Fellow, who in the midst of immense Wealth had always refused the least Contribution to Charity. Our Hearts were hardened with this Reflection, and we all filled our Pockets with his Money. I remarked a poetical Spirit in particular, who swore he would have a hearty Gripe at him: 'For,' says he, 'the Rascal not only refused to subscribe to my Works; but sent back my Letter unanswered, tho' I'm a better Gentleman than himself.'

We now returned from this miserable Object, greatly admiring the Propriety, as well as Justice of his Punishment, which consisted, as our Host informed us, merely in the delivering forth his Money; and he observed we could not wonder at the Pain this gave him, since it was as reasonable that the bare parting with Money should make him miserable, as that the bare having Money without using it should have made him happy.

Other Tie-wig Porters, (for those we had summoned before refused to *visit* us again) now attended us; and we having feed them the instant they entered the Room, according to the Instructions of our Host, they bowed and smiled, and offered to introduce us to whatever Disease we pleased.

We sat out several Ways, as we were all to pay our Respects to different Ladies. I directed my Porter to shew me to the *Fever on the Spirits*,* being the Disease which had delivered me from the Flesh. My Guide and I traversed many Streets, and knocked at several Doors, but to no purpose. At one we were told, lived the *Consumption*; at another, the *Maladie Alamode*,* a *French* Lady; at the third, the *Dropsy*; at the fourth, the *Rheumatism*; at the fifth, *Intemperance*; at the sixth, *Misfortune*. I was tired, and had exhausted my Patience, and almost my Purse; for I gave my Porter a new Fee at every Blunder he made: when my Guide, with a solemn Countenance, told me, *he could do no more*; and marched off without any farther Ceremony.

He was no sooner gone, than I met another Gentleman with a Ticket, *i.e.* an amber-headed Cane in his Hand. I first fee'd him, and then acquainted him with the Name of the Disease. He cast himself for two or three Minutes into a thoughtful Posture, then pulled a piece of Paper out of his Pocket, on which he writ something in one of the oriental Languages, I believe; for I could not read a Syllable: he bad me carry it to such a particular Shop, and telling me *it would do my Business*, he took his Leave.

Secure, as I now thought myself of my Direction, I went to the Shop, which very much resembled an Apothecary's. The Person who officiated, having read the Paper, took down about twenty different Jars, and pouring something out of every one of them, made a mixture, which he delivered to me in a Bottle, having first tied a Paper around the Neck of it, on which were written three or four Words, the last containing eleven Syllables. I mentioned the Name of the Disease I wanted to find out; but received no other answer, than that he had done as he was ordered, and the Drugs were excellent.

I began now to be enraged, and quitting the Shop with some anger in my Countenance, I intended to find out my Inn: but meeting in the way a Porter, whose Countenance had in it something more pleasing than ordinary, I resolved to try once more, and clapt a Fee into his Hand. As soon as I mentioned the Disease to him, he laughed heartily, and told me I had been imposed on: for in reality, no such Disease was to be found in that City. He then enquired into the Particulars of my Case, and was no sooner acquainted with them, than he informed me that the *Maladie Alamode* was the Lady, to whom I was obliged. I thanked him, and immediately went to pay my Respects to her.

The House, or rather Palace, of this Lady, was one of the most beautiful and magnificent in the City. The Avenue to it was planted with Sycamore Trees, with Beds of Flowers on each side; it was extremely pleasant, but short. I was conducted through a magnificent Hall, adorned with several Statues and Bustoes, most of them maimed, whence I concluded them all to be true Antiques; but was informed they were the Figures of several modern Heroes, who had died Martyrs to her Ladyship's Cause. I next mounted through a large painted Stair-Case, where several Persons were depictured in Caracatura; and upon enquiry, was told they were the Portraits of those who had distinguished themselves against the Lady in the lower World. I suppose, I should have known the Faces of many Physicians and Surgeons, had they not been so violently distorted by the Painter. Indeed, he had exerted so much Malice in his Work, that I believe he had himself received some particular Favours from the Lady of this Mansion: It is difficult to conceive a Groupe of stranger Figures. I then entered a long Room hung round with the Pictures of Women of such exact Shapes and Features, that I should have thought my self in a Gallery of Beauties, had not a certain sallow Paleness in their Complexions given me a more distasteful Idea. Through this, I proceeded to a second Apartment, adorned, if I may so call it, with the Figures of old Ladies. Upon my seeming to admire at this Furniture, the Servant told me with a Smile, that these had been very good Friends of his Lady, and had done her eminent service in the lower World. I immediately recollected the Faces of one or two of my Acquaintance, who had formerly kept Bagnio's: but was very much surprized to see the Resemblance of a Lady of great Distinction in such Company. The Servant, upon my mentioning this, made no other Answer than that his Lady had Pictures of all degrees.

I was now introduced into the Presence of the Lady herself. She was a thin, or rather meagre Person, very wan in the Countenance, had no Nose, and many Pimples in her Face. She offered to rise at my entrance, but could not stand. After many Compliments, much Congratulation on her side, and the most fervent Expressions of Gratitude on mine, she asked me many Questions concerning the Situation of her Affairs in the lower World; most of which I answered to her intire Satisfaction. At last with a kind of forced Smile, she said, 'I suppose the *Pill* and *Drop** go on swimmingly.' I told her, they were reported to have done great Cures. She replied, she could apprehend no danger from any Person, who was not of regular Practice; 'for however simple Mankind are,' said she, 'or however afraid they are of Death, they prefer dying in a regular manner to being cured by a Nostrum. She then exprest great pleasure at the Account I gave her of the Beau-Monde. She said, she had, herself, removed the Hundreds of *Drury* to the Hundreds of *Charing-Cross*, and was very much delighted to find they had spread into *St James's*;* That she imputed this chiefly to several of her dear and worthy Friends, who had lately published their excellent Works, endeavouring to extirpate all Notions of Religion and Virtue; and particularly to the deserving Author of the *Batchelor's Estimate*,* 'to whom,' said she, 'if I had not reason to think he was a Surgeon, and had therefore written from mercenary Views, I could never sufficiently own my Obligations.' She spoke likewise greatly in approbation of the Method so generally used by Parents, of marrying Children very young, and without the least affection between the Parties; and concluded by saying, that if these Fashions continued to spread, she doubted not, but she should shortly be the only Disease who would ever receive a Visit from any Person of considerable Rank.

While we were discoursing, her three Daughters entered the Room. They were all called *by hard Names*, the eldest was named[2] *Lepra*, the second *Chœras*, and the third *Scorbutia*. They were all genteel, but ugly. I could not help observing the little respect they paid their Parent; which the old Lady remarking in my Countenance, as soon as they quitted the Room, which soon happened, acquainted me with her Unhappiness in her Offspring, every one of which had the confidence to deny themselves to be her Children, though she said she had been a very indulgent Mother, and had plentifully provided for them all. As Family Complaints generally as much tire the Hearer, as they relieve him who makes them, when I found her launching farther into this Subject, I resolved to put an end to my Visit; and taking my leave, with many Thanks for the Favour she had done me, I returned to the Inn, where I found my Fellow-Travellers just mounting into their Vehicle. I shook hands with my Host, and accompanied them into the Coach, which immediately after proceeded on its Journey.

CHAPTER IV

Discourses on the Road, and a Description of the Palace of Death.

WE were all silent for some Minutes, till being well shaken into our several Seats, I opened my Mouth first, and related what had happened to me after our Separation in the City we had just left. The rest of the Company, except the grave female Spirit, whom our Reader may remember to have refused giving an Account of the Distemper, which occasioned her Dissolution, did the same. It might be tedious to relate these at large, we shall therefore only mention a very remarkable Inveteracy, which the *Surfeit* declared to all the other Diseases, especially to the Fever, who she said, by the Roguery of the Porters, received Acknowledgements from numberless Passengers, which were due to

[2] These Ladies, I believe, by their Names, presided over the *Leprosy*, *King's-Evil*, and *Scurvy*.

herself.* 'Indeed (says she) those *cane-headed* Fellows (for so she called them, alluding, I suppose, to their Ticket) are constantly making such Mistakes: there is no Gratitude in those Fellows; for I am sure they have greater Obligations to me, than to any other Disease, except the Vapours.* These Relations were no sooner over, than one of the Company informed us, we were approaching to the most noble Building he had ever beheld, and which we learnt from our Coachman, was the *Palace of Death*. Its Outside, indeed, appeared extremely magnificent. Its Structure was of the Gothic Order: vast beyond Imagination, the whole Pile consisting of black Marble. Rows of immense Yews form an Amphitheatre round it of such Height and Thickness, that no Ray of the Sun ever perforates this Grove; where black eternal Darkness would reign, was it not excluded by innumerable Lamps, which are placed in Pyramids round the Grove. So that the distant Reflection they cast on the Palace, which is plentifully gilt with Gold on the outside, is inconceivably solemn. To this I may add, the hollow Murmur of Winds constantly heard from the Grove, and the very remote Sound of roaring Waters. Indeed, every Circumstance seems to conspire to fill the Mind with Horrour and Consternation as we approach to this Palace. Which we had scarce time to admire, before our Vehicle stopped at the Gate, and we were desired to alight in order to pay our Respects to his most mortal Majesty, (this being the Title which it seems he assumes.) The outward Court was all full of Soldiers, and, indeed, the whole very much resembled the State of an earthly Monarch, only more magnificent. We past through several Courts, into a vast Hall, which led to a spacious Stair-case, at the bottom of which stood two Pages, with very grave Countenances; whom I recollected afterwards to have formerly been very eminent Undertakers, and were in reality the only dismal Faces I saw here: for this Palace, so awful and tremendous without, is all gay and spritely within, so that we soon lost all those dismal and gloomy Ideas we had contracted in approaching it. Indeed, the still Silence maintained among the Guards and Attendants resembled rather the stately Pomp of Eastern Courts, but there was on every Face such Symptoms of Content and Happiness, that diffused an Air of Cheerfulness all round. We ascended the Stair-case, and past through many noble Apartments, whose Walls were adorned with various Battle-pieces in Tapistry, and which we spent some time in observing. These brought to my mind those beautiful ones I had in my Life-time seen at *Blenheim*, nor could I prevent my Curiosity from enquiring where the Duke of *Marlborough's* Victories were placed; (for I think they were almost the only Battles of any Eminence I had read of, which I did not meet with:) when the Skeleton of a Beef-eater shaking his Head, told me, a certain Gentleman, one *Lewis* the 14th, who had great Interest with his most mortal Majesty, had prevented any such from being hung up there; besides, (says he) his Majesty, hath no great Respect for that Duke,* for he never sent him a Subject, he could keep from him, nor did he ever get a single Subject by his means, but he lost 1,000 others for him. We found the Presence-Chamber, at our Entrance, very full, and a Buz ran through it, as in all Assemblies, before the principal Figure enters: for his Majesty was not yet come out. At the bottom of the Room were two Persons in close Conference, one with a square black Cap on his Head, and the other with a Robe embroidered with Flames of Fire. These, I was informed, were a Judge long since dead, and an Inquisitor-General. I overheard them disputing with great Eagerness, whether the one had hanged, or the other burnt the most. While I was listning to this Dispute, which seemed to be in no likelihood of a speedy Decision, the Emperor entred the Room, and placed himself between two Figures, one of which was remarkable for the Roughness, and the other for the Beauty of his Appearance. These were, it seems, *Charles* the 12th of *Sweden*, and *Alexander* of *Macedon*. I was at too great a Distance to hear any of the Conversation, so could only satisfy my Curiosity by contemplating the several Personages present, of whose Names I informed myself by a Page, who looked as pale and meagre as any Court Page in the other World, but was somewhat more modest. He shewed me here two or three *Turkish* Emperors, to whom his most mortal Majesty seemed to express much Civility. Here were likewise several of the *Roman* Emperors, among whom none seemed so much caressed as *Caligula*, on account, as the Page told me, of his *pious* Wish, that he could send all the *Romans* hither at one blow. The Reader may be perhaps surprized, that I saw no Physicians here; as, indeed, I was myself till informed that they were all departed to the City of Diseases, where they were busy in an Experiment to purge away the Immortality of the Soul.

It would be tedious to recollect the many Individuals I saw here: but I cannot omit a fat Figure well drest in the *French* Fashion, who was received with extraordinary Complacence by the Emperor, and whom I imagined to be *Lewis* the 14th himself; but the Page acquainted me he was a celebrated *French* Cook.*

We were at length introduced to the Royal Presence, and had the Honour to kiss Hands. His Majesty asked us a few Questions, not very material to relate, and soon after retired.

When we returned into the Yard, we found our Caravan ready to set out, at which we all declared ourselves well pleased; for we were sufficiently tired with the Formality of a Court, notwithstanding its outward Splendor and Magnificence.

CHAPTER V

The Travellers proceed on their Journey, and meet several Spirits, who are coming into the Flesh.

WE now came to the Banks of the great River *Cocytus*, where we quitted our Vehicle, and past the Water in a Boat, after which we were obliged to travel on foot the rest of our Journey; and now we met, for the first time, several Passengers travelling to the World we had left, who informed us they were Souls going into the Flesh.

The two first we met were walking Arm in Arm in very close and friendly Conference; they informed us, that one of them was intended for a Duke, and the other for a Hackney Coachman. As we had not yet arrived at the Place where we were to deposite our Passions, we were all surprized at the Familiarity, which subsisted between Persons of such different Degrees, nor could the grave Lady help expressing her Astonishment at it. The future Coachman then replied with a Laugh, that they had exchanged Lots: for that the Duke had with his Dukedom drawn a Shrew of a Wife, and the Coachman only a single State.

As we proceeded on our Journey, we met a solemn Spirit walking alone with great Gravity in his Countenance: our Curiosity invited us, notwithstanding his Reserve, to ask what Lot he had drawn. He answered with a Smile, he was to have the Reputation of a wise Man with 100000 *l.* in his Pocket, and that he was practicing the Solemnity, which he was to act in the other World.

A little farther we met a Company of very merry Spirits, whom we imagined by their Mirth to have drawn some mighty Lot, but on enquiry, they informed us they were to be Beggars.

The farther we advanced, the greater Numbers we met, and now we discovered two large Roads leading different Ways, and of very different Appearance; the one all craggy with Rocks, full as it seemed of boggy Grounds, and every where beset with Briars, so that it was impossible to pass through it without the utmost Danger and Difficulty; the other, the most delightful imaginable, leading through the most verdant Meadows, painted and perfumed with all kinds of beautiful Flowers; in short, the most wanton Imagination could imagine nothing more lovely. Notwithstanding which, we were surprized to see great Numbers crouding into the former, and only one or two solitary Spirits chusing the latter. On enquiry we were acquainted that the bad Road was the way to *Greatness*, and the other to *Goodness*, When we exprest our surprize at the Preference given to the former, we were acquainted that it was chosen for the sake of the Music of Drums and Trumpets, and the perpetual Acclamations of the Mob; with which, those who travelled this way, were constantly saluted. We were told likewise, that there were several noble Palaces to be seen, and lodged in on this Road, by those who had past through the Difficulties of it, (which indeed many were not able to surmount) and great Quantities of all sorts of Treasure to be found in it; whereas the other had little inviting more than the Beauty of the way, scarce a handsome Building, save one greatly resembling a certain House by the *Bath*,* to be seen during that whole Journey; and lastly, that it was thought very scandalous and mean-spirited to travel through this, and as highly honourable and noble to pass by the other.

We now heard a violent Noise, when casting our Eyes forwards, we perceived a vast Number of Spirits advancing in pursuit of one, whom they mocked and insulted with all kinds of Scorn. I cannot give my Reader a more adequate Idea of this Scene, than by comparing it to an *English* Mob conducting a Pick-pocket to the Water; or by supposing that an incensed Audience at a Play-house had unhappily possess'd themselves of the miserable damned Poet. Some laughed, some hiss'd, some squawled, some groaned, some bawled, some spit at him, some threw dirt at him. It was impossible not to ask who or what the wretched Spirit was, whom they treated in this barbarous manner; when, to our great Surprize, we were informed that it was a King: we were likewise told, that this manner of Behaviour was usual among the Spirits, to those who drew the Lots of Emperors, Kings, and other great Men, not from Envy or Anger, but mere Derision and Contempt of earthly Grandeur: That nothing was more common, than for those who had drawn these great Prizes, (as to us they seemed) to exchange them with Taylors and Coblers; and that *Alexander the Great* and *Diogenes* had formerly done so; he that was afterwards *Diogenes* having originally fallen on the Lot of *Alexander*.

And now on a sudden, the Mockery ceased, and the King Spirit having obtained a Hearing, began to speak as follows: for we were now near enough to hear him distinctly.

'Gentlemen,

I am justly surprized at your treating me in this manner; since whatever Lot I have drawn, I did not chuse: if therefore it be worthy of Derision, you should compassionate me, for it might have fallen to any of your shares. I know in how low a Light the Station to which Fate hath assigned me is considered here, and that, when Ambition doth not support it, it becomes generally so intolerable, that there is scarce any other Condition for which it is not gladly exchanged: for what Portion, in the World to which we are going, is so miserable as that of Care? Should I therefore consider my self as become by this Lot essentially your Superiour, and of a higher Order of Being than the rest of my Fellow-Creatures: Should I foolishly imagine my self without Wisdom superiour to the Wise, without Knowledge to the Learned, without Courage to the Brave, and without Goodness and Virtue to the Good and Virtuous; surely so preposterous, so absurd a Pride, would justly render me the Object of Ridicule. But far be it from me to entertain it. And yet, Gentlemen, I prize the Lot I have drawn, nor would I exchange it with any of your's, seeing it is in my eye so much greater than the rest. Ambition, which I own my self possest of, teaches me this. Ambition, which makes me covet Praise, assures me, that I shall enjoy a much larger Proportion of it than can fall within your power either to deserve or obtain. I am then superiour to you all, when I am able to do more good, and when I execute that Power. What the Father is to the Son, the Guardian to the Orphan, or the Patron to his Client, that am I to you. You are my Children, to whom I will be a Father, a Guardian, and a Patron. Not one Evening in my long Reign (for so it is to be) will I repose my self to rest, without the glorious, the heart-warming Consideration, that thousands that Night owe their sweetest Rest to me. What a delicious Fortune is it to him whose strongest Appetite is doing good, to have every day the Opportunity and the Power of satisfying it! If such a Man hath Ambition, how happy is it for him to be seated so on high, that every Act blazes abroad, and attracts to him Praises tainted with neither Sarcasm nor Adulation; but such as the nicest and most delicate Mind may relish? Thus therefore, while you derive your Good from me, I am your Superiour. If to my strict Distribution of Justice you owe the Safety of your Property from domestic Enemies: If by my Vigilance and Valour you are protected from foreign Foes; If by my Encouragement of genuine Industry, every Science, every Art which can embellish or sweeten Life is produced and flourishes among you; will any of you be so insensible or ungrateful, as to deny Praise and Respect to him, by whose Care and Conduct you enjoy these Blessings? I wonder not at the Censure which so frequently falls on those in my Station: but I wonder that those in my Station so frequently deserve it. What strange Perverseness of Nature! What wanton Delight in Mischief must taint his Composition, who prefers Danger, Difficulty and Disgrace, by doing evil, to Safety, Ease and Honour, by doing good? who refuses Happiness in the other World, and Heaven in this, for Misery there, and Hell here? But be assured, my Intentions are different. I shall always endeavour the Ease, the Happiness, and the Glory of my People, being confident that by so doing, I take the most certain Method of procuring them all to my self.'—He then struck directly into the Road of *Goodness*, and received such a Shout of Applause, as I never remember to have heard equalled.

He was gone a little way, when a Spirit limped after him, swearing he would fetch him back. This Spirit, I was presently informed, was one who had drawn the Lot of his Prime Minister.

CHAPTER VI

An Account of the Wheel of Fortune, with a Method of preparing a Spirit for this World.

WE now proceeded on our Journey, without staying to see whether he fulfilled his Word or no; and without encountering any thing worth mentioning, came to the Place where the Spirits on their Passage to the other World were obliged to decide by Lot the Station in which every one was to act there. Here was a monstrous Wheel, infinitely larger than those in which I had formerly seen Lottery Tickets deposited. This was called the WHEEL OF FORTUNE. The Goddess herself was present. She was one of the most deformed Females I ever beheld; nor could I help observing the Frowns she exprest when any beautiful Spirit of her own Sex passed by her, nor the Affability which smiled in her Countenance on the Approach of any handsome Male Spirits. Hence I accounted for the Truth of an Observation I had often made on Earth, that nothing is more fortunate than handsome Men, nor more unfortunate than handsome Women. The Reader may be perhaps pleased with an Account of the whole Method of equipping a Spirit for his Entrance into the Flesh.

First then, he receives from a very sage Person, whose Look much resembled that of an Apothecary, (his Warehouse likewise bearing an affinity to an Apothecary's Shop) a small Phial inscribed, THE PATHETIC POTION, *to be taken just before you are born*. This Potion is a Mixture of all the Passions, but in no exact Proportion, so that sometimes one predominates and sometimes another; nay, often in the hurry of making up, one particular

Ingredient is as we were informed left out. The Spirit receiveth at the same time another Medicine called the NOUSPHORIC DECOCTION, of which he is to drink *ad Libitum*. This Decoction is an Extract from the Faculties of the Mind, sometimes extremely strong and spirituous, and sometimes altogether as weak: for very little Care is taken in the Preparation. This Decoction is so extremely bitter and unpleasant, that notwithstanding its Wholesomeness, several Spirits will not be persuaded to swallow a Drop of it; but throw it away, or give it to any other who will receive it: by which means some who were not disgusted by the Nauseousness, drank double and treble Portions. I observed a beautiful young Female, who tasting it immediately from Curiosity, screwed up her Face and cast it from her with great disdain, whence advancing presently to the Wheel, she drew a Coronet, which she clapped up so eagerly, that I could not distinguish the Degree;* and indeed, I observed several of the same Sex, after a very small sip, throw the Bottles away.

As soon as the Spirit is dismissed by the Operator, or Apothecary, he is at liberty to approach the Wheel, where he hath a Right to extract a single Lot: but those whom Fortune favours, she permits sometimes secretly to draw three or four. I observed a comical kind of Figure who drew forth a Handful, which when he opened, were a Bishop, a General, a Privy-Counsellor, a Player and a Poet Laureate, and returning the three first, he walked off smiling with the two last.*

Every single Lot contained two or more Articles, which were generally disposed so as to render the Lots as equal as possible to each other.

On one was written *Earl,*
Riches,
Health,
Disquietude.

On another, *Cobler,*
Sickness,
Good-Humour.

On a Third, *Poet,*
Contempt,
Self-Satisfaction.

On a Fourth,	*General,*
	Honour,
	Discontent.
On a Fifth,	*Cottage,*
	Happy-Love.
On a Sixth,	*Coach and Six,*
	Impotent jealous Husband.
On a Seventh,	*Prime-Minister,*
	Disgrace.
On an Eighth,	*Patriot,*
	Glory.
On a Ninth,	*Philosopher,*
	Poverty,
	Ease.
On a Tenth,	*Merchant,*
	Riches,
	Care.

And indeed the whole seemed to contain such a Mixture of Good and Evil, that it would have puzzled me which to chuse. I must not omit here, that in every Lot was directed, whether the Drawer should marry or remain in Celibacy, the married Lots being all marked with a large Pair of Horns.

We were obliged, before we quitted this Place, to take each of us an Emetic from the Apothecary, which immediately purged us of all our earthly Passions, and presently the Cloud forsook our Eyes, as it doth those of *Æneas* in *Virgil* when removed by *Venus*,* and we discerned Things in a much clearer Light than before. We began to compassionate those Spirits who were making their Entry into the Flesh, whom we had till then secretly envied, and to long eagerly for those delightful Plains which now opened themselves to our Eyes, and to which we now hastened with the utmost Eagerness. On our way, we met with several Spirits with very dejected Countenances: but our Expedition would not suffer us to ask any Questions.

At length, we arrived at the Gate of *Elysium*. Here was a prodigious Croud of Spirits waiting for Admittance, some of whom were admitted and some were rejected: for all were strictly examined by the Porter, whom I soon discovered to be the celebrated Judge *Minos*.

CHAPTER VII

The Proceedings of Judge Minos,* *at the Gate of* Elysium.

I NOW got near enough to the Gate, to hear the several Claims of those who endeavoured to pass. The first, among other Pretensions, set forth, that he had been very liberal to an Hospital; but *Minos* answered, *Ostentation*, and repulsed him. The second exhibited, that he had constantly frequented his Church, been a rigid Observer of Fast-Days. He likewise represented the great Animosity he had shewn to Vice in others, which never escaped his severest Censure; and as to his own Behaviour, he had never been once guilty of Whoring, Drinking, Gluttony, or any other Excess. He said, he had disinherited his Son for getting a Bastard.—Have you so, said *Minos*, then pray return into the other World and beget another; for such an unnatural Rascal shall never pass this Gate. A dozen others, who had advanced with very confident Countenances, seeing him rejected, turned about of their own accord, declaring, if he could not pass, they had no Expectation, and accordingly they followed him back to Earth; which was the Fate of all who were repulsed, they being obliged to take a farther Purification, unless those who were guilty of some very heinous Crimes, who were hustled in at a little back Gate, whence they tumbled immediately into the Bottomless Pit.

The next Spirit that came up, declared, he had done neither Good nor Evil in the World: for that since his Arrival at Man's Estate, he had spent his whole Time in search of Curiosities; and particularly in the Study of Butterflies, of which he had collected an immense Number. *Minos* made him no Answer, but with great Scorn pushed him back.

There now advanced a very beautiful Spirit indeed. She began to ogle *Minos* the moment she saw him. She said, she hoped, there was some Merit in refusing a great Number of Lovers, and dying a Maid, tho' she had had the Choice of a hundred. *Minos* told her she had not refused enow yet, and turned her back.

She was succeeded by a Spirit, who told the Judge, he believed his Works would speak for him.—What Works? answered

Minos.—My Dramatic Works, replied the other, which have done so much Good in recommending Virtue and punishing Vice.—Very well, said the Judge, if you please to stand by, the first Person who passes the Gate, by your means, shall carry you in with him: but if you will take my Advice, I think, for Expedition sake, you had better return and live another Life upon Earth. The Bard grumbled at this, and replied, that besides his Poetical Works, he had done some other good Things: for that he had once lent the whole Profits of a Benefit Night to a Friend, and by that Means had saved him and his Family from Destruction. Upon this, the Gate flew open, and *Minos* desired him to walk in, telling him, if he had mentioned this at first, he might have spared the Remembrance of his Plays. The Poet answered, he believed, if *Minos* had read his Works, he would set a higher Value on them. He was then beginning to repeat, but *Minos* pushed him forward, and turning his Back to him, applied himself to the next Passenger; a very genteel Spirit, who made a very low Bow to *Minos*, and then threw himself into an erect Attitude, and imitated the Motion of taking Snuff with his right Hand.—*Minos* asked him, what he had to say for himself? He answered, he would dance a Minuet with any Spirit in *Elysium*: that he could likewise perform all his other Exercises very well, and hoped he had in his Life deserved the Character of a perfect *fine Gentleman. Minos* replied, it would be great pity to rob the World of so *fine a Gentleman*, and therefore desired him to take the other Trip. The Beau bowed, thanked the Judge, and said he desired no better. Several Spirits expressed much Astonishment at this his Satisfaction; but we were afterwards informed, he had not taken the Emetic above mentioned.

A miserable old Spirit now crawled forwards, whose Face I thought I had formerly seen near *Westminster-Abbey*.* He entertained *Minos* with a long Harangue of what he had done *when in the House*; and then proceeded to inform him how much he was worth, without attempting to produce a single Instance of any one good Action. *Minos* stopt the Career of his Discourse, and acquainted him, he must take a Trip back again.——What, to S——House,* said the Spirit in an Extasy? But the Judge without making him any Answer, turned to another, who with a very solemn Air and great Dignity, acquainted him, he was a

Duke.—To the Right about, Mr Duke, cried *Minos*, you are infinitely too great a Man for *Elysium*; and then giving him a Kick on the B——ch, he addressed himself to a Spirit, who with Fear and Trembling begged he might not go to the Bottomless Pit: he said, he hoped *Minos* would consider, that tho' he had gone astray, he had suffered for it, that it was Necessity which drove him to the Robbery of eighteen Pence, which he had committed, and for which he was hanged: that he had done some good Actions in his Life, that he had supported an aged Parent with his Labour, that he had been a very tender Husband and a kind Father, and that he had ruined himself by being Bail for his Friend. At which Words the Gate opened, and *Minos* bid him enter, giving him a slap on the Back as he past by him.

A great Number of Spirits now came forwards, who all declared they had the same Claim, and that the Captain should speak for them. He acquainted the Judge, that they had been all slain in the Service of their Country. *Minos* was going to admit them, but had the Curiosity to ask who had been the Invader, in order, as he said, to prepare the back Gate for him. The Captain answered, they had been the Invaders themselves, that they had entered the Enemies Country, and burnt and plundered several Cities.—And for what Reason? said *Minos*.—By the Command of him who paid us, said the Captain, that is the Reason of a Soldier. We are to execute whatever we are commanded, or we should be a Disgrace to the Army, and very little deserve our Pay.—You are brave Fellows indeed, said *Minos*, but be pleased to face about, and obey my Command for once, in returning back to the other World: for what should such Fellows as you do, where there are no Cities to be burnt, nor People to be destroy'd? But let me advise you to have a stricter Regard to Truth for the future, and not call the depopulating other Countries the Service of your own.—The Captain answered, in a Rage, D——n me, do you give me the Lye? and was going to take *Minos* by the Nose, had not his Guards prevented him, and immediately turned him and all his Followers back the same Road they came.

Four Spirits informed the Judge, that they had been starved to death through Poverty; being the Father, Mother, and two

Children. That they had been honest, and as industrious as possible, till Sickness had prevented the Man from Labour.—All that is very true, cried a grave Spirit, who stood by: I know the Fact; for these poor People were under my Cure.—You was, I suppose, the Parson of the Parish, cries *Minos*; I hope you had a good Living, Sir.—That was but a small one, replied the Spirit: but I had another a little better.—Very well, said *Minos*, let the poor People pass.—At which the Parson was stepping forwards with a stately Gait before them; but *Minos* caught hold of him, and pulled him back, saying, 'Not so fast, Doctor; you must take one step more into the other World first; for no Man enters that Gate without Charity.'

A very stately Figure now presented himself, and informing *Minos* he was a Patriot, began a very florid Harangue on public Virtue, and the Liberties of his Country. Upon which, *Minos* shewed him the utmost Respect, and ordered the Gate to be opened. The Patriot was not contented with this Applause—he said, he had behaved as well in Place as he had done in the Opposition; and that, tho' he was now obliged to embrace the Court-Measures, yet he had behaved very honestly to his Friends, and brought as many in as was possible.—Hold a moment, says *Minos*, on second Consideration, Mr *Patriot*, I think a Man of your great Virtue and Abilities will be so much miss'd by your Country, that if I might advise you, you should take a Journey back again. I am sure you will not decline it, for I am certain you will with great Readiness sacrifice your own Happiness to the public Good. The Patriot smiled, and told *Minos*, he believed he was in jest; and was offering to enter the Gate, but the Judge laid fast hold of him, and insisted on his Return, which the Patriot still declining, he at last ordered his Guards to seize him, and conduct him back.

A Spirit now advanced, and the Gate was immediately thrown open to him, before he had spoken a Word. I heard some whisper,—*That is our last Lord Mayor.**

It now came to our Company's turn. The fair Spirit, which I mentioned with so much Applause, in the Beginning of my Journey, past through very easily; but the grave Lady was rejected on her first Appearance, *Minos* declaring, there was not a single Prude in *Elysium*.

The Judge then address'd himself to me, who little expected to pass this fiery Trial. I confess'd I had indulged myself very freely with Wine and Women in my Youth, but had never done an Injury to any Man living, nor avoided an Opportunity of doing good; that I pretended to very little Virtue more than general Philanthropy, and private Friendship.—I was proceeding, when *Minos* bid me enter the Gate, and not indulge myself with trumpeting forth my Virtues. I accordingly past forward with my lovely Companion, and embracing her with vast Eagerness, but spiritual Innocence, she returned my Embrace in the same manner, and we both congratulated ourselves on our Arrival in this happy Region, whose Beauty, no Painting of the Imagination can describe.

CHAPTER VIII

The Adventures which the Author met on his first Entrance into Elysium.

We pursued our way through a delicious Grove of Orange-Trees, where I saw infinite Numbers of Spirits, every one of whom I knew, and was known by them: (for Spirits here know one another by Intuition.) I presently met a little Daughter, whom I had lost several Years before.* Good Gods! what Words can describe the Raptures, the melting passionate Tenderness, with which we kiss'd each other, continuing in our Embrace, with the most extatic Joy, a Space, which if Time had been measured here as on Earth, could not be less than half a Year.

The first Spirit, with whom I entered into Discourse, was the famous *Leonidas* of *Sparta*. I acquainted him with the Honours which had been done him by a celebrated Poet of our Nation; to which he answered, he was very much obliged to him.*

We were presently afterwards entertained with the most delicious Voice I had ever heard, accompanied by a Violin, equal to Signior *Piantanida*.* I presently discovered the Musician and Songster to be *Orpheus* and *Sappho*.

Old *Homer* was present at this Consort, (if I may so call it) and Madam *Dacier* sat in his Lap.* He asked much after Mr *Pope*, and said he was very desirous of seeing him: for that he had read his *Iliad* in his Translation with almost as much delight, as he believed he had given others in the Original. I had the Curiosity to enquire whether he had really writ that Poem in detached Pieces, and sung it about as Ballads all over *Greece*, according to the Report which went of him? He smiled at my Question, and asked me whether there appeared any Connection in the Poem; for if there did, he thought I might answer myself. I then importuned him to acquaint me in which of the Cities, which contended for the Honour of his Birth, he was really born? To which he answered,—Upon my Soul I can't tell.*

Virgil then came up to me, with Mr *Addison* under his Arm. 'Well, Sir,' said he, 'how many Translations have these few last Years produced of my *Æneid?*' I told him, I believed several, but I could not possibly remember; for that I had never read any but Dr *Trapp's*.—Ay, said he, that is a curious Piece indeed!* I then acquainted him with the Discovery made by Mr *Warburton* of the *Eleusinian* Mysteries couched in his 6th Book.* 'What Mysteries?' said Mr *Addison*. 'The *Eleusinian*,' answered *Virgil*, 'which I have disclosed in my 6th Book.' 'How!' replied *Addison*. 'You never mentioned a word of any such Mysteries to me in all our Acquaintance.' 'I thought it was unnecessary,' cried the other, 'to a Man of your infinite Learning: besides, you always told me, you perfectly understood my meaning.' Upon this I thought the Critic looked a little out of countenance, and turned aside to a very merry Spirit, one *Dick Steele*, who embraced him, and told him, He had been the greatest Man upon Earth; that he readily resigned up all the Merit of his own Works to him, Upon which, *Addison* gave him a gracious Smile, and clapping him on the Back with much Solemnity, cried out, *Well said, Dick*.

I then observed *Shakespeare* standing between *Betterton* and *Booth*,* and deciding a Difference between those two great Actors, concerning the placing an Accent in one of his Lines: this was disputed on both sides with a Warmth, which surprized me in *Elysium*, till I discovered by Intuition, that every Soul retained its principal Characteristic, being, indeed, its very Essence. The Line was that celebrated one in *Othello*;

Put out the Light, and then put out the Light,

according to *Betterton*. Mr *Booth* contended to have it thus;

Put out the Light, and then put out the *Light.*

I could not help offering my Conjecture on this Occasion, and suggested it might perhaps be,

Put out the Light, and then put out thy *Light.*

Another hinted a Reading very *sophisticated* in my Opinion,

Put out the Light, and then put out thee, *Light*;

making Light to be the vocative Case. Another would have altered the last Word, and read,

Put out thy Light, and then put out thy Sight.

But *Betterton* said, if the Text was to be *disturbed*, he saw no reason why a Word might not be changed as well as a Letter, and instead of *put out thy* Light, you might read *put out thy* Eyes. At last it was agreed on all sides, to refer the matter to the Decision of *Shakespeare* himself, who delivered his Sentiments as follows: 'Faith, Gentlemen, it is so long since I wrote the Line, I have forgot my Meaning. This I know, could I have dreamt so much Nonsense would have been talked, and writ about it, I would have blotted it out of my Works: for I am sure, if any of these be my Meaning, it doth me very little Honour.'

He was then interrogated concerning some other ambiguous Passages in his Works; but he declined any satisfactory Answer: Saying, if Mr *Theobald** had not *writ about it* sufficiently, there were three or four more new Editions of his Plays coming out, which he hoped would satisfy every one. Concluding, 'I marvel nothing so much as that Men will gird themselves at discovering obscure Beauties in an Author. Certes the greatest and most pregnant Beauties are ever the plainest and most evidently striking; and when two Meanings of a Passage can in the least ballance our Judgements which to prefer, I hold it matter of unquestionable Certainty, that neither of them are worth a farthing.'

From his Works our Conversation turned on his Monument;* upon which, *Shakespeare* shaking his Sides, and addressing himself to *Milton*, cried out; 'On my word, Brother *Milton*, they have brought a noble Set of Poets together, they would have been hanged erst have convened such a Company at their Tables, when alive.' 'True, Brother,' answered *Milton*, 'unless we had been as incapable of eating then as we are now.'

CHAPTER IX

More Adventures in Elysium.

A CROUD of Spirits now joined us, whom I soon perceived to be the Heroes, who here frequently pay their Respects to the several Bards, the Recorders of their Actions. I now saw *Achilles* and *Ulysses* addressing themselves to *Homer*, and *Æneas* and *Julius Cæsar* to *Virgil: Adam* went up to *Milton*, upon which I whispered Mr *Dryden*, that I thought the Devil should have paid his Compliments there, according to his Opinion.* *Dryden* only answered, 'I believe the Devil was in me, when I said so.' Several applied themselves to *Shakespeare*, amongst whom *Henry* V made a very distinguishing Appearance. While my Eyes were fixed on that Monarch, a very small Spirit came up to me, shook me heartily by the Hand, and told me his Name was THOMAS THUMB. I expressed great Satisfaction in seeing him, nor could I help speaking my Resentment against the Historian, who had done such Injustice to the Stature of this Great little Man; which he represented to be no bigger than a Span; whereas I plainly perceived at first sight, he was a full Foot and a half, (and the 37th Part of an Inch more, as he himself informed me) being indeed little shorter than some considerable Beaus of the present Age.

I asked this little Hero, concerning the Truth of those Stories related of him, *viz.* of the Pudding, and the Cow's Belly. As to the former, he said it was a ridiculous Legend, worthy to be laughed at; but as to the latter, he could not help owning there was some Truth in it: nor, had he any reason to be ashamed of it, as he was swallowed by Surprize; adding with great Fierceness, that if he had had any Weapon in his Hand, the Cow should have as soon swallowed the Devil.

He spoke the last Word with so much Fury, and seemed so

confounded, that perceiving the Effect it had on him, I immediately waved the Story, and passing to other Matters, we had much Conversation touching Giants. He said, So far from killing any, he had never seen one alive; that he believed those Actions were by mistake recorded of him, instead of *Jack* the Giant-killer, whom he knew very well, and who had, he fancied, extirpated the Race. I assured him to the contrary, and told him I had myself seen a huge tame Giant, who very complacently staid in *London* a whole Winter, at the special Request of several Gentlemen and Ladies; tho' the Affairs of his Family called him home to *Sweden*.*

I now beheld a stern-looking Spirit leaning on the Shoulder of another Spirit, and presently discerned the former to be *Oliver Cromwell*, and the latter *Charles Martel*.* I own I was a little surprized at seeing *Cromwell* here; for I had been taught by my Grandmother, that he was carried away by the Devil himself in a Tempest: but he assured me on his Honour, there was not the least Truth in that Story.* However, he confessed he had narrowly escaped the Bottomless Pit; and, if the former Part of his Conduct had not been more to his Honour than the latter, he had been certainly soused into it. He was nevertheless sent back to the upper World with this Lot,

Army.
Cavalier.
Distress.

He was born for the second Time, the day of *Charles* II's Restoration, into a Family which had lost a very considerable Fortune in the Service of that Prince and his Father, for which they received the Reward very often conferred by Princes on real Merit, *viz.*—ooo. At 16, his Father bought a small Commission for him in the Army, in which he served without any Promotion all the Reigns of *Charles* II and of his Brother. At the Revolution he quitted his Regiment, and followed the Fortunes of his former Master, and was in his Service dangerously wounded at the famous Battle of the *Boyne*, where he fought in the Capacity of a private Soldier.* He recovered of this Wound, and retired after the unfortunate King to *Paris*, where he was reduced to support a Wife, and seven Children, (for his Lot had Horns in it) by cleaning Shoes, and snuffing Candles at the Opera. In which Situation after he had spent a few miserable Years, he died half-starved and broken-hearted. He then revisited *Minos*, who compassionating his Sufferings, by means of that Family, to whom he had been in his former Capacity so bitter an Enemy, suffered him to enter here.

My Curiosity could not refrain asking him one Question, *i.e.* Whether in reality he had any desire to obtain the Crown? He smiled and said, 'No more than an Ecclesiastic hath to the Mitre, when he cries *Nolo Episcopari*.'* Indeed, he seemed to express some Contempt at the Question, and presently turned away.

A venerable Spirit appeared next, whom I found to be the great Historian *Livy*. *Alexander the Great*, who was just arrived from the Palace of Death, past by him with a Frown. The Historian observing it, said, 'Ay, you may frown: but those Troops which conquered the base *Asiatic* Slaves, would have made no Figure against the *Romans*.' We then privately lamented the Loss of the most valuable Part of his History, after which he took occasion to commend the judicious Collection made by Mr *Hooke*, which he said was infinitely preferable to all others; and at my mentioning *Echard's*,* he gave a Bounce, not unlike the going off of a Squib, and was departing from me, when I begged him to satisfy my Curiosity in one Point, Whether he was really superstitious or no? For I had always believed he was, till Mr *Leibnitz* had assured me to the contrary. He answered sullenly,—'Doth Mr *Leibnitz* know my Mind better than myself?' and then walked away.*

CHAPTER X

The Author is surprized at meeting Julian *the Apostate in* Elysium: *but is satisfied by him, by what means he procured his Entrance there.* Julian *relates his Adventures in the Character of a Slave.**

As he was departing, I heard him salute a Spirit by the Name of Mr *Julian* the Apostate. This exceedingly amazed me: for I had concluded, that no Man ever had a better Title to the Bottomless Pit than he. But I soon found, that this same *Julian* the Apostate was also the very individual Arch-Bishop *Latimer*.* He told me, that several Lyes had been raised on him in his former Capacity, nor was he so bad a Man as he had been represented. However, he had been denied Admittance, and forced to undergo several subsequent Pilgrimages on Earth, and to act in the different Characters of a Slave, a Jew, a General, an Heir, a Carpenter, a Beau, a Monk, a Fidler, a wise Man, a King, a Fool, a Beggar, a Prince, a Statesman, a Soldier, a Taylor, an Alderman, a Poet, a Knight, a Dancing-Master, and three times a Bishop, before his Martyrdom, together with his other Behaviour in this last Character, satisfied the Judge, and procured him a Passage to the blessed Regions.

I told him, such various Characters must have produced Incidents extremely entertaining; and if he remembered all, as I supposed he did, and had Leisure, I should be obliged to him for the Recital. He answered, he perfectly recollected every Circumstance; and as to Leisure, the only Business of that happy Place was to contribute to the Happiness of each other. He therefore thanked me for increasing his, in proposing to him a Method of pleasing mine. I then took my little Darling in one Hand, and my Favourite Fellow-Traveller in the other, and going with him to a sunny Bank of Flowers, we all sat down, and he began as follows:

'I suppose, you are sufficiently acquainted with my Story, during the Time I acted the Part of the Emperor *Julian*, tho' I assure you, all which hath been related of me is not true, particularly with regard to the many Prodigies forerunning my Death. However, they are now very little worth disputing; and if they can serve any Purpose of the Historian, they are extremely at his service.

'My next Entrance into the World, was at *Laodicea* in *Syria*, in a *Roman* Family of no great Note; and being of a roving Disposition, I came at the Age of Seventeen to *Constantinople*, where after about a Year's stay, I set out for *Thrace* at the Time when the Emperor *Valens* admitted the *Goths* into that Country.* I was there so captivated with the Beauty of a *Gothic* Lady, the Wife of one *Rodoric* a Captain, whose Name, out of the most delicate Tenderness for her lovely Sex, I shall even at this Distance conceal; since her Behaviour to me was more consistent with Good-Nature, than with that Virtue which Women are obliged to preserve against every Assailant. In order to procure an Intimacy with this Woman, I sold my self a Slave to her Husband, who being of a Nation not over-inclined to Jealousy, presented me to his Wife, for those very Reasons, which would have induced one of a jealous Complexion to have with-held me from her, namely, for that I was young and handsome.

'Matters succeeded so far according to my Wish, and the Sequel answered those Hopes which this Beginning had raised. I soon perceived my Service was very acceptable to her, I often met her Eyes, nor did she withdraw them without a Confusion which is scarce consistent with entire Purity of Heart. Indeed, she gave me every day fresh Encouragement, but the unhappy Distance which Circumstances had placed between us, deterred me long from making any direct Attack; and she was too strict an Observer of Decorum, to violate the severe Rules of Modesty by advancing first: but Passion, at last, got the better of my Respect, and I resolved to make one bold Attempt, whatever was the Consequence. Accordingly, laying hold of the first kind Opportunity, when she was alone, and my Master abroad, I stoutly assailed the Citadel, and carried it by Storm. Well may I say by Storm: for the Resistance I met was extremely resolute, and indeed, as much as the most perfect Decency would require. She swore often she would cry out for Help: but I answered, it was in vain, seeing there was no Person near to assist her; and probably she believed me, for she did not once actually cry out; which if she had, I might very likely have been prevented.

'When she found her Virtue thus subdued against her Will, she patiently submitted to her Fate, and quietly suffered me a long time to enjoy the most delicious Fruits of my Victory: but envious Fortune resolved to make me pay a dear Price for my Pleasure. One day, in the midst of our Happiness, we were suddenly surprized by the unexpected Return of her Husband, who coming directly into his Wife's Apartment, just allowed me time to creep under the Bed. The Disorder in which he found his Wife, might have surprized a jealous Temper; but his was so far otherwise, that possibly no Mischief might have happened, had he not by a cross Accident discovered my Legs, which were not well hid. He immediately drew me out by them, and then turning to his Wife with a stern Countenance, began to handle a Weapon he wore by his Side, with which I am persuaded he would have instantly dispatched her, had I not very gallantly and with many Imprecations asserted her Innocence and my own Guilt; which, however, I protested had hitherto gone no farther than Design. She so well seconded my Plea, (for she was a Woman of wonderful Art) that he was at length imposed upon; and now all his Rage was directed against me, threatning all manner of Tortures, which the poor Lady was in too great a Fright and Confusion to dissuade him from executing; and perhaps, if her Concern for me had made her attempt it, it would have raised a Jealousy in him not afterwards to be removed.

'After some Hesitation, *Rodoric* cried out, he had luckily hit on the most proper Punishment for me in the World, by a Method which would at once do severe Justice on me for my criminal Intention, and at the same time, prevent me from any Danger of executing my wicked Purpose hereafter. This cruel Resolution was immediately executed, and I was no longer worthy the Name of a Man.

'Having thus disqualified me from doing him any future Injury, he still retained me in his Family: but the Lady, very probably repenting of what she had done, and looking on me as the Author of her Guilt, would never, for the future, give me either a kind Word or Look: and shortly after, a great Exchange being made between the *Romans* and the *Goths* of Dogs for Men, my Lady exchanged me with a *Roman* Widow for a small Lap-Dog, giving a considerable Sum of Money to boot.

'In this Widow's Service I remained seven Years, during all which time I was very barbarously treated. I was worked without the least Mercy, and often severely beat by a swinging Maid-Servant, who never called me by any other Names than those of *the Thing* and *the Animal*. Though I used my utmost Industry to please, it never was in my power. Neither the Lady nor her Woman would eat any thing I touched, saying, they did not believe me wholesome. It is unnecessary to repeat Particulars; in a word, you can imagine no kind of ill Usage which I did not suffer in this Family.

'At last, a Heathen Priest, an Acquaintance of my Lady's, obtained me of her for a Present. The Scene was now totally changed, and I had as much reason to be satisfied with my present Situation, as I had to lament my former. I was so absolutely my Master's Favourite, that the rest of the Slaves paid me almost as much Regard as they shewed to him, well knowing, that it was entirely in my power to command and treat them as I pleased. I was intrusted with all my Master's Secrets, and used to assist him in privately conveying away by Night the Sacrifices from the Altars, which the People believed the Deities themselves devoured. Upon these we feasted very elegantly, nor could Invention suggest a Rarity which we did not pamper ourselves with. Perhaps you may admire at the close Union between this Priest and his Slave: but we lived in an Intimacy which the Christians thought criminal: but my Master, who knew the Will of the Gods, with whom he told me he often conversed, assured me it was perfectly innocent.

'This happy Life continued about four Years, when my Master's Death, occasioned by a Surfeit got by over-feeding on several exquisite Dainties, put an end to it.

'I now fell into the hands of one of a very different Disposition, and this was no other than the celebrated St *Chrysostome*,* who dieted me with Sermons instead of Sacrifices, and filled my Ears with good Things, but not my Belly. Instead of high Food to fatten and pamper my Flesh, I had Receipts to mortify and reduce it. With these I edified so well, that within a few Months I became a Skeleton. However, as he had converted me to his Faith, I was well enough satisfied with this new Manner of living, by which he taught me I might insure myself an eternal Reward in a future State. The Saint was a good-natured Man, and never gave me an ill Word but once, which was occasioned by my neglecting to place *Aristophanes*, which was his constant Bed-fellow, on his Pillow. He was, indeed, extremely fond of that *Greek* Poet, and frequently made me read his Comedies to him: when I came to any of the loose Passages, he would smile, and say, *It was pity his Matter was not as pure as his Style*; of which latter, he was so immoderately fond, that notwithstanding the Detestation he expressed for Obscenity, he hath made me repeat those Passages ten times over. The Character of this good

Man hath been very unjustly attacked by his Heathen Cotemporaries, particularly with regard to Women; but his severe Invectives against that Sex, are his sufficient Justification.

'From the Service of this Saint, from whom I received Manumission, I entered into the Family of *Timasius*, a Leader of great Eminence in the Imperial Army, into whose Favour I so far insinuated myself, that he preferred me to a good Command, and soon made me Partaker of both his Company and his Secrets. I soon grew intoxicated with this Preferment, and the more he loaded me with Benefits, the more he raised my Opinion of my own Merit; which still outstripping the Rewards he conferred on me, inspired me rather with Dissatisfaction than Gratitude. And thus, by preferring me beyond my Merit or first Expectation, he made me an envious aspiring Enemy, whom perhaps, a more moderate Bounty, would have preserved a dutiful Servant.

'I fell now acquainted with one *Lucilius*, a Creature of the Prime-Minister *Eutropius*, who had by his Favour been raised to the Post of a Tribune; a Man of low Morals, and eminent only in that meanest of all Qualities, Cunning. This Gentleman imagining me a fit Tool for the Minister's Purpose, having often sounded my Principles of Honour and Honesty; both which he declared to me were Words without Meaning: and finding my ready Concurrence in his Sentiments, recommended me to *Eutropius*, as very proper to execute some wicked Purposes he had contrived against my Friend *Timasius*. The Minister embraced this Recommendation, and I was accordingly acquainted by *Lucilius*, (after some previous Accounts of the great Esteem *Eutropius* entertained of me, from the Testimony he had born of my Parts) that he would introduce me to him; adding, that he was a great Encourager of Merit, and that I might depend upon his Favour.

'I was with little difficulty prevailed on to accept this Invitation. A late Hour therefore the next Evening being appointed, I attended my Friend *Lucilius* to the Minister's House. He received me with the utmost Civility and Chearfulness, and affected so much Regard to me, that I, who knew nothing of these high Scenes of Life, concluded I had in him a most disinterested Friend, owing to the favourable Report which *Lucilius* had made of me. I was however soon cured of this Opinion: for immediately after Supper, our Discourse turned on the Injustice which the Generality of the World were guilty of in their Conduct to Great Men, expecting that they should reward their private Merit, without ever endeavouring to apply it to their Use. *What avail* (said *Eutropius*) *the Learning, Wit, Courage, or any Virtue which a Man may be possest of to me, unless I receive some Benefit from them? Hath he not more Merit to me, who doth my Business, and obeys my Commands, without any of these Qualities?* I gave such entire Satisfaction in my Answers on this Head, that both the Minister and his Creature grew bolder, and after some Preface, began to accuse *Timasius*. At last, finding I did not attempt to defend him, *Lucilius* swore a great Oath, that he was not fit to live, and that he would destroy him. *Eutropius* answered, that it would be too dangerous a Task: *Indeed*, says he, *his Crimes are of so black a Dye, and so well known to the Emperor, that his Death must be a very acceptable Service, and could not fail meeting a proper Reward; but I question whether you are capable of executing it. If he is not*, cried I, *I am; and surely, no Man can have greater Motives to destroy him than my self: for, besides his Disloyalty to my Prince, for whom I have so perfect a Duty, I have private Disobligations to him. I have had Fellows put over my head, to the great Scandal of the Service in general, and to my own Prejudice and Disappointment in particular.*—I will not repeat you my whole Speech: but to be as concise as possible, when we parted that Evening, the Minister squeezed me heartily by the Hand, and with great Commendation of my Honesty, and Assurances of his Favour, he appointed me, the next Evening, to come to him alone; when finding me, after a little more Scrutiny, ready for his Purpose, he proposed to me, to accuse *Timasius* of High-Treason: promising me the highest Rewards, if I would undertake it. The Consequence to him, I suppose you know, was Ruin: but what was it to me? Why truly, when I waited on *Eutropius*, for the fulfilling his Promises, he received me with great Distance and Coldness; and on my dropping some Hints of my Expectations from him, he affected not to understand me; saying, he thought Impunity was the utmost I could hope for, on discovering my Accomplice, whose Offence was only greater than mine, as he was in a higher Station; and telling me, he had great difficulty to obtain a Pardon for me from the Emperor, which, he said he had struggled very hardly for, as he had worked the Discovery out of me, he turned away, and addressed himself to another Person.

'I was so incensed at this Treatment, that I resolved Revenge, and should certainly have pursued it, had he not cautiously prevented me, by taking effectual Means to dispatch me soon after out of the World.

'You will, I believe, now think, I had a second good Chance for the Bottomless Pit, and indeed *Minos* seemed inclined to tumble me in, till he was informed of the Revenge taken on me by *Rodoric*, and my seven Years subsequent Servitude to the Widow; which he said he thought sufficient to make Atonement for all the Crimes a single Life could admit of, and so sent me back to try my Fortune a third time.'

CHAPTER XI

In which Julian *relates his Adventures in the Character of an avaricious* Jew.

'THE next Character in which I was destined to appear in the Flesh, was that of an avaricious *Jew*. I was born in *Alexandria* in *Egypt*. My Name was *Balthazar*. Nothing very remarkable happened to me, till the Year of the memorable Tumult, in which the *Jews* of that City are reported in History to have massacred more Christians, than at that time dwelt in it. Indeed, the truth is, they did maul the Dogs pretty handsomely; but I my self was not present: for as all our People were ordered to be armed, I took that opportunity of selling two Swords, which probably I might otherwise never have disposed of, they being extremely old and rusty: so that having no Weapon left, I did not care to venture abroad. Besides, tho' I really thought it an Act meriting Salvation to murder the *Nazarenes*, as the Fact was to be committed at Midnight, at which Time, to avoid Suspicion, we were all to sally from our own Houses; I could not persuade my self to consume so much Oil in sitting up till that Hour: for these Reasons therefore, I remained at home that Evening.

'I was at this time greatly enamoured with one *Hypatia*, the Daughter of a Philosopher;* a young Lady of the greatest Beauty and Merit: indeed, she had every imaginable Ornament both of Mind and Body. She seemed not to dislike my Person: but there were two Obstructions to our Marriage, *viz.* my Religion and her Poverty: both which might probably have been got over, had not those Dogs the Christians murdered her; and, what is worse, afterwards burnt her Body: worse, I say, because I lost by that means a Jewel of some Value, which I had presented to her, designing, if our Nuptials did not take place, to demand it of her back again.

'Being thus disappointed in my Love, I soon after left *Alexandria*, and went to the Imperial City, where I apprehended I should find a good Market for Jewels on the approaching Marriage of the Emperor with *Athenais*.* I disguised my self as a Beggar on this Journey, for these Reasons: first, as I imagined I should thus carry my Jewels with greater Safety; and secondly, to lessen my Expences: which latter Expedient succeeded so well, that I begged two Oboli on my way more than my Travelling cost me, my Diet being chiefly Roots, and my Drink Water.

'But perhaps, it had been better for me if I had been more lavish, and more expeditious: for the Ceremony was over before I reached *Constantinople*; so that I lost that glorious Opportunity of disposing of my Jewels, with which many of our People were greatly enriched.

'The Life of a Miser is very little worth relating, as it is one constant Scheme of getting or saving Money. I shall therefore repeat to you some few only of my Adventures, without regard to any Order.

'A Roman *Jew*, who was a great Lover of *Falernian* Wine, and who indulged himself very freely with it, came to dine at my House; when knowing he should meet with little Wine, and that of the cheaper sort, sent me in half a dozen Jars of *Falernian*. Can you believe I would not give this Man his own Wine? Sir, I adulterated it so, that I made six Jars of them; three, which he and his Friend drank; the other three I afterwards sold to the very Person who originally sent them me, knowing he would give a better Price than any other.

'A noble *Roman* came one day to my House in the Country,

which I had purchased, for half the Value, of a distressed Person. My Neighbours paid him the Compliment of some Music, on which account, when he departed, he left a Piece of Gold with me, to be distributed among them. I pocketed this Money, and ordered them a small Vessel of sour Wine, which I could not have sold for above two Drachmas, and afterwards made them pay in Work three times the Value of it.

'As I was not entirely void of Religion, tho' I pretended to infinitely more than I had, so I endeavoured to reconcile my Transactions to my Conscience as well as possible. Thus I never invited any one to eat with me, but those on whose Pockets I had some Design. After our Collation, it was constantly my Method to set down in a Book I kept for that purpose, what I thought they owed me for their Meal. Indeed, this was generally a hundred times as much as they could have dined elsewhere for: but however, it was *quid pro quo*, if not *ad valorem*. Now whenever the Opportunity offered of imposing on them, I considered it only as paying my self what they owed me: indeed, I did not always confine my self strictly to what I had set down, however extravagant that was; but I reconciled taking the Overplus to my self as Usance.

'But I was not only too cunning for others, I sometimes overreached my self. I have contracted Distempers for want of Food and Warmth, which have put me to the Expence of a Physician: Nay, I once very narrowly escaped Death by taking bad Drugs, only to save one Seven Eighths *per Cent*. in the Price.

'By these and such like Means, in the midst of Poverty and every kind of Distress, I saw my self Master of an immense Fortune: the casting up and ruminating on which was my daily and only Pleasure. This was however obstructed and embittered by two Considerations, which against my Will often invaded my Thoughts. One would have been intolerable (but that indeed seldom troubled me) was, that I must one day leave my darling Treasure. The other haunted me continually, *viz.* that my Riches were no greater. However, I comforted my self against this Reflection, by an Assurance that they would increase daily: On which Head, my Hopes were so extensive, that I may say with *Virgil*,

*His ego nec Metas Rerum nec Tempora pono.**

Indeed I am convinced, that had I possessed the whole Globe of Earth, save one single Drachma, which I had been certain never to be master of, I am convinced, I say, that single Drachma, would have given me more Uneasiness than all the rest could afford me Pleasure.

'To say the truth, between my Solicitude in contriving Schemes to procure Money, and my extreme Anxiety in preserving it, I never had one Moment of Ease while awake, nor of Quiet when in my Sleep. In all the Characters through which I have passed, I have never undergone half the Misery I suffered in this, and indeed *Minos* seemed to be of the same Opinion: for while I stood trembling and shaking in Expectation of my Sentence, he bid me go back about my Business; for that no body was to be d——n'd in more Worlds than one. And indeed, I have since learnt, that the Devil will not receive a Miser.'

CHAPTER XII

What happened to Julian *in the Characters of a General, an Heir, a Carpenter, and a Beau.*

'THE next Step I took into the World, was at *Apollonia* in *Thrace*; where I was born of a beautiful *Greek* Slave, who was the Mistress of *Eutyches*, a great Favourite of the Emperor *Zeno*.* That Prince, at his Restoration, gave me the Command of a Cohort, I being then but fifteen Years of Age; and a little afterwards, before I had ever seen an Army, preferred me, over the Heads of all the old Officers, to be a Tribune.

'As I found an easy Access to the Emperor, by means of my Father's Intimacy with him, he being a very good Courtier, or in other Words, a most prostitute Flatterer; so I soon ingratiated myself with *Zeno*, and so well imitated my Father in flattering him, that he would never part with me from about his Person. So that the first armed Force I ever beheld, was that with which *Martian* surrounded the Palace, where I was then shut up with the rest of the Court.*

'I was after put at the Head of a Legion, and ordered to march into *Syria*, with *Theodoric* the *Goth*,* that is, I mean my Legion was so ordered: for as to myself, I remained at Court, with the Name and Pay of a General, without the Labour or the Danger.

'As nothing could be more gay, *i.e.* debauched, than *Zeno's* Court, so the Ladies of gay Disposition had great sway in it; particularly one, whose Name was *Fausta*, who, tho' not extremely handsome, was by her Wit and Spriteliness very agreeable to the Emperor. With her I lived in good Correspondence, and we together disposed of all kinds of Commissions in the Army, not to those who had most Merit, but who would purchase at the highest Rate. My Levee was now prodigiously thronged by Officers, who returned from the Campaigns; who, tho' they might have been convinced, by daily Example, how ineffectual a Recommendation their Services were, still continued indefatigable in Attendance, and behaved to me with as much Observance and Respect, as I should have been entitled to, for making their Fortunes, while I suffered them and their Families to starve.

'Several Poets, likewise, addressed Verses to me, in which they celebrated my Military Atchievements; and what, perhaps, may seem strange to us at present, I received all this Incense with most greedy Vanity, without once reflecting, that as I did not deserve these Compliments, they should rather put me in mind of my Defects.

'My Father was now dead, and I became so absolute in the Emperor's Grace, that one unacquainted with Courts would scarce believe the Servility with which all kinds of Persons, who entered the Walls of the Palace, behaved towards me. A Bow, a Smile, a Nod from me, as I past through cringing Crouds, were esteemed as signal Favours, but a gracious Word made any one happy; and, indeed, had this real Benefit attending it, that it drew on the Person, on whom it was bestowed, a very great Degree of Respect from all others; for these are of current Value in Courts, and, like Notes in trading Communities, are assignable from one to the other. The Smile of a Court-Favourite immediately raises the Person who receives it, and gives a Value to his Smile when conferred on an Inferiour: thus the Smile is transferred from one to the other, and the Great Man at last is the Person to discount it. For instance, a very low Fellow hath a desire for a Place. To whom is he to apply? Not to the Great Man; for to him he hath no Access. He therefore applies to *A*, who is the Creature of *B*, who is the Tool of *C*, who is the Flatterer of *D*, who is the Catamite of *E*, who is the Pimp of *F*, who is the Bully of *G*, who is the Buffoon of *I*, who is the Husband of *K*, who is the Whore of *L*, who is the Bastard of *M*, who is the Instrument of the Great Man. Thus the Smile descending regularly from the Great Man to *A*, is discounted back again, and at last paid by the Great Man.

'It is manifest, that a Court would subsist as difficultly without this kind of Coin, as a trading City without Paper Credit. Indeed, they differ in this, that their Value is not quite so certain, and a Favourite may protest his Smile without the Danger of Bankruptcy.

'In the midst of all this Glory, the Emperor died, and *Anastasius* was preferred to the Crown.* As it was yet uncertain whether I should not continue in favour, I was received as usual at my Entrance into the Palace, to pay my Respects to the new Emperor; but I was no sooner rumped by him, than I received the same Compliment from all the rest; the whole Room, like a Regiment of Soldiers, turning their Backs to me all at once, my Smile now was become of equal Value with the Note of a broken Banker, and every one was as cautious not to receive it.

'I made as much haste as possible from the Court, and shortly after from the City, retreating to the Place of my Nativity, where I spent the Remainder of my Days in a retired Life in Husbandry, the only Amusement for which I was qualified, having neither Learning nor Virtue.

'When I came to the Gate, *Minos* again seemed at first doubtful, but at length dismissed me; saying, tho' I had been guilty of many heinous Crimes, in as much as I had, tho' a General, never been concerned in spilling human Blood, I might return again to Earth.

'I was now again born in *Alexandria*, and, by great Accident, entring into the Womb of my Daughter-in-Law, came forth my own Grandson, inheriting that Fortune which I had before amassed.

'Extravagance was now as notoriously my Vice, as Avarice had been formerly; and I spent, in a very short Life, what it had cost me the Labour of a very long one to rake together. Perhaps, you will think my present Condition was more to be envied than my former: but upon my Word it was very little so; for by possessing every thing almost before I desired it, I could hardly ever say, I enjoyed my Wish: I scarce ever knew the Delight of satisfying a craving Appetite. Besides, as I never once thought, my Mind was useless to me, and I was an absolute Stranger to all the Pleasures arising from it. Nor, indeed, did my Education qualify me for any Delicacy in other Enjoyments; so that in the midst of Plenty I loathed every thing. Taste for Elegance, I had none; and the greatest of corporeal Blisses I felt no more from, than the lowest Animal. In a word, as while a Miser I had Plenty without daring to use it, so now I had it without Appetite.

'But if I was not very happy in the height of my Enjoyment, so I afterward became perfectly miserable; being soon overtaken by Disease, and reduced to Distress, 'till at length with a broken Constitution, and broken Heart, I ended my wretched Days in a Gaol: nor can I think the Sentence of *Minos* too mild, who condemned me, after having taken a large Dose of Avarice, to wander three Years on the Banks of *Cocytus*, with the Knowledge of having spent the Fortune in the Person of the Grandson, which I had raised in that of the Grandfather.

'The Place of my Birth, on my return to the World, was *Constantinople*, where my Father was a Carpenter. The first Thing I remember was, the Triumph of *Belisarius*; which was, indeed, a most noble Shew: but nothing pleased me so much as the Figure of *Gelimer*, King of the *African Vandals*, who being led Captive on this Occasion, reflecting with Disdain on the Mutation of his own Fortune, and on the ridiculous empty Pomp of the Conqueror, cried out, VANITY, VANITY, ALL IS MERE VANITY.*

'I was bred up to my Father's Trade, and you may easily believe so low a Sphere could produce no Adventures worth your Notice. However, I married a Woman I liked, and who proved a very tolerable Wife. My Days were past in hard Labour, but this procured me Health, and I enjoyed a homely Supper at night with my Wife, with more Pleasure than I apprehend greater Persons find at their luxurious Meals. My Life had scarce any Variety in it, and at my Death, I advanced to *Minos* with great

Confidence of entring the Gate: but I was unhappily obliged to discover some Frauds I had been guilty of in the Measure of my Work, when I worked by the Foot, as well as my Laziness, when I was employed by the Day. On which account when I attempted to pass, the angry Judge laid hold on me by the Shoulders, and turned me back so violently, that had I had a Neck of Flesh and Bone, I believe he would have broke it.'

CHAPTER XIII

Julian *passes into a Fop.*

'MY next Scene of Action was *Rome*. I was born into a noble Family, and Heir to a considerable Fortune. On which my Parents, thinking I should not want any Talents, resolved very kindly and wisely to throw none away upon me. The only Instructors of my Youth were therefore one *Saltator*,* who taught me several Motions for my Legs; and one *Ficus*,* whose Business was to shew me the cleanest way (as he called it) of cutting off a Man's Head. When I was well accomplished in these Sciences, I thought nothing more wanting, but what was to be furnished by the several Mechanics in *Rome*, who dealt in dressing and adorning the Pope. Being therefore well equipped with all which their Art could produce, I became at the Age of Twenty, a complete finished Beau. And now during 45 Years I drest, I sang and danced, and danced and sang, I bowed and ogled, and ogled and bowed, 'till in the 66th Year of my Age, I got cold by over-heating myself with dancing, and died.

'Minos told me as I was unworthy of *Elysium*, so I was too insignificant to be damned, and therefore bad me walk back again.'

CHAPTER XIV

Adventures in the Person of a Monk.

'FORTUNE now placed me in the Character of a younger Brother of a good House, and I was in my Youth sent to School; but

Learning was now at so low an Ebb, that my Master himself could hardly construe a Sentence of *Latin*; and as for *Greek*, he could not read it. With very little Knowledge therefore, and with altogether as little Virtue, I was set apart for the Church, and at the proper Age commenced Monk.* I lived many Years retired in a Cell, a Life very agreeable to the Gloominess of my Temper, which was much inclined to despise the World; that is, in other Words, to envy all Men of superiour Fortune and Qualifications, and in general, to hate and detest the human Species. Notwithstanding which, I could, on proper Occasions, submit to flatter the vilest Fellow in Nature, which I did one *Stephen* an Eunuch, a Favourite of the Emperor *Justinian* II, one of the wickedest Wretches whom perhaps the World ever saw. I not only wrote a Panegyric on this Man, but I commended him as a Pattern to all others in my Sermons, by which means I so greatly ingratiated my self with him, that he introduced me to the Emperor's Presence, where I prevailed so far by the same Methods, that I was shortly taken from my Cell, and preferred to a Place at Court. I was no sooner established in the Favour of *Justinian*, than I prompted him to all kind of Cruelty. As I was of a sour morose Temper, and hated nothing more than the Symptoms of Happiness appearing in any Countenance, I represented all kind of Diversion and Amusement as the most horrid Sins. I inveighed against Chearfulness as Levity, and encouraged nothing but Gravity, or, to confess the Truth to you, Hypocrisy. The unhappy Emperor followed my Advice, and incensed the People by such repeated Barbarities, that he was at last deposed by them and banished.*

'I now retired again to my Cell, (for Historians mistake in saying I was put to death) where I remained safe from the Danger of the irritated Mob, whom I cursed in my own Heart, as much as they could curse me.

'Justinian, after three Years of his Banishment, returned to *Constantinople* in disguise, and paid me a Visit. I at first affected not to know him, and without the least Compunction of Gratitude for his former Favours, intended not to receive him, till a Thought immediately suggesting it self to me, how I might convert him to my Advantage, I pretended to recollect him; and blaming the shortness of my Memory and badness of my Eyes, I sprung forward and embraced him with great Affection.

'My Design was to betray him to *Apsimar*, who, I doubted not, would generously reward such a Service. I therefore very earnestly requested him to spend the whole Evening with me; to which he consented. I formed an Excuse for leaving him a few Minutes, and ran away to the Palace to acquaint *Apsimar* with the Guest whom I then had in my Cell. He presently ordered a Guard to go with me and seize him: but whether the Length of my Stay gave him any Suspicion, or whether he changed his Purpose after my Departure, I know not: for at my Return, we found he had given us the slip; nor could we with the most diligent Search discover him.

'Apsimar being disappointed of his Prey, now raged at me; at first denouncing the most dreadful Vengeance, if I did not produce the deposed Monarch: However, by soothing his Passion when at the highest, and afterwards by Canting and Flattery, I made a shift to escape his Fury.

'When *Justinian* was restored, I very confidently went to wish him Joy of his Restoration: but it seems, he had unfortunately heard of my Treachery, so that he at first received me coldly, and afterwards upbraided me openly with what I had done. I persevered stoutly in denying it, as I knew no Evidence could be produced against me; till finding him irreconcileable, I betook my self to reviling him in my Sermons, and on every other Occasion, as an Enemy to the Church, and good Men, and as an Infidel, an Heretic, an Atheist, a Heathen, and an Arian. This I did immediately on his Return, and before he gave those flagrant Proofs of his Inhumanity, which afterwards sufficiently verified all I had said.

'Luckily, I died on the same Day, when a great Number of those Forces which *Justinian* had sent against the *Thracian Bosphorus*, and who had executed such unheard of Cruelties there, perished. As every one of these was cast into the Bottomless Pit, *Minos* was so tired with Condemnation, that he proclaimed that all present, who had not been concerned in that bloody Expedition, might, if they pleased, return to the other World. I took him at his Word, and presently turning about, began my Journey.'

CHAPTER XV

Julian *passes into the Character of a Fiddler.*

'ROME was now the Seat of my Nativity. My Mother was an *African*, a Woman of no great Beauty, but a Favourite, I suppose from her Piety, to Pope *Gregory* II.* Who was my Father, I know not; but I believe no very considerable Man: for after the Death of that Pope, who was, out of his Religion, a very good Friend of my Mother, we fell into great Distress, and were at length reduced to walk the Streets of *Rome*; nor had either of us any other Support but a Fiddle, on which I played with pretty tolerable skill: for as my Genius turned naturally to Music, so I had been in my Youth very early instructed at the Expence of the good Pope. This afforded us but a very poor Livelihood: for tho' I had often a numerous Croud of Hearers, few ever thought themselves obliged to contribute the smallest Pittance to the poor starving Wretch who had given them Pleasure. Nay, some of the Graver Sort after an Hour's Attention to my Music, have gone away shaking their Heads, and crying, it was a shame such Vagabonds were suffered to stay in the City.

'To say the truth, I am confident the Fiddle would not have kept us alive, had we entirely depended on the Generosity of my Hearers. My Mother therefore was forced to use her own Industry; and while I was soothing the Ears of the Croud, she applied to their Pockets, and that generally with such good Success, that we now began to enjoy a very comfortable Subsistence; and indeed, had we had the least Prudence or Forecast, might have soon acquired enough to enable us to quit this dangerous and dishonourable Way of Life: but I know not what is the reason, that Money got with Labour and Safety is constantly preserved, while the Produce of Danger and Ease is commonly spent as easily, and often as wickedly, as acquired. Thus we proportioned our Expences rather by what we had than what we wanted, or even desired; and on obtaining a considerable Booty, we have even forced Nature into the most profligate Extravagance; and have been wicked without Inclination.

'We carried on this Method of Thievery for a long time without Detection: but as Fortune generally leaves Persons of extraordinary Ingenuity in the lurch at last; so did she us: for my poor Mother was taken in the Fact, and together with my self, as her Accomplice, hurried before a Magistrate.

'Luckily for us, the Person who was to be our Judge, was the greatest Lover of Music in the whole City, and had often sent for me to play to him, for which, as he had given me very small Rewards, perhaps his Gratitude now moved him: but, whatever was his Motive, he browbeat the Informers against us, and treated their Evidence with so little Favour, that their Mouths were soon stopped, and we dismissed with Honour; acquitted, I should rather have said: for we were not suffered to depart, till I had given the Judge several Tunes on the Fiddle.

'We escaped the better on this Occasion, because the Person robbed happened to be a Poet; which gave the Judge, who was a facetious Person, many Opportunities of jesting. He said, Poets and Musicians should agree together, seeing they had married Sisters, which he afterwards explained to be the Sister Arts. And when the Piece of Gold was produced, he burst into a loud Laugh, and said it must be the golden Age when Poets had Gold in their Pockets, and in that Age there could be no Robbers. He made many more Jests of the same kind, but a small Taste will suffice.

'It is a common Saying, that Men should take Warning by any signal Delivery; but I cannot approve the Justice of it: for to me it seems, that the Acquittal of a guilty Person should rather inspire him with Confidence, and it had this Effect on us: for we now laughed at the Law and despised its Punishments, which we found were to be escaped even against positive Evidence. We imagined the late Example was rather a Warning to the Accuser than the Criminal, and accordingly proceeded in the most impudent and flagitious manner.

'Among other Robberies, one Night being admitted by the Servants into the House of an opulent Priest, my Mother took an opportunity whilst the Servants were dancing to my Tunes, to convey away a Silver Vessel; this she did without the least sacrilegious Intention: but it seems the Cup, which was a pretty large one, was dedicated to holy Uses, and only borrowed by the Priest on an Entertainment which he made for some of his Brethren. We were immediately pursued upon this Robbery, (the Cup being taken in our possession,) and carried before the same Magistrate, who had before behaved to us with so much Gentleness: but his Countenance was now changed; for the moment the Priest appeared against us, his Severity was as remarkable as his Candour had been before, and we were both ordered to be stript and whipt through the Streets.

'This Sentence was executed with great Severity, the Priest himself attending and encouraging the Executioner, which he said he did for the good of our Souls: but though our Backs were both flea'd, neither my Mother's Torments nor my own afflicted me so much, as the Indignity offered to my poor Fiddle, which was carried in Triumph before me, and treated with a Contempt by the Multitude, intimating a great Scorn for the Science I had the Honour to profess; which, as it is one of the noblest Inventions of Men, and as I had been always in the highest degree proud of my Excellence in it, I suffered so much from the ill Treatment my Fiddle received, that I would have given all my Remainder of Skin to have preserved it from this Affront.

'My Mother survived the Whipping a very short time, and I was now reduced to great Distress and Misery; till a young *Roman* of considerable Rank took a fancy to me, received me into his Family, and conversed with me in the utmost Familiarity. He had a violent Attachment to Music, and would learn to play on the Fiddle: but through want of Genius for the Science, he never made any considerable progress. However, I flattered his Performance, and he grew extravagantly fond of me for so doing. Had I continued this Behaviour, I might possibly have reaped the greatest Advantages from his Kindness; but I had raised his own Opinion of his musical Abilities so high, that he now began to prefer his Skill to mine, a Presumption I could not bear. One day as we were playing in Concert he was horribly out; nor was it possible, as he destroyed the Harmony, to avoid telling him of it. Instead of receiving my Correction, he answered, It was my Blunder, and not his, and that I had mistaken the Key. Such an Affront from my own Scholar was beyond human Patience; I flew into a violent Passion, I flung down my Instrument in a Rage, and swore, I was not to be taught Music at my Age. He answered with as much Warmth, nor was he to be instructed by a stroling Fiddler. The Dispute ended in a

Challenge to play a Prize before Judges. This Wager was determined in my favour: but the Purchase was a dear one; for I lost my Friend by it, who now twitting me with all his Kindness, with my former ignominious Punishment, and the destitute Condition from which I had been by his Bounty relieved, discarded me for ever.

'While I lived with this Gentleman, I became known, among others to *Sabina*, a Lady of Distinction, and who valued her self much on her Taste for Music. She no sooner heard of my being discarded, than she took me into her House, where I was extremely well cloathed and fed. Notwithstanding which, my Situation was far from agreeable: for I was obliged to submit to her constant Reprehensions before Company; which gave me the greater Uneasiness, because they were always wrong; nor am I certain that she did not by these Provocations contribute to my Death: for as Experience had taught me to give up my Resentment to my Bread, so my Passions, for want of outward Vent, preyed inwardly on my Vitals, and perhaps occasioned the Distemper of which I sicken'd.

'The Lady who, amidst all the Faults she found, was very fond of me; nay, probably was the fonder of me the more Faults she found; immediately called in the Aid of three celebrated Physicians. The Doctors (being well feed,) made me seven Visits in three Days; and two of them were at the Door to visit me the eighth time, when being acquainted that I was just dead, they shook their Heads and departed.

'When I came to *Minos*, he asked me with a Smile, whether I had brought my Fiddle with me; and receiving an Answer in the Negative, he bid me get about my business, saying, it was well for me that the Devil was no Lover of Music.'

CHAPTER XVI

The History of the Wise Man.

'I NOW returned to *Rome*, but in a very different Character. Fortune had now allotted me a serious Part to act. I had even in my Infancy a grave Disposition, nor was I ever seen to smile; which infused an Opinion into all about me, that I was a Child of great Solidity: some foreseeing that I should be a Judge, and others a Bishop. At two Years old my Father presented me with a Rattle, which I broke to pieces with great indignation. This the good Parent, being extremely wise, regarded as an eminent Symptom of my Wisdom, and cried out in a kind of Extasy, *Well said, Boy, I warrant thou makest a Great Man.*

'At School, I could never be persuaded to play with my Mates; not that I spent my Hours in Learning, to which I was not in the least addicted, nor indeed had I any Talents for it. However, the Solemnity of my Carriage won so much on my Master, who was a most sagacious Person, that I was his chief Favourite, and my Example on all Occasions was recommended to the other Boys, which filled them with Envy, and me with Pleasure: but though they envied me, they all paid me that involuntary Respect, which it is the Curse attending this Passion to bear towards its Object.

'I had now obtained universally the Character of a very wise young Man, which I did not altogether purchase without Pains; for the Restraint I laid on my self in abstaining from the several Diversions adapted to my Years, cost me many a yearning: but the Pride which I inwardly enjoyed in the fancied Dignity of my Character, made me some Amends.

'Thus I past on, without any thing very memorable happening to me, till I arrived at the Age of Twenty-three; when unfortunately I fell acquainted with a young *Neapolitan* Lady, whose Name was *Ariadne*. Her Beauty was so exquisite, that her first Sight made a violent Impression on me; this was again improved by her Behaviour, which was most genteel, easy, and affable: Lastly, her Conversation compleated the Conquest. In this she discovered a strong and lively Understanding, with the sweetest and most benign Temper. This lovely Creature was about Eighteen when I first unhappily beheld her at *Rome*, in a Visit to a Relation, with whom I had great Intimacy. As our Interviews at first were extremely frequent, my Passions were captivated before I apprehended the least Danger; and the sooner probably, as the young Lady herself, to whom I consulted every Method of Recommendation, was not displeased with my being her Admirer.

'Ariadne having spent three Months at *Rome*, now returned to

Naples, bearing my Heart with her; on the other hand, I had all the Assurances consistent with the constraint under which the most perfect Modesty lays a young Woman, that her own Heart was not entirely unaffected. I soon found her Absence gave me an Uneasiness not easy to be born, or to remove. I now first applied to Diversions (of the graver sort, particularly to Music) but in vain; they rather raised my Desires, and heightened my Anguish. My Passion at length grew so violent, that I began to think of satisfying it. As the first Step to this, I cautiously enquired into the Circumstances of *Ariadne's* Parents, with which I was hitherto unacquainted; tho' indeed, I did not apprehend they were extremely great, notwithstanding the handsome Appearance of their Daughter at *Rome*. Upon Examination, her Fortune exceeded my Expectation; but was not sufficient to justify my Marriage with her, in the Opinion of the Wise and Prudent. I had now a violent Struggle between Wisdom and Happiness, in which, after several grievous Pangs, Wisdom got the better. I could by no means prevail with my self to sacrifice that Character of profound Wisdom, which I had with such uniform Conduct obtained, and with such Caution hitherto preserved. I therefore resolved to conquer my Affection, whatever it cost me, and indeed it did not cost me a little.

'While I was engaged in this Conflict, (for it lasted a long time) *Ariadne* returned to *Rome*: Her Presence was a terrible Enemy to my Wisdom, which even in her Absence had with great difficulty stood its ground. It seems (as she hath since told me in *Elysium* with much merriment) I had made the same Impressions on her which she had made on me. Indeed, I believe my Wisdom would have been totally subdued by this Surprize, had it not cunningly suggested to me a Method of satisfying my Passion without doing any Injury to my Reputation. This was by engaging her privately as a Mistress, which was at that time reputable enough at *Rome*, provided the Affair was managed with an Air of Slyness and Gravity, tho' the Secret was known to the whole City.

'I immediately set about this Project, and employed every Art and Engine to effect it. I had particularly bribed her Priest, and an old Female Acquaintance and distant Relation of hers into my Interest: but all was in vain; her Virtue opposed the Passion in her Breast as strongly as Wisdom had opposed it in mine. She received my Proposals with the utmost Disdain, and presently refused to see or hear from me any more.

'She returned again to *Naples*, and left me in a worse Condition, than before. My Days I now passed with the most irksome Uneasiness, and my Nights were restless and sleepless. The Story of our Amour was now pretty public, and the Ladies talked of our Match as certain; but my Acquaintance denied their Assent, saying, No, no, he is too wise to marry so imprudently. This their Opinion gave me, I own, very great Pleasure: but to say the truth, scarce compensated the Pangs I suffered to preserve it.

'One day, while I was balancing with myself, and had almost resolved to enjoy my Happiness, at the Price of my Character, a Friend brought me word, that *Ariadne* was married. This News struck me to the Soul, and tho' I had Resolution enough to maintain my Gravity before him, (for which I suffered not a little the more) the Moment I was alone, I threw myself into the most violent Fit of Despair, and would willingly have parted with Wisdom, Fortune, and every thing else, to have retrieved her: but that was impossible, and I had now nothing but Time to hope a Cure from. This was very tedious in performing it, and the longer as *Ariadne* had married a *Roman* Cavalier, was now become my near Neighbour, and I had the mortification of seeing her make the best of Wives, and of having the Happiness, which I had lost, every day before my Eyes.

'If I suffered so much on account of my Wisdom, in having refused *Ariadne*, I was not much more obliged to it, for procuring me a rich Widow, who was recommended to me by an old Friend, as a very prudent Match, and, indeed, so it was; her Fortune being superiour to mine, in the same Proportion as that of *Ariadne* had been inferiour. I therefore embraced this Proposal, and my Character of Wisdom soon pleaded so effectually for me with the Widow, who was herself a Woman of great Gravity and Discretion, that I soon succeeded; and as soon as Decency would permit, (or which this Lady was the strictest Observer) we were married; being the second Day of the second Week, of the second Year, after her Husband's Death: for she said, she thought some Period of Time above the Year had a great Air of Decorum.*

'But prudent as this Lady was, she made me miserable. Her Person was far from being lovely; but her Temper was intolerable. During fifteen Years Habitation, I never passed a single Day without heartily cursing her, and the Hour in which we came together. The only Comfort I received in the midst of the highest Torments, was from continually hearing the Prudence of my Match commended by all my Acquaintance.

'Thus you see in the Affairs of Love, I bought the Reputation of Wisdom pretty dear. In other Matters, I had it somewhat cheaper; not that Hypocrisy, which was the Price I gave for it, gives one no pain. I have refused myself a thousand little Amusements with a feign'd Contempt, while I have really had an Inclination to them. I have often almost choaked myself to restrain from laughing at a Jest, and (which was perhaps to myself the least hurtful of all my Hypocrisy) have heartily enjoyed a Book in my Closet, which I have spoke with detestation of in public. To sum up my History in short, as I had few Adventures worth remembring, my whole Life was one constant Lye; and happy would it have been for me, if I could as thoroughly have imposed on myself, as I did on others: for Reflection, at every turn, would often remind me I was not so wise as People thought me; and this considerably embittered the Pleasure I received from the public Commendation of my Wisdom. This Self-Admonition, like a *Memento mori*, or *Mortalis es*, must be, in my opinion, a very dangerous Enemy to Flattery: indeed, a Weight sufficient to counter-ballance all the false Praise of the World. But whether it be, that the generality of wise Men do not reflect at all, or whether they have, from a constant Imposition on others, contracted such a Habit of Deceit, as to deceive themselves; I will not determine: it is, I believe, most certain, that very few wise Men know themselves what Fools they are, more than the World doth. Good Gods! could one but see what passes in the Closet of Wisdom! how ridiculous a Sight must it be to behold the wise Man, who despises gratifying his Palate, devouring Custard; the sober wise Man with his Dram-bottle; or, the Anti-Carnalist (if I may be allowed the Expression) chuckling over a B——y Book or Picture, and perhaps caressing his House-Maid!

'But to conclude a Character, in which I apprehend I made

as absurd a Figure, as in any in which I trod the Stage of Earth, my Wisdom at last put an end to itself; that is, occasioned my Dissolution.

'A relation of mine in the Eastern Part of the Empire, disinherited his Son, and left me his Heir. This happened in the depth of Winter, when I was in my grand Climacteric, and had just recovered of a dangerous Disease.* As I had all the Reason imaginable to apprehend the Family of the Deceased would conspire against me, and embezzle as much as they could, I advised with a grave and wise Friend, what was proper to be done; whether I should go myself, or employ a Notary on this occasion, and defer my Journey to the Spring. To say the truth, I was most inclined to the latter; the rather, as my Circumstances were extremely flourishing, as I was advanced in Years, and had not one Person in the World, to whom I should with pleasure bequeath any Fortune at my Death.

'My Friend told me, he thought my Question admitted no manner of Doubt or Debate; that common Prudence absolutely required my immediate Departure; adding, that if the same good luck had happened to him, he would have been already on his Journey: "For," continued he, "a Man who knows the World so well as you, would be inexcusable to give Persons such an Opportunity of cheating you, who, you must be assured, will be too well inclined; and as for employing a Notary, remember that excellent Maxim, *Ne facias per alium, quod fieri potest per te*.* I own the Badness of the Season, and your very late Recovery are unlucky Circumstances: but a wise Man must get over Difficulties, when Necessity obliges him to encounter them."

'I was immediately determined by this Opinion. The Duty of a wise Man made an irresistible Impression, and I took the Necessity for granted, without Examination. I accordingly set forward the next Morning; very tempestuous Weather soon overtook me; I had not travelled three Days before I relapsed into my Fever, and died.

'I was now as cruelly disappointed by *Minos*, as I had formerly been happily so. I advanced with the utmost Confidence to the Gate, and really imagined I should have been admitted by the Wisdom of my Countenance, even without any Questions asked: but this was not my Case; and to my great Surprize,

Minos, with a menacing Voice, called out to me—You Mr there, with the grave Countenance, whither so fast, pray? Will you please, before you move any farther forwards, to give me a short Account of your Transactions below? I then began, and recounted to him my whole History, still expecting, at the end of every Period, that the Gate would be ordered to fly open: but I was obliged to go quite through with it, and then *Minos*, after some little Consideration, spoke to me as follows.

'"You, Mr *Wise-man*; stand forth, if you please. Believe me, Sir, a trip back again to Earth, will be one of the wisest Steps you ever took, and really more to the Honour of your Wisdom, than any you have hitherto taken. On the other side, nothing could be simpler, than to endeavour at *Elysium*; for who, but a Fool, would carry a Commodity, which is of such infinite Value in one Place, into another where it is of none. But without attempting to offend your Gravity with a Jest, you must return to the Place from whence you came: for *Elysium* was never designed for those who are too wise to be happy."

'This Sentence confounded me greatly, especially as it seemed to threaten me with carrying my Wisdom back again to Earth. I told the Judge, tho' he would not admit me at the Gate, I hoped I had committed no Crime, while alive, which merited my being wise any longer. He answered me, I must take my Chance as to that matter, and immediately we turned our backs to each other.'

CHAPTER XVII

Julian *enters into the Person of a King.**

'I WAS now born at *Oviedo* in *Spain*. My Father's Name was *Veremond*, and I was adopted by my Uncle, King *Alphonso* the Chaste. I don't recollect in all the Pilgrimages I have made on Earth, that I ever past a more miserable Infancy than now; being under the utmost Confinement and Restraint, and surrounded with Physicians, who were ever dosing me; and Tutors, who were continually plaguing me with their Instructions; even those Hours of Leisure, which my Inclination would have spent in Play, were allotted to tedious Pomp and Ceremony, which at an

Age wherein I had no Ambition to enjoy the Servility of Courtiers, enslaved me more than it could the meanest of them. However, as I advanced towards Manhood, my Condition made me some Amends: for the most beautiful Women of their own accord threw out Lures for me, and I had the Happiness, which no Man in an inferiour Degree can arrive at, of enjoying the most delicious Creatures, without the previous and tiresome Ceremonies of Courtship, unless with the most simple, young and unexperienced. As for the Court Ladies, they regarded me rather as Men do the most lovely of the other Sex; and tho' they outwardly retained some Appearance of Modesty, they in reality rather considered themselves as receiving than conferring Favours.

'Another Happiness I enjoyed, was in conferring Favours of another sort; for as I was extremely good-natured and generous, so I had daily Opportunities of satisfying those Passions. Besides my own princely Allowance, which was very bountiful, and with which I did many liberal and good Actions, I recommended numberless Persons of Merit in Distress to the King's Notice, most of whom were provided for.

'Indeed, had I sufficiently known my blest Situation at this time, I should have grieved at nothing more than the Death of *Alphonso*, by which the Burden of Government devolved upon me: but so blindly fond is Ambition, and such Charms doth it fancy in the Power, and Pomp, and Splendor of a Crown, that tho' I vehemently loved that King, and had the greatest Obligations to him, the Thoughts of succeeding him obliterated my Regret at his Loss, and the Wish for my approaching Coronation dryed my Eyes at his Funeral.

'But my Fondness for the Name of King, did not make me forgetful of those, over whom I was to reign. I considered them in the Light in which a tender Father regards his Children, as Persons whose Wellbeing God had intrusted to my Care; and again, in that in which a prudent Lord respects his Tenants, as those on whose Wealth and Grandeur he is to build his own. Both these Considerations inspired me with the greatest Care for their Welfare, and their Good was my first and ultimate Concern.

'The Usurper *Mauregas* had impiously obliged himself, and

his Successors, to pay to the *Moors* every Year an infamous Tribute of a hundred young Virgins: from this cruel and scandalous Imposition, I resolved to relieve my Country.* Accordingly, when their Emperor *Abderames* the Second had the Audaciousness to make this Demand of me, instead of complying with it, I ordered his Ambassadors to be driven away with all imaginable Ignominy, and would have condemned them to Death, could I have done it without a manifest Violation of the Law of Nations.

'I now raised an immense Army. At the levying of which, I made a Speech from my Throne, acquainting my Subjects with the Necessity, and the Reasons of the War in which I was going to engage: which I convinced them I had undertaken for their Ease and Safety, and not for satisfying any wanton Ambition, or revenging any private Pique of my own. They all declared unanimously, that they would venture their Lives, and every thing dear to them in my Defence, and in the Support of the Honour of my Crown. Accordingly my Levies were instantly complete, sufficient Numbers being only left to till the Land; Churchmen, even Bishops themselves, enlisting themselves under my Banners.

'The Armies met at *Alvelda*, where we were discomfited with immense Loss, and nothing but the lucky Intervention of the Night could have saved our whole Army.*

'I retreated to the Summit of a Hill, where I abandoned myself to the highest Agonies of Grief, not so much for the Danger in which I then saw my Crown, as for the Loss of those miserable Wretches, who had exposed their Lives at my Command. I could not then avoid this Reflection; That if the Deaths of these People in a War, undertaken absolutely for their Protection, could give me such Concern; what Horrour must I have felt, if, like Princes greedy of Dominion, I had sacrificed such Numbers to my own Pride, Vanity, and ridiculous Lust of Power.

'After having vented my Sorrows for some time in this manner, I began to consider by what means I might possibly endeavour to retrieve this Misfortune; when reflecting on the great number of Priests I had in my Army, and on the prodigious Force of Superstition, a Thought luckily suggested itself to me, to counterfeit that St *James* had appeared to me in a Vision, and had promised me the Victory. While I was ruminating on this, the Bishop of *Najara* came opportunely to me. As I did not intend to communicate the Secret to him, I took another Method, and instead of answering any thing the Bishop said to me, I pretended to talk to St *James*, as if he had been really present; till at length, after having spoke those things, which I thought sufficient, and thanked the Saint aloud for his Promise of the Victory, I turned about to the Bishop, and embracing him with a pleased Countenance, protested I did not know he was present; and then informing him of this supposed Vision, I asked him, if he had not himself seen the Saint? He answered me, he had; and afterwards proceeded to assure me, that this Appearance of St *James* was entirely owing to his Prayers; for that he was his tutelar Saint. He added, he had a Vision of him a few hours before, when he promised him a Victory over the Infidels, and acquainted him at the same time of the Vacancy of the See of *Toledo*. Now this News being really true, tho' it had happened so lately, that I had not heard of it, (nor, indeed, was it well possible I should, considering the great Distance of the Way) when I was afterwards acquainted with it, a little staggered me, tho' far from being superstitious; till being informed, that the Bishop had lost three Horses on a late Expedition, I was satisfied.

'The next Morning, the Bishop, at my Desire, mounted the Rostrum, and trumpeted forth this Vision so effectually, which he said he had that Evening twice seen with his own Eyes, that a Spirit began to be infused through the whole Army, which rendered them superiour to almost any Force: the Bishop insisted, that the least Doubt of Success was giving the lye to the Saint, and a damnable Sin, and he took upon him in his Name to promise them Victory.

'The Army being drawn out, I soon experienced the Effect of Enthusiasm, for having contrived another Stratagem[1] to strengthen what the Bishop had said, the Soldiers fought more like Furies than Men. My Stratagem was this: I had about me a dextrous Fellow, who had been formerly a Pimp in my Amours. Him I drest up in a strange antick Dress, with a Pair of white Colours

[1] This silly Story is told as a Solemn Truth, (i.e. that St James really appeared in the manner this Fellow is described) by *Mariana*, L. 7, 78.

in his right Hand, a red Cross in his left, and having disguised him so, that no one could know him, I placed him on a white Horse, and ordered him to ride to the Head of the Army, and cry out, *Follow St James!* These Words were reiterated by all the Troops, who attacked the Enemy with such Intrepidity, that notwithstanding our Inferiority of Numbers, we soon obtained a complete Victory.

'The Bishop was come up by the time that the Enemy was routed, and acquainting us, that he had met St *James* by the way, and that he had informed him of what had past, he added, that he had express Orders from the Saint, to receive a considerable Sum for his Use, and that a certain Tax on Corn and Wine should be settled on his Church for ever; and lastly, that a Horseman's Pay should be allowed for the future to the Saint himself, of which he and his Successors were appointed Receivers. The Army received these Demands with such Acclamations, that I was obliged to comply with them, as I could by no means discover the Imposition, nor do I believe I should have gained any Credit if I had.

'I had now done with the Saint, but the Bishop had not; for about a Week afterwards, Lights were seen in a Wood near where the Battle was fought; and in a short time afterwards, they discovered his Tomb at the same Place. Upon this, the Bishop made me a Visit, and forced me to go thither to build a Church to him, and largely endow it. In a word, the good Man so plagued me with Miracle after Miracle, that I was forced to make interest with the Pope to convey him to *Toledo*, to get rid of him.

'But to proceed to other Matters.—There was an inferiour Officer, who had behaved very bravely in the Battle against the *Moors*, and had received several Wounds, who solicited me for Preferment; which I was about to confer on him, when one of my Ministers came to me in a Fright, and told me, that he had promised the Post I designed for this Man to the Son of Count *Alderedo*; and that the Count, who was a powerful Person, would be greatly disobliged at the Refusal, as he had sent for his Son from School to take possession of it. I was obliged to agree with my Minister's Reasons, and at the same time recommended the wounded Soldier to be preferred by him, which he faithfully promised he would: but I met the poor Wretch since in *Elysium*, who informed me he was afterwards starved to death.

'None, who hath not been himself a Prince, nor any Prince, till his Death, can conceive the Impositions daily put on them by their Favourites and Ministers; so that Princes are often blamed for the Faults of others. The Count of *Saldagne*, had been long confined in Prison, when his Son D. *Bernard del Carpio*, who had performed the greatest Actions against the *Moors*, entreated me as a Reward for his Service, to grant him his Father's Liberty. The old Man's Punishment had been so tedious, and the Services of the young one so singularly eminent, that I was very inclinable to grant the Request: but my Ministers strongly opposed it. They told me, *My Glory demanded Revenge for the Dishonour offered to my Family; that so positive a Demand carried with it rather the Air of Menace than Entreaty. That the vain Detail of his Services, and the Recompence due to them, was an injurious Reproach. That to grant what had been so haughtily demanded, would argue in the Monarch both Weakness and Timidity; in a word, that to remit the Punishment inflicted by my Predecessors, would be to condemn their Judgment. Lastly, one told me in a Whisper, his whole Family are Enemies to your House.* By these means the Ministers prevailed. The young Lord took the Refusal so ill, that he retired from Court, and abandoned himself to Despair, whilst the old one languished in Prison. By which means, as I have since discovered, I lost the Use of two of my best Subjects.

'To confess the Truth, I had by means of my Ministers conceived a very unjust Opinion of my whole People, whom I fancied to be daily conspiring against me, and to entertain the most disloyal Thoughts; when in reality (as I have known since my death) they held me in universal Respect and Esteem. This is a Trick, I believe, too often played with Sovereigns, who by such Means are prevented from that open Intercourse with their Subjects, which as it would greatly endear the Person of the Prince to the People, so might it often prove dangerous to a Minister, who was consulting his own Interest only at the expence of both. I believe I have now recounted to you the most material Passages of my Life; for I assure you, there are some Incidents in the Lives of Kings not extremely worth relating. Every thing which passes in their Minds and Families, is not attended with the Splendor which surrounds their Throne: indeed, there are some Hours wherein the naked King and the naked Cobler can scarce be distinguished from each other.

'Had it not been, however, for my Ingratitude to *Bernard del Carpio*, I believe this would have been my last Pilgrimage on Earth: for as to the Story of St *James*, I thought *Minos* would have burst his Sides at it: but he was so displeased with me on the other account, that with a Frown, he cried out, "Get thee back again, King." Nor would he suffer me to say another Word.'

CHAPTER XVIII

Julian *passes into a Fool.*

'THE next Visit I made to the World, was performed in *France*, where I was born in the Court of *Lewis* III and had afterwards the Honour to be preferred to be Fool to the Prince, who was surnamed *Charles the Simple*.* But in reality, I know not whether I might so properly be said to have acted the Fool in his Court, as to have made Fools of all others in it. Certain it is, I was very far from being what is generally understood by that Word, being a most cunning, designing, arch Knave. I knew very well the Folly of my Master and of many others, and how to make my advantage of this Knowledge. I was as dear to *Charles the Simple*, as the Player *Paris* was to *Domitian*,* and, like him, bestowed all manner of Offices and Honours on whom I pleased. This drew me a great Number of Followers among the Courtiers, who really mistook me for a Fool, and yet flattered my Understanding. There was particularly in the Court a Fellow, who had neither Honour, Honesty, Sense, Wit, Courage, Beauty, nor indeed any one good Quality either of Mind or Body, to recommend him: but was at the same time, perhaps, as cunning a Monster as ever lived. This Gentleman took it into his head to list under my Banner, and pursued me so very assiduously with Flattery, constantly reminding me of my good Sense, that I grew immoderately fond of him: for tho' Flattery is not most judiciously applied to Qualities which the Persons flattered possess, yet as, notwithstanding my being well assured of my own Parts, I past in the whole Court for a Fool, this Flattery was a very sweet Morsel to me. I therefore got this Fellow preferred to a Bishopric, but I lost my Flatterer by it: for he never afterwards said a civil Thing to me.

'I never baulked my Imagination for the Grossness of the Reflection on the Character of the greatest Noble, nay even the King himself; of which, I will give you a very bold Instance. One day, his simple Majesty told me, he believed I had so much Power, that his People looked on me as the King, and himself as my Fool. At this I pretended to be angry as with an Affront. "Why, how now," says the King; "Are you ashamed of being a King?" "No Sir," says I, "but I am devilishly ashamed of my Fool."

'Hebert, Earl of *Vermandois*, had by my means been restored to the Favour of *The Simple*, (for so I used always to call Charles.)* He afterwards prevailed with the King to take the City of *Arras* from Earl *Baldwin*, by which means *Hebert* in exchange for this City had *Peronne* restored to him by Count *Altmar*. *Baldwin* came to Court, in order to procure the Restoration of his City; but, either through Pride or Ignorance, neglected to apply to me. As I met him at Court during his Solicitation, I told him he did not apply the right way; he answered roughly, he should not ask a Fool's Advice. I replied, I did not wonder at his Prejudice; since he had miscarried already by following a Fool's Advice: but I told him, there were Fools, who had more Interest than that he had brought with him to Court. He answered me surlily, he had no Fool with him, for that he travelled alone.—Ay, my Lord, says I, I often travel alone, and yet they will have it I always carry a Fool with me. This raised a Laugh among the By-standers, on which he gave me a Blow. I immediately complained of this Usage to *The Simple*, who dismissed the Earl from Court with very hard Words, instead of granting him the Favour he solicited.

'I give you these rather as a Specimen of my Interest and Impudence than of my Wit; indeed my Jests were commonly more admired than they ought to be: for perhaps, I was not in reality much more a Wit than a Fool. But with the Latitude of unbounded Scurrility, it is easy enough to attain the Character of Wit, especially in a Court, where, as all Persons hate and envy one another heartily, and are at the same time obliged by the constrained Behaviour of Civility to profess the greatest Liking, so it is and must be wonderfully pleasant to them to see the Follies of their Acquaintance exposed by a third Person. Besides, the Opinion of the Court is as uniform as the Fashion, and is always guided by the Will of the Prince or of the Favourite. I doubt not that *Caligula's* Horse was universally held in his Court to be a good and able Consul. In the same manner was I universally acknowledged to be the wittiest Fool in the World. Every Word I said raised Laughter, and was held to be a Jest, especially by the Ladies; who sometimes laughed before I had discovered my Sentiment, and often repeated that as a Jest which I did not even intend as one.

'I was as severe on the Ladies as on the Men, and with the same Impunity; but this at last cost me dear: for once having joked the Beauty of a Lady, whose Name was *Adelaide*, a Favourite of *the Simple's*; she pretended to smile and be pleased at my Wit with the rest of the Company; but in reality, she highly resented it, and endeavoured to undermine me with the King. In which she so greatly succeeded (for what can't a favourite Woman do with one who deserves the Surname of *Simple?*) that the King grew every day more reserved to me, and when I attempted any Freedom, gave me such Marks of his Displeasure; that the Courtiers (who have all Hawk's Eyes at a Slight from the Sovereign) soon discerned it; and indeed, had I been blind enough not to have discovered that I had lost ground in the *Simple's* Favour, by his own Change in his Carriage towards me, I must have found it, nay even felt it, in the Behaviour of the Courtiers: for as my Company was two days before solicited with the utmost Eagerness, it was now rejected with as much Scorn. I was now the Jest of the Ushers and Pages; and an Officer of the Guards, on whom I was a little jocose, gave me a Box on the Ear, bidding me make free with my Equals. This very Fellow had been my Butt for many Years, without daring to lift his Hand against me.

'But tho' I visibly perceived the Alteration in the *Simple*, I was utterly unable to make any Guess at the Occasion. I had not the least Suspicion of *Adelaide*: for besides her being a very good-humour'd Woman, I had often made severe Jests on her Reputation, which I had all the reason imaginable to believe had given her no Offence. But I soon perceived, that a Woman will bear the most bitter Censures on her Morals, easier than the smallest Reflection on her Beauty: for she now declared publickly, that I ought to be dismist from Court, as the stupidest of Fools, and one in whom there was no Diversion; and that she wondered how any Person could have so little Taste, as to imagine I had any Wit. This Speech was echoed through the Drawing Room, and agreed to by all present. Every one now put on an unusual Gravity on their Countenance whenever I spoke; and it was as much out of my power to raise a Laugh, as formerly it had been for me to open my Mouth without one.

'While my Affairs were in this posture, I went one day into the Circle, without my Fool's Dress. The *Simple*, who would still speak to me, cried out, "So, Fool, what's the matter now?" "Sir," answered I, "Fools are like to be so common a Commodity at Court, that I am weary of my Coat." "How dost thou mean," answered the *Simple*; "What can make them commoner now than usual?"—"O, Sir," said I, "there are Ladies here make your Majesty a Fool every Day of their Lives." The *Simple* took no notice of my Jest, and several present said my Bones ought to be broke for my Impudence; but it pleased the Queen, who knowing *Adelaide*, whom she hated, to be the Cause of my Disgrace, obtained me of the King, and took me into her Service; so that I was henceforth called the Queen's Fool, and in her Court received the same Honour, and had as much Wit as I had formerly had in the King's. But as the Queen had really no Power unless over her own Domestics, I was not treated in general with that Complacence, nor did I receive those Bribes and Presents, which had once fallen to my share.

'Nor did this confined Respect continue long: for the Queen, who had in fact no Taste for Humour, soon grew sick of my Foolery, and forgetting the Cause for which she had taken me, neglected me so much, that her Court grew intolerable to my Temper, and I broke my Heart and died.

'Minos laughed heartily at several things in my Story, and then telling me, No one played the Fool in *Elysium*, bid me go back again.'

CHAPTER XIX

Julian *appears in the Character of a Beggar.*

'I NOW returned to *Rome*, and was born into a very poor and numerous Family, which, to be honest with you, procured its Livelihood by Begging. This, if you was never yourself of the Calling, you do not know, I suppose, to be as regular a Trade as any other; to have its several Rules and Secrets, or Mysteries, which to learn require perhaps as tedious an Apprenticeship as those of any Craft whatever.

'The first thing we are taught is *the Countenance miserable*. This indeed Nature makes much easier to some than others: but there are none who cannot accomplish it, if they begin early enough in Youth, and before the Muscles are grown too stubborn.

'The second Thing is, *the Voice lamentable*. In this Qualification too, Nature must have her share in producing the most consummate Excellence: however, Art will here, as in every other Instance, go a great way with Industry and Application, even without the Assistance of Genius; especially if the Student begins young.

'There are many other Instructions: but these are the most considerable. The Women are taught one Practice more than the Men; for they are instructed in the Art of Crying, that is, to have their Tears ready on all Occasions: but this is attained very easily by most. Some indeed arrive at the utmost Perfection in this Art with incredible Facility.

'No Profession requires a deeper Insight into human Nature, than the Beggar's. Their Knowledge of the Passions of Men is so extensive, that I have often thought, it would be of no little service to a Politician to have his Education among them. Nay, there is a much greater Analogy between these two Characters than is imagined: for both concur in their first and grand Principle, it being equally their Business to delude and impose on Mankind. It must be confest, that they differ widely in the Degree of Advantage, which they make by their Deceit: for, whereas the Beggar is contented with a little, the Politician leaves but a little behind.

'A very great *English* Philosopher hath remarked our Policy, in taking Care never to address any one with a Title inferiour to what he really claims. My Father was of the same Opinion: for I remember when I was a Boy, the Pope happening to pass by, I attended him with *Pray Sir; for God's sake, Sir; for the Lord's sake, Sir.*—To which he answered gravely, *Sirrah, Sirrah, you ought to be whipt, for taking the Lord's Name in vain*; and in vain it was indeed, for he gave me nothing. My Father over-hearing this, took his Advice and whipt me very severely. While I was under Correction, I promised often never to take the Lord's Name in vain any more. My Father then said, "Child, I do not whip you for taking his Name in vain: I whip you for not calling the Pope *his Holiness.*"

'If all Men were so wise and good to follow the Clergy's Example, the Nusance of Beggars would soon be removed. I do not remember to have been above twice relieved by them during my whole State of Beggary. Once was by a very well-looking Man, who gave me a small Piece of Silver, and declared, he had given me more than he had left himself; the other was by a spruce young Fellow, who had that very day first put on his Robes, whom I attended with *Pray, Reverend Sir, good Reverend Sir, consider your Cloth.* He answered, *I do, Child, consider my Office, and I hope all of our Cloth do the same.* He then threw down some Money, and strutted off with great Dignity.

'With the Women, I had one general Formulary: *Sweet pretty Lady, God bless your Ladyship, God bless your handsome Face.* This generally succeeded; but I observed, the uglier the Woman was, the surer I was of Success.

'It was a constant Maxim among us, that the greater Retinue any one travelled with, the less Expectation we might promise ourselves from them; but whenever we saw a Vehicle with a single, or no Servant, we imagined our Booty sure, and were seldom deceived.

'We observed great Difference introduced by Time and Circumstance in the same Person: for instance, a losing Gamester is sometimes generous; but from a Winner, you will as easily obtain his Soul, as a single Groat. A Lawyer travelling from his Country Seat to his Clients at *Rome*, and a Physician going to visit a Patient, were always worth asking: but the same on their Return were (according to our Cant Phrase) *untouchable.*

'The most general, and indeed, the truest Maxim among us, was, That those who possess'd the least were always the readiest to give. The chief Art of a Beggarman is therefore to discern the rich from the Poor, which, tho' it be only distinguishing Substance from Shadow, is by no means attainable without a pretty good Capacity, and a vast Degree of Attention: for these two are eternally industrious in endeavouring to counterfeit each other. In this Deceit, the poor Man is more heartily in earnest to deceive you, than the Rich; who amidst all the Emblems of Poverty which he puts on, still permits some mark of his Wealth to strike the Eye. Thus, while his Apparel is not worth a Groat, his Finger wears a Ring of Value, or his Pocket a Gold Watch. In a word, he seems rather to affect Poverty to insult, than impose on you. Now the poor Man, on the contrary, is very sincere in his Desire of passing for rich; but the Eagerness of this Desire, hurries him to overact his Part, and he betrays himself, as one who is drunk by his overacted Sobriety. Thus, instead of being attended by one Servant well mounted, he will have two; and not being able to purchase or maintain a second Horse of Value, one of his Servants at least is mounted on a hired Rascallion.* He is not contented to go plain and neat in his Clothes; he therefore claps on some taudry Ornament, and what he adds to the Fineness of his Vestment, he detracts from the Fineness of his Linnen. Without descending into more minute Particulars, I believe I may assert it as an Axiom of indubitable Truth, That whoever shews you he is either in himself, or his Equipage, as gaudy as he can, convinces you he is more so than he can afford. Now whenever a Man's Expence exceeds his Income, he is indifferent in the Degree; we had therefore nothing more to do with such, than to flatter them with their Wealth and Splendor, and were always certain of Success.

'There is, indeed, one kind of rich Man, who is commonly more liberal, namely, where Riches surprize him as it were, in the midst of Poverty and Distress, the Consequence of which is, I own, sometimes excessive Avarice; but oftner extreme Prodigality. I remember one of these, who having received a pretty large Sum of Money, gave me, when I begged an Obolus, a whole Talent;* on which his Friend having reproved him, he answered with an Oath, "Why not? Have I not fifty left?"

'The Life of a Beggar, if Men estimated things by their real Essence, and not by their outward false Appearance, would be, perhaps, a more desirable Situation than any of those, which Ambition persuades us with such Difficulty, Danger, and often Villany, to aspire to. The Wants of a Beggar are commonly as chimerical as the Abundance of a Nobleman; for besides Vanity, which a judicious Beggar will always apply to with wonderful Efficacy, there are in reality very few Natures so hardened, as not to compassionate Poverty and Distress, when the Predominancy of some other Passion doth not prevent them.

'There is one Happiness which attends Money got with ease, namely, that it is never hoarded; otherwise, as we have frequent Opportunities of growing rich, that Canker Care might prey on our Quiet, as it doth on others: but our Money Stock we spend as fast as we acquire it; usually at least, for I speak not without exception; thus it gives us mirth only, and no trouble. Indeed, the Luxury of our Lives might introduce Diseases, did not our daily Exercise prevent them. This gives us Appetite and Relish for our Dainties, and at the same time, an Antidote against the evil Effects, which Sloth, united with Luxury, induces on the Habit of a human Body. Our Women we enjoy with Extasies, at least equal to what the greatest Men feel in their Embraces. I can, I am assured, say of myself, that no Mortal could reap more perfect Happiness from the tender Passion, than my Fortune had decreed me. I married a charming young Woman for Love; she was the Daughter of a neighbouring Beggar, who with an Improvidence too often seen, spent a very large Income, which he procured by his Profession, so that he was able to give her no Fortune down; however, at his Death, he left her a very well-accustomed Begging-Hut, situated on the side of a steep Hill, where Travellers could not immediately escape from us, and a Garden adjoining, being the 28th Part of an Acre, well planted. She made the best of Wives, bore me nineteen Children, and never failed, unless on her Lying-in, which generally lasted three Days, to get my Supper ready, against my return home in an Evening; this being my favourite Meal, and at which I, as well as my whole Family, greatly enjoyed ourselves; the principal Subject of our Discourse, being generally the Boons we had that day obtained, on which occasions laughing at the Folly of the Donors, made no inconsiderable Part of the Entertainment: for whatever might be their Motive for giving, we constantly imputed our Success to our having flattered their Vanity, or over-reached their Understanding.

'But, perhaps, I have dwelt too long on this Character; I shall conclude therefore with telling you, that after a Life of 102 Years Continuance, during all which I had never known any Sickness or Infirmity, but that which Old Age necessarily induced, I at last, without the least Pain, went out like the Snuff of a Candle.

'Minos having heard my History, bid me compute, if I could, how many Lyes I had told in my Life. As we are here by a certain fated Necessity, obliged to confine ourselves to Truth, I answered, I believed about 50,000,000. He then replyed with a Frown, "Can such a Wretch conceive any Hopes of entering *Elysium?*" I immediately turned about, and, upon the whole, was rejoiced at his not calling me back.'

CHAPTER XX

Julian *performs the Part of a Statesman.*

'It was now my fortune to be born of a *German* Princess; but a Man-Midwife pulling my Head off, in delivering my Mother, put a speedy end to my princely Life.

'Spirits, who end their Lives before they are at the Age of five Years, are immediately ordered into other Bodies; and it was now my fortune to perform several Infancies, before I could again entitle myself to an Examination of *Minos*.

'At length I was destined once more to play a considerable Part on the Stage.* I was born in *England*, in the Reign of *Ethelred* II. My Father's Name was *Ulnoth*. He was Earl or Thane of *Sussex*: I was afterwards known by the Name of Earl *Goodwin*, and began to make a considerable Figure in the World, in the time of *Harold Harefoot*, whom I procured to be made King of *Wessex*, or the *West Saxons*, in prejudice of *Hardicanute*, whose Mother *Emma* endeavoured afterwards to set another of her Sons on the Throne: but I circumvented her, and communicating her Design to the King, at the same time acquainted him with a Project, which I had formed for the Murder of these two young Princes. *Emma* had sent for these her Sons from *Normandy*, with the King's Leave, whom she had deceived by her religious Behaviour, and pretended Neglect of all worldly Affairs; but I prevailed with *Harold* to invite these Princes to his Court, and put them to death. The prudent Mother sent only *Alfred*, retaining *Edward* to herself, as she suspected my ill Designs, and thought I should not venture to execute them on one of her Sons, while she secured the other: but she was deceived, for I had no sooner *Alfred* in my possession, than I caused him to be conducted to *Ely*, where I ordered his Eyes to be put out, and afterwards to be confined in a Monastery.

'This was one of those cruel Expedients, which great Men satisfy themselves well in executing, by concluding them to be necessary to the Service of their Prince, who is the Support of their Ambition.

'Edward, the other Son of *Emma*, escaped again to *Normandy*; whence, after the Death of *Harold* and *Hardicanute*, he made no scruple of applying to my Protection and Favour, tho' he had before prosecuted me with all the Vengeance he was able, for the Murder of his Brother: but in all great Affairs, private Relation must yield to public Interest. Having therefore concluded very advantagious Terms for myself with him, I made no scruple of patronizing his Cause, and soon placed him on the Throne. Nor did I conceive the least Apprehension from his Resentment, as I knew my Power was too great for him to encounter.

'Among other stipulated Conditions, one was to marry my Daughter *Editha*. This *Edward* consented to, with great Reluctance, and I had afterwards no reason to be pleased with it: for it raised her, who had been my favourite Child, to such an Opinion of Greatness, that instead of paying me the usual Respect, she frequently threw in my teeth, (as often at least as I gave her any Admonition) that she was now a Queen, and that the Character and Title of Father merged in that of Subject. This Behaviour, however, did not cure me of my Affection towards her, nor lessen the Uneasiness, which I afterwards bore on *Edward's* dismissing her from his Bed.

'One thing, which principally induced me to labour the Promotion of *Edward*, was the Simplicity or Weakness of that Prince, under whom I promised myself absolute Dominion, under another Name. Nor did this Opinion deceive me: for during his whole Reign, my Administration was in the highest degree despotic. I had every thing of Royalty, but the outward Ensigns: No Man ever applying for a Place, or any kind of Preferment, but to me only. A Circumstance, which as it greatly enriched my Coffers, so it no less pampered my Ambition, and satisfied my Vanity with a numerous Attendance; and I had the pleasure of seeing those, who only bowed to the King, prostrating themselves before me.

'Edward the Confessor, or St *Edward*, as some have called him in derision, I suppose, being a very silly Fellow, had all the Faults incident, and almost inseparable, to Fools. He married my Daughter *Editha*, from his fear of disobliging me; and afterwards, out of hatred to me, refused even to consummate his Marriage, tho' she was one of the most beautiful Women of her Age. He was likewise guilty of the basest Ingratitude to his Mother, (a Vice to which Fools are chiefly, if not only liable) and in return for her Endeavours to procure him a Throne in his Youth, confined her in a loathsome Prison, in her old Age. This, it is true, he did by my Advice: but as to her walking over nine Plowshares red-hot, and giving nine Manors, when she had not one in her possession, there is not a syllable of Veracity in it.

'The first great Perplexity I fell into, was on the account of my Son *Swane*, who had deflowered the Abbess of *Leon*, since called *Leominster* in *Herefordshire*. After this Fact, he retired into *Denmark*, whence he sent to me, to obtain his Pardon. The King at first refused it; being moved thereto, as I afterwards found, by some Churchmen, particularly by one of his Chaplains, whom I had prevented from obtaining a Bishoprick. Upon this, my Son *Swane* invaded the Coasts with several Ships, and committed many outragious Cruelties; which, indeed, did his business, as they served me to apply to the Fear of this King, which I had long since discovered to be his predominant Passion. And at last, he who had refused Pardon to his first Offence, submitted to give it him, after he had committed many other more monstrous Crimes; by which his Pardon lost all Grace to the Offended, and received double Censure from all others.

'The King was greatly inclined to the *Normans*, had created a

Norman Archbishop of *Canterbury*, and had heaped extraordinary Favours on him.* I had no other Objection to this Man, than that he rose without my Assistance; a Cause of Dislike, which in the Reign of great and powerful Favourites, hath often proved fatal to the Persons who have given it, as the Persons thus raised, inspire us constantly with Jealousies and Apprehensions. For when we promote any one ourselves, we take effectual Care to preserve such an Ascendant over him, that we can at any time reduce him to his former Degree, should he dare to act in opposition to our Wills: for which reason we never suffer any to come near the Prince, but such as we are assured it is impossible should be capable of engaging or improving his Affection; no Prime-Minister, as I apprehend, esteeming himself to be safe, while any other shares the Ear of his Prince, of whom we are as jealous as the fondest Husband can be of his Wife. Whoever, therefore, can approach him by any other Channel than that of ourselves, is in our opinion a declared Enemy, and one, whom the first Principles of Policy oblige us to demolish with the utmost expedition. For the Affection of Kings, is as precarious as that of Women, and the only Way to secure either to ourselves, is to keep all others from them.

'But the Arch-Bishop did not let Matters rest on Suspicion. He soon gave open Proofs of his Interest with the Confessor, in procuring an Office of some Importance for one *Rollo*, a *Norman* of mean Extraction and very despicable Parts. When I represented to the King the Indecency of conferring such an Honour on such a Fellow, he answered me, that he was the Arch-Bishop's Relation. "Then, Sir," replied I, "he is related to your Enemy." Nothing more past at that time: but I soon perceived by the Arch-Bishop's Behaviour, that the King had acquainted him with our private Discourse, a sufficient Assurance of his Confidence in him and Neglect of me.

'The Favour of Princes, when once lost, is recoverable only by the gaining a Situation which may make you terrible to them. As I had no doubt of having lost all Credit with this King, which indeed had been originally founded and constantly supported by his Fear, so I took the Method of Terror to regain it.

'The Earl of *Boulogne* coming over to visit the King, gave me an Opportunity of breaking out into open Opposition: for as the

Earl was on his return to *France*, one of his Servants, who was sent before to procure Lodgings at *Dover*, and insisted on having them in the House of a private Man in spite of the Owner's teeth, was, in a Fray which ensued, killed on the spot; and the Earl himself arriving there soon after, very narrowly escaped with his Life. The Earl, enraged at this Affront, returned to the King at *Gloucester*, with loud Complaints and Demands of Satisfaction. *Edward* consented to his Demands, and ordered me to chastise the Rioters, who were under my Government as Earl of *Kent*: but instead of obeying these Orders, I answered with some warmth, That the *English* were not used to punish People unheard; nor ought their Rights and Privileges to be violated: that the Accused should be first summoned; if guilty, should make Satisfaction both with Body and Estate; but if innocent, should be discharged. Adding, with great ferocity, that as Earl of *Kent* it was my Duty to protect those under my Government against the Insults of Foreigners.

'This Accident was extremely lucky, as it gave my Quarrel with the King a popular Colour; and so ingratiated me with the People, that when I set up my Standard, which I soon after did, they readily and chearfully listed under my Banners, and embraced my Cause, which I persuaded them was their own: for that it was to protect them against Foreigners that I had drawn my Sword. The word Foreigners with an *Englishman* hath a kind of magical Effect, they having the utmost Hatred and Aversion to them, arising from the Cruelties they suffered from the *Danes* and some other foreign Nations. No wonder therefore they espoused my Cause, in a Quarrel which had such a Beginning.

'But what may be somewhat more remarkable is, that when I afterwards returned to *England* from Banishment, and was at the Head of an Army of the *Flemish*, who were preparing to plunder the City of *London*, I still persisted that I was come to defend the *English* from the Danger of Foreigners, and gained their Credit. Indeed, there is no Lye so gross, but it may be imposed on the People by those whom they esteem their Patrons and Defenders.

'The King saved his City by being reconciled to me, and taking again my Daughter whom he had put away from him; and thus having frightened the King into what Concessions I thought proper, I dismiss'd my Army and Fleet, with which

I intended, could I not have succeeded otherwise, to have sacked the City of *London*, and ravaged the whole Country.

'I was no sooner re-established in the King's Favour, or, what was as well for me, the Appearance of it, than I fell violently on the Arch-Bishop. He had of himself retired to his Monastery in *Normandy*; but that did not content me, I had him formally banished, the See declared vacant, and then filled up by another.

'I enjoyed my Grandeur a very short time, after my Restoration to it: for the King hating and fearing me to a very great degree, and finding no means of openly destroying me, at last effected his Purpose by Poison, and then spread abroad a ridiculous Story of my wishing the next Morsel might choak me, if I had had any hand in the Death of *Alfred*; and accordingly that the next Morsel, by a divine Judgment, stuck in my Throat, and performed that Office.

'This of a Statesman was one of my worst Stages in the other World. It is a Post subjected daily to the greatest Danger and Inquietude, and attended with little Pleasure, and less Ease. In a word, it is a Pill, which, was it not gilded over by Ambition, would appear nauseous and detestable in the eye of every one; and perhaps that is one reason why *Minos* so greatly compassionates the Case of those who swallow it: for that just Judge told me, he always acquitted a Prime-Minister, who could produce one single good Action in his whole Life, let him have committed ever so many Crimes. Indeed, I understood him a little too largely, and was stepping towards the Gate: but he pulled me by the Sleeve, and telling me, no Prime-Minister ever entered there, bid me go back again; saying, he thought I had sufficient Reason to rejoice in escaping the Bottomless Pit, which half my Crimes committed in any other Capacity would have entitled me to.'

CHAPTER XXI

Julian's *Adventures in the Post of a Soldier.*

'I WAS born at *Caen* in *Normandy*. My Mother's Name was *Matilda*; as for my Father, I am not so certain: for the good

Woman on her Death-Bed assured me, she herself could bring her Guess to no greater Certainty, than to five of Duke *William's* Captains. When I was no more than Thirteen (being indeed a surprizing stout Boy of my Age) I enlisted into the Army of Duke *William*, afterwards known by the Name of *William the Conqueror*; landed with him at *Pemesey*, or *Pemsey* in *Sussex*, and was present at the famous Battle of *Hastings*.*

'At the first Onset, it was impossible to describe my Consternation, which was heightened by the Fall of two Soldiers who stood by me; but this soon abated, and by degrees as my Blood grew warm, I thought no more of my own Safety, but fell on the Enemy with great Fury, and did a good deal of Execution; till unhappily I received a Wound in my Thigh, which rendered me unable to stand any longer, so that I now lay among the Dead, and was constantly exposed to the Danger of being trampled to death; as well by my Fellow-Soldiers as by the Enemy. However, I had the fortune to escape it, and continued the remaining part of the Day, and the Night following, on the Ground.

'The next Morning, the Duke sending out Parties to bring off the wounded, I was found almost expiring with Loss of Blood; notwithstanding which, as immediate Care was taken to dress my Wounds, Youth and a robust Constitution stood my Friends, and I recovered, after a long and tedious Indisposition, and was again able to use my Limbs and do my Duty.

'As soon as *Dover* was taken, I was conveyed thither with all the rest of the sick and wounded. Here I recovered of my Wound: but fell afterwards into a violent Flux, which when it departed, left me so weak, that it was long before I could regain my Strength. And what most afflicted me was, that during my whole Illness, when I languished under Want as well as Sickness, I had daily the mortification to see and hear the Riots and Excess of my Fellow-Soldiers, who had happily escaped safe from the Battle.

'I was no sooner well, than I was ordered into Garrison at *Dover* Castle. The Officers here fared very indifferently; but the private Men much worse. We had great Scarcity of Provisions, and what was yet more intolerable, were so closely confined for want of Room (four of us being obliged to lie on the same Bundle of Straw) that many died, and most sickened.

'Here I had remained about four Months, when one Night we were alarmed with the Arrival of the Earl of *Boulogne*, who had come over privily from *France*, and endeavoured to surprize the Castle. The Design proved ineffectual: for the Garrison making a brisk Sally, most of his Men were tumbled down the Precipice, and he returned with a very few back to *France*. In this Action however, I had the misfortune to come off with a broken Arm; it was so shattered, that besides a great deal of Pain and Misery, which I endured in my Cure, I was disabled for upwards of three Months.

'Soon after my Recovery, I had contracted an Amour with a young Woman, whose Parents lived near the Garrison, and were in much better Circumstances than I had reason to expect should give their Consent to the Match. However, as she was extremely fond of me, (as I was indeed distractedly enamoured of her) they were prevailed on to comply with her Desires, and the Day was fixed for our Marriage.

'On the Evening preceding, while I was exulting with the eager Expectation of the Happiness I was the next Day to enjoy, I received Orders to march early in the Morning towards *Windsor*, where a large Army was to be formed, at the Head of which the King intended to march into the *West*. Any Person who hath ever been in love, may easily imagine what I felt in my Mind, on receiving those Orders; and what still heightened my Torments was, that the commanding Officer would not permit any one to go out of the Garrison that Evening; so that I had not even an Opportunity of taking Leave of my Beloved.

'The Morning came, which was to have put me in the Possession of my Wishes; but alas! the Scene was now changed, and all the Hopes which I had raised, were now so many Ghosts to haunt, and Furies to torment me.

'It was now the midst of Winter, and very severe Weather for the Season; when we were obliged to make very long and fatiguing Marches, in which we suffered all the Inconveniencies of Cold and Hunger. The Night in which I expected to riot in the Arms of my beloved Mistress, I was obliged to take up with a Lodging on the Ground, exposed to the Inclemencies of a rigid Frost; nor could I obtain the least Comfort of Sleep, which shunned me as its Enemy. In short, the Horrors of that Night are not to be described, or perhaps imagined. They made such an Impression on my Soul, that I was forced to be dipped three Times in the River *Lethe*, to prevent my remembering it in the Characters which I afterwards performed in the Flesh.'

Here I interrupted *Julian* for the first time, and told him, no such dipping had happened to me in my Voyage from one World to the other: but he satisfied me by saying, 'That this only happened to those Spirits which returned into the Flesh, in order to prevent the Reminiscence which *Plato* mentions, and which would otherwise cause great Confusion in the other World.

He then proceeded as follows: 'We continued a very laborious March to *Exeter*, which we were ordered to besiege. The Town soon surrendered, and his Majesty built a Castle there, which he garrisoned with his *Normans*, and unhappily I had the misfortune to be one of the Number.

'Here we were confined closer than I had been at *Dover*; for as the Citizens were extremely disaffected, we were never suffered to go without the Walls of the Castle; nor indeed could we, unless in large Bodies, without the utmost Danger. We were likewise kept to continual Duty, nor could any Sollicitations prevail with the Commanding Officer to give me a Month's Absence to visit my Love, from whom I had no Opportunity of hearing in all my long Absence.

'However, in the Spring, the People being more quiet, and another Officer of a gentler Temper, succeeding to the principal Command, I obtained Leave to go to *Dover*: but alas! what Comfort did my long Journey bring me? I found the Parents of my Darling in the utmost Misery at her Loss: for she had died about a Week before my Arrival of a Consumption, which they imputed to her pining at my sudden Departure.

'I now fell into the most violent and almost raving Fit of Despair. I cursed my self, the King, and the whole World, which no longer seemed to have any Delight for me. I threw my self on the Grave of my deceased Love, and lay there without any kind of Sustenance for two whole Days. At last Hunger, together with the Persuasions of some People who took pity on me, prevailed with me to quit that Situation, and refresh my self with Food. They then persuaded me to return to my Post, and abandon a Place where almost every Object I saw, recalled Ideas to my Mind, which, as they said, I should endeavour with my utmost Force to expel from it. This Advice at length succeeded; the rather, as the Father and Mother of my Beloved refused to see me, looking on me as the innocent but certain Cause of the Death of their only Child.

'The Loss of one we tenderly love, as it is one of the most bitter and biting Evils which attends human Life, so it wants the Lenitive which palliates and softens every other Calamity; I mean that great Reliever, Hope. No Man can be so totally undone, but that he may still cherish Expectation: but this deprives us of all such Comfort, nor can any thing but Time alone lessen it. This however, in most Minds, is sure to work a slow but effectual Remedy; so did it in mine: for within a Twelvemonth, I was entirely reconciled to my Fortune, and soon after absolutely forgot the Object of a Passion from which I had promised my self such extreme Happiness, and in the Disappointment of which I had experienced such inconceivable Misery.

'At the Expiration of the Month, I returned to my Garrison at *Exeter*; where I was no sooner arrived, than I was ordered to march into the North, to oppose a Force there levied by the Earls of *Chester* and *Northumberland*. We came to *York*, where his Majesty pardoned the Heads of the Rebels, and very severely punished some who were less guilty. It was particularly my Lot to be ordered to seize a poor Man, who had never been out of his House, and convey him to Prison. I detested this Barbarity, yet was obliged to execute it; nay, though no Reward would have bribed me in a private Capacity to have acted such a Part, yet so much Sanctity is there in the Commands of a Monarch, or General to a Soldier, that I performed it without Reluctance, nor had the Tears of his Wife and Family any Prevalence with me.

'But this, which was a very small piece of Mischief in comparison with many of my Barbarities afterwards, was however the only one which ever gave me any Uneasiness: for when the King led us afterward into *Northumberland* to revenge those People's having joined with *Osborn* the *Dane* in his Invasion, and Orders were given us to commit what Ravages we could, I was forward in fulfilling them, and among some lesser Cruelties (I remember it yet with Sorrow) I ravished a Woman, murdered a little Infant playing in her Lap, and then burnt her House. In short, for I have no pleasure in this part of my Relation, I had my share in all the Cruelties exercised on those poor Wretches; which were so grievous, that for sixty Miles together, between *York* and *Durham*, not a single House, Church, or any other public or private Edifice was left standing.

'We had pretty well devoured the Country, when we were ordered to march to the Isle of *Ely*, to oppose *Hereward*, a bold and stout Soldier, who had under him a very large Body of Rebels, who had the Impudence to rise against their King and Conqueror (I talk now in the same Style I did then) in defence of their Liberties, as they called them. These were soon subdued: but as I happened (more to my Glory than my Comfort) to be posted in that part through which *Hereward* cut his way, I received a dreadful Cut on the Forehead, a second on the Shoulder, and was run through the Body with a Pike.

'I languished a long time with these Wounds, which made me incapable of attending the King into *Scotland*. However, I was able to go over with him afterwards into *Normandy*, in his Expedition against *Philip*, who had taken the Opportunity of the Troubles in *England*, to invade that Province.* Those few *Normans* who had survived their Wounds, and had remained in the Isle of *Ely*, were all of our Nation who went, the rest of his Army being all composed of *English*. In a Skirmish near the Town of *Mans*, my Leg was broke, and so shattered that it was forced to be cut off.

'I was now disabled for serving longer in the Army, and accordingly being discharged from the Service, I retired to the Place of my Nativity, where in extreme Poverty, and frequent bad Health from the many Wounds I had received, I dragged on a miserable Life to the Age of Sixty-three; my only Pleasure being to recount the Feats of my Youth, in which Narratives I generally exceeded the Truth.

'It would be tedious and unpleasant to recount to you the several Miseries I suffered after my Return to *Caen*; let it suffice, they were so terrible, that they induced *Minos* to compassionate me, and, notwithstanding the Barbarities I had been guilty of in *Northumberland*, to suffer me to go once more back to Earth.'

CHAPTER XXII

What happened to Julian *in the Person of a Taylor.*

'FORTUNE now stationed me in a Character, which the Ingratitude of Mankind hath put them on ridiculing, tho' they owe to it not only a Relief from the Inclemencies of Cold, to which they would otherwise be exposed, but likewise a considerable Satisfaction of their Vanity. The Character I mean, was that of a Taylor; which, if we consider it with due Attention, must be confessed to have in it great Dignity and Importance. For in reality, who constitutes the different Degrees between Men but the Taylor? The Prince indeed gives the Title, but *it is the Taylor who makes the Man.* To his Labours are owing the Respect of Crouds, and the Awe which Great Men inspire into their Beholders, tho' these are too often unjustly attributed to other Motives. Lastly, the Admiration of the Fair is most commonly to be placed to his Account.

'I was just set up in my Trade, when I made three Suits of fine Clothes for King *Stephen's* Coronation.* I question whether the Person who wears the rich Coat, hath so much Pleasure and Vanity in being admired in it, as we Taylors have from that Admiration; and perhaps a Philosopher would say, he is not so well entitled to it. I bustled on the Day of the Ceremony through the Croud, and it was with incredible Delight, I heard several say, as my Clothes walked by, *Bless me was ever any thing so fine as the Earl of* Devonshire! *Sure he and Sir* Hugh Bigot *are the two best-drest Men I ever saw.* Now both those Suits were of my making.

'There would indeed be infinite Pleasure in working for the Courtiers, as they are generally genteel Men, and shew one's Clothes to the best advantage, was it not for one small Discouragement; this is, that they never pay. I solemnly protest, tho' I lost almost as much by the Court in my Life as I got by the City, I never carried a Suit into the latter with half the Satisfaction which I have done to the former; tho' from that I was certain of ready Money, and from this almost as certain of no Money at all.

'Courtiers may, however, be divided into two sorts, very essentially different from each other; into those who never intend to pay for their Clothes; and those who do intend to pay for them, but never happen to be able. Of the latter sort, are many of those young Gentlemen whom we equip out for the Army, and who are unhappily for us, cut off before they arrive at Preferment. This is the Reason that Taylors in time of War are mistaken for Politicians, by their Inquisitiveness into the Event of Battles, one Campaign very often proving the Ruin of half a dozen of us. I am sure I had frequent Reason to curse that fatal Battle of *Cardigan*, where the *Welsh* defeated some of King *Stephen's* best Troops, and where many a good Suit of mine, unpaid for, fell to the ground.

'The Gentlemen of this honourable Calling have fared much better in later Ages than when I was of it: for now it seems the Fashion is, when they apprehend their Customer is not in the best Circumstances, if they are not paid as soon as they carry home the Suit, they charge him in their Book as much again as it is worth, and then send a Gentleman with a small Scrip of Parchment to demand the Money. If this be not immediately paid, the Gentleman takes the Beau with him to his House, where he locks him up till the Taylor is contented: but in my Time, these Scrips of Parchment were not in use; and if the Beau disliked paying for his Clothes, as very often happened, we had no Method of compelling him.

'In several of the Characters which I have related to you, I apprehend, I have sometimes forgot my self, and considered my self as really interested, as I was when I personated them on Earth. I have just now caught my self in the Fact: for I have complained to you as bitterly of my Customers as I formerly used to do, when I was the Taylor: but in reality, tho' there were some few Persons of very great Quality, and some others, who never paid their Debts; yet those were but a few, and I had a Method of repairing this Loss. My Customers I divided under three Heads: those who paid ready Money, those who paid slow, and those who never paid at all. The first of these, I considered apart by themselves, as Persons by whom I got a certain but small Profit. The two last I lumped together, making those who paid slow, contribute to repair my Losses by those who did not pay at all. Thus upon the whole I was a very inconsiderable Loser, and might have left a Fortune to my Family, had I not launched forth into Expences which swallowed up all my Gains. I had a Wife and two Children. These indeed I kept frugally enough; for I half starved them: but I kept a Mistress in a finer way, for whom I had a Country House, pleasantly situated on the *Thames*, elegantly fitted up and neatly furnished. This Woman might very properly be called my Mistress: for she was most absolutely so, and tho' her Tenure was no higher than by my Will, she domineered as tyrannically, as if my Chains had been rivetted in the strongest manner. To all this I submitted, not through any Adoration of her Beauty, which was indeed but indifferent. Her Charms consisted in little Wantonnesses, which she knew admirably well to use in Hours of Dalliance, and which, I believe, are of all Things the most delightful to a Lover.

'She was so profusely extravagant, that it seemed as if she had an actual Intent to ruin me. This I am sure of, if such had been her real Intention, she could have taken no properer Way to accomplish it; nay, I my self might appear to have had the same View: for besides this extravagant Mistress, and my Country House, I kept likewise a Brace of Hunters, rather for that it was fashionable so to do, than for any great Delight I took in the Sport, which I very little attended; not for want of Leisure; for few Noblemen had so much. All the Work I ever did was taking Measure, and that only of my greatest and best Customers. I scarce ever cut a Piece of Cloth in my Life, nor was indeed much more able to fashion a Coat than any Gentleman in the Kingdom. This made a skilful Servant too necessary to me. He knew I must submit to any Terms with, or any Treatment from him. He knew it was easier for him to find another such a Taylor as me, than for me to procure such another Workman as him: for this Reason, he exerted the most notorious and cruel Tyranny, seldom giving me a civil Word; nor could the utmost Condescension on my side, tho' attended with continual Presents and Rewards, and raising his Wages, content or please him. In a word, he was as absolutely my Master, as was ever an ambitious, industrious Prime-Minister over an indolent and voluptuous King. All my other Journeymen paid more Respect to him than to me: for they considered my Favour as a necessary Consequence of obtaining his.

'These were the most remarkable Occurrences while I acted this Part. *Minos* hesitated a few Moments, and then bid me get back again, without assigning any Reason.'

CHAPTER XXIII
The Life of Alderman Julian.

'I NOW revisited *England*, and was born at *London*. My Father was one of the Magistrates of that City. He had eleven Children, of whom I was the eldest. He had great Success in Trade, and grew extremely rich, but the largeness of his Family rendered it impossible for him to leave me a Fortune sufficient to live well on, independent of Business. I was accordingly brought up to be a Fishmonger: in which Capacity, I myself afterwards acquired very considerable Wealth.

'The same Disposition of Mind, which in Princes is called Ambition, is in Subjects named Faction. To this Temper I was greatly addicted from my Youth. I was, while a Boy, a great Partizan of Prince *John's* against his Brother *Richard*, during the latter's Absence in the Holy War, and in his Captivity.* I was no more than one and twenty, when I first began to make Political Speeches in Public, and to endeavour to foment Disquietude and Discontent in the City. As I was pretty well qualified for this Office, by a great Fluency of Words, an harmonious Accent, a graceful Delivery, and above all, an invincible Assurance, I had soon acquired some Reputation among the younger Citizens, and some of the weaker and more inconsiderate of a riper Age. This cooperating with my own natural Vanity, made me extravagantly proud and supercilious. I soon began to esteem myself a Man of some Consequence, and to overlook Persons every way my Superiours.

'The famous *Robin Hood*, and his Companion *Little John*, at this time made a considerable Figure in *Yorkshire*. I took upon me to write a Letter to the former, in the Name of the City, inviting him to come to *London*, where I assured him of very good Reception, signifying to him my own great Weight and Consequence, and how much I had disposed the Citizens in his favour. Whether he received this Letter or no, I am not certain: but he never gave me any Answer to it.

'A little afterwards, one *William Fitz-Osborn*,* or, as he was nicknamed, *William Long-Beard*, began to make a Figure in the City. He was a bold and an impudent Fellow, and had raised himself to great Popularity with the Rabble, by pretending to espouse their Cause against the Rich. I took this Man's part, and made a public Oration in his favour, setting him forth as a Patriot, and one who had embarked in the Cause of Liberty: for which Service he did not receive me with the Acknowledgments I expected. However, as I thought I should easily gain the Ascendant over this Fellow, I continued still firm on his side, till the Archbishop of *Canterbury*, with an armed Force, put an end to his Progress: for he was seized in *Bow* Church, where he had taken Refuge, and with nine of his Accomplices hanged in Chains.

'I escaped narrowly myself: for I was seized in the same Church with the rest, and as I had been very considerably engaged in the Enterprize, the Archbishop was inclined to make me an Example: but my Father's Merit, who had advanced a considerable Sum to Queen *Eleanor*, towards the King's Ransom, preserved me.*

'The Consternation my Danger had occasioned, kept me some time quiet, and I applied myself very assiduously to my Trade. I invented all manner of Methods to enhance the Price of Fish, and made use of my utmost Endeavours to engross as much of the Business as possible in my own hands. By these means I acquired a Substance, which raised me to some little Consequence in the City: but far from elevating me to that Degree, which I had formerly flattered myself with possessing, at a time when I was totally insignificant: for in a trading Society, Money must at least lay the Foundation of all Power and Interest.

'But as it hath been remarked, that the same Ambition which sent *Alexander* into *Asia*, brings the Wrestler on the Green; and as this same Ambition is as incapable as Quicksilver of lying still: so I, who was possessed, perhaps, of a Share equal to what hath fired the Blood of any of the Heroes of Antiquity, was no less restless, and discontented with Ease and Quiet. My first Endeavours were to make myself head of my Company, which *Richard* I had just established, and soon afterwards I procured myself to be chosen Alderman.

'Opposition is the only State, which can give a Subject an Opportunity of exerting the Disposition I was possessed of. Accordingly King *John* was no sooner seated on his Throne, than I began to oppose his Measures, whether right or wrong. It is true, that Monarch had Faults enow. He was so abandoned to Lust and Luxury, that he addicted himself to the most extravagant Excesses in both, while he indolently suffered the King of *France* to rob him of almost all his foreign Dominions: my Opposition therefore was justifiable enough, and if my Motive from within had been as good as the Occasion from without, I should have had little to excuse: but in truth, I sought nothing but my own Preferment, by making myself formidable to the King, and then selling to him the Interest of that Party, by whose means I had become so. Indeed, had the public Good been my Care, however zealously I might have opposed the Beginning of his Reign, I should not have scrupled to lend him my utmost Assistance in the Struggle between him and Pope *Innocent* the Third, in which he was so manifestly in the right; nor have suffered the Insolence of that Pope, and the Power of the King of *France*, to have compelled him in the Issue basely to resign his Crown into the hands of the former, and receive it again as a Vassal; by means of which Acknowledgement the Pope afterwards claimed this Kingdom as a tributary Fief to be held of the Papal Chair. A Claim which occasioned great Uneasiness to many subsequent Princes, and brought numberless Calamities on the Nation.*

'As the King had among other Concessions stipulated to pay an immediate Sum of Money to *Pandulph*, which he had great difficulty to raise, it was absolutely necessary for him to apply to the City, where my Interest and Popularity were so high, that he had no Hopes without my Assistance. As I knew this, I took care to sell myself and Country as high as possible. The Terms I demanded, therefore, were a Place, a Pension, and a Knighthood. All those were immediately consented to. I was forthwith knighted, and promised the other two.

'I now mounted the *Hustings*, and without any regard to

Decency or Modesty, made as emphatical a Speech in favour of the King, as before I had done against him. In this Speech I justified all those Measures which I had before condemned, and pleaded as earnestly with my Fellow-Citizens, to open their Purses, as I had formerly done to prevail with them to keep them shut. But alas my Rhetoric had not the Effect I proposed. The Consequence of my Arguments was only Contempt to myself. The People at first stared on one another, and afterwards began unanimously to express their Dislike. An impudent Fellow among them reflecting on my Trade, cryed out, *Stinking Fish*; which was immediately reiterated through the whole Croud. I was then forced to slink a way home, but I was not able to accomplish my Retreat without being attended by the Mob, who huzza'd me along the Street with the repeated Cries of *Stinking Fish*.

'I now proceeded to Court, to inform his Majesty of my faithful Service, and how much I had suffered in his Cause. I found by my first Reception, he had already heard of my Success. Instead of thanking me for my Speech, he said, the City should repent of their Obstinacy; for that he would shew them who he was: and so saying, he immediately turned that Part to me, to which the Toe of Man hath so wonderful an Affection, that it is very difficult, whenever it presents itself conveniently, to keep our Toes from the most violent and ardent Salutation of it.

'I was a little nettled at this Behaviour, and with some Earnestness claimed the King's fulfilling his Promise: but he retired without answering me. I then applied to some of the Courtiers, who had lately professed great Friendship to me, had eat at my House, and invited me to theirs: but not one would return me any Answer, all running away from me, as if I had been seized with some contagious Distemper. I now found by Experience, that as none can be so civil, so none can be ruder than a Courtier.

'A few Moments after the King's retiring, I was left alone in the Room, to consider what I should do, or whither I should turn myself. My Reception in the City promised itself to be equal at least with what I found at Court. However, there was my Home, and thither it was necessary I should retreat for the present.

'But, indeed, bad as I apprehended my Treatment in the City

would be, it exceeded my Expectation. I rode home on an ambling Pad through Crouds, who expressed every kind of Disregard and Contempt; pelting me not only with the most abusive Language, but with Dirt. However, with much difficulty I arrived at last at my own House, with my Bones whole, but covered over with Filth.

'When I was got within my Doors, and had shut them against the Mob, who had pretty well vented their Spleen, and seemed now contented to retire; my Wife, whom I found crying over her Children, and from whom I hoped some Comfort in my Afflictions, fell upon me in the most outragious manner. She asked me, why I would venture on such a Step, without consulting her; she said, her Advice might have been civilly asked, if I was resolved not to have been guided by it. That whatever opinion I might have conceived of her Understanding, the rest of the World thought better of it. That I had never failed, when I had asked her Counsel, nor ever succeeded without it; with much more of the same kind, too tedious to mention; concluding, that it was a monstrous Behaviour to desert my Party, and come over to the Court. An Abuse, which I took worse than all the rest, as she had been constantly for several Years assiduous in railing at the Opposition, in siding with the Court-Party, and begging me to come over to it. And especially after my mentioning the Offer of Knighthood to her, since which time she had continually interrupted my Repose, with dinning in my Ears the Folly of refusing Honours, and of adhering to a Party, and to Principles, by which I was certain of procuring no Advantage to myself and my Family.

'I had now entirely lost my Trade, so that I had not the least Temptation to stay longer in a City, where I was certain of receiving daily Affronts and Rebukes. I therefore made up my Affairs with the utmost Expedition, and scraping together all I could, retired into the Country; where I spent the Remainder of my Days, in universal Contempt, being shunned by every body, perpetually abused by my Wife, and not much respected by my Children.

'Minos told me, tho' I had been a very vile Fellow, he thought my Sufferings made some Atonement, and so bid me take the other Trial.'

CHAPTER XXIV

Julian *recounts what happened to him while he was a Poet.*

'*Rome* was now the Seat of my Nativity, where I was born of a Family more remarkable for Honour than Riches. I was intended for the Church, and had a pretty good Education: but my Father dying while I was young, and leaving me nothing, for he had wasted his whole Patrimony, I was forced to enter my self in the Order of Mendicants.

'When I was at School, I had a knack of rhiming, which I unhappily mistook for Genius, and indulged to my Cost: for my Verses drew on me only Ridicule, and I was in Contempt called *The Poet.*

'This Humour pursued me through my Life. My first Composition after I left School, was a Panegyric on Pope *Alexander* IV who then pretended a Project of dethroning the King of *Sicily*.* On this Subject, I composed a Poem of about fifteen Thousand Lines, which with much difficulty I got to be presented to his Holiness, of whom I expected great Preferment as my Reward, but I was cruelly disappointed: for when I had waited a Year without hearing any of the Commendations I had flattered my self with receiving, and being now able to contain no longer, I applied to a Jesuit who was my Relation, and had the Pope's Ear, to know what his Holiness's Opinion was of my Work; he coldly answered me, that he was at that time busied in Concerns of too much Importance, to attend the reading of Poems.

'However dissatisfied I might be, and really was, with this Reception; and however angry I was with the Pope, for whose Understanding I entertained an immoderate Contempt, I was not yet discouraged from a second Attempt. Accordingly, I soon after produced another Work, entituled, *The Trojan Horse*. This was an allegorical Work, in which the Church was introduced into the World, in the same manner as that Machine had been into *Troy*. The Priests were the Soldiers in its Belly, and the Heathen Superstition the City to be destroyed by them. This Poem was written in *Latin*. I remember some of the Lines:

Mundanos scandit fatalis Machina Muros,
Farta Sacerdotum Turmis: exinde per Alvum
Visi exire omnes, magno cum Murmure olentes.
Non aliter quam cum Humanis furibundus ab Antris
It Sonus, & Nares simul Aura invadit hiantes.
Mille scatent et mille alii; trepidare Timore
Ethnica Gens cœpit: falsi per inane volantes
Effugere Dei—Desertaque Templa relinquunt.
Jam magnum crepitavit Equus, mox Orbis & alti
Ingemuere Poli: tunc tu Pater, ultimus Omnium
Maxime Alexander, ventrem maturus Equinum
*Deseris, heu Proles meliore digne Parente.**

I believe *Julian*, had I not stopt him, would have gone through the whole Poem; (for, as I observed, in most of the Characters he related, the Affections he had enjoyed while he personated them on Earth, still made some Impression on him) but I begged him to omit the Sequel of the Poem, and proceed with his History. He then recollected himself, and smiling at the Observation which by Intuition he perceived I had made, continued his Narration as follows:

'I confess to you, says he, that the Delight in repeating our own Works is so predominant in a Poet, that I find nothing can totally root it out of the Soul. Happy would it be for those Persons, if their Hearers could be delighted in the same manner: but alas! hence that *ingens Solitudo* complained of by *Horace*:* for the Vanity of Mankind is so much greedier and more general than their Avarice, that no Beggar is so ill received by them as he who solicits their Praise.

'This I sufficiently experienced in the Character of a Poet: for my Company was shunned (I believe on this account chiefly) by my whole House; nay, there were few who would submit to hearing me read my Poetry, even at the price of sharing in my Provisions. The only Person who gave me Audience was a Brother Poet; he indeed fed me with Commendation very liberally: but as I was forced to hear and commend in my turn, I perhaps bought his Attention dear enough.

'Well, Sir, if my Expectations of the Reward I hoped from my first Poem had baulked me, I had now still greater Reason to complain: for instead of being preferred or commended for the second, I was enjoined a very severe Penance by my Superiour, for ludicrously comparing the Pope to a Fart. My Poetry was now the Jest of every Company, except some few, who spoke of it with detestation; and I found, that instead of recommending me to Preferment, it had effectually barred me from all Probability of attaining it.

'These Discouragements had now induced me to lay down my Pen, and write no more. But, as *Juvenal* says,

> *—Si discedas, Laqueo tenet ambitiosi*
> *Consuetudo Mali.**

I was an Example of the Truth of this Assertion: for I soon betook my self again to my Muse. Indeed, a Poet hath the same Happiness with a Man who is doatingly fond of an ugly Woman. The one enjoys his Muse, and the other his Mistress, with a Pleasure very little abated by the Esteem of the World, and only undervalues their Taste for not corresponding with his own.

'It is unnecessary to mention any more of my Poems; they had all the same Fate; and tho' in reality some of my latter Pieces deserved (I may now speak it without the Imputation of Vanity) a better Success, as I had the Character of a bad Writer, I found it impossible ever to obtain the Reputation of a good one. Had I possessed the Merit of *Homer*, I could have hoped for no Applause; since it must have been a profound Secret: for no one would now read a Syllable of my Writings.

'The Poets of my Age were, as I believe you know, not very famous. However, there was one in some Credit at that time, tho' I have the Consolation to know his Works are all perished long ago. The Malice, Envy, and Hatred I bore this Man are inconceivable to any but an Author, and an unsuccessful one; I never could bear to hear him well spoken of, and writ anonymous Satires against him, tho' I had received Obligations from him; indeed I believe it would have been an absolute Impossibility for him at any rate to have made me sincerely his Friend.

'I have heard an Observation which was made by some one of later Days, that there are no worse Men than bad Authors. A Remark of the same kind hath been made on ugly Women, and the Truth of both stands on one and the same Reason, *viz.* that they are both tainted with that cursed and detestable Vice of

Envy; which, as it is the greatest Torment to the Mind it inhabits, so is it capable of introducing into it a total Corruption, and of inspiring it to the Commission of the most horrid Crimes imaginable.

'My Life was but short; for I soon pined my self to death with the Vice I just now mentioned. *Minos* told me, I was infinitely too bad for *Elysium*; and as for the other Place, the Devil had sworn, he would never entertain a Poet for *Orpheus's* sake: so I was forced to return again to the Place from whence I came.'

CHAPTER XXV

Julian *performs the Parts of a Knight and a Dancing-Master.*

'I NOW mounted the Stage in *Sicily*, and became a Knight Templar: but as my Adventures differ so little from those, I have recounted you in the Character of a common Soldier, I shall not tire you with Repetition. The Soldier and the Captain differ in reality so little from one another, that it requires an accurate Judgment to distinguish them; the latter wears finer Clothes, and in Time of Success lives somewhat more delicately: but as to every thing else, they very nearly resemble one another.

'My next Step was into *France*, where Fortune assigned me the Part of a Dancing-Master. I was so expert in my Profession, that I was brought to Court in my Youth, and had the Heels of *Philip de Valois*, who afterwards succeeded *Charles the Fair*, committed to my Direction.*

'I do not remember, that in any of the Characters in which I appeared on Earth, I ever assumed to my self a greater Dignity, or thought my self of more real Importance that now. I looked on Dancing as the greatest Excellence of human Nature, and on my self as the greatest Proficient in it. And indeed, this seemed to be the general Opinion of the whole Court: for I was the chief Instructor of the Youth of both Sexes, whose Merit was almost entirely defined by the Advances they made in that Science, which I had the Honour to profess. As to my self, I was so fully persuaded of this Truth, that I not only slighted and despised those who were ignorant of Dancing; but I thought the highest Character I could give of any Man, was, that he made a graceful Bow: for want of which Accomplishment, I had a sovereign Contempt for many Persons of Learning; nay, for some Officers of the Army, and a few even of the Courtiers themselves.

'Though so little of my Youth had been thrown away in what they call Literature, that I could hardly write and read, yet I composed a Treatise on Education; the first Rudiments of which, as I taught, were to instruct a Child in the Science of coming handsomely into a Room. In this I corrected many Faults of my Predecessors, particularly that of being too much in a hurry, and instituting a Child in the sublimer Parts of Dancing before they are capable of *making their Honours.*

'But as I have not now the same high Opinion of my Profession, which I had then, I shall not entertain you with a long History of a Life which consisted of *Borées* and *Coupées.** Let it suffice, that I lived to a very old Age, and followed my Business as long as I could crawl. At length I revisited my old Friend *Minos*, who treated me with very little Respect, and bad me dance back again to Earth.

'I did so, and was now once more born an *Englishman*, bred up to the Church, and at length arrived at the Station of a Bishop.

'Nothing was so remarkable in this Character, as my always voting——[1].'

[1] Here Part of the Manuscript is lost, and that a very considerable one, as appears by the Number of the next Book and Chapter, which contains, I find, the History of *Anna Boleyn*, but as to the Manner in which it was introduced, or to whom the Narrative is told, we are totally left in the dark. I have only to remark, that this Chapter is in the Original writ in a Woman's Hand: And tho' the Observations in it are, I think, as excellent as any in the whole Volume, there seems to be a Difference in Style between this and the preceding Chapters, and as it is the Character of a Woman which is related, I am inclined to fancy it was really written by one of that Sex.

BOOK XIX

CHAPTER VII

Wherein Anna Boleyn *relates the History of her Life.*

'I AM going now truly to recount a Life, which from the Time of its ceasing, has been, in the other World, the continual Subject of the Cavils of contending Parties; the one making me as black as Hell, the other as pure and innocent as the Inhabitants of this blessed Place; the Mist of Prejudice blinding their Eyes, and Zeal for what they themselves profess, making every thing appear in that Light, which they think most conduces to its Honour.*

'My Infancy was spent in my Father's House, in those childish Plays, which are most suitable to that State, and I think this was one of the happiest Parts of my Life; for my Parents were not among the Number of those who look upon their Children as so many Objects of a Tyrannic Power, but I was regarded as the dear Pledge of a virtuous Love, and all my little Pleasures were thought from their Indulgence their greatest Delight.

'At seven Years old, I was carried into *France* with the King's Sister, who was married to the *French* King, where I lived with a Person of Quality, who was an Acquaintance of my Father's. I spent my Time in learning those Things necessary to give young Persons of Fashion a polite Education, and did neither good nor evil, but day passed after day in the same easy way, till I was Fourteen; then began my Anxiety, my Vanity grew strong, and my Heart fluttered with Joy at every Compliment paid to my Beauty: and as the Lady, with whom I lived, was of a gay chearful Disposition, she kept a great deal of Company, and my Youth and Charms made me the continual Object of their Admiration. I passed some little time in those exulting Raptures, which are felt by every Woman, perfectly satisfied with her self, and with the Behaviour of others towards her.

'I was, when very young, promoted to be Maid of Honour to her Majesty. The Court was frequented by a young Nobleman, whose Beauty was the chief Subject of Conversation in all Assemblies of Ladies. The Delicacy of his Person, added to a great Softness in his Manner, gave every thing he said and did such an Air of Tenderness, that every Woman he spoke to, flattered her self with being the Object of his Love. I was one of those who was vain enough of my own Charms to hope to make a Conquest of him, whom the whole Court sighed for; I now thought every other Object below my Notice: yet the only Pleasure I proposed to myself in this Design, was, the triumphing over that Heart, which I plainly saw all the Ladies of the highest Quality, and the greatest Beauty would have been proud of possessing. I was yet too young to be very artful, but Nature, without any Assistance, soon discovers to a Man, who is used to Gallantry, a Woman's Desire to be liked by him, whether that Desire arises from any particular Choice she makes of him, or only from Vanity. He soon perceived my Thoughts, and gratified my utmost Wishes, by constantly preferring me before all other Women, and exerting his utmost Gallantry and Address to engage my Affections.

'This sudden Happiness, which I then thought the greatest I could have had, appeared visible in all my Actions; I grew so gay, and so full of Vivacity, that it made my Person appear still to a better Advantage. All my Acquaintance pretended to be fonder of me than ever; tho' young as I was, I plainly saw it was but Pretence, for through all their Endeavours to the contrary, Envy would often break forth in sly Insinuations, and malicious Sneers, which gave me fresh matter of Triumph, and frequent Opportunities of insulting them; which I never let slip, for now first my Female Heart grew sensible of the spiteful Pleasure of seeing another languish for what I enjoy'd.

'Whilst I was in the height of my Happiness, her Majesty fell ill of a languishing Distemper, which obliged her to go into the Country for the change of Air; my Place made it necessary for me to attend her, and which way he brought it about, I can't imagine, but my young Hero found means to be one of that small Train, that waited on my Royal Mistress, altho' she went as privately as possible. Hitherto all the Interviews I had ever had with him were in public, and I only looked on him as the fitter Object to feed that Pride which had no other view, but to shew its Power; but now the Scene was quite changed. My Rivals were all at a distance: the Place we went to, was as charming as the most agreeable natural Situation, assisted by the greatest Art, could make it; the pleasant solitary Walks, the singing of Birds, the thousand pretty Romantic Scenes this delightful Place afforded, gave a sudden Turn to my Mind, my whole Soul was melted into Softness, and all my Vanity was fled.

'My Spark was too much used to Affairs of this nature, not to perceive this Change; at first the profuse Transports of his Joy made me believe him wholly mine, and this belief gave me such Happiness, that no Language affords Words to express it, and can be only known to those who have felt it. But this was of a very short duration, for I soon found I had to do with one of those Men, whose only End in the persuit of a Woman, is to make her fall a Victim to an insatiable Desire to be admired. His Designs had succeeded, and now he every day grew colder, and, as if by Infatuation, my Passion every day increased; and notwithstanding all my Resolutions and Endeavours to the contrary, my Rage at the Disappointment at once both of my Love and Pride, and at the finding a Passion fixed in my Breast I knew not how to conquer, broke out into that inconsistent Behaviour, which must always be the Consequence of violent Passions. One Moment I reproach'd him, the next I grew to Tenderness, and blamed my self, and thought I fancied what was not true; he saw my Struggle, and triumphed in it: but as he had not Witnesses enough there of his Victory, to give him the full Enjoyment of it, he grew weary of the Country, and returned to *Paris*, and left me in a Condition it is utterly impossible to describe.

'My Mind was like a City up in Arms, all Confusion; and every new Thought was a fresh Disturber of my Peace. Sleep quite forsook me, and the Anxiety I suffered threw me into a Fever, which had like to have cost me my Life. With great Care I recovered; but the Violence of the Distemper left such a Weakness on my Body, that the Disturbance of my Mind was greatly assuaged; and now I began to comfort my self in the Reflection, that this Gentleman's being a finish'd Coquet, was very likely the only Thing could have preserved me; for he was the only Man from whom I was ever in any danger.

'By that time I was got tolerable well, we returned to *Paris*; and I confess, I both wished and feared to see this Cause of all my Pain: however, I hoped by the help of my Resentment, to be able to meet him with Indifference. This employed my Thoughts till our Arrival. The next day, there was a very full Court to congratulate the Queen on her Recovery; and amongst the rest, my Love appeared dressed and adorned, as if he designed some new Conquest. Instead of seeing a Woman he despised and slighted, he approached me with that assured Air which is common to successful Coxcombs. At the same time, I perceived I was surrounded by all those Ladies who were on his account my greatest Enemies; and in revenge, wished for nothing more than to see me make a ridiculous Figure. This Situation so perplexed my Thoughts, that when he came near enough to speak to me, I fainted away in his Arms. (Had I studied which way I could gratify him most, it was impossible to have done any thing to have pleased him more.) Some that stood by, brought smelling Bottles, and used means for my Recovery; and I was welcomed to returning Life, by all those ill-natured Repartees, which Women enraged by Envy are capable of venting. One cried, "Well, I never thought my Lord had any thing so frightful in his Person, or so fierce in his Manner, as to strike a young Lady dead at the sight of him." "No, no," says another, "some Ladies Senses are more apt to be hurried by agreeable, than disagreeable Objects." With many more such sort of Speeches, which shewed more Malice than Wit. This not being able to bear, trembling, and with but just Strength enough to move, I crawled to my Coach, and hurried home.

'When I was alone, and thought on what had happened to me in a public Court, I was at first driven to the utmost Despair; but afterwards, when I came to reflect, I believe this Accident contributed more to my being cured of my Passion, than any other could have done. I began to think the only Method to pique the Man, who had used me so barbarously, and to be revenged on my spightful Rivals, was to recover that Beauty, which was then languid, and had lost its Lustre, to let them see I had still Charms enough to engage as many Lovers as I could desire, and that I could yet rival them, who had thus cruelly insulted me. These pleasing Hopes revived my sinking Spirits, and worked a more effectual Cure on me, than all the Philosophy and Advice of the wisest Men could have done.

'I now employ'd all my Time and Care in adorning my Person, and studying the surest Means of engaging the Affections of others, while I myself continued quite indifferent; for I resolved for the future, if ever one soft Thought made its way to my Heart, to fly the Object of it, and by new Lovers to drive the Image from my Breast. I consulted my Glass every Morning, and got such a command of my Countenance, that I could suit it to the different Tastes of Variety of Lovers; and tho' I was young, for I was not yet above Seventeen; yet my public Way of Life gave me such continual Opportunities of conversing with Men, and the strong Desire I now had of pleasing them, led me to make such constant Observations on every thing they said or did, that I soon found out the different Methods of dealing with them. I observed that most Men generally liked in Women what was most opposite to their own Characters; therefore to the grave solid Man of Sense, I endeavoured to appear sprightly, and full of Spirit; to the Witty and Gay, soft and languishing; to the Amorous (for they want no increase of their Passions) cold and reserved; to the Fearful and Backward, warm and full of Fire, and so of all the rest. As to Beaus, and all those sort of Men, whose Desires are centered in the Satisfaction of their Vanity, I had learned by sad Experience, the only way to deal with them was to laugh at them, and let their own good Opinion of themselves be the only Support of their Hopes. I knew, while I could get other Followers, I was sure of them; for the only sign of Modesty they ever give, is that of not depending on their own Judgments, but following the Opinions of the greatest Number.

'Thus furnished with Maxims, and grown wise by past Errors, I in a manner begun the World again: I appeared in all public Places handsomer and more lively than ever, to the Amazement of every one who saw me, and had heard of the Affair between me and my Lord. He himself was much surprized, and vexed at this sudden Change, nor could he account how it was possible for me so soon to shake off those Chains he thought he had fixed on me for Life, nor was he willing to lose his Conquest in this manner. He endeavoured by all means possible to talk to me again of Love, but I stood fixed to my Resolution, (in which I was greatly assisted by the Croud of Admirers that daily surrounded me) never to let him explain himself: for notwithstanding all my

Pride, I found the first Impression the Heart receives of Love is so strong, that it requires the most vigilant Care to prevent a Relapse.

'Now I lived three Years in a constant Round of Diversions, and was made the perfect Idol of all the Men that came to Court of all Ages, and all Characters. I had several good Matches offered me, but I thought none of them equal to my Merit; and one of my greatest Pleasures was to see those Women, who had pretended to rival me, often glad to marry those whom I had refused. Yet notwithstanding this great Success of my Schemes, I cannot say I was perfectly Happy; for every Woman that was taken the least notice of, and every Man that was insensible to my Arts, gave me as much Pain as all the rest gave me Pleasure; and sometimes little underhand Plots, which were laid against my Designs, would succeed in spite of my Care: so that I really begun to grow weary of this manner of Life, when my Father returning from his Embassy in *France*, took me home with him, and carried me to a little pleasant Country House, where there was nothing grand or superfluous, but every thing neat and agreeable; there I led a Life perfectly solitary.

'At first, the time hung very heavy on my hands, and I wanted all kind of Employment, and I had very like to have fallen into the height of the Vapours, from no other Reason, but from want of knowing what to do with myself. But when I had lived here a little time, I found such a Calmness in my Mind, and such a Difference between this, and the restless Anxieties I had experienced in a Court, that I began to share the Tranquillity, that visibly appeared in every thing round me. I set myself to do Works of Fancy; and to raise little Flower-Gardens, with many such innocent rural Amusements; which, altho' they are not capable of affording any great Pleasure, yet they give that serene Turn to the Mind, which I think much preferable to any thing else Human Nature is made susceptible of. I now resolved to spend the rest of my Days here, and that nothing should allure me from this sweet Retirement, to be again tossed about with tempestuous Passions of any kind.

'Whilst I was in this Situation, my Lord *Peircy*, the Earl of *Northumberland's* eldest Son, by an Accident of losing his way after a Fox-Chace, was met by my Father, about a Mile from our House; he came home with him, only with a design of dining with us, but was so taken with me, that he stay'd three Days. I had too much Experience in all Affairs of this kind, not to see presently the Influence I had on him; but I was at that time so intirely free from all Ambition, that even the Prospect of being a Countess had no Effect on me; and I then thought nothing in the World could have bribed me to have changed my Way of Life. This young Lord, who was just in his Bloom, found his Passion so strong, he could not endure a long Absence, but returned again in a Week, and endeavoured by all the Means he could think of, to engage me to return his Affection. He addressed me with that Tenderness and Respect, which Women on Earth think can flow from nothing but real Love; and very often told me, that unless he could be so happy, as by his Assiduity and Care to make himself agreeable to me, although he knew my Father would eagerly embrace any Proposal from him, yet he would suffer that last of Miseries, of never seeing me more, rather than owe his own Happiness to any thing that might be the least Contradiction to my Inclinations.

'This manner of proceeding had something in it so noble and generous, that by degrees it raised a Sensation in me, which I know not how to describe, nor by what Name to call it; it was nothing like my former Passion; for there was no Turbulence, no uneasy waking Nights attended it, but all I could with Honour grant to oblige him, appeared to me to be justly due to his Truth and Love, and more the Effect of Gratitude, than of any Desire of my own. The Character I had heard of him from my Father, at my first returning to *England*, in discoursing of the young Nobility, convinced me, that if I was his Wife, I should have the perpetual Satisfaction of knowing every Action of his must be approved by all the sensible Part of Mankind; so that very soon I began to have no Scruple left, but that of leaving my little Scene of Quietness, and venturing again into the World. But this by his continual Application, and submissive Behaviour, by degrees entirely vanished, and I agreed he should take his own Time to break it to my Father, whose Consent he was not long in obtaining; for such a Match was by no means to be refused.

'There remained nothing now to be done, but to prevail with

the Earl of *Northumberland* to comply with what his Son so ardently desired; for which purpose, he set out immediately for *London*, and begged it as the greatest Favour, that I would accompany my Father, who was also to go thither the Week following. I could not refuse his Request, and as soon as we arrived in Town, he flew to me with the greatest Raptures, to inform me his Father was so good, that finding his Happiness depended on his Answer, he had given him free Leave to act in this Affair as would best please himself, and that he had now no Obstacle to prevent his Wishes.

'It was then the Beginning of the Winter, and the Time for our Marriage was fixed for the latter end of *March*; the Consent of all Parties made his Access to me very easy, and we conversed together both with Innocence and Pleasure. As his Fondness was so great, that he contrived all the Methods possible to keep me continually in his sight, he told me one Morning, he was commanded by his Father to attend him to Court that Evening, and begg'd I would be so good as to meet him there. I was now so used to act as he would have me, that I made no difficulty of complying with his Desire.

'Two Days after this, I was very much surprized at perceiving such a Melancholy in his Countenance, and Alteration in his Behaviour, as I could no way account for; but by Importunity, at last, I got from him, that Cardinal *Wolsey*, for what Reason he knew not, had peremptorily forbid him to think any more of me: and when he urged that his Father was not displeased with it, the Cardinal in his imperious Manner answered him, he should give his Father such convincing Reasons, why it would be attended with great Inconveniences, that he was sure he could bring him to be of his Opinion. On which he turned from him, and gave him no opportunity of replying.

'I could not imagine what Design the Cardinal could have in intermeddling in this Match, and I was still more perplexed to find that my Father treated my Lord *Peircy* with much more Coldness than usual; he too saw it, and we both wondered what could possibly be the Cause of all this. But it was not long before the Mystery was all made clear by my Father, who sending for me one day into his Chamber, let me into a Secret which was as little wished for as expected; he began with the surprizing

Effects of Youth and Beauty, and the Madness of letting go those Advantages they might procure us, till it was too late, when we might wish in vain to bring them back again. I stood amazed at this Beginning; he saw my Confusion, and bid me sit down and attend to what he was going to tell me, which was of the greatest Consequence; and he hoped I would be wise enough to take his Advice, and act as he should think best for my future Welfare.

'He then asked me, if I should not be much pleased to be a Queen? I answered with the greatest Earnestness, that so far from it, I would not live in a Court again to be the greatest Queen in the World; that I had a Lover who was both desirous and able to raise my Station, even beyond my Wishes. I found this Discourse was very displeasing; my Father frowned and called me a romantick Fool, and said, if I would hearken to him he could make me a Queen; for the Cardinal had told him, that the King, from the Time he saw me at Court the other Night, liked me; and intended to get a Divorce from his Wife, and to put me in her place; and ordered him to find some Method to make me a Maid of Honour to her present Majesty, that in the mean time he might have an Opportunity of seeing me.

'It is impossible to express the Astonishment these Words threw me into; and notwithstanding that the Moment before, when it appeared at so great a distance, I was very sincere in my Declaration, how much it was against my Will to be raised so high; yet now the Prospect came nearer, I confess my Heart fluttered, and my Eyes were dazzled with the View of being seated on a Throne. My Imagination presented before me all the Pomp, Power, and Greatness that attend a Crown; and I was so perplexed, I knew not what to answer, but remained as silent, as if I had lost the Use of my Speech. My Father, who guessed what it was that made me in this Condition, proceeded to bring all the Arguments he thought most likely to bend me to his Will; at last, I recovered from this Dream of Grandeur, and begged him by all the most endearing Names I could think of, not to urge me dishonourably to forsake the Man, whom I was convinced would raise me to an Empire, if in his power, and who had enough in his power to give me all I desired. But he was deaf to all I could say, and insisted, that by next Week, I should prepare my self to go to Court: he bid me consider of it, and not prefer a ridiculous Notion of Honour to the real Interest of my whole Family, but above all things not to disclose what he had trusted me with. On which, he left me to my own Thoughts.

'When I was alone, I reflected how little real Tenderness this Behaviour shewed to me, whose Happiness he did not at all consult; but only look'd on me as a Ladder, on which he could climb to the Height of his own ambitious Desires: and when I thought on his Fondness for me in my Infancy, I could impute it to nothing, but either the liking me as a Play-thing, or the Gratification of his Vanity in my Beauty. But I was too much divided between a Crown and my Engagement to Lord *Peircy*, to spend much Time in thinking of any thing else; and altho' my Father had positively forbid me, yet when he came next, I could not help acquainting him with all that had passed, with the Reserve only of the Struggle in my own Mind on the first mention of being a Queen.

'I expected he would have received the News with the greatest Agonies; but he shewed no vast Emotion; however he could not help turning pale; and taking me by the Hand, looked at me with an Air of Tenderness, and said, "If being a Queen will make you happy, and it's in your power to be so, I would not for the World prevent it, let me suffer what I will." This amazing Greatness of Mind had on me quite the contrary Effect, from what it ought to have had: for instead of increasing my Love for him, it almost put an end to it; and I began to think if he could part with me, the matter was not much. And I am convinced, when any Man gives up the Possession of a Woman, whose Consent he has once obtained, let his Motive be ever so generous, he will disoblige her. I could not help shewing my Dissatisfaction, and told him, I was very glad this Affair sat so easily on him. He had not power to answer, but was so suddenly struck with this unexpected ill-natur'd Turn I gave his Behaviour, that he stood amazed for some time, and then bowed and left me.

'Now I was again left to my own Reflections; but to make any thing intelligible out of them, is quite impossible; I wished to be a Queen, and wished I might not be one; I would have my Lord *Peircy* happy without me; and yet I would not have the Power of my Charms be so weak, that he could bear the Thought of Life after being disappointed in my Love. But the Result of all these confused Thoughts was a Resolution to obey my Father. I am afraid there was not much Duty in the Case, tho' at that time I was glad to take hold of that small Shadow, to save me from looking on my own Actions in the true Light.

'When my Lover came again, I looked on him with that Coldness that he could not bear, on purpose to rid my self of all Importunity: for since I had resolved to use him ill, I regarded him as the Monument of my Shame, and his every Look appeared to me to upbraid me. My Father soon carried me to Court; there I had no very hard Part to act; for with the Experience I had had of Mankind, I could find no great difficulty in managing a Man who liked me, and for whom I not only did not care, but had an utter Aversion to: but this Aversion he believed to be Virtue; for how credulous is a Man who has an Inclination to believe? And I took care sometimes to drop Words of Cottages and Love, and how happy the Woman was who fixed her Affections on a Man in such a Station of Life, that she might show her Love, without being suspected of Hypocrisy or mercenary Views.

'All this was swallowed very easily by the amorous King, who pushed on the Divorce with the utmost Impetuosity, although the Affair lasted a good while, and I remained most part of the time behind the Curtain. Whenever the King mentioned it to me, I used such Arguments against it, as I thought the most likely to make him the more eager for it; begging, that unless his Conscience was really touched, he would not on my account give any grief to his virtuous Queen; for in being her Handmaid, I thought my self highly honoured; and that I would not only forgo a Crown, but even give up the Pleasure of ever seeing him more, rather than wrong my Royal Mistress. This way of talking, joined to his eager Desire to possess my Person, convinced the King so strongly of my exalted Merit, that he thought it a meritorious Act to displace the Woman (whom he could not have so good an Opinion of, because he was tired of her) and to put me in her place.

'After about a Year's stay at Court, as the King's Love to me began to be talked of, it was thought proper to remove me, that there might be no Umbrage given to the Queen's Party; I was forced to comply with this, though greatly against my Will; for I was very jealous that Absence might change the King's Mind. I retired again with my Father to his Country Seat,* but it had no longer those Charms for me which I once enjoyed there; for my Mind was now too much taken up with Ambition to make room for any other Thoughts. During my Stay here, my Royal Lover often sent Gentlemen to me with Messages and Letters, which I always answered in the manner I thought would best bring about my Designs, which were to come back again to Court.

'In all the Letters that passed between us, there was something so kingly and commanding in his, and so deceitful and submissive in mine, that I sometimes could not help reflecting on the Difference betwixt this Correspondence, and that with Lord *Peircy*; yet I was so pressed forward by the Desire of a Crown, I could not think of turning back. In all I wrote, I continually praised his Resolution of letting me be at a distance from him, since at this time it conduced indeed to my Honour; but what was of ten times more weight with me, I thought it was necessary for his; and I would sooner suffer any thing in the World than be any means of Hurt to him, either in his Interest, or Reputation. I always gave some Hints of ill Health, with some Reflections how necessary the Peace of the Mind was to that of the Body. By these means, I brought him to recall me again by the most absolute Command, which I for a little time artfully delay'd, (for I knew the Impatience of his Temper would not bear any Contradiction;) till he made my Father in a manner force me to what I most wished, with the utmost Appearance of Reluctance on my side.

'When I had gained this Point, I began to think which way I could separate the King from the Queen, for hitherto they lived in the same House. The Lady *Mary*,* the Queen's Daughter, being then about Sixteen, I sought for Emissaries of her own Age, that I could confide in, to instil into her Mind disrespectful Thoughts of her Father, and make a Jest of the Tenderness of his Conscience about the Divorce. I knew she had naturally strong Passions, and that young People of that Age are apt to think those that pretend to be their Friends are really so, and only speak their Minds freely; I afterwards contrived to have every Word she spoke of him carried to the King; who took it all as I could wish, and fancied those things did not come at first from the young Lady, but from her Mother. He would often talk of it to me, and I agreed with him in his Sentiments; but then as a great Proof of my Goodness, I always endeavoured to excuse her, by saying, a Lady so long time used to be a Royal Queen, might naturally be a little exasperated with those, she fancied would throw her from that Station she so justly deserved. By these sort of Plots, I found the way to make the King angry with the Queen; for nothing is easier than to make a Man angry with a Woman he wants to be rid of, and who stands in the way between him and his Pleasures: so that now the King, on the Pretence of the Queen's Obstinacy, in a Point where his Conscience was so tenderly concerned, parted with her.

'Every Thing was now plain before me; I had nothing farther to do but to let the King alone to his own Desires; and I had no reason to fear, since they had carried him so far, but that they would urge him on to do every thing I aimed at. I was created Marchioness of *Pembroke*. This Dignity sat very easy on me; for the Thoughts of a much higher Title, took from me all feeling of this; and I looked upon being a Marchioness as a Trifle, not that I saw the Bauble in its true Light, but because it fell short of what I had figured to my self I should soon obtain.

'The King's Desires grew very impatient, and it was not long before I was privately married to him. I was no sooner his Wife, than I found all the Queen come upon me; I felt my self conscious of Royalty, and even the Faces of my most intimate Acquaintance seemed to me to be quite strange. I hardly knew them, Height had turned my Head, and I was like a Man placed on a Monument, to whose Sight all Creatures at a great distance below him, appear like so many little Pigmies crawling about on the Earth; and the Prospect so greatly delighted me, that I did not presently consider, that in both Cases, descending a few Steps erected by human Hands would place us in the Number of those very Pigmies who appeared so despicable.

'Our Marriage was kept private for some time, for it was not thought proper to make it public (the Affair of the Divorce not being finished) till the Birth of my Daughter *Elizabeth* made it necessary. But all who saw me knew it; for my Manner of speaking and acting was so much changed with my Station, that all around me plainly perceived, I was sure I was a Queen. While it was a Secret, I had yet something to wish for; I could not be perfectly satisfied, till all the World was acquainted with my Fortune: but when my Coronation was over,* and I was raised to the height of my Ambition, instead of finding my self happy, I was in reality more miserable than ever; for besides that the Aversion I had naturally to the King was much more difficult to dissemble after Marriage than before, and grew into a perfect Detestation, my Imagination, which had thus warmly pursued a Crown, grew cool when I was in the possession of it, and gave me time to reflect what mighty matter I had gained by all this Bustle; and I often used to think my self in the case of the Fox-hunter, who when he has toiled and sweated all day in the Chace, as if some unheard-of Blessing was to crown his Success, finds at last, all he has got by his Labour is a stinking nauseous Animal. But my Condition was yet worse than his; for he leaves the loathsome Wretch to be torn by his Hounds, whilst I was obliged to fondle mine, and meanly pretend him to be the Object of my Love.

'For the whole time I was in this envied, this exalted State, I led a continual Life of Hypocrisy, which I now know nothing on earth can compensate. I had no Companion but the Man I hated. I dared not disclose my Sentiments to any Person about me; nor did any one presume to enter into any freedom of Conversation with me; but all who spoke to me, talked to the Queen, and not to me; for they would have said just the same Things to a dress'd-up Puppet, if the King had taken a fancy to call it his Wife. And as I knew every Woman in the Court was my Enemy, from thinking she had much more right than I had to the Place I filled, I thought my self as unhappy, as if I had been placed in a wild Wood, where there was no human Creature for me to speak to, in a continual fear of leaving any Traces of my Footsteps, lest I should be found by some dreadful Monster, or stung by Snakes and Adders: for such are spiteful Women to the Objects of their Envy. In this worst of all Situations, I was obliged to hide my Melancholy, and appear chearful. This threw me into an Error the other way, and I sometimes fell into a Levity in my Behaviour, that was afterwards made use of to my disadvantage.

'I had a Son dead-born, which I perceived abated something of the King's Ardor; for his Temper could not brook the least Disappointment. This gave me no Uneasiness; for not considering the Consequences, I could not help being best pleased when I had least of his Company. Afterwards I found he had cast his Eyes on one of my Maids of Honour; and whether it was owing to any Arts of her's, or only to the King's violent Passions, I was in the End used even worse than my former Mistress had been by my means. The Decay of the King's Affection was presently seen by all those Court-Sycophants, who continually watch the Motions of Royal Eyes; and the Moment they found they could be heard against me, they turned my most innocent Actions and Words, nay even my very Looks, into Proofs of the blackest Crimes.

'The King, who was impatient to enjoy his new Love,* lent a willing Ear to all my Accusers, who found ways of making him jealous, that I was false to his Bed. He would not so easily have believed any thing against me before, but he was now glad to flatter himself that he had found a Reason to do just what he had resolved upon without a Reason; and on some slight Pretences, and hear-say Evidence, I was sent to the *Tower*, where the Lady, who was my greatest Enemy, was appointed to watch me and lie in the same Chamber with me.* This was really as bad a Punishment as my Death; for she insulted me with those keen Reproaches, and spiteful Witticisms, which threw me into such Vapours and violent Fits, that I knew not what I uttered in this Condition. She pretended, I had confess'd talking ridiculous Stuff with a Set of low Fellows, whom I had hardly ever taken notice of, as could have imposed on none but such as were resolved to believe.* I was brought to my trial, and to blacken me the more, accused of conversing criminally with my own Brother, whom indeed I loved extremely well, but never looked on him in any other Light than as my Friend. However, I was condemned to be beheaded, or burnt, as the King pleased; and he was graciously pleased, from the great Remains of his Love, to chuse the mildest Sentence.

'I was much less shocked at this manner of ending my Life, than I should have been in any other Station: but I had had so little Enjoyment from the Time I had been a Queen, that Death was the less dreadful to me. The chief Things that lay on my Conscience, were the Arts I made use of to induce the King to part with the Queen, my ill Usage of Lady *Mary*, and my jilting Lord *Peircy*. However, I endeavoured to calm my Mind as well as I could, and hoped these Crimes would be forgiven me: for in other respects I had led a very innocent Life, and always did all the good-natur'd Actions I found any opportunity of doing. From the Time I had it in my power, I gave a great deal of Money amongst the Poor, I prayed very devoutly, and went to my Execution very composedly.

'Thus I lost my Life at the Age of Twenty-nine, in which short time I believe I went through more variety of Scenes, than many People who live to be very old. I had lived in a Court, where I spent my Time in Coquetry and Gaiety: I had experienced what it was to have one of those violent Passions which makes the Mind all Turbulence and Anxiety. I had had a Lover whom I esteemed and valued, and at the latter part of my Life, I was raised to a Station as high as the vainest Woman could wish. But in all these various Changes, I never enjoyed any real Satisfaction, unless in the little time I lived retired in the Country free from all Noise and Hurry; and while I was conscious, I was the Object of the Love and Esteem of a Man of Sense and Honour.'

On the Conclusion of this History, *Minos* paused for a small time, and then ordered the Gate to be thrown open for *Anne Bullen's* Admittance; on the Consideration, That whoever had suffered being a Queen for four Years, and been sensible during all that time of the real Misery which attends that exalted Station, ought to be forgiven whatever she had done to obtain it[1].

[1] Here ends this curious Manuscript; the rest being destroyed in rolling up Pens, Tobacco, *&c.* It is to be hoped, heedless People will henceforth be more cautious what they burn or use to other vile Purposes; especially when they consider the Fate which had likely to have befallen the Divine *Milton*; and that the Works of *Homer* were probably discovered in some Chandler's Shop in *Greece*.

THE JOURNAL OF A VOYAGE TO LISBON

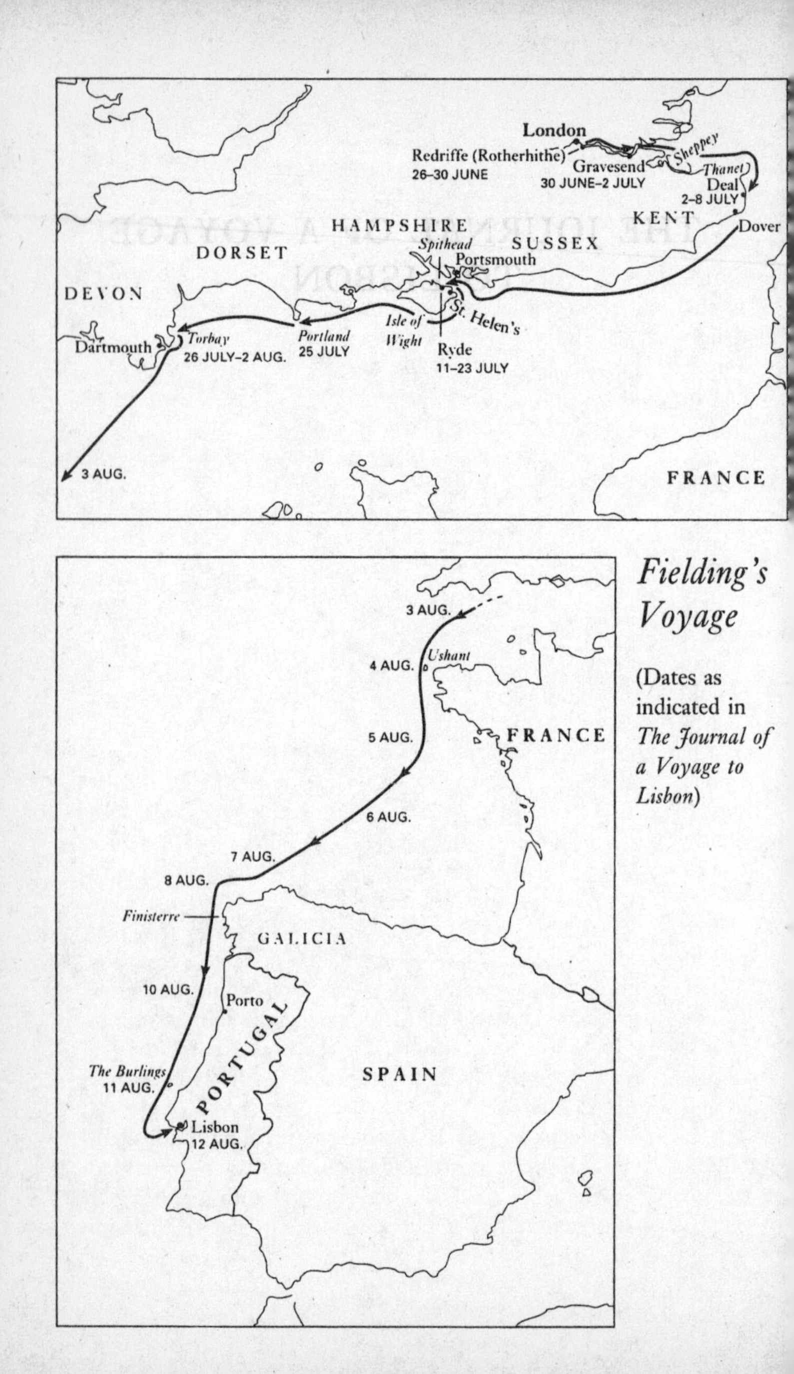

Fielding's Voyage

(Dates as indicated in *The Journal of a Voyage to Lisbon*)

DEDICATION TO THE PUBLIC*

YOUR candour is desired on the perusal of the following sheets, as they are the product of a genius that has long been your delight and entertainment. It must be acknowledged that a lamp almost burnt out does not give so steady and uniform a light, as when it blazes in its full vigour; but yet it is well known that, by its wavering, as if struggling against its own dissolution, it sometimes darts a ray as bright as ever. In like manner, a strong and lively genius will, in its last struggles, sometimes mount aloft, and throw forth the most striking marks of its original lustre.

Wherever these are to be found, do you, the genuine patrons of extraordinary capacities, be as liberal in your applauses of him who is now no more as you were of him whilst he was yet amongst you. And, on the other hand, if in this little work there should appear any traces of a weaken'd and decay'd life, let your own imaginations place before your eyes a true picture, in that of a hand trembling in almost its latest hour, of a body emaciated with pains, yet struggling for your entertainment; and let this affecting picture open each tender heart, and call forth a melting tear, to blot out whatever failings may be found in a work begun in pain, and finished almost at the same period with life.

It was thought proper, by the friends of the deceased, that this little piece should come into your hands as it came from the hands of the author, it being judged that you would be better pleased to have an opportunity of observing the faintest traces of a genius you have long admired, than have it patch'd by a different hand; by which means the marks of its true author might have been effac'd.

That the success of this last written, tho' first published, volume, of the author's posthumous pieces, may be attended with some convenience to those innocents he hath left behind, will, no doubt, be a motive to encourage its circulation through the kingdom, which will engage every future genius to exert itself for your pleasure.

The principles and spirit which breathe in every line of the small fragment begun in answer to Lord Bolingbroke* will unquestionably be a sufficient apology for its publication, altho' vital strength was wanting to finish a work so happily begun and so well designed.

THE PREFACE*

THERE would not, perhaps, be a more pleasant or profitable study, among those which have their principal end in amusement, than that of travels or voyages, if they were writ, as they might be, and ought to be, with a joint view to the entertainment and information of mankind. If the conversation of travellers be so eagerly sought after as it is, we may believe their books will be still more agreeable company, as they will, in general, be more instructive and more entertaining.

But when I say the conversation of travellers is usually so welcome, I must be understood to mean that only of such as have had good sense enough to apply their peregrinations to a proper use, so as to acquire from them a real and valuable knowledge of men and things; both which are best known by comparison. If the customs and manners of men were everywhere the same, there would be no office so dull as that of a traveller: for the difference of hills, valleys, rivers; in short, the various views in which we may see the face of the earth, would scarce afford him a pleasure worthy of his labour; and surely it would give him very little opportunity of communicating any kind of entertainment or improvement to others.

To make a traveller an agreeable companion to a man of sense, it is necessary, not only that he should have seen much, but that he should have overlooked much of what he hath seen. Nature is not, any more than a great genius, always admirable in her productions, and therefore the traveller, who may be called her commentator, should not expect to find everywhere subjects worthy of his notice.

It is certain, indeed, that one may be guilty of omission, as well as of the opposite extreme: but a fault on that side will be more easily pardoned, as it is better to be hungry than surfeited, and to miss your dessert at the table of a man whose gardens abound with the choicest fruits, than to have your taste affronted with every sort of trash that can be pick'd up at the green-stall or the wheelbarrow.

If we should carry on the analogy between the traveller and

the commentator, it is impossible to keep one's eye a moment off from the laborious much-read doctor Zachary Gray, of whose redundant notes on Hudibras I shall only say, that it is, I am confident, the single book extant in which above five hundred authors are quoted, not one of which could be found in the collection of the late doctor Mead.*

As there are few things which a traveller is to record, there are fewer on which he is to offer his observations: this is the office of the reader, and it is so pleasant a one, that he seldom chuses to have it taken from him, under the pretence of lending him assistance. Some occasions, indeed, there are, when proper observations are pertinent, and others when they are necessary; but good sense alone must point them out. I shall lay down only one general rule, which I believe to be of universal truth between relator and hearer, as it is between author and reader; this is, that the latter never forgive any observation of the former which doth not convey some knowledge that they are sensible they could not possibly have attained of themselves.

But all his pains in collecting knowledge, all his judgment in selecting, and all his art in communicating it, will not suffice, unless he can make himself, in some degree, an agreeable, as well as an instructive companion. The highest instruction we can derive from the tedious tale of a dull fellow scarce ever pays us for our attention. There is nothing, I think, half so valuable as knowledge, and yet there is nothing which men will give themselves so little trouble to attain; unless it be, perhaps, that lowest degree of it which is the object of curiosity, and which hath therefore that active passion constantly employed in its service. This, indeed, it is in the power of every traveller to gratify; but it is the leading principle in weak minds only.

To render his relation agreeable to the man of sense, it is therefore necessary that the voyager should possess several eminent and rare talents; so rare, indeed, that it is almost wonderful to see them ever united in the same person.

And if all these talents must concur in the relator, they are certainly in a more eminent degree necessary to the writer: for here the narration admits of higher ornaments of stile, and every fact and sentiment offers itself to the fullest and most deliberate examination.

It would appear, therefore, I think, somewhat strange, if such writers as these should be found extremely common: since nature hath been a most parsimonious distributor of her richest talents, and hath seldom bestowed many on the same person. But, on the other hand, why there should scarce exist a single writer of this kind worthy our regard; and whilst there is no other branch of history (for this is history) which hath not exercised the greatest pens, why this alone should be overlooked by all men of great genius and erudition, and delivered up to the Goths and Vandals as their lawful property, is altogether as difficult to determine.

And yet that this is the case, with some very few exceptions, is most manifest. Of these I shall willingly admit Burnet and Addison; if the former was not perhaps to be considered as a political essayist, and the latter as a commentator on the classics, rather than as a writer of travels; which last title perhaps they would both of them have been least ambitious to affect.*

Indeed if these two, and two or three more, should be removed from the mass, there would remain such a heap of dullness behind, that the appellation of voyage-writer would not appear very desirable.

I am not here unapprised that old Homer himself is by some considered as a voyage-writer; and indeed the beginning of his Odyssy may be urged to countenance that opinion, which I shall not controvert. But, whatever species of writing the Odyssy is of, it is surely at the head of that species, as much as the Iliad is of another; and so far the excellent Longinus* would allow, I believe, at this day.

But, in reality, the Odyssy, the Telemachus,* and all of that kind, are to the voyage-writing I here intend, what romance is to true history, the former being the confounder and corrupter of the latter. I am far from supposing that Homer, Hesiod,* and the other antient poets and mythologists, had any settled design to pervert and confuse the records of antiquity; but it is certain they have effected it; and, for my part, I must confess I should have honoured and loved Homer more had he written a true history of his own times in humble prose, than those noble poems that have so justly collected the praise of all ages; for though I read these with more admiration and astonishment, I still read

Herodotus, Thucydides and Xenophon, with more amusement and more satisfaction.

The original poets were not, however, without excuse. They found the limits of nature too strait for the immensity of their genius, which they had not room to exert, without extending fact by fiction; and that especially at a time when the manners of men were too simple to afford that variety which, they have since offered in vain to the choice of the meanest writers. In doing this, they are again excusable for the manner in which they have done it,

Ut speciosa dehinc miracula promant.*

They are not indeed so properly said to turn reality into fiction, as fiction into reality. Their paintings are so bold, their colours so strong, that everything they touch seems to exist in the very manner they represent it: their portraits are so just, and their landscapes so beautiful, that we acknowledge the strokes of nature in both, without inquiring whether nature herself, or her journeyman the poet, formed the first pattern of the piece.

But other writers (I will put Pliny at their head) have no such pretensions to indulgence: they lie for lying sake, or in order insolently to impose the most monstrous improbabilities and absurdities upon their readers on their own authority; treating them as some fathers treat children, and as other fathers do laymen, exacting their belief of whatever they relate, on no other foundation than their own authority, without ever taking the pains of adapting their lies to human credulity, and of calculating them for the meridian of a common understanding; but with as much weakness as wickedness, and with more impudence often than either, they assert facts contrary to the honour of God, to the visible order of the creation, to the known laws of nature, to the histories of former ages, and to the experience of our own, and which no man can at once understand and believe.

If it should be objected (and it can nowhere be objected better than where I now write[1], as there is nowhere more pomp of bigotry) that whole nations have been firm believers in such most absurd suppositions; I reply, the fact is not true. They have known

[1] At Lisbon.

nothing of the matter, and have believed they knew not what. It is, indeed, with me no matter of doubt, but that the pope and his clergy might teach any of those Christian Heterodoxies, the tenets of which are the most diametrically opposite to their own; nay, all the doctrines of Zoroaster, Confucius, and Mahomet, not only with certain and immediate success, but without one catholic in a thousand knowing he had changed his religion.

What motive a man can have to sit down, and to draw forth a list of stupid, senseless, incredible lies upon paper, would be difficult to determine, did not Vanity present herself so immediately as the adequate cause. The vanity of knowing more than other men is, perhaps, besides hunger, the only inducement to writing, at least to publishing, at all: why then should not the voyage-writer be inflamed with the glory of having seen what no man ever did or will see but himself? This is the true source of the wonderful, in the discourse and writings, and sometimes, I believe, in the actions of men. There is another fault, of a kind directly opposite to this, to which these writers are sometimes liable, when, instead of filling their pages with monsters which nobody hath ever seen, and with adventures which never have nor possibly could have happened to them, waste their time and paper with recording things and facts of so common a kind, that they challenge no other right of being remembered, than as they had the honour of having happened to the author, to whom nothing seems trivial that in any manner happens to himself. Of such consequence do his own actions appear to one of this kind, that he would probably think himself guilty of infidelity, should he omit the minutest thing in the detail of his journal. That the fact is true, is sufficient to give it a place there, without any consideration whether it is capable of pleasing or surprising, of diverting or informing the reader.

I have seen a play (if I mistake not, it is one of Mrs Behn's, or of Mrs Centlivre's)* where this vice in a voyage-writer is finely ridiculed. An ignorant pedant, to whose government, for I know not what reason, the conduct of a young nobleman in his travels is committed, and who is sent abroad to shew My Lord the world, of which he knows nothing himself, before his departure from a town, calls for his journal, to record the goodness of the wine and tobacco, with other articles of the same importance, which are to furnish the materials of a voyage at his return home. The humour, it is true, is here carried very far; and yet, perhaps, very little beyond what is to be found in writers who profess no intention of dealing in humour at all.

Of one or other, or both of these kinds, are, I conceive, all that vast pile of books which pass under the names of voyages, travels, adventures, lives, memoirs, histories, &c. some of which a single traveller sends into the world in many volumes, and others are, by judicious booksellers, collected into vast bodies in folio, and inscribed with their own names, as if they were indeed their own travels; thus unjustly attributing to themselves the merit of others.

Now from both these faults we have endeavoured to steer clear in the following narrative: which, however the contrary may be insinuated by ignorant, unlearned, and fresh-water critics, who have never travelled either in books or ships, I do solemnly declare doth, in my own impartial opinion, deviate less from truth than any other voyage extant; my lord Anson's alone being, perhaps, excepted.*

Some few embellishments must be allowed to every historian: for we are not to conceive that the speeches in Livy, Sallust, or Thuycidydes, were literally spoken in the very words in which we now read them. It is sufficient that every fact hath its foundation in truth, as I do seriously aver is the case in the ensuing pages; and when it is so, a good critic will be so far from denying all kind of ornament of stile or diction, or even of circumstance to his author, that he would be rather sorry if he omitted it: for he could hence derive no other advantage than the loss of an additional pleasure in the perusal.

Again, if any merely common incident should appear in this journal, which will seldom, I apprehend, be the case, the candid reader will easily perceive it is not introduced for its own sake, but for some observations and reflections naturally resulting from it; and which, if but little to his amusement, tend directly to the instruction of the reader, or to the information of the public; to whom if I chuse to convey such instruction or information with an air of joke and laughter, none but the dullest of fellows will, I believe, censure it; but if they should, I have the authority of more than one passage in Horace to alledge in my defence.*

Having thus endeavoured to obviate some censures, to which a man without the gift of fore-sight, or any fear of the imputation of being a conjurer, might conceive this work would be liable, I might now undertake a more pleasing task, and fall at once to the direct and positive praises of the work itself; of which indeed I could say a thousand good things: but the task is so very pleasant that I shall leave it wholly to the reader; and it is all the task that I impose on him. A moderation for which he may think himself obliged to me, when he compares it with the conduct of authors, who often fill a whole sheet with their own praises, to which they sometimes set their own real names, and sometimes a fictitious one. One hint, however, I must give the kind reader; which is, that if he should be able to find no sort of amusement in the book, he will be pleased to remember the public utility which will arise from it. If entertainment, as Mr Richardson observes, be but a secondary consideration in a romance; with which Mr Addison I think agrees, affirming the use of the pastry-cook to be the first;* if this, I say, be true of a mere work of invention, sure it may well be so considered in a work founded, like this, on truth; and where the political reflections form so distinguishing a part.

But perhaps I may hear, from some critic of the most saturnine complexion, that my vanity must have made a horrid dupe of my judgment, if it hath flattered me with an expectation of having anything here seen in a grave light, or of conveying any useful instruction to the public, or to their guardians. I answer with the great man, whom I just now quoted, that my purpose is to convey instruction in the vehicle of entertainment; and so to bring about at once, like the revolution in the rehearsal,* a perfect reformation of the laws relating to our maritime affairs: an undertaking, I will not say more modest, but surely more feasible, than that of reforming a whole people, by making use of a vehicular story, to wheel in among them worse manners than their own.

THE INTRODUCTION

In the beginning of August, 1753, when I had taken the Duke of Portland's medicine, as it is called, near a year, the effects of which had been the carrying off the symptoms of a lingering imperfect gout, I was persuaded by Mr Ranby,* the King's premier serjeant-surgeon, and the ablest advice, I believe, in all branches of the physical profession, to go immediately to Bath. I accordingly writ that very night to Mrs Bowden, who, by the next post, informed me she had taken me a lodging for a month certain.

Within a few days after this, whilst I was preparing for my journey, and when I was almost fatigued to death with several long examinations, relating to five different murders, all committed within the space of a week, by different gangs of street robbers, I received a message from his Grace the Duke of Newcastle,* by Mr Carrington, the King's messenger, to attend his Grace the next morning, in Lincoln's-inn-fields, upon some business of importance; but I excused myself from complying with the message, as besides being lame, I was very ill with the great fatigues I had lately undergone, added to my distemper.

His Grace, however, sent Mr Carrington, the very next morning, with another summons; with which, tho' in the utmost distress, I immediately complied; but the Duke happening, unfortunately for me, to be then particularly engaged, after I had waited some time, sent a gentleman to discourse with me on the best plan which could be invented for putting an immediate end to those murders and robberies which were every day committed in the streets: upon which, I promised to transmit my opinion, in writing, to his Grace, who, as the gentleman informed me, intended to lay it before the privy council.

Tho' this visit cost me a severe cold, I, notwithstanding, set myself down to work, and in about four days sent the Duke as regular a plan as I could form, with all the reasons and arguments I could bring to support it, drawn out in several sheets of paper; and soon received a message from the Duke by Mr Carrington, acquainting me that my plan was highly approved of, and that all the terms of it would be complied with.

The principal and most material of those terms was the immediately depositing 600 *l.* in my hands; at which small charge I undertook to demolish the then reigning gangs, and to put the civil policy into such order, that no such gangs should ever be able, for the future, to form themselves into bodies, or at least to remain any time formidable to the public.

I had delayed my Bath-journey for some time, contrary to the repeated advice of my physical acquaintance, and to the ardent desire of my warmest friends, tho' my distemper was now turned to a deep jaundice; in which case the Bath-waters are generally reputed to be almost infallible. But I had the most eager desire of demolishing this gang of villains and cut-throats, which I was sure of accomplishing the moment I was enabled to pay a fellow who had undertaken, for a small sum, to betray them into the hands of a set of thief-takers whom I had enlisted into the service, all men of known and approved fidelity and intrepidity.

After some weeks the money was paid at the Treasury, and within a few days after 200 *l.* of it had come to my hands the whole gang of cut-throats was entirely dispersed, seven of them were in actual custody, and the rest driven, some out of the town, and others out of the kingdom.

Tho' my health was now reduced to the last extremity, I continued to act with the utmost vigour against these villains; in examining whom, and in taking the depositions against them, I have often spent whole days, nay sometimes whole nights, especially when there was any difficulty in procuring sufficient evidence to convict them; which is a very common case in street-robberies, even when the guilt of the party is sufficiently apparent to satisfy the most tender conscience. But courts of justice know nothing of a cause more than what is told them on oath by a witness; and the most flagitious villain upon earth is tried in the same manner as a man of the best character, who is accused of the same crime.

Mean while, amidst all my fatigues and distresses, I had the satisfaction to find my endeavours had been attended with such success, that this hellish society were almost utterly extirpated, and that, instead of reading of murders and street-robberies in the news, almost every morning, there was, in the remaining part of the month of November, and in all December, not only no such thing as a murder, but not even a street-robbery committed. Some such, indeed, were mentioned in the public papers; but they were all found, on the strictest enquiry, to be false.

In this entire freedom from street-robberies, during the dark months, no man will, I believe, scruple to acknowledge, that the winter of 1753 stands unrival'd, during a course of many years; and this may possibly appear the more extraordinary to those who recollect the outrages with which it began.

Having thus fully accomplished my undertaking. I went into the country in a very weak and deplorable condition, with no fewer or less diseases than a jaundice, a dropsy,* and an asthma, altogether uniting their forces in the destruction of a body so entirely emaciated, that it had lost all its muscular flesh.

Mine was now no longer what was called a Bath case; nor, if it had been so, had I strength remaining sufficient to go thither, a ride of six miles only being attended with an intolerable fatigue. I now discharged my lodgings at Bath, which I had hitherto kept. I began, in earnest, to look on my case as desperate, and I had vanity enough to rank myself with those heroes who, of old times, became voluntary sacrifices to the good of the public.

But, lest the reader should be too eager to catch at the word *vanity*, and should be unwilling to indulge me with so sublime a gratification, for I think he is not too apt to gratify me, I will take my key a pitch lower, and will frankly own that I had a stronger motive than the love of the public to push me on: I will therefore confess to him that my private affairs at the beginning of the winter had but a gloomy aspect; for I had not plundered the public or the poor of those sums which men, who are always ready to plunder both as much as they can, have been pleased to suspect me of taking: on the contrary, by composing, instead of inflaming, the quarrels of porters and beggars (which I blush when I say hath not been universally practised) and by refusing to take a shilling from a man who most undoubtedly would not have had another left, I had reduced an income of about 500 *l.*[1]

[1] A predecessor of mine used to boast that he made 1,000 *l.* a year in his office: but how he did this (if indeed he did it) is to me a secret. His clerk, now mine, told me I had more business than he had ever known there; I am sure I had as much as any man could do. The truth is, the fees are so very low, when any are due, and so much is done for nothing, that if a single justice of peace had

a year of the dirtiest money upon earth, to little more than 300 *l.*; a considerable proportion of which remained with my clerk; and indeed if the whole had done so, as it ought, he would be but ill paid for sitting almost sixteen hours in the twenty-four in the most unwholesome, as well as nauseous air in the universe, and which hath in his case corrupted a good constitution without contaminating his morals.

But, not to trouble the reader with anecdotes, contrary to my own rule laid down in my preface, I assure him I thought my family was very slenderly provided for; and that my health began to decline so fast, that I had very little more of life left to accomplish what I had thought of too late. I rejoiced therefore greatly in seeing an opportunity, as I apprehended, of gaining such merit in the eye of the public, that if my life were the sacrifice to it, my friends might think they did a popular act in putting my family at least beyond the reach of necessity, which I myself began to despair of doing. And tho' I disclaim all pretence to that Spartan or Roman patriotism, which loved the public so well that it was always ready to become a voluntary sacrifice to the public good, I do solemnly declare I have that love for my family.

After this confession therefore, that the public was not the principal Deity to which my life was offered a sacrifice, and when it is farther considered what a poor sacrifice this was, being indeed no other than the giving up what I saw little likelihood of being able to hold much longer, and which, upon the terms I

business enough to employ twenty clerks, neither he nor they would get much by their labour. The public will not therefore, I hope, think I betray a secret when I inform them, that I received from the government a yearly pension out of the public service-money; which I believe indeed would have been larger, had my great patron been convinced of an error, which I have heard him utter more than once, that he could not indeed say, that the acting as a principal justice of peace in Westminster was on all accounts very desirable, but that all the world knew it was a very lucrative office. Now to have shewn him plainly, that a man must be a rogue to make a very little this way, and that he could not make much by being as great a rogue as he could be, would have required more confidence than I believe he had in me, and more of his conversation than he chose to allow me; I therefore resigned the office, and the farther execution of my plan to my brother, who had long been my assistant. And now, lest the case between me and the reader should be the same in both instances as it was between me and the great man, I will not add another world on the subject.

held it, nothing but the weakness of human nature could represent to me as worth holding at all; the world may, I believe, without envy allow me all the praise to which I have any title.

My aim, in fact, was not praise, which is the last gift they care to bestow; at least this was not my aim as an end, but rather as a means, of purchasing some moderate provision for my family, which tho' it should exceed my merit, must fall infinitely short of my service, if I succeeded in my attempt.

To say the truth, the public never act more wisely, than when they act most liberally in the distribution of their rewards; and here the good they receive is often more to be considered than the motive from which they receive it. Example alone is the end of all public punishments and rewards. Laws never inflict disgrace in resentment, nor confer honour from gratitude. For it is very hard, my lord, said a convicted felon at the bar to the late excellent judge Burnet, to hang a poor man for stealing a horse. You are not to be hanged, Sir, answered my ever-honoured and beloved friend, for stealing a horse, but you are to be hanged that horses may not be stolen. In like manner it might have been said to the late duke of Marlborough, when the parliament was so deservedly liberal to him, after the battle of Blenheim, You receive not these honours and bounties on account of a victory past, but that other victories may be obtained.*

I was now, in the opinion of all men, dying of a complication of disorders; and, were I desirous of playing the advocate, I have an occasion fair enough: but I disdain such an attempt. I relate facts plainly and simply as they are; and let the world draw from them what conclusions they please, taking with them the following facts for their instruction. The one is, That the proclamation offering 100 *l.* for the apprehending felons for certain felonies committed in certain places, which I prevented from being revived, had formerly cost the government several thousand pounds within a single year. Secondly, that all such proclamations, instead of curing the evil, had actually increased it; had multiplied the number of robberies; had propagated the worst and wickedest of perjuries; had laid snares for youth and ignorance; which, by the temptation of these rewards, had been sometimes drawn into guilt; and sometimes, which cannot be thought on without the highest horror, had destroyed them without it. Thirdly, That my plan had not put the Government to more than 300 *l.* expence, and had produced none of the ill consequences above-mentioned; but, lastly, Had actually suppressed the evil for a time, and had plainly pointed out the means of suppressing it for ever. This I would myself have undertaken, had my health permitted, at the annual expense of the abovementioned sum.

After having stood the terrible six weeks which succeeded last Christmas, and put a lucky end, if they had known their own interests, to such numbers of aged and infirm valetudinarians, who might have gasped through two or three mild winters more, I returned to town in February, in a condition less despaired of by myself than by any of my friends. I now became the patient of Dr Ward,* who wished I had taken his advice earlier.

By his advice I was tapped, and fourteen quarts of water drawn from my belly. The sudden relaxation which this caused, added to my enervate, emaciated habit of body, so weakened me that within two days I was thought to be falling into the agonies of death.

I was at the worst on that memorable day when the public lost Mr Pelham.* From that day I began slowly, as it were, to draw my feet out of the grave; till in two month's time I had again acquired some little degree of strength; but was again full of water.

During this whole time, I took Mr Ward's medicines, which had seldom any perceptible operation. Those in particular of the diaphoretic kind, the working of which is thought to require a great strength of constitution to support, had so little effect on me, that Mr Ward declared it was as vain to attempt sweating me as a deal board.

In this situation I was tapped a second time. I had one quart of water less taken from me now than before; but I bore all the consequences of the operation much better. This I attributed greatly to a dose of laudanum prescribed by my surgeon. It first gave me the most delicious flow of spirits, and afterwards as comfortable a nap.

The month of May, which was now begun, it seemed reasonable to expect would introduce the spring, and drive off that winter which yet maintained its footing on the stage. I resolved therefore to visit a little house of mine in the country, which stands at Ealing, in the county of Middlesex, in the best air, I believe, in the whole kingdom, and far superior to that of Kensington Gravel-Pits; for the gravel is here much wider and deeper, the place higher and more open towards the south, whilst it is guarded from the north wind by a ridge of hills, and from the smells and smoke of London by its distance; which last is not the fate of Kensington, when the wind blows from any corner of the east.

Obligations to Mr Ward I shall always confess; for I am convinced that he omitted no care in endeavouring to serve me, without any expectation or desire of fee or reward.

The powers of Mr Ward's remedies want indeed no unfair puffs of mine to give them credit; and tho' this distemper of the dropsy stands, I believe, first in the list of those over which he is always certain of triumphing; yet, possibly, there might be something particular in my case, capable of eluding that radical force which had healed so may thousands. The same distemper, in different constitutions, many possibly be attended with such different symptoms, that to find an infallible nostrum for the curing any one distemper in every patient, may be almost as difficult as to find a panacea for the cure of all.

But even such a panacea one of the greatest scholars and best of men did lately apprehend he had discovered. It is true, indeed, he was no physician; that is, he had not by the forms of his education acquired a right of applying his skill in the art of physic to his own private advantage; and yet, perhaps, it may be truly asserted, that no other modern hath contributed so much to make his physical skill useful to the public; at least, that none hath undergone the pains of communicating this discovery in writing to the world. The reader, I think, will scarce need to be informed that the writer I mean is the late bishop of Cloyne, in Ireland, the discovery, that of the virtues of tar-water.*

I then happened to recollect, upon a hint given me by the inimitable and shamefully distress'd author of the Female Quixote,* that I had many years before, from curiosity only, taken a cursory view of bishop Berkley's treatise on the virtues of tar-water, which I had formerly observed he strongly contends to be that real panacea which Sydenham* supposes to have an existence in nature, tho' it yet remains undiscovered, and perhaps will always remain so.

Upon the re-perusal of this book I found the bishop only asserting his opinion, that tar-water might be useful in the dropsy, since he had known it to have a surprising success in the cure of a most stubborn anasarca, which is indeed no other than, as the word implies, the dropsy of the flesh; and this was, at that time, a large part of my complaint.

After a short trial, therefore, of a milk diet, which I presently found did not suit with my case, I betook myself to the bishop's prescription, and dosed myself every morning and evening with half a pint of tar-water.

It was no more than three weeks since my last tapping, and my belly and limbs were distended with water. This did not give me the worse opinion of tar-water: for I never supposed there could be any such virtue in tar-water, as immediately to carry off a quantity of water already collected. For my delivery from this, I well knew I must be again obliged to the trochar,* and if the tar-water did me any good at all, it must be only by the slowest degrees; and that if it should ever get the better of my distemper, it must be the tedious operation of undermining; and not by a sudden attack and storm.

Some visible effects, however, and far beyond what my most sanguine hopes could with any modesty expect, I very soon experienced; the tar-water having, from the very first, lessened my illness, increased my appetite; and added, though in a very slow proportion, to my bodily strength.

But if my strength had increased a little, my water daily increased much more. So that, by the end of May, my belly became again ripe for the trochar, and I was a third time tapped; upon which two very favourable symptoms appeared. I had three quarts of water taken from me less than had been taken the last time; and I bore the relaxation with much less (indeed with scarce any) faintness.

Those of my physical friends, on whose judgment I chiefly depended, seemed to think my only chance of life consisted in having the whole summer before me; in which I might hope to gather sufficient strength to encounter the inclemencies of the ensuing winter. But this chance began daily to lessen. I saw the summer mouldering away, or rather, indeed, the year passing away without intending to bring on any summer at all. In the whole month of May the sun scarce appeared three times. So that the early fruits came to the fulness of their growth, and to some appearance of ripeness, without acquiring any real maturity; having wanted the heat of the sun to soften and meliorate their juices. I saw the dropsy gaining rather than losing ground; the distance growing still shorter between the tappings. I saw the asthma likewise beginning again to become more troublesome. I saw the Midsummer quarter drawing towards a close. So that I conceived, if the Michaelmas quarter should steal off in the same manner, as it was, in my opinion, very much to be apprehended it would, I should be delivered up to the attacks of winter, before I recruited my forces, so as to be any wise able to withstand them.

I now began to recall an intention, which from the first dawnings of my recovery I had conceiv'd, of removing to a warmer climate; and finding this to be approv'd of by a very eminent physician, I resolved to put it into immediate execution.

Aix in Provence was the place first thought on; but the difficulties of getting thither were insuperable. The journey by land, beside the expence of it, was infinitely too long and fatiguing; and I could hear of no ship that was likely to set out from London, within any reasonable time for Marseilles, or any other port in that part of the Mediterranean.

Lisbon was presently fixed on in its room. The air here, as it was near four degrees to the south of Aix, must be more mild and warm, and the winter shorter and less piercing.

It was not difficult to find a ship bound to a place with which we carry on so immense a trade.* Accordingly, my brother soon informed me of the excellent accommodations for passengers, which were to be found on board a ship that was obliged to sail for Lisbon in three days.

I eagerly embraced the offer, notwithstanding the shortness of the time; and having given my brother full power to contract for our passage, I began to prepare my family for the voyage with the utmost expedition.

But our great haste was needless; for the captain* having twice put off his sailing, I at length invited him to dinner with me at Fordhook, a full week after the time on which he had declared, and that with many asseverations, he must, and would weigh anchor.

He dined with me, according to his appointment; and when all matters were settled between us, left me with positive orders to be on board the Wednesday following; when he declared he would fall down the river to Gravesend; and would not stay a moment for the greatest man in the world.

He advised me to go to Gravesend by land, and there wait the arrival of his ship; assigning many reasons for this, every one of which was, as I well remember, among those that had before determined me to go on board near the Tower.

THE JOURNAL OF A VOYAGE TO LISBON

Wednesday, June 26, 1754.

On this day, the most melancholy sun I had ever beheld arose, and found me awake at my house at Fordhook. By the light of this sun, I was, in my own opinion, last to behold and take leave of some of those creatures on whom I doated with a mother-like fondness, guided by nature and passion, and uncured and unhardened by all the doctrine of that philosophical school where I had learnt to bear pains and to despise death.

In this situation, as I could not conquer nature, I submitted entirely to her, and she made as great a fool of me as she had ever done of any woman whatsoever: under pretence of giving me leave to enjoy, she drew me in to suffer the company of my little ones, during eight hours; and I doubt not whether, in that time, I did not undergo more than in all my distemper.

At twelve precisely my coach was at the door, which was no sooner told me than I kiss'd my children round, and went into it with some little resolution. My wife, who behaved more like a heroine and philosopher, tho' at the same time the tenderest mother in the world, and my eldest daughter* followed me; some friends went with us, and others here took their leave; and I heard my behaviour applauded, with many murmurs and praises to which I well knew I had no title; as all other such philosophers may, if they have any modesty, confess on the like occasions.

In two hours we arrived in Redriffe,* and immediately went on board, and were to have sailed the next morning; but as this was the king's proclamation-day, and consequently a holiday at the Custom-house, the captain could not clear his vessel till the Thursday; for these holidays are as strictly observed as those in the popish calendar, and are almost as numerous. I might add, that both are opposite to the genius of trade, and consequently *contra bonum publicum.**

To go on board the ship it was necessary first to go into a boat; a matter of no small difficulty, as I had no use of my limbs, and was to be carried by men, who tho' sufficiently strong for their burden, were, like Archimedes, puzzled to find a steady footing.* Of this, as few of my readers have not gone into wherries* on the Thames, they will easily be able to form to themselves an idea. However, by the assistance of my friend Mr Welch, whom I never think or speak of but with love and esteem, I conquered this difficulty, as I did afterwards that of ascending the ship, into which I was hoisted with more ease by a chair lifted with pullies. I was soon seated in a great chair in the cabin, to refresh myself after a fatigue which had been more intolerable, in a quarter of a mile's passage from my coach to the ship, than I had before undergone in a land-journey of twelve miles, which I had travelled with the utmost expedition.

This latter fatigue was, perhaps, somewhat heightened by an indignation which I could not prevent arising in my mind. I think, upon my entrance into the boat, I presented a spectacle of the highest horror. The total loss of limbs was apparent to all who saw me, and my face contained marks of a most diseased state, if not of death itself. Indeed so ghastly was my countenance, that timorous women with child had abstained from my house, for fear of the ill consequences of looking at me. In this condition, I ran the gauntlope* (so, I think I may justly call it) through rows of sailors and watermen, few of whom failed of paying their compliments to me, by all manner of insults and jests on my misery. No man who knew me will think I conceived any personal resentment at this behaviour; but it was a lively picture of that cruelty and inhumanity, in the nature of men, which I have often contemplated with concern; and which leads the mind into a train of very uncomfortable and melancholy thoughts. It may be said, that this barbarous custom is peculiar to the English, and of them only to the lowest degree; that it is an excrescence of an uncontroul'd licentiousness mistaken for liberty, and never shews itself in men who are polish'd and refin'd, in such manner as human nature requires, to produce that perfection of which it is susceptible, and to purge away that malevolence of disposition, of which, at our birth we partake in common with the savage creation.

This may be said, and this is all that can be said; and it is, I am afraid, but little satisfactory to account for the inhumanity of those, who, while they boast of being made after God's own image, seem to bear in their minds a resemblance of the vilest species of brutes; or rather, indeed, of our idea of devils: for I don't know that any brutes can be taxed with such malevolence.

A surloin of beef was now placed on the table, for which, tho' little better than carrion, as much was charged by the master of the little paltry alehouse who dressed it, as would have been demanded for all the elegance of the King's Arms, or any other polite tavern, or eating-house; for indeed the difference between the best house and the worst is, that at the former you pay largely for luxury, at the latter for nothing.

Thursday, June 27. This morning the captain, who lay on shore at his own house, paid us a visit in the cabin; and behaved like an angry bashaw,* declaring, that had he known we were not to be pleased, he would not have carried us for 500 *l.* He added many asseverations that he was a gentleman, and despised money; not forgetting several hints of the presents which had been made him for his cabin, of 20, 30, and 40 guineas, by several gentlemen, over and above the sum for which they had contracted. This behaviour greatly surprised me, as I knew not how to account for it, nothing having happened since we parted from the captain the evening before in perfect good humour; and all this broke forth on the first moment of his arrival this morning. He did not, however, suffer my amazement to have any long continuance, before he clearly shewed me that all this was meant only as an apology to introduce another procrastination (being the fifth) of his weighing anchor; which was now postponed till Saturday, for such was his will and pleasure.*

Besides the disagreeable situation in which we then lay, in the confines of Wapping and Redriffe, tasting a delicious mixture of the air of both these sweet places, and enjoying the concord of sweet sounds of seamen, watermen, fish-women, oyster-women, and of all the vociferous inhabitants of both shores, composing altogether a greater variety of harmony than Hogarth's imagination hath brought together in that print of his, which is enough to make a man deaf to look at;* I had a more urgent cause to press our departure, which was, that the dropsy, for which I had undergone three tappings, seemed to threaten me with a fourth discharge, before I should reach Lisbon, and when I should have no body on board capable of performing the operation; but I was obliged to hearken to the voice of reason, if I may use the captain's own words, and to rest myself contented. Indeed there was no alternative within my reach, but what would have cost me much too dear.

There are many evils in society, from which people of the highest rank are so entirely exempt, that they have not the least knowledge or idea of them; nor indeed of the characters which are formed by them. Such, for instance, is the conveyance of goods and passengers from one place to another. Now there is no such thing as any kind of knowledge contemptible in itself; and as the particular knowledge I here mean is entirely necessary to the well understanding and well enjoying this journal; and, lastly, as in this case the most ignorant will be those very readers whose amusement we chiefly consult, and to whom we wish to be supposed principally to write, we will here enter somewhat largely into the discussion of this matter; the rather, for that no antient or modern author (if we can trust the catalogue of Dr Mead's library) hath ever undertaken it; but that it seems (in the stile of Don Quixotte)* a task reserved for my pen alone.

When I first conceived this intention, I began to entertain thoughts of enquiring into the antiquity of travelling; and, as many persons have performed in this way (I mean have travelled) at the expence of the public, I flattered myself that the spirit of improving arts and sciences, and of advancing useful and substantial learning, which so eminently distinguishes this age, and hath given rise to more speculative societies in Europe than I at present can recollect the names of; perhaps indeed than I or any other, besides their very near neighbours ever heard mentioned, would assist in promoting so curious a work; a work begun with the same views, calculated for the same purposes, and fitted for the same uses with the labours which those right honourable societies have so cheerfully undertaken themselves, and encouraged in others; sometimes with the highest honours, even with admission into their colleges, and with inrolment among their members.*

From these societies I promised myself all assistance in their power, particularly the communication of such valuable manuscripts and records as they must be supposed to have collected from those obscure ages of antiquity, when history yields us such imperfect accounts of the residence, and much more imperfect, of the travels of the human race; unless, perhaps, as a curious and learned member of the young society of antiquarians is said to have hinted his conjectures, that their residence and their travels were one and the same; and this discovery (for such it seems to be) he is said to have owed to the lighting by accident on a book, which we shall have occasion to mention presently, the contents of which were then little known to the society.

The King of Prussia,* moreover, who from a degree of benevolence and taste, which in either case is a rare production in so northern a climate, is the great encourager of art and science, I was well assured would promote so useful a design, and order his archives to be searched in my behalf.

But after well weighing all these advantages, and much meditation on the order of my work, my whole design was subverted in a moment by hearing of the discovery just mentioned to have been made by the young antiquarian, who from the most antient record in the world (tho' I don't find the society are all agreed on this point) one long preceding the date of the earliest modern collections, either of books or butterflies, none of which pretend to go beyond the flood, shews us, that the first man was a traveller, and that he and his family were scarce settled in Paradise before they disliked their own home, and became passengers to another place. Hence it appears, that the humour of travelling is as old as the human race, and that it was their curse from the beginning.

By this discovery my plan became much shortened, and I found it only necessary to treat of the conveyance of goods and passengers from place to place; which not being universally known, seemed proper to be explained before we examined into its original. There are, indeed, two different ways of tracing all things, used by the historian and the antiquary; these are upwards and downwards. The former shews you how things are, and leaves to others to discover when they began to be so. The latter shews you how things were, and leaves their present existence to be examined by others. Hence the former is more useful, the latter more curious. The former receives the thanks of mankind; the latter of that valuable part, the virtuosi.

In explaining, therefore, this mystery of carrying goods and passengers from one place to another, hitherto so profound a secret to the very best of our readers, we shall pursue the historical method, and endeavour to shew by what means it is at present performed, referring the more curious enquiry either to some other pen, or to some other opportunity.

Now there are two general ways of performing (if God permit) this conveyance; viz. by land and water, both of which have much variety; that by land being performed in different vehicles, such as coaches, caravans, waggons, &c. and that by water in ships, barges, and boats, of various sizes and denominations. But as all these methods of conveyance are formed on the same principles, they agree so well together, that it is fully sufficient to comprehend them all in the general view, without descending to such minute particulars, as would distinguish one method from another.

Common to all of these is one general principle, that as the goods to be conveyed are usually the larger, so they are to be chiefly considered in the conveyance; the owner being indeed little more than an appendage to his trunk, or box, or bale, or at best a small part of his own baggage, very little care is to be taken in stowing or packing them up with convenience to himself; for the conveyance is not of passengers and goods, but of goods and passengers.

Secondly, From this conveyance arises a new kind of relation, or rather of subjection, in the society; by which the passenger becomes bound in allegiance to his conveyer. This allegiance is indeed only temporary and local, but the most absolute during its continuance, of any known in Great-Britain, and, to say truth, scarce consistent with the liberties of a free people; nor could it be reconciled with them, did it not move downwards, a circumstance universally apprehended to be incompatible to all kinds of slavery. For Aristotle in his Politicks hath proved abundantly to my satisfaction, that no men are born to be slaves, except barbarians; and these only to such as are not themselves barbarians: and indeed Mr Montesquieu* hath carried it very little farther, in the case of the Africans; the real truth being, that no man is born to be a slave, unless to him who is able to make him so.

Thirdly, This subjection is absolute, and consists of a perfect resignation both of body and soul to the disposal of another; after which resignation, during a certain time, his subject retains no more power over his own will, than an Asiatic slave, or an English wife, by the laws of both countries, and by the customs of one of them.* If I should mention the instance of a stage-coachman, many of my readers would recognize the truth of what I have here observed; all indeed, that ever have been under the dominion of that tyrant, who, in this free country, is as absolute as a Turkish Bashaw. In two particulars only his power is defective; he cannot press you into his service, and if you enter yourself at one place, on condition of being discharged at a certain time at another, he is obliged to perform his agreement, if God permit: but all the intermediate time you are absolutely under his government; he carries you how he will, when he will, and whither he will, provided it be not much out of the road; you have nothing to eat, or to drink, but what, and when, and where he pleases. Nay, you cannot sleep, unless he pleases you should; for he will order you sometimes out of bed at midnight, and hurry you away at a moment's warning: indeed, if you can sleep in his vehicle, he cannot prevent it; nay, indeed, to give him his due, this he is ordinarily disposed to encourage; for the earlier he forces you to rise in the morning, the more time he will give you in the heat of the day, sometimes even six hours at an alehouse, or at their doors, where he always gives you the same indulgence which he allows himself; and for this he is generally very moderate in his demands. I have known a whole bundle of passengers charged no more than half a crown for being suffered to remain quiet at an alehouse door, for above a whole hour, and that even in the hottest day in summer.

But as this kind of tyranny, tho' it hath escaped our political writers, hath been, I think, touched by our dramatic, and is more trite among the generality of readers; and as this and all other kinds of such subjection are alike unknown to my friends, I will quit the passengers by land, and treat of those who travel by water; for whatever is said on this subject is applicable to both alike, and we may bring them together as closely as they are brought in the liturgy, when they are recommended to the prayers of all Christian congregations; and (which I have often thought very remarkable) where they are joined with other miserable wretches, such as, women in labour, people in sickness, infants just born, prisoners and captives.*

Goods and passengers are conveyed by water in divers vehicles, the principal of which being a ship, it shall suffice to mention that alone. Here the tyrant doth not derive his title, as the stage-coachman doth, from the vehicle itself, in which he stows his goods and passengers, but he is called the captain; a word of such various use and uncertain signification, that it seems very difficult to fix any positive idea to it: if indeed there be any general meaning which may comprehend all its different uses, that of the head, or chief, of any body of men, seems to be most capable of this comprehension; for whether they be a company of soldiers, a crew of sailors, or a gang of rogues, he who is at the head of them is always stiled the captain.

The particular tyrant, whose fortune it was to stow us aboard, laid a farther claim to this appellation than the bare command of a vehicle of conveyance. He had been the captain of a privateer,* which he chose to call being in the king's service, and thence derived a right of hoisting the military ornament of a cockade over the button of his hat. He likewise wore a sword of no ordinary length by his side, with which he swaggered in his cabin, among the wretches his passengers, whom he had stowed in cupboards on each side. He was a person of a very singular character. He had taken it into his head that he was a gentleman, from those very reasons that proved he was not one; and to shew himself a fine gentleman, by a behaviour which seemed to insinuate he had never seen one. He was, moreover, a man of gallantry; at the age of seventy he had the finicalness of Sir Courtly Nice, with the roughness of Surly; and, while he was deaf himself, had a voice capable of deafening all others.*

Now, as I saw myself in danger by the delays of the captain, who was, in reality, waiting for more freight, and as the wind had been long nested, as it were, in the south-west, where it constantly blew hurricanes, I began with great reason to apprehend that our voyage might be long, and that my belly, which began already to be much extended, would require the water to be let out at a time when no assistance was at hand; though, indeed, the captain comforted me with assurances, that he had a pretty young fellow on board, who acted as his surgeon, as I found he likewise did as steward, cook, butler, sailor. In short, he had as many offices as Scrub in the play,* and went through them all with great dexterity; this of surgeon, was, perhaps, the only one in which his skill was somewhat deficient, at least that branch of tapping for the dropsy; for he very ingenuously and modestly confessed, he had never seen the operation performed, nor was possessed of that chirurgical instrument with which it is performed.

Friday, June 28. By way of prevention, therefore, I this day sent for my friend Mr Hunter, the great surgeon and anatomist of Covent-garden; and, though my belly was not yet very full and tight, let out ten quarts of water, the young sea-surgeon attended the operation, not as a performer, but as a student.

I was now eased of the greatest apprehension which I had from the length of the passage; and I told the captain, I was become indifferent as to the time of his sailing. He expressed much satisfaction in this declaration, and at hearing from me, that I found myself, since my tapping, much lighter and better. In this, I believe, he was sincere; for he was, as we shall have occasion to observe more than once, a very good-natured man; and as he was a very brave one too, I found that the heroic constancy with which I had born an operation that is attended with scarce any degree of pain had not a little raised me in his esteem. That he might adhere, therefore, in the most religious and rigorous manner to his word, when he had no longer any temptation from interest to break it, as he had no longer any hopes of more goods or passengers, he ordered his ship to fall down to Gravesend on Sunday morning, and there to wait his arrival.

Sunday, June 30. Nothing worth notice pass'd till that morning, when my poor wife, after passing a night in the utmost torments of the tooth-ach, resolved to have it drawn. I dispatched, therefore, a servant into Wapping, to bring in haste the best toothdrawer he could find. He soon found out a female of great eminence in the art; but when he brought her to the boat, at the water-side, they were informed that the ship was gone; for, indeed, she had set out a few minutes after his quitting her; nor did the pilot, who well knew the errand on which I had sent my servant, think fit to wait a moment for his return, or to give me any notice of his setting out, though I had, very patiently, attended the delays of the captain four days, after many solemn promises of weighing anchor every one of the three last.

But of all the petty bashaws, or turbulent tyrants I ever beheld, this soure-faced pilot was the worst tempered; for, during the time that he had the guidance of the ship, which was till we arrived in the Downs,* he complied with no one's desires, nor did he give a civil word, or, indeed, a civil look, to any on board.

The toothdrawer, who, as I said before, was one of great eminence among her neighbours, refused to follow the ship; so that my man made himself the best of his way, and with some difficulty, came up with us before we were got under full sail, for, after that, as we had both wind and tide with us, he would have found it impossible to overtake the ship, till she was come to an anchor at Gravesend.

The morning was fair and bright, and we had a passage thither, I think, as pleasant as can be conceived; for, take it with all its advantages, particularly the number of fine ships you are always sure of seeing by the way, there is nothing to equal it in all the rivers of the world. The yards of Deptford and of Woolwich are noble sights; and give us a just idea of the great perfection to which we are arrived in building those floating castles, and the figure which we may always make in Europe among the other maritime powers. That of Woolwich, at least, very strongly imprinted this idea on my mind; for there was now on the stocks there the Royal Anne, supposed to be the largest ship ever built, and which contains ten carriage guns more than had ever yet equipped a first rate.*

It is true, perhaps, that there is more of ostentation than of real utility, in ships of this vast and unwieldy burthen, which are rarely capable of acting against an enemy; but if the building such contributes to preserve, among other nations, the notion of the British superiority in naval affairs, the expence, though very great, is well incurred, and the ostentation is laudable and truly political. Indeed I should be sorry to allow that Holland, France, or Spain, possessed a vessel larger and more beautiful than the largest and most beautiful of ours; for this honour I would always administer to the pride of our sailors, who should challenge it from all their neighbours with truth and success. And sure I am that not our honest tars alone, but every inhabitant of this island, may exult in the comparison, when he considers the king of Great-Britain as a maritime prince, in opposition to any other prince in Europe; but I am not so certain that the same idea of superiority will result from comparing our land-forces with those of many other crowned heads. In numbers they all far exceed us, and in the goodness and splendour of their troops, many nations, particularly, the Germans and French, and perhaps the Dutch, cast us at a distance; for, however we may flatter ourselves with the Edwards and Henrys of former ages, the change of the whole art of war since those days, by which the advantage of personal strength is, in a manner, entirely lost, hath produced a change in military affairs to the advantage of our enemies. As for our successes in later days, if they were not entirely owing to the superior genius of our general, they were not a little due to the superior force of his money. Indeed, if we should arraign marshal Saxe of ostentation, when he shewed his army, drawn up, to our captive general, the day after the battle of La Val, we cannot say that the ostentation was intirely vain; since he certainly shewed him an army, which had not been often equalled, either in the number or goodness of the troops, and which, in those respects, so far exceeded ours, that none can ever cast any reflection on the brave young prince who could not reap the lawrels of conquest in that day; but his retreat will be always mentioned as an addition to his glory.*

In our marine the case is entirely the reverse, and it must be our own fault if it doth not continue so; for, continue so it will, as long as the flourishing state of our trade shall support it, and this support it can never want, till our legislature shall cease to give sufficient attention to the protection of our trade, and our magistrates want sufficient power, ability, and honesty to execute the laws: a circumstance not to be apprehended, as it cannot happen, till our senates and our benches shall be filled with the blindest ignorance, or with the blackest corruption.

Besides the ships in the docks, we saw many on the water: the yatchts are sights of great parade, and the king's body yatcht is,

I believe, unequalled in any country for convenience as well as magnificence; both which are consulted in building and equipping her with the most exquisite art and workmanship.

We saw likewise several Indiamen just returned from their voyage. These are, I believe, the largest and finest vessels which are anywhere employed in commercial affairs. The colliers, likewise, which are very numerous, and even assemble in fleets, are ships of great bulk; and if we descend to those used in the American, African, and European trades, and pass through those which visit our own coasts, to the small craft that ly between Chatham and the Tower, the whole forms a most pleasing object to the eye, as well as highly warming to the heart of an Englishman, who has any degree of love for his country, or can recognize any effect of the patriot in his constitution.

Lastly, the Royal Hospital of Greenwich,* which presents so delightful a front to the water, and doth such honour at once to its builder and the nation, to the great skill and ingenuity of the one, and to the no less sensible gratitude of the other, very properly closes the account of this scene; which may well appear romantic to those who have not themselves seen, that, in this one instance, truth and reality are capable, perhaps, of exceeding the power of fiction.

When we had passed by Greenwich, we saw only two or three gentlemen's houses, all of very moderate account, till we reached Gravesend; these are all on the Kentish shore, which affords a much drier, wholsomer and pleasanter situation than doth that of its opposite, Essex. This circumstance, I own, is somewhat surprising to me, when I reflect on the numerous villas that crowd the river from Chelsea upwards as far as Shepperton, where the narrower channel affords not half so noble a prospect, and where the continual succession of the small craft, like the frequent repetition of all things, which have nothing in them great, beautiful, or admirable, tire the eye, and give us distaste and aversion instead of pleasure. With some of these situations, such as Barnes, Mortlake, &c. even the shore of Essex, might contend, not upon very unequal terms; but on the Kentish borders, there are many spots to be chosen by the builder, which might justly claim the preference over almost the very finest of those in Middlesex and Surry.

How shall we account for this depravity in taste? for, surely, there are none so very mean and contemptible, as to bring the pleasure of seeing a number of little wherries, gliding along after one another, in competition with what we enjoy in viewing a succession of ships, with all their sails expanded to the winds, bounding over the waves before us.

And here I cannot pass by another observation on the deplorable want of taste in our enjoyments, which we shew by almost totally neglecting the pursuit of what seems to me the highest degree of amusement: this is, the sailing ourselves in little vessels of our own, contrived only for our ease and accommodation, to which such situations of our villas, as I have recommended, would be so convenient and even necessary.

This amusement, I confess, if enjoyed in any perfection, would be of the expensive kind; but such expence would not exceed the reach of a moderate fortune, and would fall very short of the prices which are daily paid for pleasures of a far inferior rate. The truth, I believe, is, that sailing in the manner I have just mentioned, is a pleasure rather unknown, or unthought of, than rejected by those who have experienced it; unless, perhaps, the apprehension of danger, or sea-sickness, may be supposed, by the timorous and delicate, to make too large deductions; insisting, that all their enjoyments shall come to them pure and unmixed, and being ever ready to cry out,

*—Nocet empta dolore voluptas.**

This, however, was my present case; for the ease and lightness which I felt from my tapping, the gaiety of the morning, the pleasant sailing with wind and tide, and the many agreeable objects with which I was constantly entertained during the whole way, were all suppressed and overcome by the single consideration of my wife's pain, which continued incessantly to torment her till we came to an anchor, when I dispatched a messenger in great haste, for the best reputed operator in Gravesend. A surgeon of some eminence now appeared, who did not decline tooth-drawing, tho' he certainly would have been offended with the appellation of tooth drawer, no less than his brethren, the members of that venerable body, would be with that of barber, since the late separation between those long united companies, by which, if the surgeons have gained much, the barbers are supposed to have lost very little.

This able and careful person (for so I sincerely believe he is), after examining the guilty tooth, declared, that it was such a rotten shell, and so placed at the very remotest end of the upper jaw, where it was, in a manner, covered and secured by a large, fine, firm tooth, that he despaired of his power of drawing it.

He said, indeed, more to my wife, and used more rhetoric to dissuade her from having it drawn, than is generally employed to persuade young ladies, to prefer a pain of three moments to one of three months continuance, especially, if those young ladies happen to be past forty or fifty years of age, when, by submitting to support a racking torment, the only good circumstance attending which is, 'tis so short, that scarce one in a thousand can cry out, I feel it, they are to do a violence to their charms, and lose one of those beautiful holders, with which alone Sir Courtly Nice declares, a lady can ever lay hold of his heart.*

He said at last so much, and seemed to reason so justly, that I came over to his side, and assisted him in prevailing on my wife (for it was no easy matter) to resolve on keeping her tooth a little longer, and to apply palliatives only for relief. These were opium applied to the tooth, and blisters behind the ears.

Whilst we were at dinner this day, in the cabin, on a sudden the window on one side was beat into the room, with a crash, as if a twenty-pounder had been discharged among us. We were all alarmed at the suddenness of the accident, for which, however, we were soon able to account: for the sash, which was shivered all to pieces, was pursued into the middle of the cabin by the bowsprit of a little ship, called a cod-smack, the master of which made us amends for running (carelessly at best) against us, and injuring the ship, in the sea-way; that is to say, by damning us all to hell, and uttering several pious wishes that it had done us much more mischief. All which were answered in their own kind and phrase by our men; between whom, and the other crew, a dialogue of oaths and scurrility was carried on, as long as they continued in each other's hearing.

It is difficult, I think, to assign a satisfactory reason why sailors in general should, of all others, think themselves entirely discharged from the common bands of humanity, and should seem to glory in the language and behaviour of savages? They see more of the world, and have, most of them, a more erudite education, than is the portion of land-men of their degree. Nor do I believe that in any country they visit (Holland itself not excepted) they can ever find a parallel to what daily passes on the River Thames. Is it that they think true courage (for they are the bravest fellows upon earth) inconsistent with all the gentleness of a humane carriage, and that the contempt of civil order springs up in minds but little cultivated at the same time, and from the same principles, with the contempt of danger and death? Is it——? In short, it is so; and how it comes to be so, I leave to form a question in the Robin Hood society,* or to be propounded for solution among the aenigmas in the Woman's Almanac for the next year.

Monday, July 1. This day Mr Welch took his leave of me after dinner, as did a young lady* of her sister, who was proceeding with my wife to Lisbon. They both set out together in a post-chaise for London.

Soon after their departure our cabin, where my wife and I were sitting together, was visited by two ruffians, whose appearance greatly corresponded with that of the sheriff's, or rather the knight marshal's bailiffs. One of these, especially, who seemed to affect a more than ordinary degree of rudeness and insolence, came in without any kind of ceremony, with a broad gold lace on his hat, which was cocked with much military fierceness on his head. An inkhorn at his button-hole, and some papers in his hand, sufficiently assured me what he was, and I asked him if he and his companion were not custom-house officers; he answered with sufficient dignity, that they were, as an information which he seemed to conclude would strike the hearer with awe, and suppress all further inquiry; but, on the contrary I proceeded to ask of what rank he was in the Custom-house, and receiving an answer from his companion, as I remember, that the gentleman was a riding surveyor; I replied that he might be a riding surveyor, but could be no gentleman, for that none who had any title to that denomination, would break into the presence of a lady, without an apology, or even moving his hat. He then took his covering from his head, and laid it on the table, saying, he asked pardon, and blamed the mate, who should, he said, have informed him if any persons of distinction were below. I told him, he might guess by our appearance (which, perhaps, was rather more than could be said with the strictest adherence to truth) that he was before a gentleman and lady, which should teach him to be very civil in his behaviour, tho' we should not happen to be of that number whom the world calls people of fashion and distinction. However, I said, that, as he seemed sensible of his error, and had asked pardon, the lady would permit him to put his hat on again if he chose it. This he refused with some degree of surliness, and failed not to convince me that, if I should condescend to become more gentle, he would soon grow more rude.

I now renewed a reflection, which I have often seen occasion to make, that there is nothing so incongruous in nature as any kind of power, with lowness of mind and of ability, and that there is nothing more deplorable than the want of truth in the whimsical notion of Plato; who tells us that 'Saturn, well knowing the state of human affairs, gave us kings and rulers, not of human, but divine original: for as we make not shepherds of sheep, nor oxherds of oxen, nor goatherds of goats; but place some of our own kind over all, as being better and fitter to govern them: in the same manner, were demons by the Divine Love, set over us, as a race of beings of a superior order to men, and who, with great ease to themselves, might regulate our affairs, and establish peace, modesty, freedom and justice, and totally destroying all sedition, might complete the happiness of the human race. So far, at least, may even now be said with truth, that in all states which are under the government of mere man, without any divine assistance, there is nothing but labour and misery to be found. From what I have said therefore, we may at least learn, with our utmost endeavours, to imitate the Saturnian institution; borrowing all assistance from our immortal part, while we pay to this the strictest obedience, we should form both our private œconomy, and public policy, from its dictates. By this dispensation of our immortal minds, we are to establish a law, and to call it by that name. But if any government be in the hands of a single person, of the few, or of the many; and such governor or governors shall abandon himself or themselves to the unbridled pursuit of the wildest pleasures or desires, unable to restrain any passion, but possessed with an insatiable bad disease; if such shall attempt to govern; and at the same time to trample on all laws, there can be no means of preservation left for the wretched people,'—*Plato de Leg., lib.* 4. *p.* 713. *c.*714. *edit. Serrani.**

It is true that Plato is here treating of the highest or sovereign power in a state; but it is as true, that his observations are general, and may be applied to all inferior powers: and, indeed, every subordinate degree is immediately derived from the highest; and as it is equally protected by the same force, and sanctified by the same authority, is alike dangerous to the well-being of the subject.

Of all powers, perhaps, there is none so sanctified and protected, as this which is under our present consideration. So numerous, indeed, and strong are the sanctions given to it by many acts of parliament that having once established the laws of customs on merchandize, it seems to have been the sole view of the legislature to strengthen the hands, and to protect the persons of the officers, who became established by those laws; many of whom are so far from bearing any resemblance to the Saturnian institution, and to be chosen from a degree of beings superior to the rest of the human race, that they sometimes seem industriously picked out of the lowest and vilest orders of mankind.

There is, indeed, nothing so useful to man in general, nor so beneficial to particular societies and individuals, as trade. This is that *alma mater** at whose plentiful breast all mankind are nourished. It is true, like other parents, she is not always equally indulgent to all her children; but tho' she gives to her favourites a vast proportion of redundancy and superfluity, there are very few whom she refuses to supply with the conveniencies, and none with the necessaries, of life.

Such a benefactress as this must naturally be beloved by mankind in general; it would be wonderful, therefore, if her interest was not considered by them, and protected from the fraud and violence of some of her rebellious offspring, who coveting more than their share, or more than she thinks proper to allow them, are daily employed in meditating mischief against her, and in endeavouring to steal from their brethren those shares which this great *alma mater* had allowed them.

At length our Governor came on board, and about six in the evening we weighed anchor, and fell down to the Nore,* whither our passage was extremely pleasant, the evening being very delightful, the moon just past the full, and both wind and tide favourable to us.

Tuesday, July 2. This morning we again set sail under all the advantages we had enjoy'd the evening before: this day we left the shore of Essex, and coasted along Kent, passing by the pleasant island of Thanet, which is an island,* and that of Sheppy, which is not an island, and about three o'clock, the wind being now full in our teeth, we came to an anchor in the Downs, within two miles of Deal. My wife, having suffered intolerable pain from her tooth, again renewed her resolution of having it drawn, and another surgeon was sent for from Deal, but with no better success than the former. He likewise declined the operation, for the same reason which had been assigned by the former: however, such was her resolution, backed with pain, that he was obliged to make the attempt, which concluded more in honour of his judgment, than of his operation; for, after having put my poor wife to inexpressible torment, he was obliged to leave her tooth *in statu quo*; and she had now the comfortable prospect of a long fit of pain, which might have lasted her whole voyage, without any possibility of relief.

In these pleasing sensations, of which I had my just share, nature, overcome with fatigue, about eight in the evening resign'd her to rest; a circumstance which would have given me some happiness, could I have known how to employ those spirits which were raised by it: but unfortunately for me, I was left in a disposition of enjoying an agreeable hour, without the assistance of a companion, which has always appeared to me necessary to such enjoyment; my daughter and her companion were both retired sea-sick to bed; the other passengers were a rude schoolboy of fourteen years old, and an illiterate Portuguese friar, who understood no language but his own, in which I had not the least smattering. The captain was the only person left, in whose conversation I might indulge myself; but unluckily, besides a total ignorance of everything in the world but a ship, he had the misfortune of being so deaf, that to make him hear, I will not say understand, my words, I must run the risque of conveying them to the ears of my wife, who, tho' in another room (called, I think, the state-room; being, indeed a most stately apartment capable of containing one human body in length, if not very tall, and three bodies in breadth) lay asleep within a yard of me. In this situation necessity and choice were one and the same thing; the captain and I sat down together to a small bowl of punch, over which we both soon fell fast asleep, and so concluded the evening.

Wednesday, July 3. This morning I awaked at four o'clock, for my distemper seldom suffered me to sleep later. I presently got up, and had the pleasure of enjoying the sight of a tempestuous sea for four hours before the captain was stirring; for he loved to indulge himself in morning slumbers, which were attended with a wind music, much more agreeable to the performers than to the hearers, especially such as have, as I had, the privilege of sitting in the orchestra. At eight o'clock the captain rose, and sent his boat on shore. I ordered my man likewise to go in it, as my distemper was not of that kind which entirely deprives us of appetite. Now tho' the captain had well victualled his ship with all manner of salt provisions for the voyage, and had added great quantities of fresh stores, particularly of vegetables at Gravesend, such as beans and peas, which had been on board only two days, and had, possibly, not been gathered above two more, I apprehended I could provide better for myself at Deal, than the ship's ordinary seemed to promise. I accordingly sent for fresh provisions of all kinds from the shore, in order to put off the evil day of starving as long as possible. My man returned with most of the articles I sent for, and I now thought myself in a condition of living a week on my own provisions. I therefore ordered my own dinner, which I wanted nothing but a cook to dress, and a proper fire to dress it at; but those were not to be had, nor indeed any addition to my roast mutton, except the pleasure of the captain's company, with that of the other passengers; for my wife continued the whole day in a state of dozing, and my other females, whose sickness did not abate by the rolling of the ship at anchor, seemed more inclined to empty their stomachs than to fill them. Thus I pass'd the whole day (except about an hour at dinner) by myself, and the evening concluded with the captain as the preceding one had done; one comfortable piece of news he communicated to me, which was, that he had no doubt of a prosperous wind in the morning; but as he did not divulge the reasons of this confidence, and as I saw none myself besides the wind being directly opposite, my faith in this prophecy was not strong enough to build any great hopes upon.

Thursday, July 4. This morning, however, the captain seem'd resolved to fulfil his own predictions, whether the wind would or no; he accordingly weighed anchor, and, taking the advantage of the tide, when the wind was not very boisterous, he hoisted his sails, and, as if his power had been no less absolute over Eolus than it was over Neptune, he forced the wind to blow him on in its own despight.

But as all men who have ever been at sea well know how weak such attempts are, and want no authorities of Scripture to prove, that the most absolute power of a captain of a ship is very contemptible in the wind's eye, so did it befall our noble commander; who having struggled with the wind three or four hours, was obliged to give over, and lost, in a few minutes, all that he had been so long a gaining; in short, we returned to our former station, and once more cast anchor in the neighbourhood of Deal.

Here, though we lay near the shore, that we might promise ourselves all the emolument which could be derived from it, we found ourselves deceived; and that we might with as much conveniency be out of the sight of land; for, except when the captain launch'd forth his own boat, which he did always with great reluctance, we were incapable of procuring anything from Deal, but at a price too exorbitant, and beyond the reach even of modern luxury; the fare of a boat from Deal, which lay at two miles distance, being at least three half-crowns, and if we had been in any distress for it, as many half guineas; for these good people consider the sea as a large common, appendant to their mannor, in which, when they find any of their fellow creatures impounded, they conclude, that they have a full right of making them pay at their own discretion for their deliverance: to say the truth, whether it be that men, who live on the sea-shore, are of an amphibious kind, and do not entirely partake of human nature, or whatever else may be the reason, they are so far from taking any share in the distresses of mankind, or of being moved with any compassion for them, that they look upon them as blessings shower'd down from above; and which the more they improve to their own use, the greater is their gratitude and piety. Thus at Gravesend, a sculler requires a shilling for going less way than he would row in London for threepence; and, at Deal, a boat often brings more profit in a day, than it can produce in London in a week, or, perhaps in a month; in both places the owner of the boat founds his demand on the necessity and distress of one, who stands more or less in absolute want of his assistance; and with the urgency of these, always rises in the exorbitancy of his demand, without ever considering, that, from these very circumstances, the power or ease of gratifying such demand is in like proportion lessened. Now, as I am unwilling that some conclusions, which may be, I am aware, too justly drawn from these observations, should be imputed to human nature in general, I have endeavoured to account for them in a way more consistent with the goodness and dignity of that nature: however it be, it seems a little to reflect on the governors of such monsters, that they do not take some means to restrain these impositions, and prevent them from triumphing any longer in the miseries of those, who are, in many circumstances at least, their fellow-creatures, and considering the distresses of a wretched seaman, from his being wrecked to his being barely wind-bound, as a blessing sent among them from above, and calling it by that blasphemous name.

Friday, July 5. This day I sent a servant on board a man of war that was stationed here, with my compliments to the captain, to represent to him the distress of the ladies, and to desire the favour of his long-boat to conduct us to Dover, at about seven miles distance; and, at the same time, presumed to make use of a great lady's* name, the wife of the first lord commissioner of the admiralty; who would, I told him, be pleased with any kindness shewn by him towards us in our miserable condition. And this I am convinced was true, from the humanity of the lady, though she was entirely unknown to me.

The captain returned a verbal answer to a long letter; acquainting me, that what I desired could not be complied with, it being a favour not in his power to grant. This might be, and I suppose was true; but it is as true, that if he was able to write, and had pen, ink and paper aboard, he might have sent a written answer, and that it was the part of a gentleman so to have done; but this is a character seldom maintained on the watery element, especially by those who exercise any power on it. Every commander of a vessel here seems to think himself entirely free from all those rules of decency and civility, which direct and restrain the conduct of the members of a society on shore; and each, claiming absolute dominion in his little wooden world, rules by his own laws and his own discretion. I do not, indeed, know so pregnant an instance of the dangerous consequences of absolute power, and its aptness to intoxicate the mind, as that of those petty tyrants, who become such in a moment, from very well-disposed and social members of that communion, in which they affect no superiority, but live in an orderly state of legal subjection with their fellow-citizens.

Saturday, July 6. This morning our commander, declaring he was sure the wind would change, took the advantage of an ebbing tide, and weighed his anchor. His assurance, however, had the same completion, and his endeavours the same success, with his former trial; and he was soon obliged to return once more to his old quarters. Just before we let go our anchor, a small sloop, rather than submit to yield us an inch of way, ran foul of our ship, and carried off her bowsprit. This obstinate frolic would have cost those aboard the sloop very dear, if our steersman had not been too generous to exert his superiority, the certain consequence of which would have been the immediate sinking of the other. This contention of the inferior, with a might capable of crushing it in an instant, may seem to argue no small share of folly or madness, as well as of impudence; but I am convinced there is very little danger in it: contempt is a port to which the pride of man submits to fly with reluctance, but those who are within it are always in a place of the most assured security; for whosoever throws away his sword, prefers, indeed, a less honourable, but much safer means of avoiding danger, than he who defends himself with it. And here we shall offer another distinction, of the truth of which much reading and experience have well convinced us, that as in the most absolute governments, there is a regular progression of slavery downwards, from the top to the bottom, the mischief of which is seldom felt with any great force and bitterness, but by the next immediate degree; so in the most dissolute and anarchical states, there is as regular an ascent of what is called rank or condition, which is always laying hold of the head of him, who is advanced but one step higher on the ladder, who might, if he did not too much despise such efforts, kick his pursuer headlong to the bottom. We will conclude this digression with one general and short observation, which will, perhaps, set the whole matter in a clearer light than the longest and most laboured harangue. Whereas envy of all things most exposes us to danger from others; so, contempt of all things best secures us from them. And thus, while the dungcart and the sloop are always meditating mischief against the coach and the ship, and throwing themselves designedly in their way, the latter consider only their own security, and are not ashamed to break the road, and let the other pass by them.

Monday, July 8. Having passed our Sunday without anything remarkable, unless the catching a great number of whitings in the afternoon may be thought so; we now set sail on Monday at six o'clock, with a little variation of wind; but this was so very little, and the breeze itself so small, that the tide was our best, and indeed almost our only friend. This conducted us along the short remainder of the Kentish shore. Here we passed that cliff of Dover, which makes so tremendous a figure in Shakespear, and which, whoever reads without being giddy, must, according to Mr Addison's observation,* have either a very good head, or a very bad one; but, which, whoever contracts any such ideas from the sight of, must have, at least, a poetic, if not a Shakespearian genius. In truth, mountains, rivers, heroes and gods owe great part of their existence to the poets; and Greece and Italy do so plentifully abound in the former, because they furnished so glorious a number of the latter; who, while they bestowed immortality on every little hillock and blind stream, left the noblest rivers and mountains in the world to share the same obscurity with the eastern and western poets, in which they are celebrated.

This evening we beat the sea* off Sussex in sight of Dungeness, with much more pleasure than progress; for the weather was almost a perfect calm, and the moon, which was almost at the full, scarce suffered a single cloud to veil her from our sight.

Tuesday, Wednesday, July 9, 10. These two days we had much the same fine weather, and made much the same way; but, in the evening of the latter day, a pretty fresh gale sprung up, at N. N. W. which brought us by the morning in sight of the Isle of Wight.

Thursday, July 11. This gale continued till towards noon; when the east end of the island bore but little a-head of us. The captain swaggered, and declared he would keep the sea; but the wind got the better of him, so that about three he gave up the victory, and, making a sudden tack, stood in for the shore, passed by Spithead and Portsmouth, and came to an anchor at a place called Ryde on the island.*

A most tragical incident fell out this day at sea. While the ship was under sail, but making, as will appear, no great way, a kitten, one of four of the feline inhabitants of the cabin, fell from the window into the water: an alarm was immediately given to the captain, who was then upon deck, and received it with the utmost concern and many bitter oaths. He immediately gave orders to the steersman in favour of the poor thing, as he called it; the sails were instantly slackened, and all hands, as the phrase is, employed to recover the poor animal. I was, I own, extremely surprised at all this; less, indeed, at the captain's extreme tenderness, than at his conceiving any possibility of success; for, if puss had had nine thousand, instead of nine lives, I concluded they had been all lost. The boatswain, however, had more sanguine hopes; for, having stripped himself of his jacket, breeches, and shirt, he leapt boldly into the water, and to my great astonishment, in a few minutes, returned to the ship, bearing the motionless animal in his mouth. Nor was this, I observed, a matter of such great difficulty as it appeared to my ignorance, and possibly may seem to that of my fresh-water reader: the kitten was now exposed to air and sun on the deck, where its life, of which it retained no symptoms, was despaired of by all.

The captain's humanity, if I may so call it, did not so totally destroy his philosophy, as to make him yield himself up to affliction on this melancholy occasion. Having felt his loss like a man, he resolved to shew he could bear it like one,* and, having declared, he had rather have lost a cask of rum or brandy, betook himself to threshing* at backgammon with the Portuguese friar, in which innocent amusement they had passed about two-thirds of their time.

But, as I have, perhaps, a little too wantonly endeavoured to raise the tender passions of my readers, in this narrative, I should think myself unpardonable if I concluded it, without giving them the satisfaction of hearing that the kitten at last recovered, to the great joy of the good captain; but to the great disappointment of some of the sailors, who asserted that the drowning a cat was the very surest way of raising a favourable wind: a supposition of which, though we have heard several plausible accounts, we will not presume to assign the true original reason.

Friday, July 12. This day our ladies went a-shore at Ryde, and drank their afternoon tea at an alehouse there with great satisfaction: here they were regaled with fresh cream, to which they had been strangers since they left the Downs.

Saturday, July 13. The wind seeming likely to continue in the same corner, where it had been almost constantly for two months together, I was persuaded by my wife to go ashore, and stay at Ryde till we sailed. I approved the motion much; for, though I am a great lover of the sea, I now fancied there was more pleasure in breathing the fresh air of the land; but, how to get thither was the question: for, being really that dead luggage, which I considered all passengers to be in the beginning of this narrative, and incapable of any bodily motion without external impulse, it was in vain to leave the ship, or to determine to do it, without the assistance of others. In one instance, perhaps, the living luggage is more difficult to be moved, or removed, than an equal or much superior weight of dead matter; which, if of the brittle kind, may indeed be liable to be broken through negligence; but this, by proper care, may be almost certainly prevented; whereas, the fractures to which the living lumps are exposed, are sometimes by no caution avoidable, and often by no art to be amended.

I was deliberating on the means of conveyance, not so much out of the ship to the boat, as out of a little tottering boat to the land. A matter which, as I had already experienced in the Thames, was not extremely easy, when to be performed by any other limbs than your own. Whilst I weighed all that could suggest itself on this head, without strictly examining the merit of the several schemes which were advanced by the captain and sailors, and, indeed, giving no very deep attention even to my wife, who, as well as her friend and my daughter, were exerting their tender concern for my ease and safety; fortune, for I am convinced she had a hand in it, sent me a present of a buck; a present, welcome enough of itself, but more welcome on account of the vessel in which it came, being a large hoy,* which in some places would pass for a ship, and many people would go some miles to see the sight. I was pretty easily conveyed on board this hoy, but to get from hence to the shore was not so easy a task; for, however strange it may appear, the water itself did not extend so far; an instance which seems to explain those lines of Ovid,

*Omnia Pontus erant, deerant quoque littora Ponto**

in a less tautological sense, than hath generally been imputed to them.

In fact, between the sea and the shore, there was, at low water, an impassable gulf, if I may so call it, of deep mud, which could neither be traversed by walking nor swimming; so that for near one half of the twenty-four hours, Ryde was inaccessible by friend or foe. But as the magistrates of this place seemed more to desire the company of the former, than to fear that of the latter, they had begun to make a small causeway to the low water mark, so that foot passengers might land whenever they pleased; but as this work was of a publick kind, and would have cost a large sum of money, at least ten pounds, and the magistrates, that is to say, the church-wardens, the overseers, constable and tithingman, and the principal inhabitants had every one of them some separate scheme of private interest to advance at the expence of the publick, they fell out among themselves; and after having thrown away one half of the requisite sum, resolved at least to save the other half, and rather be contented to sit down losers themselves, than to enjoy any benefit which might bring in a greater profit to another. Thus that unanimity which is so necessary in all publick affairs, became wanting, and every man, from the fear of being a bubble* to another, was, in reality, a bubble to himself.

However, as there is scarce any difficulty, to which the strength of men, assisted with the cunning of art, is not equal, I was at last hoisted into a small boat, and being rowed pretty near the shore, was taken up by two sailors, who waded with me through the mud, and placed me in a chair on the land, whence they afterwards conveyed me a quarter of a mile farther, and brought me to a house, which seemed to bid the fairest for hospitality of any in Ryde.

We brought with us our provisions from the ship, so that we wanted nothing but a fire to dress our dinner, and a room in which we might eat it. In neither of these had we any reason to apprehend a disappointment, our dinner consisting only of beans and bacon, and the worst apartment in his Majesty's dominions, either at home or abroad, being fully sufficient to answer our present ideas of delicacy.

Unluckily, however, we were disappointed in both; for when we arrived about four at our inn, exulting in the hopes of immediately seeing our beans smoking on the table, we had the mortification of seeing them on the table indeed, but without the circumstance which would have made the sight agreeable, being in the same state in which we had dispatched them from our ship.

In excuse for this delay, tho' we had exceeded, almost purposely, the time appointed, and our provision had arrived three hours before, the mistress of the house acquainted us, that it was not for want of time to dress them that they were not ready, but for fear of their being cold or over-done before we should come; which she assured us was much worse than waiting a few minutes for our dinner. An observation so very just, that it is impossible to find any objection in it; but indeed it was not altogether so proper at this time: for we had given the most absolute orders to have them ready at four, and had been ourselves, not without much care and difficulty, most exactly punctual in keeping to the very minute of our appointment. But tradesmen, inn-keepers, and servants never care to indulge us in matters contrary to our true interest, which they always know better than ourselves, nor can any bribes corrupt them to go out of their way, whilst they are consulting our good in our own despight.

Our disappointment in the other particular, in defiance of our humility, as it was more extraordinary, was more provoking. In short, Mrs Francis* (for that was the name of the good woman of the house) no sooner received the news of our intended arrival, than she considered more the gentility, than the humanity of her guests, and applied herself not to that which kindles, but to that which extinguishes fire, and forgetting to put on her pot, fell to washing her house.

As the messenger who had brought my venison was impatient to be dispatched, I ordered it to be brought and laid on the table, in the room where I was seated; and the table not being large enough, one side, and that a very bloody one, was laid on the brick floor. I then ordered Mrs Francis to be called in, in order to give her instructions concerning it; in particular, what I would have roasted, and what baked; concluding that she would be highly pleased with the prospect of so much money being spent in her house, as she might have now reason to expect, if the wind continued only a few days longer to blow from the same points whence it had blown for several weeks past.

I soon saw good cause, I must confess, to despise my own sagacity. Mrs Francis having received her orders, without making any answer, snatched the side from the floor, which remained stained with blood, and bidding a servant to take up that on the table, left the room with no pleasant countenance, muttering to herself, that had she known the litter which was to have been made, she would not have taken such pains to wash her house that morning. 'If this was gentility, much good may it do such gentlefolks, for her part she had no notion of it!'

From these murmurs I received two hints. The one, that it was not from a mistake of our inclination that the good woman had starved us, but from wisely consulting her own dignity, or rather, perhaps, her vanity, to which our hunger was offered up as a sacrifice. The other, that I was now sitting in a damp room; a circumstance, tho' it had hitherto escaped my notice, from the colour of the bricks, which was by no means to be neglected in a valetudinary state.

My wife, who, besides discharging excellently well her own, and all the tender offices becoming the female character; who, besides being a faithful friend, an amiable companion, and a tender nurse, could likewise supply the wants of a decrepit husband, and occasionally perform his part, had, before this, discovered the immoderate attention to neatness in Mrs Francis, and provided against its ill consequences. She had found, tho' not under the same roof, a very snug apartment belonging to Mr Francis, and which had escaped the mop by his wife's being satisfied it could not possibly be visited by gentlefolks.

This was a dry, warm, oaken floored barn, lined on both sides with wheaten straw, and opening at one end into a green field, and a beautiful prospect. Here, without hesitation, she ordered the cloth to be laid, and came hastily to snatch me from worse perils by water than the common dangers of the sea.

Mrs Francis, who could not trust her own ears, or could not believe a footman in so extraordinary a phænomenon, followed my wife, and asked her if she had indeed ordered the cloth to be laid in the barn: she answered in the affirmative; upon which Mrs Francis declared she would not dispute her pleasure, but it was the first time, she believed, that quality had ever preferred a barn to a house. She shewed at the same time the most pregnant marks of contempt, and again lamented the labour she had undergone, through her ignorance of the absurd taste of her guests.

At length we were seated in one of the most pleasant spots, I believe, in the kingdom, and were regaled with our beans and bacon, in which there was nothing deficient but the quantity. This defect was, however, so deplorable, that we had consumed our whole dish, before we had visibly lessened our hunger. We now waited with impatience the arrival of our second course, which necessity and not luxury had dictated. This was a joint of mutton which Mrs Francis had been ordered to provide; but when being tired with expectation, we ordered our servants *to see for something else*, we were informed that there was nothing else; on which Mrs Francis being summoned, declared there was no such thing as mutton to be had at Ryde. When I expressed some astonishment at their having no butcher in a village so situated, she answered they had a very good one, and one that killed all sorts of meat in season, beef two or three times a year, and mutton the whole year round; but that it being then beans and pease time, he killed no meat, by reason he was not sure of selling it. This she had not thought worthy of communication, any more than that there lived a fisherman at next door, who was then provided with plenty of soals, and whitings, and lobsters, far superior to those which adorn a city-feast. This discovery being made by accident, we completed the best, the pleasantest, and the merriest meal, with more appetite, more real, solid luxury, and more festivity, than was ever seen in an entertainment at White's.*

It may be wondered at, perhaps, that Mrs Francis should be so negligent of providing for her guests, as she may seem to be thus inattentive to her own interest; but this was not the case; for having clapt a poll-tax on our heads at our arrival, and determined at what price to discharge our bodies from her house, the less she suffered any other to share in the levy, the clearer it came into her own pocket; and that it was better to get twelve pence in a shilling than ten-pence, which latter would be the case if she afforded us fish at any rate.

Thus we passed a most agreeable day, owing to good appetites and good humour; two hearty feeders, which will devour with satisfaction whatever food you place before them: whereas without these, the elegance of St James's, the charde, the perigord-pye, or the ortolan,* the venison, the turtle, or the custard, may titillate the throat, but will never convey happiness to the heart, or cheerfulness to the countenance.

As the wind appeared still immoveable, my wife proposed my lying on shore. I presently agreed, tho' in defiance of an act of parliament, by which persons wandering abroad, and lodging in alehouses, are decreed to be rogues and vagabonds; and this too after having been very singularly officious in putting that law in execution.

My wife, having reconnoitred the house, reported, that there was one room in which were two beds. It was concluded, therefore, that she and Harriot should occupy one, and myself take possession of the other. She added likewise an ingenious recommendation of this room, to one who had so long been in a cabin, which it exactly resembled, as it was sunk down with age on one side, and was in the form of a ship with gunnels to.

For my own part I make little doubt but this apartment was an ancient temple, built with the materials of a wreck, and, probably, dedicated to Neptune, in honour of THE BLESSING sent by him to the inhabitants, such blessings having, in all ages, been very common to them. The timber employed in it confirms this opinion, being such as is seldom used by any but shipbuilders. I do not find, indeed, any mention of this matter in Hern;* but, perhaps, its antiquity was too modern to deserve his notice. Certain it is that this island of Wight was not an early convert to christianity; nay, there is some reason to doubt whether it was ever entirely converted. But I have only time to touch slightly on things of this kind, which, luckily for us, we have a society whose peculiar profession it is to discuss and develope.

Sunday, July 19. This morning early I summoned Mrs Francis, in order to pay her the preceding day's account. As I could recollect only two or three articles, I thought there was no necessity of pen and ink. In a single instance only we had exceeded what the law allows gratis to a foot soldier on his march, viz. vinegar, salt, &c. and dressing his meat. I found, however, I was mistaken in my calculation; for when the good woman attended with her bill, it contained as follow.

	l.	*s.*	*d.*
Bread and beer	0	2	4
Wind	0	2	0
Rum.	0	2	0
Dressing dinner.	0	3	0
Tea	0	1	6
Firing	0	1	0
Lodging	0	1	6
Servants lodging	0	0	6
	£0	13	10

Now that five people, and two servants* should live a day and night at a public house for so small a sum, will appear incredible to any person in London above the degree of a chimney-sweeper; but more astonishing will it seem, that these people should remain so long at such a house, without tasting any other delicacy than bread, small beer, a tea cup full of milk called cream, a glass of rum converted into punch by their own materials, and one bottle of *wind*, of which we only tasted a single glass, tho' possibly, indeed, our servants drank the remainder of the bottle.

This *wind* is a liquor of English manufacture, and its flavour is thought very delicious by the generality of the English, who drink it in great quantities. Every seventh year is thought to produce as much as the other six. It is then drank so plentifully, that the whole nation are in a manner intoxicated by it, and consequently, very little business is carried on at that season.

It resembles in colour the red wine, which is imported from Portugal, as it doth in its intoxicating quality; hence, and from this agreement in the orthography, the one is often confounded with the other, tho' both are seldom esteemed by the same person. It is to be had in every parish of the kingdom, and a pretty large quantity is consumed in the metropolis, where several taverns are set apart solely for the vendition of this liquor, the masters never dealing in any other.*

The disagreement in our computation produced some small remonstrance to Mrs Francis on my side; but this received an immediate answer, 'She scorned to overcharge gentlemen: her house had been always frequented by the very best gentry of the island; and she had never had a bill found fault with in her life, tho' she had lived upwards of forty years in the house, and within that time the greatest gentry in Hampshire had been at it, and that Lawyer Willis never went to any other, when he came to those parts. That for her part she did not get her livelihood by travellers, who were gone and away, and she never expected to see them more, but that her neighbours might come again; wherefore, to be sure, they had the only right to complain.'

She was proceeding thus, and from her volubility of tongue seemed likely to stretch the discourse to an immoderate length, when I suddenly cut all short by paying the bill.

This morning our ladies went to church, more, I fear, from curiosity than religion; they were attended by the captain in a most military attire, with his cockade in his hat, and his sword by his side. So unusual an appearance in this little chappel drew the attention of all present, and probably disconcerted the women, who were in dishabille, and wished themselves drest, for the sake of the curate, who was the greatest of their beholders.

While I was left alone I received a visit from Mr Francis himself, who was much more considerable as a farmer than as an innholder. Indeed he left the latter entirely to the care of his wife, and he acted wisely, I believe, in so doing.

As nothing more remarkable past on this day, I will close it with the account of these two characters, as far as a few days residence could inform me of them. If they should appear as new to the reader as they did to me, he will not be displeased at finding them here.

This amiable couple seemed to border hard on their grand climacteric;* nor indeed were they shy of owning enough to fix their ages within a year or two of that time. They appeared to be rather proud of having employed their time well, than ashamed of having lived so long; the only reason which I could ever assign, why some fine ladies, and fine gentlemen too, should desire to be thought younger than they really are by the cotemporaries of their grand children. Some, indeed, who too hastily credit appearances, might doubt whether they had made so good a use of their time as I would insinuate, since there was no appearance of anything but poverty, want, and wretchedness about their house; nor could they produce any thing to a customer in exchange for his money, but a few bottles of *wind*, and spirituous liquors, and some very bad ale, to drink; with rusty bacon and worse cheese to eat. But then it should be considered, on the other side, that whatever they received was almost as entirely clear profit as the blessing of a wreck itself; such an inn being the very reverse of a coffee-house: for here you can neither sit for nothing, nor have anything for your money.

Again, as many marks of want abounded everywhere, so were the marks of antiquity visible. Scarce any thing was to be seen which had not some scar upon it, made by the hand of time; not an utensil, it was manifest, had been purchased within a dozen years last past; so that whatever money had come into the house during that period, at least, must have remained in it, unless it had been sent abroad for food, or other perishable commodities; but these were supplied by a small portion of the fruits of the farm, in which the farmer allowed he had a very good bargain. In fact, it is inconceivable what sums may be collected by starving only, and how easy it is for a man to die rich, if he will but be contented to live miserable.

Nor is there in this kind of starving anything so terrible as some apprehend. It neither wastes a man's flesh, nor robs him of his cheerfulness. The famous Cornaro's* case well proves the contrary, and so did farmer Francis, who was of a round stature, had a plump round face, with a kind of smile on it, and seemed to borrow an air of wretchedness, rather from his coat's age, than from his own.

The truth is, there is a certain diet which emaciates men more than any possible degree of abstinence; tho' I do not remember to have seen any caution against it, either in Cheney, Arbuthnot, or in any other modern writer on regimen. Nay, the very name is not, I believe, in the learned Dr James's dictionary;* all which is the more extraordinary, as it is a very common food in this kingdom, and the college themselves were not long since very liberally entertained with it, by the present attorney* and other eminent lawyers, in Lincoln's-inn hall, and were all made horribly sick by it.

But though it should not be found among our English physical writers, we may be assured of meeting with it among the Greeks; for nothing considerable in nature escapes their notice; though many things considerable in them, it is to be feared, have escaped the notice of their readers. The Greeks then, to all such as feed too voraciously on this diet give the name of HEAUTOFAGI, which our physicians will, I suppose, translate men that eat themselves.

As nothing is so destructive to the body as this kind of food, so nothing is so plentiful and cheap; but it was perhaps the only cheap thing the farmer disliked. Probably living much on fish might produce this disgust; for Diodorus Siculus* attributes the same aversion in a people of Æthiopia to the same cause: he calls them the fish-eaters; and asserts, that they cannot be brought to eat a single meal with the Heautofagi by any persuasion, threat, or violence whatever, not even though they should kill their children before their faces.

What hath puzzled our physicians, and prevented them from setting this matter in the clearest light, is possibly one simple mistake, arising from a very excusable ignorance; that the passions of men are capable of swallowing food as well as their appetites; that the former, in feeding resemble that state of those animals who chew the cud; and therefore, such men, in some sense, may be said to prey on themselves, and as it were, to devour their own entrails. And hence ensues a meagre aspect, and thin habit of body, as surely as from what is called a consumption.

Our farmer was one of these. He had no more passion than an Ichthuofagus or Ethiopian fisher. He wished not for any thing, thought not of any thing; indeed, he scarce did any thing or said any thing. Here I cannot be understood strictly; for then I must describe a non-entity, whereas I would rob him of nothing but that free agency which is the cause of all the corruption, and of all the misery of human nature. No man, indeed, ever did more than the farmer, for he was an absolute slave to labour all the week; but in truth, as my sagacious reader must have at first apprehended, when I said, he resigned the care of the house to his wife, I meant more than I then expressed; even the house and all that belonged to it; for he was really a farmer, only under the direction of his wife. In a word, so composed, so serene, so placid a countenance, I never saw; and he satisfied himself by answering to every question he was asked; 'I don't know anything about it, Sir, I leaves all that to my wife.'

Now as a couple of this kind would, like two vessels of oil, have made no composition in life, and for want of all savour must have palled every taste; nature, or fortune, or both of them, took care to provide a proper quantity of acid, in the materials that formed the wife, and to render her a perfect *Help-mate* for so tranquil a husband. She abounded in whatsoever he was defective; that is to say, in almost every thing. She was indeed as vinegar to oil, or a brisk wind to a standing-pool, and preserved all from stagnation and corruption.

Quin the player, on taking a nice and severe survey of a fellow-comedian, burst forth into this exclamation, 'If that fellow be not a rogue, God Almighty doth not write a legible hand.'* Whether he guessed right or no, is not worth my while to examine. Certain it is that the latter having wrought his features into a proper harmony to become the characters of Iago, Shylock, and others of the same cast, gave us a semblance of truth to the observation, that was sufficient to confirm the wit of it. Indeed, we may remark, in favour of the physiognomist, though the law has made him a rogue and vagabond, that nature is seldom curious in her works within; without employing some little pains on the outside; and this more particularly in mischievous characters, in forming which, as Mr Derham observes, in venomous insects, as the sting or saw of a wasp, she is sometimes wonderfully industrious.* Now, when she hath thus completely armed her hero, to carry on a war with man, she never fails of furnishing that innocent lambkin with some means of knowing his enemy, and foreseeing his designs. Thus she hath been observed to act in the case of a rattle-snake, which never meditates a human prey without giving warning of his approach.

This observation will, I am convinced, hold most true, if applied to the most venomous individuals of human insects. A tyrant, a trickster, and a bully, generally wear the marks of their several dispositions in their countenances; so do the vixen, the shrew, the scold, and all other females of the like kind. But, perhaps, nature hath never afforded a stronger example of all this than in the case of Mrs Francis. She was a short, squat woman; her head was closely joined to her shoulders, where it was fixed somewhat awry; every feature of her countenance was sharp and pointed; her face was furrowed with the smallpox; and her complexion, which seemed to be able to turn milk to curds, not a little resembled in colour such milk as had already undergone that operation. She appeared indeed to have many symptoms of a deep jaundice in her look; but the strength and firmness of her voice overbalanced them all; the tone of this was a sharp treble at a distance, for, I seldom heard it on the same floor; but was usually waked with it in the morning, and entertained with it almost continually through the whole day.

Though vocal be usually put in opposition to instrumental music; I question whether this might not be thought to partake of the nature of both; for she played on two instruments, which she seemed to keep for no other use from morning till night; these were two maids, or rather scolding-stocks, who, I suppose, by some means or other, earned their board, and she gave them their lodging gratis, or for no other service than to keep her lungs in constant exercise.

She differed, as I have said, in every particular from her husband; but very remarkably in this, that as it was impossible to displease him, so it was as impossible to please her; and as no art could remove a smile from his countenance, so could no art carry it into hers. If her bills were remonstrated against, she was offended with the tacit censure of her fair-dealing; if they were not, she seemed to regard it as a tacit sarcasm on her folly, which might have set down larger prices with the same success. On this latter hint she did indeed improve; for she daily raised some of her articles. A pennyworth of fire was to-day rated at a shilling, to-morrow at eighteen-pence; and if she drest us two dishes for two shillings on the Saturday, we paid half a crown for the cookery of one on the Sunday; and whenever she was paid, she never left the room without lamenting the small amount of her bill; saying, she knew not how it was that others got their money by gentlefolks, but for her part she had not the art of it. When she was asked, why she complained, when she was paid all she demanded, she answered, she could not deny that, nor did she know she had omitted anything, but that it was but a poor bill for gentlefolks to pay.

I accounted for all this by her having heard, that it is a maxim with the principal innholders on the continent, to levy considerable sums on their guests, who travel with many horses and servants, though such guests should eat little or nothing in their houses. The method being, I believe, in such cases, to lay a capitation on the horses, and not on their masters. But she did not consider, that in most of these inns a very great degree of hunger, without any degree of delicacy, may be satisfied; and that in all such inns there is some appearance, at least, of provision, as well as of a man cook to dress it, one of the hostlers being always furnished with a cook's cap, waistecoat and apron, ready to attend gentlemen and ladies on their summons; that the case therefore of such inns differed from hers, where there was nothing to eat or to drink; and in reality no house to inhabit, no chair to sit upon, nor any bed to lie in; that one third or fourth part therefore of the levy imposed at inns was in truth a higher tax than the whole was when laid on in the other, where, in order to raise a small sum, a man is obliged to submit to pay as many various ways for the same thing as he doth to the government, for the light which enters through his own window into his own house, from his own estate;* such are the articles of bread and beer, firing, eating, and dressing dinner.

The foregoing is a very imperfect sketch of this extraordinary couple; for every thing is here lowered instead of being heightened. Those who would see them set forth in more lively colours, and with the proper ornaments, may read the descriptions of the furies in some of the classical poets, or of the stoic philosophers in the works of Lucian.*

Monday, July 20. This day nothing remarkable passed; Mrs Francis levied a tax of fourteen shillings for the Sunday. We regaled ourselves at dinner with venison and good claret of our own; and, in the afternoon, the women, attended by the Captain, walked to see a delightful scene two miles distant, with the beauties of which they declared themselves most highly charmed at their return, as well as with the goodness of the lady of the mansion, who had slipt out of the way, that my wife and their company might refresh themselves with the flowers and fruits with which her garden abounded.

Tuesday, July 21. This day, having paid our taxes of yesterday, we were permitted to regale ourselves with more venison. Some of this we would willingly have exchanged for mutton; but no such flesh was to be had nearer than Portsmouth, from whence it would have cost more to convey a joint to us, than the freight of a Portugal ham from Lisbon to London amounts to: for tho' the water-carriage be somewhat cheaper here than at Deal, yet can you find no watermen who will go on board his boat, unless by two or three hours rowing he can get drunk for the residue of the week.

And here I have an opportunity, which possibly may not offer again, of publishing some observations on that political œconomy of this nation, which, as it concerns only the regulation of the mob, is below the notice of our great men; tho', on the due regulation of this order depend many emoluments which the great men themselves, or, at least, many who tread close on their heels, may enjoy, as well as some dangers, which may some time or other arise from introducing a pure state of anarchy among them. I will represent the case as it appears to me very fairly and impartially between the mob and their betters.

The whole mischief which infects this part of our œconomy, arises from the vague and uncertain use of a word called Liberty, of which, as scarce any two men with whom I have ever conversed, seem to have one and the same idea, I am inclined to doubt whether there be any simple universal notion represented by this word, or whether it conveys any clearer or more determinate idea, than some of those old punic compositions of syllables, preserved in one of the comedies of Plautus;* but at present, as I conceive, not supposed to be understood by any one.

By liberty, however, I apprehend, is commonly understood the power of doing what we please: not absolutely; for then it would be inconsistent with law, by whose control the liberty of the freest people, except only the Hottentots and wild Indians, must always be restrained.

But, indeed, however largely we extend, or however moderately we confine the sense of the word, no politician will, I presume, contend that it is to pervade in an equal degree, and be with the same extent enjoyed by every member of society; no such polity having been ever found, unless among those vile people just before commemorated. Among the Greeks and Romans, the servile and free conditions were opposed to each other; and no man who had the misfortune to be enrolled under the former, could lay any claim to liberty, 'till the right was conveyed to him by that master whose slave he was, either by the means of conquest, of purchase, or of birth.

This was the state of all the free nations in the world; and this, 'till very lately, was understood to be the case of our own. I will not indeed say this is the case at present, the lowest class of our people having shaken off all the shackles of their superiors, and become not only as free, but even freer, than most of their superiors. I believe it cannot be doubted, tho' perhaps we have no recent instance of it, that the personal attendance of every man who hath 300 l. *per annum*, in parliament, is indispensibly his duty; and that, if the citizens and burgesses of any city or borough shall chuse such a one, however reluctant he appear he may be obliged to attend, and be forcibly brought to his duty by the serjeant at arms.*

Again, there are numbers of subordinate offices, some of which are of burthen, and others of expence in the civil government: all of which, persons who are qualified, are liable to have imposed on them, may be obliged to undertake and properly execute, notwithstanding any bodily labour, or even danger, to which they may subject themselves, under the penalty of fines and imprisonment; nay, and what may appear somewhat hard, may be compelled to satisfy the losses which are eventually incident to that of sheriff in particular, out of their own private fortunes; and tho' this should prove the ruin of a family, yet the public, to whom the price is due, incurs no debt or obligation to preserve its officer harmless, let his innocence appear ever so clearly.

I purposely omit the mention of those military or military duties, which our old constitution laid upon its greatest members. These might, indeed, supply their posts with some other able-bodied men; but, if no such could have been found, the obligation nevertheless remained, and they were compellable to serve in their own proper persons.

The only one, therefore, who is possessed of absolute liberty, is the lowest member of the society, who, if he prefers hunger or the wild product of the fields, hedges, lanes and rivers, with the indulgence of ease and laziness, to a food a little more delicate, but purchased at the expence of labour, may lay himself under a shade; nor can be forced to take the other alternative from that which he hath, I will not affirm whether wisely or foolishly, chosen.

Here I may, perhaps, be reminded of the last vagrant act,* where all such persons are compellable to work for the usual and accustomed wages allowed in the place; but this is a clause little known to the justices of the peace, and least likely to be executed by those who do know it, as they know likewise that it is formed on the antient power of the justices to fix and settle these wages every year, making proper allowances for the scarcity and plenty of the times, the cheapness and dearness of the place; and that *the usual and accustomed wages*, are words without any force or meaning, when there are no such; but every man spunges and raps* whatever he can get; and will haggle as long and struggle as hard to cheat his employer of two pence in a day's labour, as an honest tradesman will to cheat his customers of the same sum in a yard of cloth or silk.

It is a great pity then that this power, or rather this practice, was not revived; but this having been so long omitted that it is become obsolete, will be best done by a new law, in which this power, as well as the consequent power of forcing the poor to labour at a moderate and reasonable rate, should be well considered, and their execution facilitated: for gentlemen who give their time and labour gratis, and even voluntarily, to the public, have a right to expect that all their business be made as easy as possible; and to enact laws without doing this, is to fill our statute-books, much too full already, still fuller with dead letter, of no use but to the printer of the acts of parliament.

That the evil which I have here pointed at is of itself worth redressing, is, I apprehend, no subject of dispute: for why should any persons in distress be deprived of the assistance of their fellow-subjects, when they are willing amply to reward them for their labour? or, why should the lowest of the people be permitted to exact ten times the value of their work? For those exactions increase with the degrees of necessity in their object, insomuch that on the former side many are horribly imposed upon, and that often in no trifling matters. I was very well assured that at Deal no less than ten guineas was required, and paid by the supercargo of an Indiaman, for carrying him on board two miles from the shore, when she was just ready to sail; so that his necessity, as his pillager well understood, was absolute. Again, many others, whose indignation will not submit to such plunder, are forced to refuse the assistance, tho' they are often great sufferers by so doing. On the latter side, the lowest of the people are encouraged in laziness and idleness; while they live by a twentieth part of the labour that ought to maintain them, which is diametrically opposite to the interest of the public; for that requires a great deal to be done, not to be paid, for a little. And moreover, they are confirm'd in habits of exaction, and are taught to consider the distresses of their superiors as their own fair emolument.

But enough of this matter, of which I at first intended only to convey a hint to those who are alone capable of applying the remedy, tho' they are the last to whom the notice of those evils would occur, without some such monitor as myself, who am forced to travel about the world in the form of a passenger. I cannot but say I heartily wish our governors would attentively consider this method of fixing the price of labour, and by that means of compelling the poor to work, since the due execution of such powers will, I apprehend, be found the true and only means of making them useful, and of advancing trade, from its present visibly declining state, to the height to which Sir William Petyt, in his Political Arithmetic, thinks it capable of being carried.*

In the afternoon the lady of the above-mentioned mansion called at our inn, and left her compliments to us with Mrs Francis, with an assurance, that while we continued wind-bound in that place, where she feared we could be but indifferently accommodated, we were extremely welcome to the use of any thing which her garden or her house afforded. So polite a message convinced us, in spite of some arguments to the contrary, that we were not on the coast of Africa, or on some island where the few savage inhabitants have little of human in them besides their form.

And here I mean nothing less than to derogate from the merit of this lady, who is not only extremely polite in her behaviour to strangers of her own rank, but so extremely good and charitable to all her poor neighbours, who stand in need of her assistance, that she hath the universal love and praises of all who live near her. But, in reality, how little doth the acquisition of so valuable a character, and the full indulgence of so worthy a disposition, cost those who possess it? Both are accomplished by the very offals which fall from a table moderately plentiful. That they are enjoyed therefore by so few, arises truly from there being so few who have such disposition to gratify, or who aim at any such character.

Wednesday, July 22. This morning, after having been mulcted as usual, we dispatched a servant with proper acknowledgments of the lady's goodness; but confined our wants entirely to the productions of her garden. He soon returned, in company with the gardener, both richly laden with almost every particular which a garden at this most fruitful season of the year produces.

While we were regaling ourselves with these, towards the close of our dinner, we received orders from our commander, who had dined that day with some inferior officers on board a man of war, to return instantly to the ship; for that the wind was become favourable, and he should weigh that evening. These orders were soon followed by the captain himself, who was still in the utmost hurry, tho' the occasion of it had long since ceased: for the wind had, indeed, a little shifted that afternoon, but was before this very quietly set down in its old quarters.

This last was a lucky hit for me: for, as the captain, to whose orders we resolved to pay no obedience, unless delivered by himself, did not return till past six; so much time seemed requisite to put up the furniture of our bed-chamber or dining-room, for almost every article, even to some of the chairs, were either our own or the captain's property; so much more in conveying it as well as my self, as dead a luggage as any, to the shore, and thence to the ship, that the night threatened first to overtake us. A terrible circumstance to me, in my decayed condition; especially as very heavy showers of rain, attended with a high wind, continued to fall incessantly; the being carried through which two miles in the dark, in a wet and open boat, seemed little less than certain death.

However, as my commander was absolute, his orders peremptory, and my obedience necessary, I resolved to avail myself of a philosophy which hath been of notable use to me in the latter part of my life, and which is contained in this hemistich of Virgil.

——*Superanda omnis fortuna ferendo est.**

The meaning of which, if Virgil had any, I think I rightly understood, and rightly applied.

As I was therefore to be entirely passive in my motion, I resolved to abandon myself to the conduct of those who were to carry me into a cart when it returned from unloading the goods.

But before this the captain perceiving what had happened in the clouds, and that the wind remained as much his enemy as ever, came upstairs to me, with a reprieve till the morning. This was, I own, very agreeable news, and I little regreted the trouble of refurnishing my apartment, by sending back for the goods.

Mrs Francis was not well pleased with this. As she understood the reprieve to be only till the morning, she saw nothing but lodging to be possibly added, out of which she was to deduct fire and candle, and the remainder, she thought, would scarce pay her for her trouble. She exerted therefore all the ill humour of which she was mistress, and did all she could to thwart and perplex everything during the whole evening.

Thursday, July 23. Early in the morning the captain, who had remained on shore all night, came to visit us, and to press us to make haste on board. 'I am resolved,' says he, 'not to lose a moment, now the wind is coming about fair: for my own part, I never was surer of a wind in all my life.' I use his very words; nor will I presume to interpret or comment upon them farther, than by observing that they were spoke in the utmost hurry.

We promised to be ready as soon as breakfast was over but

this was not so soon as was expected: for in removing our goods the evening before, the tea-chest was unhappily lost.

Every place was immediately searched, and many where it was impossible for it to be; for this was a loss of much greater consequence than it may at first seem to many of my readers. Ladies and valetudinarians do not easily dispense with the use of this sovereign cordial, in a single instance; but to undertake a long voyage without any probability of being supplied with it the whole way, was above the reach of patience. And yet, dreadful as this calamity was, it seemed unavoidable. The whole town of Ryde could not supply a single leaf; for as to what Mrs Francis and the shop called by that name, it was not of Chinese growth. It did not indeed in the least resemble tea, either in smell or taste, or in any particular, unless in being a leaf: for it was in truth no other than a tobacco of the mundungus* species. And as for the hopes of relief in any other port, they were not to be depended upon; for the captain had positively declared he was sure of a wind, and would let go his anchor no more till he arrived in the Tajo.*

When a good deal of time had been spent, most of it indeed wasted on this occasion, a thought occurred which every one wondered at its not having presented itself the first moment. This was to apply to the good lady, who could not fail of pitying and relieving such distress. A messenger was immediately dispatched, with an account of our misfortune, till whose return we employed ourselves in preparatives for our departure, that we might have nothing to do but to swallow our breakfast when it arrived. The tea-chest, tho' of no less consequence to us than the military chest to a general, was given up as lost, or rather as stolen; for tho' I would not, for the world, mention any particular name, it is certain we had suspicions, and all, I am afraid, fell on the same person.

The man returned from the worthy lady with much expedition, and brought with him a canister of tea, dispatched with so true a generosity, as well as politeness, that if our voyage had been as long again, we should have incurred no danger of being brought to a short allowance in this most important article. At the very same instant likewise arrived William the footman, with our own tea-chest. It had been, indeed, left in the hoy, when the other goods were re-landed, as William, when he first heard it was missing, had suspected; and whence, had not the owner of the hoy been unluckily out of the way, he had retrieved it soon enough to have prevented our giving the lady an opportunity of displaying some part of her goodness.

To search the hoy was, indeed, too natural a suggestion to have escaped any one, nor did it escape being mentioned by many of us; but we were dissuaded from it by my wife's maid, who perfectly well remembered she had left the chest in the bed-chamber; for that she had never given it out of her hand in her way to or from the hoy; but William, perhaps, knew the maid better, and best understood how far she was to be believed; for otherwise he would hardly of his own accord, after hearing her declaration, have hunted out the hoyman, with much pains and difficulty.

Thus ended this scene, which begun with such appearance of distress, and ended with becoming the subject of mirth and laughter.

Nothing now remained but to pay our taxes, which were indeed laid with inconceivable severity. Lodging was raised six-pence, fire in the same proportion, and even candles, which had hitherto escaped, were charged with a wantonness of imposition, from the beginning, and placed under the stile of oversight. We were raised a whole pound, whereas we had only burned ten, in five nights, and the pound consisted of twenty-four.

Lastly, an attempt was made, which almost as far exceeds human credulity to believe, as it did human patience to submit to. This was to make us pay as much for existing an hour or two as for existing a whole day; and dressing dinner was introduced as an article, tho' we left the house before either pot or spit had approached the fire. Here I own my patience failed me, and I became an example of the truth of the observation, that all tyranny and oppression may be carried too far, and that a yoke may be made too intolerable for the neck of the tamest slave. When I remonstrated with some warmth against this grievance, Mrs Francis gave me a look, and left the room without making any answer. She returned in a minute, running to me with pen, ink, and paper in her hand, and desired me to make my own bill; for she hoped, she said, I did not expect that her house was to be dirtied, and her goods spoiled and consumed, for nothing. 'The whole is but thirteen shillings. Can gentlefolks lie a whole night at a public house for less? If they can, I am sure it is time to give off being a landlady: but pay me what you please; I would have people know that I value money as little as other folks. But I was always a fool, as I says to my husband, and never knows which side my bread is buttered of. And yet to be sure your honour shall be my warning not to be bit so again. Some folks knows better than other some how to make their bills. Candles! why, yes, to be sure; why should not travellers pay for candles? I am sure I pays for my candles, and the chandler pays the King's Majesty for them; and if he did not, I must, so as it comes to the same thing in the end. To be sure I am out of sixteens at present, but these burn as white and as clear, tho' not quite so large. I expects my chandler here soon, or I would send to Portsmouth, if your honour was to stay any time longer. But when folks stays only for a wind, you knows, there can be no dependence on such!' Here she put on a little slyness of aspect, and seemed willing to submit to interruption. I interrupted her, accordingly, by throwing down half a guinea, and declared I had no more English money, which was indeed true; and as she could not immediately change the thirty-six shilling pieces, it put a final end to the dispute. Mrs Francis soon left the room, and we soon after left the house; nor would this good woman see us, or wish us a good voyage.

I must not, however, quit this place, where we had been so ill-treated, without doing it impartial justice, and recording what may with the strictest truth be said in its favour.

First then, as to its situation, it is, I think, most delightful, and in the most pleasant spot in the whole island. It is true it wants the advantage of that beautiful river, which leads from Newport to Cowes: but the prospect here extending to the sea, and taking in Portsmouth, Spithead, and St Helen's, would be more than a recompence for the loss of the Thames itself, even in the most delightful part of Berkshire or Buckinghamshire, tho' another Denham, or another Pope, should unite in celebrating it.* For my own part, I confess myself so entirely fond of a sea prospect, that I think nothing on the land can equal it; and if it be set off with shipping, I desire to borrow no ornament from the *terra firma*. A fleet of ships is, in my opinion, the noblest object which the art of man hath ever produced; and far beyond the power of those architects who deal in brick, in stone, or in marble.

When the late Sir Robert Walpole, one of the best of men and of ministers, used to equip us a yearly fleet at Spithead, his enemies of taste must have allowed that he, at least, treated the nation with a fine sight for their money. A much finer, indeed, than the same expence in an encampment could have produced. For what, indeed, is the best idea which the prospect of a number of huts can furnish to the mind? but of a number of men forming themselves into a society, before the art of building more substantial houses was known. This, perhaps, would be agreeable enough; but in truth, there is a much worse idea ready to step in before it, and that is of a body of cut-throats, the supports of tyranny, the invaders of the just liberties and properties of mankind, the plunderers of the industrious, the ravishers of the chaste, the murderers of the innocent, and, in a word, the destroyers of the plenty, the peace, and the safety of their fellow-creatures.

And what, it may be said, are these men of war, which seem so delightful an object to our eyes? Are they not alike the support of tyranny, and oppression of innocence, carrying with them desolation and ruin wherever their masters please to send them. This is indeed too true, and however the ship of war may, in its bulk and equipment, exceed the honest merchant-man, I heartily wish there was no necessity for it; for, tho' I must own the superior beauty of the object on one side, I am more pleased with the superior excellence of the idea, which I can raise in my mind on the other; while I reflect on the art and industry of mankind, engaged in the daily improvements of commerce, to the mutual benefit of all countries, and to the establishment and happiness of social life.

This pleasant village is situated on a gentle ascent from the water, whence it affords that charming prospect I have above described. Its soil is a gravel, which assisted with its declivity, preserves it always so dry that immediately after the most violent rain, a fine lady may walk without wetting her silken shoes. The fertility of the place is apparent from its extraordinary verdure, and it is so shaded with large and flourishing elms, that its narrow lanes are a natural grove or walk, which in the regularity of its plantation vies with the power of art, and in its wanton exuberancy greatly exceeds it.

In a field in the ascent of this hill, about a quarter of a mile from the sea, stands a neat little chapel. It is very small, but adequate to the number of inhabitants: for the parish doth not seem to contain above thirty houses.

At about two miles distant from this parish, lives that polite and good lady to whose kindness we were so much obliged. It is placed on a hill, whose bottom is washed by the sea, and which, from its eminence at top, commands a view of great part of the island, as well as it does that of the opposite shore. This house was formerly built by one Boyce, who from a blacksmith at Gosport, became possessed, by great success in smuggling, of 40000 *l.* With part of this, he purchased an estate here, and by chance probably, fixed on this spot for building a large house. Perhaps the convenience of carrying on his business, to which it is so well adapted, might dictate the situation to him. We can hardly, at least, attribute it to the same taste with which he furnished his house, or at least his library, by sending an order to a bookseller in London, to pack him up 500 pound's worth of his handsomest books. They tell here several almost incredible stories of the ignorance, the folly, and the pride which this poor man and his wife discovered during the short continuance of his prosperity; for he did not long escape the sharp eyes of the revenue-solicitors, and was by extents* from the Court of Exchequer, soon reduced below his original state, to that of confinement in the Fleet. All his effects were sold, and among the rest his books by an auction at Portsmouth, for a very small price; for the bookseller was now discovered to have been perfectly a master of his trade, and, relying on Mr Boyce's finding little time to read, had sent him not only the most lasting wares of his shop, but duplicates of the same, under different titles.

His estate and house were purchased by a gentleman of these parts, whose widow now enjoys them, and who hath improved them, particularly her gardens, with so elegant a taste, that the painter who would assist his imagination in the composition of a most exquisite landscape, or the poet who would describe an earthly paradise, could nowhere furnish themselves with a richer pattern.

We left this place about eleven in the morning, and were again conveyed with more sunshine than wind aboard our ship.

Whence our captain had acquired his power of prophecy, when he promised us and himself a prosperous wind, I will not determine; it is sufficient to observe that he was a false prophet, and that the weathercocks continued to point as before.

He would not, however, so easily give up his skill in prediction. He persevered in asserting that the wind was changed, and, having weighed his anchor fell down that afternoon to St Helen's, which was at about the distance of five miles; and whither his friend the tide, in defiance of the wind, which was most manifestly against him, softly wafted him in as many hours.

Here, about seven in the evening, before which time we could not procure it, we sat down to regale ourselves with some roasted venison, which was much better drest than we imagined it would be, and an excellent cold pasty which my wife had made at Ryde, and which we had reserved uncut to eat on board our ship, whither we all chearfully exulted in being returned from the presence of Mrs Francis, who, by the exact resemblance she bore to a fury, seemed to have been with no great propriety settled in paradise.

Friday, July 24. As we passed by Spithead on the preceding evening, we saw the two regiments of soldiers who were just returned from Gibraltar and Minorca* and this day a lieutenant belonging to one of them, who was the captain's nephew, came to pay a visit to his uncle. He was what is called by some a very pretty fellow; indeed much too pretty a fellow at his years; for he was turned of thirty-four, though his address and conversation would have become him more before he had reached twenty. In his conversation, it is true, there was something military enough, as it consisted chiefly of oaths, and of the great actions and wise sayings of Jack, and Will, and Tom of our regiment, a phrase eternally in his mouth; and he seemed to conclude, that it conveyed to all the officers such a degree of public notoriety and importance, that it entitled him, like the head of a profession, or a first minister, to be the subject of conversation among those who had not the least personal acquaintance with him. This did not much surprize me, as I have seen several examples of the same; but the defects in his address, especially to the women, were so great, that they seemed absolutely inconsistent with the behaviour of a pretty fellow, much less of one in a red coat; and yet, besides having been eleven years in the army, he had had, as his uncle informed me, an education in France. This, I own, would have appeared to have been absolutely thrown away, had not his animal spirits, which were likewise thrown away upon him in great abundance, borne the visible stamp of the growth of that country. The character, to which he had an indisputable title, was that of a merry fellow; so very merry was he, that he laughed at everything he said, and always before he spoke. Possibly, indeed, he often laughed at what he did not utter, for every speech began with a laugh, tho' it did not always end with a jest. There was no great analogy between the characters of the uncle and the nephew, and yet they seem'd intirely to agree in enjoying the honour which the red-coat did to his family. This the uncle expressed with great pleasure in his countenance, and seemed desirous of shewing all present the honour which he had for his nephew, who, on his side, was at some pains to convince us of his concurring in this opinion, and at the same time of displaying the contempt he had for the parts as well as the occupation of his uncle, which he seemed to think reflected some disgrace on himself, who was a member of that profession which makes every man a gentleman. Not that I would be understood to insinuate, that the nephew endeavoured to shake off or disown his uncle, or indeed, to keep him at any distance. On the contrary, he treated him with the utmost familiarity, often calling him Dick, and dear Dick, and old Dick, and frequently beginning an oration with D—n me, Dick.

All this condescension on the part of the young man, was received with suitable marks of complaisance and obligation by the old one; especially, when it was attended with evidences of the same familiarity with general officers, and other persons of rank; one of whom, in particular, I know to have the pride and insolence of the devil himself, and who, without some strong bias of interest, is no more liable to converse familiarly with a lieutenant, than of being mistaken in his judgment of a fool; which was not, perhaps, so certainly the case of the worthy lieutenant, who, in declaring to us the qualifications which recommended men to his countenance and conversation, as well as what effectually set a bar to all hopes of that honour, exclaimed, 'No, Sir, by the D—, I hate all fools—No, d—n me, excuse me for that. That's a little too much, old Dick. There are two or three officers of our regiment, whom I know to be fools; but d—n me if I am ever seen in their company. If a man hath a fool of a relation, Dick, you know he can't help that, old boy.'

Such jokes as these the old man not only took in good part, but glibly gulped down the whole narrative of his nephew; nor did he, I am convinced, in the least doubt of our as readily swallowing the same. This made him so charmed with the lieutenant, that it is probable we should have been pestered with him the whole evening, had not the north-wind, dearer to our sea-captain, even than this glory of his family, sprung suddenly up, and called aloud to him to weigh his anchor.

While this ceremony was performing, the sea-captain ordered out his boat to row the land-captain to shore; not indeed on an uninhabited island, but one which, in this part, looked but little better, not presenting us the view of a single house. Indeed, our old friend, when his boat returned on shore, perhaps being no longer able to stifle his envy of the superiority of his nephew, told us, with a smile, that the young man had a good five mile to walk, before he could be accommodated with a passage to Portsmouth.

It appeared now, that the captain had been only mistaken in the date of his prediction, by placing the event a day earlier than it happened; for the wind which now arose, was not only favourable but brisk, and was no sooner in reach of our sails than it swept us away by the back of the Isle of Wight, and having in the night carried us by Christ-church and Peveral-point, brought us the next noon, *Saturday, July* 25 off the island of Portland, so famous for the smallness and sweetness of its mutton, of which a leg seldom weighs four pounds. We would have bought a sheep, but our captain would not permit it; though he needed not have been in such a hurry, for presently the wind, I will not positively assert in resentment of his surliness, shewed him a dog's trick, and slily slipt back again to his summer-house in the south-west.

The captain now grew outrageous, and declaring open war with the wind, took a resolution, rather more bold than wise, of sailing in defiance of it, and in its teeth. He swore he would let go his anchor no more, but would beat the sea while he had either yard or sail left. He accordingly stood from the shore, and made so large a tack, that before night, though he seemed to advance but little on his way, he was got out of sight of land.

Towards the evening the wind began, in the captain's own language, and indeed it freshned so much, that before ten it blew a perfect hurricane.* The captain having got, as he supposed, to a safe distance, tacked again towards the English shore; and now the wind veered a point only in his favour, and continued to blow with such violence, that the ship ran above eight knots or miles an hour, during this whole day and tempestuous night, till bed-time. I was obliged to betake myself once more to my solitude; for my women were again all down in their sea-sickness, and the captain was busy on deck; for he began to grow uneasy, chiefly, I believe, because he did not well know where he was, and would, I am convinced, have been very glad to have been in Portland-road, eating some sheep's-head broth.

Having contracted no great degree of good-humour, by living a whole day alone, without a single soul to converse with, I took but ill physic to purge it off, by a bed conversation with the captain; who, amongst many bitter lamentations of his fate, and protesting he had more patience than a Job, frequently intermixed summons to the commanding officer on the deck, who now happened to be one Morrison, a carpenter, the only fellow that had either common sense or common civility in the ship. Of Morrison he inquired every quarter of an hour concerning the state of affairs; the wind, the care of the ship, and other matters of navigation. The frequency of these summons, as well as the solicitude with which they were made, sufficiently testified the state of the captain's mind; he endeavoured to conceal it, and would have given no small alarm to a man, who had either not learnt what it is to die, or known what it is to be miserable. And my dear wife and child must pardon me, if what I did not conceive to be any great evil to myself, I was not much terrified with the thoughts of happening to them: in truth, I have often thought they are both too good, and too gentle, to be trusted to the power of any man I know, to whom they could possibly be so trusted.

Can I say then I had no fear; indeed I cannot, reader, I was afraid for thee, lest thou shouldst have been deprived of that pleasure thou art now enjoying; and that I should not live to draw out on paper, that military character which thou didst peruse in the journal of yesterday.

From all these fears we were relieved, at six in the morning, by the arrival of Mr Morrison, who acquainted us that he was sure he beheld land very near; for he could not see half a mile, by reason of the haziness of the weather. This land, he said, was, he believed, the Berry head, which forms one side of Torbay; the captain declared that it was impossible, and swore, on condition he was right, he would give him his mother for a maid. A forfeit which became afterwards strictly due, and payable; for the captain, whipping on his night-gown, ran up, without his breeches, and within half an hour returning into the cabin, wished me joy of our lying safe at anchor in the bay.

Sunday, July 26. Things now began to put on an aspect very different from what they had lately worn: the news that the ship had almost lost its mizen, and that we had procured very fine clouted cream and fresh bread and butter from the shore, restored health and spirits to our women, and we all sat down to a very chearful breakfast.

But however pleasant our stay promised to be here, we were all desirous it should be short: I resolved immediately to dispatch my man into the country, to purchase a present of cyder, for my friends of that which is called Southam, as well as to take with me a hogshead of it to Lisbon; for it is, in my opinion, much more delicious than that which is the growth of Herefordshire. I purchased three hogsheads for five pounds ten shillings, all which I should have scarce thought worth mentioning, had I not believed it might be of equal service to the honest farmer who sold it me, and who is by the neighbouring gentleman reputed to deal in the very best, and to the reader, who from ignorance of the means of providing better for himself, swallows at a dearer rate the juice of Middlesex turnip, instead of that Vinum Pomonæ, which Mr Giles Leverance of Cheeshurst, near Dartmouth in Devon, will, at the price of forty shillings per hogshead, send in double casks to any part of the world. Had the wind been very sudden in shifting, I had lost my cyder, by an attempt of a boatman to exact, according to custom. He required five shillings for conveying my man a mile and a half to the shore, and four more if he staid to bring him back. This I thought to be such insufferable impudence, that I ordered him to be immediately chased from the ship, without any answer. Indeed, there are few inconveniences that I would not rather encounter than encourage the insolent demands of these wretches, at the expence of my own indignation, of which I own, they are not the only objects, but rather those who purchase a paultry convenience by encouraging them. But of this I have already spoken very largely. I shall conclude, therefore, with the leave which this fellow took of our ship; saying, he should know it again, and would not put off from the shore to relieve it in any distress whatever.

It will, doubtless, surprize many of my readers to hear, that when we lay at anchor within a mile or two of a town several days together, and even in the most temperate weather, we should frequently want fresh provisions and herbage, and other emoluments of the shore, as much as if we had been a hundred leagues from land. And this too, while numbers of boats were in our sight, whose owners get their livelihood by rowing people up and down, and could be at any time summoned by a signal to our assistance, and while the captain had a little boat of his own with men always ready to row it at his command.

This, however, hath been partly accounted for already, by the imposing disposition of the people; who asked so much more than the proper price of their labour. And as to the usefulness of the captain's boat, it requires to be a little expatiated upon, as it will tend to lay open some of the grievances which demand the utmost regard of our legislature, as they affect the most valuable part of the king's subjects, those by whom the commerce of the nation is carried into execution.

Our captain then, who was a very good and experienced seaman, having been above thirty years the master of a vessel, part of which he had served, so he phrased it, as commander of a privateer; and had discharged himself with great courage and conduct, and with as great success, discovered the utmost aversion to the sending his boat ashore, whenever we lay wind-bound in any of our harbours. This aversion did not arise from any fear of wearing out his boat by using it, but was, in truth, the result of experience, that it was easier to send his men on shore than to recall them. They acknowledged him to be their master while they remained on shipboard, but did not allow his power to extend to the shores, where they had no sooner set their foot, than every man became sui juris, and thought himself at full liberty to return when he pleased. Now it is not any delight that these fellows have in the fresh air, or verdant fields on the land. Every one of them would prefer his ship and his hammock to all the sweets of Arabia the happy; but, unluckily for them, there are in every sea port in England certain houses, whose chief livelihood depends on providing entertainment for the gentlemen of the jacket. For this purpose, they are always well-furnished with those cordial liquors, which do immediately inspire the heart with gladness, banishing all careful thoughts, and indeed all others from the mind, and opening the mouth with songs of chearfulness and thanksgiving, for the many wonderful blessings with which a sea-faring life overflows.

For my own part, however whimsical it may appear, I confess, I have thought the strange story of Circe* in the Odyssey, no other than an ingenious allegory; in which Homer intended to convey to his countrymen the same kind of instruction, which we intend to communicate to our own in this digression. As teaching the art of war to the Greeks, was the plain design of the Iliad; so was teaching them the art of navigation the no less manifest intention of the Odyssey. For the improvement of this, their situation was most excellently adapted; and accordingly we find Thucydides, in the beginning of his history, considers the Greeks as a set of pirates, or privateers, plundering each other by sea. This being probably the first institution of commerce before the Ars Cauponaria was invented, and merchants, instead of robbing, began to cheat and outwit each other, and by degrees changed the Metabletic, the only kind of traffic allowed by Aristotle in his Politics, into the Chrematistic.*

By this allegory then I suppose Ulysses to have been the captain of a merchant-ship, and Circe some good ale-wife, who made his crew drunk with the spirituous liquors of those days. With this the transformation into swine, as well as all other incidents of the fable, will notably agree; and thus a key will be found out for unlocking the whole mystery, and forging, at least, some meaning to a story which, at present, appears very strange and absurd.

Hence, moreover, will appear the very near resemblance between the sea-faring men of all ages and nations; and here perhaps may be established the truth and justice of that observation, which will occur oftener than once in this voyage, that all human flesh is not the same flesh, but that there is one kind of flesh of landmen, and another of seamen.

Philosophers, divines, and others, who have treated the gratification of human appetites with contempt, have, among other instances, insisted very strongly on that satiety which is so apt to overtake them, even in the very act of enjoyment. And here they more particularly deserve our attention, as most of them may be supposed to speak from their own experience; and very probably gave us their lessons with a full stomach. Thus hunger and thirst, whatever delight they may afford while we are eating and drinking, pass both away from us with the plate and the cup; and though we should imitate the Romans, if indeed they were such dull beasts which I can scarce believe, to unload the belly like a dungpot, in order to fill it again with another load, yet would the pleasure be so considerably lessened, that it would scarce repay us the trouble of purchasing it with swallowing a basin of camomile tea. A second haunch of venison, or a second dose of turtle, would hardly allure a city glutton with its smell. Even the celebrated Jew himself, when well filled with Calipash and Calipee,* goes contentedly home to tell his money, and expects no more pleasure from his throat, during the next twenty-four hours. Hence I suppose Dr South took that elegant comparison of the joys of a speculative man to the solemn silence of an Archimedes over a problem, and those of a glutton to the stillness of a sow at her wash.* A simile, which, if it became the pulpit at all, could only become it in the afternoon.

Whereas, in those potations which the mind seems to enjoy, rather than the bodily appetite, there is happily no such satiety; but the more a man drinks the more he desires; as if, like Mark Anthony in Dryden, his appetite increased with feeding, and this to such an immoderate degree, *ut nullus sit desiderio aut pudor* *aut modus*.* Hence, as with the gang of Captain Ulysses, ensues so total a transformation, that the man no more continues what he was. Perhaps he ceases for a time to be at all; or, tho' he may retain the same outward form and figure he had before, yet is his nobler part, as we are taught to call it, so changed, that, instead of being the same man, he scarce remembers what he was a few hours before. And this transformation, being once obtained, is so easily preserved by the same potations, which induce no satiety, that the captain in vain sends or goes in quest of his crew. They know him no longer; or, if they do, they acknowledge not his power, having indeed, as entirely forgotten themselves as if they had taken a large draught of the river of Lethe.

Nor is the captain always sure of even finding out the place to which Circe hath conveyed them. There are many of those houses in every port-town. Nay, there are some where the sorceress doth not trust only to her drugs; but hath instruments of a different kind to execute her purposes, by whose means the tar is effectually secreted from the knowledge and pursuit of his captain. This would, indeed, be very fatal, was it not for one circumstance; that the sailor is seldom provided with the proper bait for these harpies. However, the contrary sometimes happens, as these harpies will bite at almost any thing, and will snap at a pair of silver buttons or buckles, as surely as at the specie itself. Nay, sometimes they are so voracious, that the very naked hook will go down, and the jolly young sailor is sacrificed for his own sake.

In vain, at such a season as this, would the vows of a pious heathen have prevailed over Neptune, Æolus, or any other marine deity. In vain would the prayers of a Christian captain be attended with the like success. The wind may change, how it pleases, while all hands are on shore; the anchor would remain firm in the ground, and the ship would continue in durance, unless, like other forcible prison-breakers, it forcibly got loose for no good purpose.

Now, as the favour of winds and courts, and such like, is always to be laid hold on at the very first motion, for within twenty-four hours all may be changed again; so, in the former case, the loss of a day may be the loss of a voyage: for, tho' it may appear to persons not well skilled in navigation, who see ships meet and sail by each other, that the wind blows sometimes east and west, north and south, backwards and forwards, at the same instant; yet, certain it is, that the land is so contrived, that even the same wind will not, like the same horse, always bring a man to the end of his journey; but, that the gale which the mariner prayed heartily for yesterday, he may as heartily deprecate to-morrow; while all use and benefit, which would have arisen to him from the westerly wind of to-morrow, may be totally lost and thrown away, by neglecting the offer of the easterly blast which blows to-day.

Hence ensues grief and disreputation to the innocent captain, loss and disappointment to the worthy merchant, and not seldom great prejudice to the trade of a nation, whose manufactures are thus liable to lye unsold in a foreign warehouse, the market being forestall'd by some rival whose sailors are under a better discipline. To guard against these inconveniences the prudent captain takes every precaution in his power: he makes the strongest contracts with his crew, and thereby binds them so firmly, that none but the greatest or least of men can break through them with impunity: but for one of these two reasons, which I will not determine, the sailor, like his brother fish the eel, is too slippery to be held, and plunges into his element with perfect impunity.

To speak a plain truth, there is no trusting to any contract with one whom the wise citizens of London call a bad man; for, with such a one, tho' your bond be ever so strong, it will prove in the end good for nothing.

What then is to be done in this case? What, indeed! but to call in the assistance of that tremendous magistrate, the justice of peace, who can, and often doth lay good and bad men in equal durance; and, tho' he seldom cares to stretch his bonds to what is great, never finds any thing too minute for their detention, but will hold the smallest reptile alive so fast in his noose, that he can never get out 'till he is let drop through it.

Why, therefore, upon the breach of those contracts, should not an immediate application be made to the nearest magistrate of this order, who should be empower'd to convey the delinquent, either to ship or to prison, at the election of the captain, to be fettered by the leg in either place.

But, as the case now stands, the condition of this poor captain, without any commission, and of this absolute commander without any power, is much worse than we have hitherto shewn it to be; for notwithstanding all the aforesaid contracts to sail in the good ship the Elizabeth, if the sailor should, for better wages, find it more his interest to go on board the better ship the Mary, either before their setting out, or on their speedy meeting in some port, he may prefer the latter without any other danger, than that of 'doing what he ought not to have done,' contrary to a rule which he is seldom Christian enough to have much at heart, while the captain is generally too good a Christian to punish a man out of revenge only, when he is to be at a considerable expence for so doing. There are many other deficiencies in our laws, relating to maritime affairs, and which would probably have been long since corrected, had we any seamen in the House of Commons. Not that I would insinuate that the legislature wants a supply of many gentlemen in the sea-service: but, as these gentlemen are, by their attendance in the house, unfortunately prevented from even going to sea, and there learning what they might communicate to their landed brethren, these latter remain as ignorant in that branch of knowledge, as they would be if none but courtiers and fox-hunters had been elected into parliament, without a single fish among them. The following seems to me to be an effect of this kind, and it strikes me the stronger, as I remember the case to have happened, and remember it to have been dispunishable. A captain of a trading vessel, of which he was part-owner, took in a large freight of oats at Liverpool, consign'd to the market at Bear key;* this he carried to a port in Hampshire, and there sold it as his own, and freighting his vessel with wheat for the port of Cadiz in Spain, dropt it at Oporto in his way, and there selling it for his own use, took in a lading of wine, with which he sailed again, and having converted it in the same manner, together with a large sum of money with which he was entrusted, for the benefit of certain merchants, sold the ship and cargo in another port, and then wisely sat down contented with the fortune he had made, and returned to London to enjoy the remainder of his days, with the fruits of his former labours and a good conscience.

The sum he brought home with him, consisted of near six

thousand pounds, all in specie, and most of it in that coin which Portugal distributes so liberally over Europe.

He was not yet old enough to be past all sense of pleasure, nor so puff'd up with the pride of his good fortune, as to overlook his old acquaintance the journeymen taylors, from among whom he had been formerly press'd into the sea-service, and having there laid the foundation of his future success, by his shares in prizes, had afterwards become captain of a trading vessel, in which he purchased an interest, and had soon begun to trade in the honourable manner above-mentioned.

The captain now took up his residence at an alehouse in Drury-lane,* where, having all his money by him in a trunk, he spent about five pounds a day among his old friends the gentlemen and ladies of those parts.

The merchant of Liverpool having luckily had notice from a friend during the blaze of his fortune, did, by the assistance of a justice of peace, without the assistance of the law, recover his whole loss. The captain, however, wisely chose to refund no more; but perceiving with what hasty strides envy was pursuing his fortune, he took speedy means to retire out of her reach, and to enjoy the rest of his wealth in an inglorious obscurity; nor could the same justice overtake him time enough to assist a second merchant, as he had done the first.

This was a very extraordinary case, and the more so, as the ingenious gentleman had steered entirely clear of all crimes in our law.

Now, how it comes about that a robbery so very easy to be committed, and to which there is such immediate temptation always before the eyes of these fellows, should receive the encouragement of impunity, is to be accounted for only from the oversight of the legislature, as that oversight can only be, I think, derived from the reasons I have assigned for it.

But I will dwell no longer on this subject. If what I have here said should seem of sufficient consequence to engage the attention of any man in power, and should thus be the means of applying any remedy, to the most inveterate evils at least, I have obtained my whole desire, and shall have lain so long windbound in the ports of this kingdom to some purpose. I would indeed, have this work, which, if I should live to finish it, a matter of no great certainty, if indeed of any great hope to me, will be probably the last I shall ever undertake, to produce some better end than the mere diversion of the reader.

Monday. This day our captain went ashore, to dine with a gentleman who lives in these parts, and who so exactly resembles the character given by Homer of Axylus,* that the only difference I can trace between them is, the one living by the highway, erected his hospitality chiefly in favour of land-travellers; and the other living by the water-side, gratifies his humanity by accommodating the wants of the mariner.

In the evening our commander received a visit from a brother bashaw, who lay wind-bound in the same harbour. This latter captain was a Swiss. He was then master of a vessel bound to Guinea, and had formerly been a privateering, when our own hero was employed in the same laudable service. The honesty and freedom of the Switzer, his vivacity, in which he was in no respect inferior to his near neighbours the French, the aukward and affected politeness, which was likewise of French extraction, mixed with the brutal roughness of the English tar; for he had served under the colours of this nation, and his crew had been of the same, made such an odd variety, such a hotch-potch of character, that I should have been much diverted with him, had not his voice, which was as loud as a speaking trumpet, unfortunately made my head ach. The noise which he conveyed into the deaf ears of his brother captain, who sat on one side of him, the soft addresses, with which, mixed with aukward bows, he saluted the ladies on the other, were so agreeably contrasted, that a man must not only have been void of all taste of humour, and insensible of mirth, but duller than Cibber is represented in the Dunciad,* who could be unentertained with him a little while: for, I confess, such entertainments should always be very short, as they are very liable to pall. But he suffered not this to happen at present, for having given us his company a quarter of an hour only, he retired, after many apologies for the shortness of his visit.

Tuesday. The wind being less boisterous than it had hitherto been since our arrival here, several fishing boats, which the tempestuous weather yesterday had prevented from working, came on board us with fish. This was so fresh, so good in kind, and so very cheap, that we supplied ourselves in great numbers, among which were very large soals at four-pence a pair, and whitings, of almost preposterous size, at nine-pence a score.

The only fish which bore any price was a john dorée, as it is called. I bought one of at least four pounds weight for as many shillings. It resembles a turbut in shape, but exceeds it in firmness and flavour. The price had the appearance of being considerable, when opposed to the extraordinary cheapness of others of value; but was, in truth, so very reasonable, when estimated by its goodness, that it left me under no other surprize, than how the gentlemen of this country, not greatly eminent for the delicacy of their taste, had discovered the preference of the dorée to all other fish: but I was informed that Mr Quin, whose distinguishing tooth hath been so justly celebrated, had lately visited Plymouth, and had done those honours to the dorée, which are so justly due to it from that sect of modern philosophers, who with Sir Epicure Mammon, or Sir Epicure Quin, their head, seem more to delight in a fish-pond than in a garden, as the old Epicureans are said to have done.*

Unfortunately for the fishmongers of London, the dorée resides only in those seas; for, could any of this company but convey one to the temple of luxury under the Piazza, where Macklin* the high-priest daily serves up his rich offerings to that goddess, great as would be the reward of that fishmonger, in blessings poured down upon him from the goddess, as great would his merit be towards the high priest, who could never be thought to over-rate such valuable incense.

And here having mentioned the extreme cheapness of fish in the Devonshire sea, and given some little hint of the extreme dearness with which this commodity is dispensed by those who deal in it in London, I cannot pass on without throwing forth an observation or two, with the same view with which I have scattered my several remarks through this voyage, sufficiently satisfied in having finished my life, as I have, probably, lost it, in the service of my country, from the best of motives, tho' it should be attended with the worst of success. Means are always in our power; ends are very seldom so.

Of all the animal foods with which man is furnished, there are none so plenty as fish. A little rivulet, that glides almost unperceived through a vast tract of rich land, will support more hundreds with the flesh of its inhabitants, than the meadow will nourish individuals. But if this be true of rivers, it is much truer of the sea-shores, which abound with such immense variety of fish, that the curious fisherman, after he hath made his draught, often culls only the daintiest part, and leaves the rest of his prey to perish on the shore.

If this be true, it would appear, I think, that there is nothing which might be had in such abundance, and consequently so cheap, as fish, of which nature seems to have provided such inexhaustible stores with some peculiar design. In the production of terrestrial animals, she proceeds with such slowness, that in the larger kind a single female seldom produces more than one a year, and this again requires three, four, or five years more to bring it to perfection. And tho' the lesser quadrupeds, those of the wild kind particularly, with the birds, do multiply much faster, yet can none of these bear any proportion with the aquatic animals, of whom every female matrix is furnished with an annual offspring, almost exceeding the power of numbers, and which, in many instances at least, a single year is capable of bringing to some degree of maturity.

What then ought in general to be so plentiful, what so cheap as fish? What then so properly the food of the poor? So in many places they are, and so might they always be in great cities which are always situated near the sea, or on the conflux of large rivers. How comes it then, to look no farther abroad for instances, that in our city of London the case is so far otherwise, that except that of sprats, there is not one poor palate in a hundred that knows the taste of fish?

It is true, indeed, that this taste is generally of such excellent flavour, that it exceeds the power of French cookery to treat the palates of the rich with anything more exquisitely delicate; so that was fish the common food of the poor it might put them too much upon an equality with their betters, in the great article of eating, in which, at present, in the opinion of some, the great difference in happiness between man and man consists. But this argument I shall treat with the utmost disdain: for if ortolans were as big as bustards, and at the same time as plenty as sparrows, I should hold it yet reasonable to indulge the poor with the dainty, and that for this cause especially, that the rich would soon find a sparrow, if as scarce as an ortolan, to be much the greater, as it would certainly be the rarer, dainty of the two.

Vanity or scarcity will be always the favourite of luxury, but honest hunger will be satisfied with plenty. Not to search deeper into the cause of the evil, I shall think it abundantly sufficient to propose the remedies of it. And, first, I humbly submit the absolute necessity of immediately hanging all the fishmongers within the bills of mortality;* and however it might have been some time ago the opinion of mild and temporizing men, that the evil complained of might be removed by gentler methods, I suppose at this day there are none who do not see the impossibility of using such with any effect. *Cuncta prius tentanda* might have been formerly urged with some plausibility, but *cuncta prius tentata* may now be replied: for surely if a few monopolizing fishmongers could defeat that excellent scheme of the Westminster market,* to the erecting which so many justices of peace, as well as other wise and learned men, did so vehemently apply themselves, that they might be truely said not only to have laid the whole strength of their heads, but of their shoulders too, to the business, it would be a vain endeavour for any other body of men to attempt to remove so stubborn a nuisance.

If it should be doubted, whether we can bring this case within the letter of any capital law now subsisting? I am ashamed to own it cannot; for surely no crime better deserves such punishment; but the remedy may, nevertheless, be immediate, and if a law was made the beginning of next session, to take place immediately, by which the starving thousands of poor was declared to be felony, without benefit of clergy, the fishmongers would be hanged before the end of the session.

A second method of filling the mouths of the poor, if not with loaves, at least with fishes, is to desire the magistrates to carry into execution one, at least, out of near a hundred acts of parliament, for preserving the small fry of the river of Thames, by which means as few fish would satisfy thousands, as may now be devoured by a small number of individuals. But while a fisherman can break through the strongest meshes of an act of parliament, we may be assured he will learn so to contrive his own meshes, that the smallest fry will not be able to swim thro' them.

Other methods may, we doubt not, be suggested by those who shall attentively consider the evil here hinted at; but we have dwelt too long on it already, and shall conclude with observing, that it is difficult to affirm, whether the atrocity of the evil itself, the facility of curing it, or the shameful neglect of the cure, be the more scandalous or more astonishing.

After having, however, gloriously regaled myself with this food, I was washing it down with some good claret with my wife and her friend, in the cabin,* when the captain's valet de chambre, head cook, house and ship steward, footman in livery and out on't, secretary and fore-mast-man, all burst into the cabin at once, being indeed all but one person, and, without saying, by your leave, began to pack half a hogshead of small beer in bottles, the necessary consequence of which must have been, either a total stop to conversation at that chearful season, when it is most agreeable, or the admitting that polyonymous officer aforesaid to the participation of it. I desired him, therefore, to delay his purpose a little longer, but he refused to grant my request; nor was he prevailed on to quit the room till he was threatened with having one bottle to pack more than his number, which then happened to stand empty within my reach.

With these menaces he retired at last, but not without muttering some menaces on his side, and which, to our great terror, he failed not to put into immediate execution.

Our captain was gone to dinner this day with his Swiss brother; and tho' he was a very sober man, was a little elevated with some champaign, which, as it cost the Swiss little or nothing, he dispensed at his table more liberally than our hospitable English noblemen put about those bottles, which the ingenious Peter Taylor teaches a led captain to avoid by distinguishing by the name of that generous liquor, which all humble companions are taught to postpone to the flavour of methuen, or honest port.*

While our two captains were thus regaling themselves, and celebrating their own heroic exploits, with all the inspiration which the liquor, at least, of wit could afford them, the polyonymous officer arrived, and being saluted by the name of honest Tom, was ordered to sit down and take his glass before he delivered his message; for every sailor is by turns his captain's mate over a can, except only that captain bashaw who presides in a man of war, and who upon earth has no other mate, unless it be another of the same bashaws.

Tom had no sooner swallowed his draught, than he hastily began his narrative, and faithfully related what had happened on board our ship; we say faithfully, tho' from what happened it may be suspected that Tom chose to add, perhaps, only five or six immaterial circumstances, as is always, I believe, the case, and may possibly have been done by me in relating this very story, tho' it happened not many hours ago.

No sooner was the captain informed of the interruption which had been given to his officer, and indeed to his orders, for he thought no time so convenient as that of his absence for causing any confusion in the cabin, than he leapt with such haste from his chair, that he had like to have broke his sword, with which he always begirt himself when he walked out of his ship, and sometimes when he walked about in it, at the same time grasping eagerly that other implement called a cockade, which modern soldiers wear on their helmets, with the same view as the antients did their crests, to terrify the enemy; he muttered something, but so inarticulately, that the word *damn* was only intelligible; he then hastily took leave of the Swiss captain, who was too well bred to press his stay on such an occasion, and leapt first from the ship to his boat, and then from his boat to his own ship, with as much fierceness in his looks as he had ever express'd on boarding his defenceless prey in the honourable calling of a privateer.

Having regained the middle deck, he paused a moment, while Tom and the others loaded themselves with bottles, and then descending into the cabin exclaimed with a thundering voice, D—n me, why arn't the bottles stoed in, according to my orders?

I answered him very mildly, that I had prevented his man from doing it, as it was at an inconvenient time to me, and as in his absence, at least, I esteemed the cabin to be my own. Your cabin, repeated he many times, no, d—n me, 'tis my cabin. Your cabin! D—n me! I have brought my hogs to a fair market. I suppose, indeed, you think it your cabin, and your ship, by your commanding in it; but I will command in it, d—n me! I will shew the world I am the commander, and nobody but I! Did you think I sold you the command of my ship for that pitiful thirty pounds? I wish I had not seen you nor your thirty pounds aboard of her. He then repeated the words thirty pounds often, with great disdain, and with a contempt which, I own, the sum did not seem to deserve in my eye, either in itself, or on the present occasion; being, indeed, paid for the freight of——weight of human flesh, which is above 50 per cent. dearer than the freight of any other luggage, whilst in reality it takes up less room, in fact, no room at all.

In truth, the sum was paid for nothing more, than for a liberty to six persons, (two of them servants)* to stay on board a ship while she sails from one port to another, every shilling of which comes clear into the captain's pocket. Ignorant people may perhaps imagine, especially when they are told that the captain is obliged to sustain them, that their diet, at least, is worth something; which may probably be now and then so far the case, as to deduct a tenth part from the neat profits on this account; but it was otherwise at present: for when I had contracted with the captain at a price which I by no means thought moderate, I had some content in thinking I should have no more to pay for my voyage; but I was whispered that it was expected the passengers should find themselves in several things; such as tea, wine, and such like; and particularly that gentlemen should stowe of the latter a much larger quantity than they could use, in order to leave the remainder as a present to the captain, at the end of the voyage; and it was expected, likewise, that gentlemen should put aboard some fresh stores, and the more of such things were put aboard, the welcomer they would be to the captain.

I was prevailed with by these hints, to follow the advice proposed, and accordingly, besides tea, and a large hamper of wine, with several hams and tongues, I caused a number of live chickens and sheep to be conveyed aboard; in truth, treble the quantity of provisions which would have supported the persons I took with me, had the voyage continued three weeks, as it was supposed, with a bare possibility, it might.

Indeed it continued much longer; but, as this was occasioned by our being wind-bound in our own ports, it was by no means of any ill consequence to the captain, as the additional stores of fish, fresh meat, butter, bread, &c. which I constantly laid in, greatly exceeded the consumption, and went some way in maintaining the ship's crew. It is true, I was not obliged to do this; but it seemed to be expected; for the captain did not think himself obliged to do it; and I can truly say, I soon ceased to expect it of him. He had, I confess, on board, a number of fowls and ducks sufficient for a West India voyage: all of them, as he often said, 'Very fine birds, and of the largest breed.' This, I believe, was really the fact, and, I can add, that they were all arrived at the full perfection of their size. Nor was there, I am convinced, any want of provisions of a more substantial kind; such as dried beef, pork, and fish; so that the captain seemed ready to perform his contract, and amply to provide for his passengers. What I did then was not from necessity, but, perhaps, from a less excusable motive, and was, by no means, chargeable to the account of the captain.

But, let the motive have been what it would, the consequence was still the same, and this was such, that I am firmly persuaded the whole pitiful 30 *l.* came pure and neat into the captain's pocket, and not only so, but attended with the value of 10 *l.* more in sundries, into the bargain. I must confess myself therefore at a loss how the epithet *pitiful* came to be annexed to the above sum: for, not being a pitiful price for what it was given, I cannot conceive it to be pitiful in itself; nor do I believe it is thought by the greatest men in the kingdom; none of whom would scruple to search for it in the dirtiest kennel,* where they had only a reasonable hope of success.

How, therefore, such a sum should acquire the idea of pitiful, in the eyes of the master of a ship, seems not easy to be accounted for; since it appears more likely to produce in him ideas of a different kind. Some men, perhaps, are no more sincere in the contempt for it which they express, than others in their contempt of money in general; and I am the rather inclined to this persuasion, as I have seldom heard of either, who have refused or refunded this their despised object. Besides, it is sometimes impossible to believe these professions, as every action of the man's life is a contradiction to it. Who can believe a tradesman, who says he would not tell his name for the profit he gets by the selling such a parcel of goods, when he hath told a thousand lies in order to get it?

Pitiful, indeed, is often applied to an object, not absolutely, but comparatively with our expectations, or with a greater object: In which sense it is not easy to set any bounds to the use of the word. Thus, a handful of halfpence daily appear pitiful to a porter, and a handful of silver to a drawer. The latter, I am convinc'd, at a polite tavern, will not tell his name (for he will not give you any answer) under the price of gold. And, in this sense, 30 *l.* may be accounted pitiful by the lowest mechanic.

One difficulty only seems to occur, and that is this: How comes it that, if the profits of the meanest arts are so considerable, the professors of them are not richer than we generally see them? One answer to this shall suffice. Men do not become rich by what they get, but by what they keep. He who is worth no more than his annual wages or salary, spends the whole; he will be always a beggar, let his income be what it will; and so will be his family when he dies. This we see daily to be the case of ecclesiastics, who, during their lives, are extremely well provided for, only because they desire to maintain the honour of the cloth by living like gentlemen, which would, perhaps, be better maintained by living unlike them.

But, to return from so long a digression, to which the use of so improper an epithet gave occasion, and to which the novelty of the subject allured, I will make the reader amends by concisely telling him, that the captain poured forth such a torrent of abuse, that I very hastily, and very foolishly, resolved to quit the ship. I gave immediate orders to summons a hoy to carry me that evening to Dartmouth, without considering any consequence. Those orders I gave in no very low voice; so that those above stairs might possibly conceive there was more than one master in the cabin. In the same tone I likewise threatened the captain with that which, he afterwards said, he feared more than any rock or quick sand. Nor can we wonder at this, when we are told he had been twice obliged to bring to, and cast anchor there before, and had neither time escaped without the loss of almost his whole cargo.

The most distant sound of law thus frightened a man, who had often, I am convinced, heard numbers of cannon roar round him with intrepidity. Nor did he sooner see the hoy approaching the vessel, than he ran down again into the cabin, and, his rage being perfectly subsided, he tumbled on his knees, and a little too abjectly implored for mercy.

I did not suffer a brave man and an old man, to remain a moment in this posture; but I immediately forgave him.

And here, that I may not be thought the sly trumpeter of my own praises, I do utterly disclaim all praise on the occasion. Neither did the greatness of my mind dictate, nor the force of my Christianity exact this forgiveness. To speak truth, I forgave him from a motive which would make men much more forgiving, if they were much wiser than they are; because it was convenient for me so to do.

Wednesday. This morning the captain drest himself in scarlet, in order to pay a visit to a Devonshire squire, to whom a captain of a ship is a guest of no ordinary consequence, as he is a stranger and a gentleman, who hath seen a great deal of the world in foreign parts, and knows all the news of the times.

The squire, therefore, was to send his boat for the captain; but a most unfortunate accident happened: for, as the wind was extremely rough and against the hoy, while this was endeavouring to avail itself of great seamanship, in hawling up against the wind, a sudden squall carried off sail and yard; or, at least, so disabled them, that they were no longer of any use, and unable to reach the ship; but the captain, from the deck, saw his hopes of venison disappointed, and was forced either to stay on board his ship, or to hoist forth his own long-boat, which he could not prevail with himself to think of, tho' the smell of the venison had had twenty times its attraction. He did, indeed, love his ship as his wife, and his boats as children, and never willingly trusted the latter, poor things! to the dangers of the seas.

To say truth, notwithstanding the strict rigour with which he preserved the dignity of his station, and the hasty impatience with which he resented any affront to his person or orders, disobedience to which he could in no instance brook in any person on board, he was one of the best-natur'd fellows alive. He acted the part of a father to his sailors; he expressed great tenderness for any of them when ill, and never suffered any, the least work of supererogation to go unrewarded by a glass of gin. He even extended his humanity, if I may so call it, to animals, and even his cats and kittens had large shares in his affections. An instance of which we saw this evening, when the cat, which had shewn it could not be drowned, was found suffocated under a feather-bed in the cabin. I will not endeavour to describe his lamentations with more prolixity than barely by saying, they were grievous, and seemed to have some mixture of the Irish howl in them. Nay, he carried his fondness even to inanimate objects, of which we have above set down a pregnant example in his demonstration of love and tenderness towards his boats and ship. He spoke of a ship which he had commanded formerly, and which was long since no more, which he had called the Princess of Brasil, as a widower of a deceased wife. This ship, after having followed the honest business of carrying goods and passengers for hire many years, did at last take to evil courses and turn privateer, in which service, to use his own words, she received many dreadful wounds, which he himself had felt as if they had been his own.

Thursday. As the wind did not yesterday discover any purpose of shifting, and the water in my belly grew troublesome, and rendered me short-breathed; I began a second time to have apprehensions of wanting the assistance of a trochar, when none was to be found: I therefore concluded to be tapped again, by way of precaution; and accordingly I this morning summoned on board a surgeon from a neighbouring parish, one whom the captain greatly recommended, and who did indeed perform his office with much dexterity. He was, I believe likewise, a man of great judgment and knowledge in the profession; but of this I cannot speak with perfect certainty; for when he was going to open on the dropsy at large, and on the particular degree of the distemper under which I laboured, I was obliged to stop him short, for the wind was changed, and the captain in the utmost hurry to depart; and to desire him, instead of his opinion, to assist me with his execution.

I was now once more delivered from my burthen, which was not indeed so great as I had apprehended, wanting two quarts of what was let out at the last operation.

While the surgeon was drawing away my water, the sailors were drawing up the anchor; both were finished at the same time, we unfurled our sails, and soon passed the Berry-head, which forms the mouth of the bay.

We had not however sailed far when the wind, which had,

tho' with a slow pace, kept us company about six miles, suddenly turned about, and offered to conduct us back again: a favour, which, though sorely against the grain, we were obliged to accept.

Nothing remarkable happened this day; for as to the firm persuasion of the captain that he was under the spell of witchcraft, I would not repeat it too often, though indeed he repeated it an hundred times every day; in truth, he talked of nothing else, and seemed not only to be satisfied in general of his being bewitched, but actually to have fixed, with good certainty, on the person of the witch, whom, had he lived in the days of Sir Matthew Hale, he would have infallibly indicted, and very possibly have hanged for the detestable sin of witchcraft,* but that law, and the whole doctrine that supported it, are now out of fashion; and witches, as a learned divine once chose to express himself, are put down by act of parliament. This witch, in the captain's opinion, was no other than Mrs Francis of Ryde, who, as he insinuated, out of anger to me, for not spending more money in her house than she could produce any thing to exchange for, or any pretence to charge for, had laid this spell on his ship.

Tho' we were again got near our harbour by three in the afternoon, yet it seemed to require a full hour or more, before we could come to our former place of anchoring, or birth, as the captain called it. On this occasion we exemplified one of the few advantages, which the travellers by water have over the travellers by land. What would the latter often give for the sight of one of those hospitable mansions, where he is assured *that there is good entertainment for man and horse*; and where both may consequently promise themselves to assuage that hunger which exercise is so sure to raise in a healthy constitution.

At their arrival at this mansion, how much happier is the state of the horse than that of the master? The former is immediately led to his repast, such as it is, and, whatever it is, he falls to it with appetite. But the latter is in a much worse situation. His hunger, however violent, is always in some degree delicate, and his food must have some kind of ornament, or as the more usual phrase is, of dressing, to recommend it. Now all dressing requires time; and therefore, though perhaps, the sheep might be just killed before you came to the inn, yet in cutting him up, fetching the joint, which the landlord by mistake said he had in the house, from the butcher at two miles distance, and afterwards warming it a little by the fire, two hours at least must be consumed, while hunger for want of better food, preys all the time on the vitals of the man.

How different was the case with us? we carried our provision, our kitchen, and our cook with us, and we were at one and the same time travelling on our road, and sitting down to a repast of fish, with which the greatest table in London can scarce at any rate be supplied.

Friday. As we were disappointed of our wind, and obliged to return back the preceding evening, we resolved to extract all the good we could out of our misfortune, and to add considerably to our fresh stores of meat and bread, with which we were very indifferently provided when we hurried away yesterday. By the captain's advice we likewise laid in some stores of butter, which we salted and potted ourselves, for our use at Lisbon, and we had great reason afterwards to thank him for his advice.

In the afternoon, I persuaded my wife, whom it was no easy matter for me to force from my side, to take a walk on shore, whither the gallant captain declared he was ready to attend her. Accordingly, the ladies set out, and left me to enjoy a sweet and comfortable nap after the operation of the preceding day.

Thus we enjoyed our separate pleasures full three hours, when we met again; and my wife gave the foregoing account of the gentleman, whom I have before compared to Axylus, and of his habitation, to both which she had been introduced by the captain, in the stile of an old friend and acquaintance, though this foundation of intimacy seemed to her to be no deeper laid than in an accidental dinner, eaten many years before, at this temple of hospitality, when the captain lay wind-bound in the same bay.

Saturday. Early this morning the wind seemed inclined to change in our favour. Our alert captain snatched its very first motion, and got under sail with so very gentle a breeze that, as the tide was against him, he recommended to a fishing hoy to bring after him a vast salmon and some other provisions which lay ready for him on shore.

Our anchor was up at six, and before nine in the morning we had doubled the Berry-head, and were arrived off Dartmouth, having gone full three miles in as many hours, in direct opposition to the tide, which only befriended us out of our harbour; and though the wind was, perhaps, our friend, it was so very silent, and exerted itself so little in our favour, that, like some cool partisans, it was difficult to say whether it was with us or against us. The captain, however, declared the former to be the case, during the whole three hours; but at last he perceived his error, or rather, perhaps, this friend, which had hitherto wavered in chusing his side, became now more determined. The captain then suddenly tacked about, and asserting that he was bewitched, submitted to return to the place from whence he came. Now, though I am as free from superstition as any man breathing, and never did believe in witches, notwithstanding all the excellent arguments of my Lord Chief Justice Hale in their favour, and long before they were put down by act of parliament, yet by what power a ship of burthen should sail three miles against both wind and tide, I cannot conceive; unless there was some supernatural interposition in the case: nay, could we admit that the wind stood neuter, the difficulty would still remain. So that we must of necessity conclude, that the ship was either bewinded or bewitched.

The captain, perhaps, had another meaning. He imagined himself, I believe, bewitched, because the wind, instead of persevering in its change in his favour, for change it certainly did that morning, should suddenly return to its favourite station, and blow him back towards the bay. But if this was his opinion, he soon saw cause to alter; for he had not measured half the way back, when the wind again declared in his favour, and so loudly that there was no possibility of being mistaken.

The orders for the second tack were given, and obeyed with much more alacrity, than those had been for the first. We were all of us indeed in high spirits on the occasion; though some of us a little regretted the good things we were likely to leave behind us by the fisherman's neglect: I might give it a werse name, for he faithfully promised to execute the commission, which he had had abundant opportunity to do; but *Nautica fides* deserves as much to be proverbial as ever *Punica fides* could formerly have done.* Nay, when we consider that the Carthaginians came from the Phenicians, who are supposed to have produced the first mariners, we may probably see the true reason of the adage, and it may open a field of very curious discoveries to the antiquarian.

We were, however, too eager to pursue our voyage, to suffer anything we left behind us to interrupt our happiness, which indeed many agreeable circumstances conspired to advance. The weather was inexpressibly pleasant, and we were all seated on the deck, when our canvas began to swell with the wind. We had likewise in our view above thirty other sail around us, all in the same situation. Here an observation occurred to me which, perhaps, though extremely obvious, did not offer itself to every individual in our little fleet: when I perceived with what different success we proceeded under the influence of a superior power, which while we lay almost idle ourselves, pushed us forward on our intended voyage, and compared this with the slow progress which we had made in the morning, of ourselves and without any such assistance, I could not help reflecting how often the greatest abilities lie wind-bound as it were in life; or if they venture out, and attempt to beat the seas, they struggle in vain against wind and tide, and if they have not sufficient prudence to put back, are most probably cast away on the rocks and quicksands, which are every day ready to devour them.

It was now our fortune to set out *melioribus avibus*.* The wind freshned so briskly in our poop, that the shore appeared to move from us, as fast as we did from the shore. The captain declared he was sure of a wind, meaning its continuance; but he had disappointed us so often, that he had lost all credit. However, he kept his word a little better now, and we lost sight of our native land, as joyfully, at least, as it is usual to regain it.

Sunday. The next morning, the captain told me he thought himself thirty miles to the westward of Plymouth, and before evening declared that the Lizard Point, which is the extremity of Cornwall, bore several leagues to leeward. Nothing remarkable past this day, except the captain's devotion, who, in his own phrase, summoned all hands to prayers, which were read by a common sailor upon deck, with more devout force and address, than they are commonly read by a country curate, and received with more decency and attention by the sailors than are usually preserved in city congregations. I am indeed assured, that if any such affected disregard of the solemn office in which they were engaged, as I have seen practised by fine gentlemen and ladies, expressing a kind of apprehension lest they should be suspected of being really in earnest in their devotion, had been shewn here, they would have contracted the contempt of the whole audience. To say the truth, from what I observed in the behaviour of the sailors in this voyage, and on comparing it with what I have formerly seen of them at sea and on shore, I am convinced that on land there is nothing more idle and dissolute; in their own element, there are no persons near the level of their degree who live in the constant practise of half so many good qualities. They are, for much the greater part, perfect masters of their business, and always extremely alert, and ready in executing it, without any regard to fatigue or hazard. The soldiers themselves are not better disciplined, nor more obedient to orders than these whilst aboard; they submit to every difficulty which attends their calling with chearfulness, and no less virtues than patience and fortitude are exercised by them every day of their lives.

All these good qualities, however, they always leave behind them on shipboard: the sailor out of water is, indeed, as wretched an animal as the fish out of water; for tho' the former hath, in common with amphibious animals the bare power of existing on the land, yet if he be kept there any time, he never fails to become a nuisance.

The ship having had a good deal of motion since she was last under sail, our women returned to their sickness, and I to my solitude; having, for twenty-four hours together, scarce opened my lips to a single person. This circumstance of being shut up within the circumference of a few yards, with a score of human creatures, with not one of whom it was possible to converse, was perhaps so rare, as scarce ever to have happened before, nor could it ever happen to one who disliked it more than myself, or to myself at a season when I wanted more food for my social disposition, or could converse less wholsomely and happily with my own thoughts. To this accident, which fortune opened to me in the Downs, was owing the first serious thought which I ever entertained of enrolling myself among the voyage-writers; some of the most amusing pages, if indeed there be any which deserve that name, were possibly the production of the most disagreeable hours which ever haunted the author.

Monday. At noon the captain took an observation, by which it appeared that Ushant bore some leagues northward of us, and that we were just entering the bay of Biscay. We had advanced a very few miles in this bay before we were entirely becalmed; we furl'd our sails, as being of no use to us, while we lay in this most disagreeable situation, more detested by the sailors than the most violent tempest; we were alarmed with the loss of a fine piece of salt beef, which had been hung in the sea to freshen it; this being, it seems, the strange property of salt water. The thief was immediately suspected, and presently afterwards taken by the sailors. He was indeed no other than a huge shark, who, not knowing when he was well off, swallowed another piece of beef, together with a great iron crook on which it was hung, and by which he was dragged into the ship.

I should scarce have mentioned the catching this shark, though so exactly conformable to the rules and practice of voyage-writing, had it not been for a strange circumstance that attended it. This was the recovery of the stolen beef out of the shark's maw, where it lay unchewed and undigested, and whence being conveyed into the pot, the flesh, and the thief that had stoln it, joined together in furnishing variety to the ship's crew.

During this calm we likewise found the mast of a large vessel, which the captain thought had lain at least three years in the sea. It was stuck all over with a little shell-fish or reptile called a barnacle, and which probably are the prey of the rock-fish, as our captain calls it, asserting that it is the finest fish in the world; for which we are obliged to confide entirely to his taste; for, though he struck the fish with a kind of harping-iron, and wounded him, I am convinced, to death, yet he could not possess himself of his body; but the poor wretch escaped to linger out a few hours, with probably great torments.

In the evening our wind returned, and so briskly, that we ran upwards of twenty leagues before the next day's [*Tuesday's*] Observation, which brought us to Lat. 47°42′.* The captain promised us a very speedy passage through the bay, but he deceived us, or the wind deceived him, for it so slackened at sun-set, that it scarce carried us a mile in an hour during the whole succeeding night.

Wednesday. A gale struck up a little after sun-rising, which carried us between three and four knots or miles an hour. We were this day at noon about the middle of the bay of Biscay, when the wind once more deserted us, and we were so entirely becalmed, that we did not advance a mile in many hours. My fresh-water reader will perhaps conceive no unpleasant idea from this calm; but it affected us much more than a storm could have done; for, as the irascible passions of men are apt to swell with indignation long after the injury which first raised them is over, so fared it with the sea. It rose mountains high, and lifted our poor ship up and down, backwards and forwards, with so violent an emotion, that there was scarce a man in the ship better able to stand than myself. Every utensil in our cabin rolled up and down, as we should have rolled ourselves, had not our chairs been fast lashed to the floor. In this situation, with our tables likewise fastened by ropes, the captain and myself took our meal with some difficulty, and swallowed a little of our broth, for we spilt much the greater part. The remainder of our dinner being an old, lean, tame duck roasted, I regretted but little the loss of, my teeth not being good enough to have chewed it.

Our women, who began to creep out of their holes in the morning, retired again within the cabin to their beds, and were no more heard of this day, in which my whole comfort was to find, by the captain's relation, that the swelling was sometimes much worse; he did, indeed, take this occasion to be more communicative than ever, and informed me of such misadventures that had befallen him within forty-six years at sea, as might frighten a very bold spirit from undertaking even the shortest voyage. Were these indeed but universally known, our matrons of quality would possibly be deterred from venturing their tender offspring at sea; by which means our navy would lose the honour of many a young commodore, who at twenty-two is better versed in maritime affairs than real seamen are made by experience at sixty.

And this may, perhaps, appear the more extraordinary, as the education of both seems to be pretty much the same; neither of them having had their courage tried by Virgil's description of a storm,* in which, inspired as he was, I doubt whether our captain doth not exceed him.

In the evening the wind, which continued in the N. W. again

freshened, and that so briskly that Cape Finister appeared by this day's observation to bear a few miles to the southward. We now indeed sailed, or rather flew, near ten knots an hour; and the captain, in the redundancy of his good-humour, declared he would go to church at Lisbon on Sunday next, for that he was sure of a wind; and indeed we all firmly believed him. But the event again contradicted him: for we were again visited by a calm in the evening.

But here, tho' our voyage was retarded, we were entertained with a scene, which as no one can behold without going to sea, so no one can form an idea of any thing equal to it on shore. We were seated on the deck, women and all, in the serenest evening that can be imagined. Not a single cloud presented itself to our view, and the sun himself was the only object which engrossed our whole attention. He did indeed set with a majesty which is incapable of description, with which while the horizon was yet blazing with glory, our eyes were called off to the opposite part to survey the moon, which was then at full, and which in rising presented us with the second object that this world hath offered to our vision. Compared to these the pageantry of theatres, or splendour of courts, are sights almost below the regard of children.

We did not return from the deck till late in the evening: the weather being inexpressibly pleasant, and so warm, that even my old distemper perceived the alteration of the climate. There was indeed a swell, but nothing comparable to what we had felt before, and it affected us on the deck much less than in the cabin.

Friday. The calm continued till sun-rising, when the wind likewise arose, but unluckily for us, it came from a wrong quarter: it was S. S. E. which is that very wind which Juno would have solicited of Æolus, had Æneas been in our latitude bound for Lisbon.*

The captain now put on his most melancholy aspect, and resumed his former opinion, that he was bewitched. He declared, with great solemnity, that this was worse and worse, for that a wind directly in his teeth was worse than no wind at all. Had we pursued the course which the wind persuaded us to take, we had gone directly for Newfoundland, if we had not fallen in with Ireland in our way. Two ways remained to avoid this; one was to put into a port of Galicia; the other, to beat to the westward with as little sail as possible; and this was our captain's election.

As for us, poor passengers, any port would have been welcome to us; especially, as not only our fresh provisions, except a great number of old ducks and fowls, but even our bread was come to an end, and nothing but sea-biscuit remained, which I could not chew. So that now, for the first time in my life, I saw what it was to want a bit of bread.

The wind, however, was not so unkind as we had apprehended; but, having declined with the sun, it changed at the approach of the moon, and became again favourable to us; tho' so gentle, that the next day's observation carried us very little to the southward of cape Finister. This evening at six the wind, which had been very quiet all day, rose very high, and continuing in our favour, drove us seven knots an hour.

This day we saw a sail, the only one, as I heard of, we had seen in our whole passage through the bay. I mention this on account of what appeared to me somewhat extraordinary. Tho' she was at such a distance that I could only perceive she was a ship, the sailors discovered that she was a snow* bound to a port in Galicia.

Sunday. After prayers, which our good captain read on the deck with an audible voice, and with but one mistake, of a lion for Elias, in the second lesson for this day, we found ourselves far advanced in 42°, and the captain declared we should sup off Porte.* We had not much wind this day; but, as this was directly in our favour, we made it up with sail, of which we crowded all we had. We went only at the rate of four miles an hour, but with so uneasy a motion, continually rolling from side to side, that I suffered more than I had done in our whole voyage; my bowels being almost twisted out of my belly. However, the day was very serene and bright, and the captain, who was in high spirits, affirmed he had never passed a pleasanter at sea.

The wind continued so brisk that we ran upward of six knots an hour the whole night.

Monday. In the morning, our captain concluded that he was got into lat. 40°, and was very little short of the Burlings,* as they are called in the charts. We came up with them at five in the afternoon, being the first land we had distinctly seen since we left Devonshire. They consist of abundance of little rocky islands, a little distant from the shore, three of them only shewing themselves above the water.

Here the Portuguese maintain a kind of garrison, if we may allow it that name. It consists of malefactors, who are banished hither for a term, for divers small offences. A policy which they may have copied from the Egyptians, as we may read in Diodorus Siculus. That wise people, to prevent the corruption of good manners by evil communication, built a town on the Red Sea, whither they transported a great number of their criminals, having first set an indelible mark on them, to prevent their returning and mixing with the sober part of their citizens.

These rocks lie about 15 leagues north-west of cape Roxent; or, as it is commonly called, the rock of Lisbon; which we past early the next morning. The wind, indeed, would have carried us thither sooner; but the captain was not in a hurry, as he was to lose nothing by his delay. *Tuesday*. This is a very high mountain, situated on the northern side of the mouth of the river Tajo, which rising about Madrid, in Spain, and soon becoming navigable for small craft, empties itself, after a long course, into the sea, about four leagues below Lisbon.

On the summit of the rock stands a hermitage, which is now in the possession of an Englishman, who was formerly master of a vessel trading to Lisbon; and, having changed his religion and his manners, the latter of which, at least, were none of the best, betook himself to this place, in order to do penance for his sins. He is now very old, and hath inhabited this hermitage for a great number of years, during which he hath received some countenance from the royal family; and particularly from the present queen dowager, whose piety refuses no trouble or expence by which she may make a proselyte; being used to say, that the saving one soul would repay all the endeavours of her life.

Here we waited for the tide, and had the pleasure of surveying the face of the country, the soil of which, at this season, exactly resembles an old brick kiln, or a field where the green-sward is pared up and set a-burning, or rather a-smoaking, in little heaps, to manure the land. This sight will, perhaps, of all others, make an Englishman proud of and pleased with his own country, which in verdure excels, I believe, every other country. Another deficiency here, is the want of large trees, nothing above a shrub being here to be discovered in the circumference of many miles.

At this place we took a pilot on board, who, being the first Portuguese we spoke to, gave us an instance of that religious observance which is paid by all nations to their laws: for, whereas it is here a capital offence to assist any person in going on shore from a foreign vessel, before it hath been examined, and every person in it viewed by the magistrates of health, as they are called, this worthy pilot, for a very small reward, rowed the Portuguese priest to shore at this place, beyond which he did not dare to advance; and, in venturing whither he had given sufficient testimony of love for his native country.

We did not enter the Tajo till noon, when after passing several old castles, and other buildings, which had greatly the aspect of ruins, we came to the castle of Bellisle, where we had a full prospect of Lisbon, and were indeed within three miles of it.

Here we were saluted with a gun, which was a signal to pass no farther, till we had complied with certain ceremonies, which the laws of this country require to be observed by all ships which arrive in this port. We were obliged then to cast anchor, and expect the arrival of the officers of the customs, without whose passport no ship must proceed farther than this place.

Here likewise we received a visit from one of those magistrates of health before-mentioned. He refused to come on board the ship, till every person in her had been drawn up on deck, and personally viewed by him. This occasioned some delay on my part, as it was not the work of a minute to lift me from the cabin to the deck. The captain thought my particular case might have been excused from this ceremony; and that it would be abundantly sufficient if the magistrate, who was obliged afterwards to visit the cabin, surveyed me there. But this did not satisfy the magistrate's strict regard to his duty. When he was told of my lameness, he called out, with a voice of authority, 'Let him be brought up,' and his orders were presently complied with. He was indeed a person of great dignity, as well as of the most exact fidelity in the discharge of his trust. Both which are the more admirable, as his salary is less than 30 *l*. English, *per annum*.

Before a ship hath been visited by one of those magistrates, no person can lawfully go on board her; nor can any on board depart from her. This I saw exemplified in a remarkable instance. The young lad, whom I have mentioned as one of our passengers, was here met by his father, who, on the first news of the captain's arrival, came from Lisbon to Bellisle in a boat, being eager to embrace a son whom he had not seen for many years. But when he came along-side our ship, neither did the father dare ascend, nor the son descend, as the magistrate of health had not yet been on board.

Some of our readers will, perhaps, admire the great caution of this policy, so nicely calculated for the preservation of this country from all pestilential distempers. Others will as probably regard it as too exact and formal to be constantly persisted in, in seasons of the utmost safety, as well as in times of danger. I will not decide either way; but will content myself with observing, that I never yet saw or heard of a place where a traveller had so much trouble given him at his landing as here. The only use of which, as all such matters begin and end in form only, is to put it into the power of low and mean fellows to be either rudely officious, or grossly corrupt, as they shall see occasion to prefer the gratification of their pride or of their avarice.

Of this kind, likewise, is that power which is lodged with other officers here, of taking away every grain of snuff, and every leaf of tobacco, brought hither from other countries, tho' only for the temporary use of the person, during his residence here. This is executed with great insolence, and, as it is in the hands of the dregs of the people, very scandalously: for, under pretence of searching for tobacco and snuff, they are sure to steal whatever they can find, insomuch that when they came on board, our sailors address'd us in the Covent Garden language, 'Pray, gentlemen and ladies, take care of your swords and watches.' Indeed I never yet saw any thing equal to the contempt and hatred which our honest tars every moment express'd for these Portuguese officers.

At Bellisle lies buried Catharine of Arragon, widow of Prince Arthur, eldest son of our Henry VII, afterwards married to, and divorced from, Henry VIII. Close by the church where her remains are deposited, is a large convent of Geronymites, one of the most beautiful piles of building in all Portugal.

In the evening, at twelve, our ship having received previous visits from all the necessary parties, took the advantage of the tide, and having sailed up to Lisbon, cast anchor there, in a calm, and a moonshiny night, which made the passage incredibly pleasant to the women, who remained three hours enjoying it, whilst I was left to the cooler transports of enjoying their pleasures at second-hand; and yet, cooler as they may be, whoever is totally ignorant of such sensation, is at the same time void of all ideas of friendship.

Wednesday. Lisbon, before which we now lay at anchor, is said to be built on the same number of hills with old Rome; but these do not all appear to the water; on the contrary, one sees from thence one vast high hill and rock, with buildings arising above one another, and that in so steep and almost perpendicular a manner, that they all seem to have but one foundation.

As the houses, convents, churches, &c. are large, and all built with white stone, they look very beautiful at a distance, but as you approach nearer, and find them to want every kind of ornament, all idea of beauty vanishes at once. While I was surveying the prospect of this city, which bears so little resemblance to any other that I have ever seen, a reflection occurred to me, that if a man was suddenly to be removed from Palmyra* hither; and should take a view of no other city, in how glorious a light would the antient architecture appear to him? and what desolation and destruction of arts and sciences would he conclude had happened between the several æra's of these cities?

I had now waited full three hours upon deck, for the return of my man, whom I had sent to bespeak a good dinner (a thing which had been long unknown to me) on shore, and then to bring a Lisbon chaise with him to the sea-shore; but, it seems, the impertinence of the providore* was not yet brought to a conclusion. At three o'clock, when I was, from emptiness rather faint than hungry, my man returned, and told me, there was a new law lately made, that no passenger should set his foot on shore without a special order from the providore; and that he himself would have been sent to prison for disobeying it, had he not been protected as the servant of the captain. He informed me, likewise, that the captain had been very industrious to get this order, but that it was then the providore's hour of sleep, a time when no man, except the king himself, durst disturb him.

To avoid prolixity, tho' in a part of my narrative which may be more agreeable to my reader than it was to me; the providore having at last finished his nap, dispatched this absurd matter of form, and gave me leave to come, or rather to be carried, on shore.

What it was that gave the first hint of this strange law is not easy to guess. Possibly, in the infancy of their defection,* and before their government could be well established, they were willing to guard against the bare possibility of surprize, of the success of which bare possibility the Trojan horse will remain for ever on record, as a great and memorable example. Now the Portuguese have no walls to secure them, and a vessel of two or three hundred tuns will contain a much larger body of troops than could be concealed in that famous machine, tho' Virgil tells us (somewhat hyperbolically, I believe) that it was as big as a mountain.*

About seven in the evening I got into a chaise on shore, and was driven through the nastiest city in the world, tho' at the same time one of the most populous, to a kind of coffee-house, which is very pleasantly situated on the brow of a hill, about a mile from the city, and hath a very fine prospect of the River Taio from Lisbon to the sea.

Here we regaled ourselves with a good supper, for which we were as well charged, as if the bill had been made on the Bath road, between Newbury and London.

And now we could joyfuily say,

*Egressi optata Troes potiuntur œrena.**

Therefore in the words of Horace,

*——his Finis chartæq; viæq;.**

EXPLANATORY NOTES

A Journey from This World to the Next

3 *New Bethlehem*: better known as 'Bedlam', a London madhouse.

Powney . . . Strand: Robert Powney conducted a stationer's business here between 1705 and 1753.

Bustos: busts.

4 *Abraham Adams*: Parson Abraham Adams is a central comic figure in Fielding's *Joseph Andrews*, also appearing more briefly towards the end of *Tom Jones*, and sporadically in two periodicals written by Fielding, *The True Patriot* and *The Jacobite's Journal*.

conjugate a Verb: the conjugation of 'mi' verbs is an elementary part of learning Greek.

8 *Warwick-Lane*: in 1743 Warwick-Lane housed the Royal College of Physicians, which for many patients proved to be the doorway into the next world.

9 *Great Peter*: Fielding ironically identifies the historical figure of Peter the Great with a contemporary money-lender, Peter Walter (1664?–1746). Walter may also be the basis for the character of Peter Pounce in *Joseph Andrews*.

10 *Mr Locke*: in his *Essay concerning Human Understanding* (bk. 4, ch. 11, para. 12), Locke emphatically denies that spirits are ever visible or knowable to the senses in any way.

hot Regimen: a traditional treatment for smallpox had been to raise the patient's temperature and encourage perspiration. By the 1740s, it had been replaced by the contending notion that the patient's temperature should be kept as low as possible.

13 *Tie-wigs . . . hands*: the conventional appearance of doctors of medicine.

15 *Patriots*: the 'Patriots' were one of the loosely defined political groups in opposition to Robert Walpole. Although Fielding accepts many of the emphases of this grouping, it was not the one to which he was most closely aligned. As Walpole's career drew to an end, the 'patriots' became notorious for their unseemly race for high office.

Privilege at your A——: peers enjoyed the privilege of exemption from corporal punishment.

16 *Fever on the Spirits*: a catch-all medical term used to diagnose all nervous illnesses, fashionable at this time. The fact that it cannot be found in the City of Diseases shows Fielding's distrust of such jargon.

Maladie Alamode: syphilis, all the symptoms of which are displayed by the 'Lady' below.

18 *Pill and Drop*: the 'pill' and the 'drop' were patent medicines employed by the popular 'quack' Joshua Ward (1685–1761), also mentioned in the 'Author's Introduction' to the *Journal of a Voyage to Lisbon*.

Drury . . . St James's: the Lady describes the spread of venereal disease from the brothels and stews of Drury Lane to the more salubrious parts of London.

Batchelor's Estimate: the text referred to is the controversial and popular anti-marriage pamphlet by Edward Ward, *The Batchelor's Estimate of the Expenses of a Married Life* (1725).

20 *Surfeit*: the great enemy of the 'surfeit' in contemporary medical theory was Dr George Cheyne (1671–1743), whose popular textbook *An Essay on Regimen* (1740) gave advice about the benefits of an austere and regulated diet. There had been a serious fever epidemic in London in 1741–2, which had claimed over 7,000 lives.

Vapours: another catch-call medical diagnosis, covering almost anything.

21 *that Duke*: John Churchill (1650–1722), first Duke of Marlborough, whose troops defeated those of Louis XIV in the war against France (1702–11).

22 *French Cook*: the identity of the cook remains unclear, but the most famous French chef of the day was Cloué, employed by the Duke of Newcastle.

23 *House by the Bath*: the reference is to Prior Park, the home of Fielding's friend and benefactor Ralph Allen (1693–1764).

27 *Coronet*: coronets, worn by distinguished commoners, carried conventional emblems signifying the rank and status of the wearer.

a Player and a Poet Laureate: the reference is to the actor and poet laureate Colley Cibber (1671–1757), a constant adversary of Fielding's, ridiculed mercilessly throughout the author's work.

28 *Venus*: see Virgil, *Aeneid*, ii. 605–6.

29 *Minos*: Minos, child of Zeus and Europa, appears in the *Odyssey* (xi. 568–71). A just ruler of Crete during his lifetime, he became one of the judges in Hades after his death.

30 *miserable old Spirit*: another reference to the money-lender Peter Walter, who spent time as an MP.

S——House: Peter Walter lived at Stalbridge House in Dorset.

32 *our last Lord Mayor*: at the time of writing, the most recent Lord Mayor of London had been Sir Robert Godschall (1692–1742), a political ally of Fielding's.

33 *a little Daughter*: Fielding's 5-year-old daughter Charlotte had died in March 1741/2.

celebrated Poet: Richard Glover (1712–85), who had eulogized the figure of Leonidas in an epic poem of 1737. Its anti-tyrannical stance made it very popular with the opposition, including Fielding.

Signior Piantanida: Giovanni Piantanida (1705–82) was a fashionable Italian violinist resident in London between 1739 and 1743.

34 *Madam Dacier*: Madame Anne Lefevre Dacier (1654?–1720) was a widely admired translator of the classics, including Homer.

which of the Cities: fuelled by speculation in Thomas Parnell's *Essay on the Life, Writings, and Learning of Homer* (1715), there had recently been a great deal of controversy over the exact location of Homer's birth.

Dr Trapp's: Joseph Trapp (1679–1747), Professor of Poetry at the University of Oxford, had produced a much-mocked literal translation of Virgil in 1731.

Mr Warburton: Bishop William Warburton (1698–1779) had argued in 1738 that Book 6 of the *Aeneid* should be read as a representation of the secret forms of religious worship conducted in ancient times at Eleusis near Athens.

Betterton and Booth: Thomas Betterton (1635–1710) and Barton Booth (1681–1731) were celebrated tragedians of the day. The following passage ridicules contemporary acting styles and some of the more absurd guesses of eighteenth-century editors of Shakespeare, principally Lewis Theobald, mocked more forcefully in the early editions of Pope's *Dunciad*. The reference is to a disputed passage in *Othello*, V. ii.

35 *Mr Theobald*: Lewis Theobald edited *The Works of Shakespeare* (1733), and in doing so acquired a reputation for pedantry and dullness.

Monument: the monument to Shakespeare designed by Peter Scheemakers had been erected in Westminster Abbey in February 1740/1.

36 *his Opinion*: in *Dedication to the Aeneis* (1697), Dryden argued that it was Satan, not Adam, who was the hero of Milton's *Paradise Lost*.

37 *tame Giant*: Daniel Cajanus (1703–49), known as the 'Swedish Giant', lived in London in 1734 and made a number of appearances on stage.

Charles Martel: (*c*.688–741), the grandfather of Charlemagne.

that Story: there was a well-known legend that, having granted Oliver Cromwell victory at the Battle of Worcester (1651), the devil reclaimed his soul seven years later to the day.

Battle of the Boyne: the Battle of the Boyne was fought on 1 July 1690, and saw the defeat of the followers of James II by the new monarch William III.

38 *Nolo Episcopari*: Cromwell's refusal of the crown in 1657 had recently become controversial through revisionist histories of the period. When offered a bishopric, a supplicant traditionally responds with the ritual rejection '*nolo episcopari*'. It is a purely formal statement, disguising genuine ambition.

Hooke . . . Echard's: in 1738, the first volume of Richard Hooke's *Roman History from the Building of Rome to the Ruin of the Commonwealth* was published, replacing the earlier, unpopular work by Laurence Echard, *Roman History* (1695, 1698).

Leibnitz: the superstitiousness of Livy had become a recurrent topic of controversy, most notably in an acerbic exchange between the English writer John Toland and the German philosopher Gottfried Leibniz published in 1726.

Julian: Julian the Apostate is Fielding's version of the Roman emperor Flavius Claudius Julianus (331–63), famous for his conversion to paganism. Julian had been demonized by earlier Christian writers, but by Fielding's time his reputation was being recovered, and he had come to be seen by Montaigne and Shaftesbury, among others, as an unusually mild and temperate ruler.

39 *Arch-Bishop Latimer*: Hugh Latimer (1485?–1555), Bishop of Worcester, a Protestant martyr burned at the stake for heresy.

Emperor Valens: the East Roman Emperor Valens (364–78) permitted the Goths into Thrace in 376. As Julian goes on to recount, they were then allowed to starve there, ignored by corrupt local Roman generals.

42 *St Chrysostome*: St John Chrysostom (*c*.307–407), Archbishop of Constantinople, was the famously ascetic Greek Father of the Church.

46 *Hypatia*: (370?–415), a neoplatonist mathematician in Alexandria. Christian hostility to her views led to her apprehension, torture, and eventual burning at the stake.

Athenais: married Emperor Theodosius II (401–50) in 421.

48 *His . . . pono*: 'for these I set neither bounds nor periods of empire' (*Aeneid*, i. 278).

Zeno: Zeno Augustus was Emperor of the East between 474 and 491, notorious for his debauched court. His reign was briefly interrupted by usurpation, but he resumed power in 476. 'Eutyches' cannot be identified and may be Fielding's invention.

Martian: Marcian led an unsuccessful rebellion against Zeno in 479.

49 *Theodoric*: Theodoric, King of the Ostrogoths (*c*.454–526), was one of Zeno's military commanders.

50 *Anastasius*: with the help of Zeno's widow Ariadne, Anastasius I (*c*.430–518) succeeded him to the throne.

51 *Belarius . . . Gelimer*: the famous general Belarius (*c*.505–65) defeated Gelimer, king of the Vandals, in 533. Led captive back to Constantinople to appear before the Emperor, Gelimer is said to have delivered this verse from Ecclesiastes.

52 *Saltator*: 'dancer' (Latin).

Ficus: according to Bertrand A. Goldgar, 'Ficus' may be a play upon the name of the well-known swordsman James Figg (d. 1734). See *Miscellanies by Henry Fielding, Esq.*, ii, ed. B. A. Goldgar (The Wesleyan Edition of the Works of Henry Fielding; Oxford, 1993), 60.

53 *Monk*: Julian is here transformed into a version of the historical personage Theodotus (d. 695), who lived as a monk during the reign of Justinian II. Although Fielding artificially prolongs his life until at least 705, his career broadly fits the pattern described.

banished: Justinian was overthrown and banished in 695 after a coup organized by one of his generals, Leontius. In 698 Leontius was deposed by Apsimar, later crowned Emperor Tiberius III. He in turn was executed when Justinian returned to power in 705.

55 *Pope Gregory II*: held the papacy from 715 until 731.

61 *Air of Decorum*: Roman widows were required by law to refrain from remarrying until the statutory period of mourning—usually defined as one year—had elapsed.

63 *grand Climacteric*: a critical point in human life, when a person is liable to drastic changes. This was sometimes defined as the period

between 45 and 60, sometimes as the sixty-third year, and sometimes as the eighty-first year. Fielding exploits the ambiguities to create uncertainty about his character's age.

63 *Ne . . . te*: a traditional maxim, usually translated as 'Do not rely on others to do something you can manage by yourself.'

64 *King*: Fielding here identifies Julian with the character of King Ramiro I of Asturias and Leon, a ninth-century Spanish monarch, drawing on the account of his career in Juan de Marina's *General History of Spain* (1699). Ramiro took up office on the death of Alfonso in 843.

66 *Mauregas*: (d. 788), a pretender to the throne who enlisted the support of the Moors by promising an annual payment of 100 virgins.

Alvelda: the battle of Alveda took place in 844.

70 *Charles the Simple*: (879–929), ruled France between 898 and 923.

Paris, Domitian: Paris, a dancer, was a great favourite of the Roman emperor Domitian. What the text ironically does not mention is that in AD 87 Domitian had Paris executed for having an affair with the empress.

71 *Hebert . . . Charles*: this passage is an oblique account of the turmoil and court rivalry which led to the assassination of the Archbishop of Reims in AD 900.

76 *Rascallion*: an inferior animal.

Obolus . . . talent: an obolus is a trifling coin, and a talent is a substantial one worth 36,000 times more.

78 *considerable Part*: Julian here becomes Godwin, Earl of the West Saxons (d. 1053), under the reign of Edward the Confessor, as described in Paul Rapin de Throyas's *History of England* (1732).

81 *Norman Archbishop of Canterbury*: Robert of Jumièges was controversially made Archbishop of Canterbury in 1051.

84 *Pemesey*: William (later 'the Conqueror') landed at Pevensey on 28 September 1066, fought the Battle of Hastings on 14 October, and was crowned king at Westminster on Christmas Day.

88 *Philip*: King Philip I of France attacked Normandy in 1073.

89 *King Stephen*: King Stephen (1097?–1154) was crowned in 1135, one year before the Battle of Cardigan.

92 *Richard*: King Richard I was imprisoned abroad during the Crusades, allowing his regent John to make efforts to seize power.

93 *William Fitz-Osborn*: William Fitzosbert was hanged for sedition in 1196.

Queen Eleanor: Eleanor of Aquitaine (1122?–1204) was trying to fund the ransom for her son Richard.

94 *Calamities*: in 1212 John was excommunicated from the Catholic Church after a long feud with Pope Innocent III. He returned to the Church in 1213, with some reluctance, paying the papal legate Pandulph 1,000 marks annually thereafter.

97 *Pope Alexander IV*: under the papal name of Alexander IV, Rinaldo Conti waged a campaign against Manfred, ruler of Sicily between 1254 and 1261.

98 *Mundanos . . . Parente*: the translation offered by B. A. Goldgar in the 1993 Wesleyan edition reads: 'The deadly machine scales the walls of the world, stuffed with squadrons of priests: from there they all seemed to exit through the belly, redolent with a mighty rumble—not otherwise than when a frenzied noise emanates from human caverns, and a gust at the same time assaults gaping nostrils. A thousand spew forth, and another thousand; the heathen begin to tremble with fear; false gods fled flying through the void—they abandon their deserted temples. Now the horse rumbled mightily; then the world and the heavens on high groaned; then last of all, O Father, almighty Alexander, ripe you forsake the horse's womb, O thou offspring worthy of a better parent.'

Horace: the *ingens Solitudo* (vast solitude) actually comes from an epigram by Martial, where it is seen as the natural habitat of poets.

99 *Si . . . Mali*: 'For if you would give it up, the habit of ambitious evil holds you fast as with a noose' (Juvenal, *Satires*, vii. 50–2).

100 *Philip de Valois*: took on the regency of France in 1328 when Charles IV died without leaving a male heir to the throne. He was later crowned Philip VI and reigned until 1350.

101 *Borées . . . Coupées*: elaborate dance steps.

102 *Honour*: in keeping with Fielding's Protestant historiography, his version of Anne Boleyn explicitly takes sides against the Catholic demonizing which presented her as the architect of the Reformation, emphasizing instead her generosity. He also takes the orthodox Protestant line on a number of other controversial matters, including the date of Anne's return to England from France and the nature of her relationship with Henry Percy.

113 *Country Seat*: Anne's return to the family home at Hever took place in September 1528.

The Lady Mary: Mary Tudor (1516–58), who reigned as Queen Mary between 1553 and 1558.

115 *Coronation*: the marriage is thought to have taken place in January 1532/3, and Anne was crowned on 1 June 1533.

116 *his new Love*: Jane Seymour (1509?–37).

Chamber: the date of committal is 2 May 1536 and the 'Lady' is Elizabeth Wood.

low Fellows: in a string of executions, the 'low Fellows'—Francis Weston, Henry Norris, William Brererton, and Mark Smeton and George Boleyn, Anne's brother, were beheaded on 17 May 1536. Two days later Anne herself was executed.

The Journal of a Voyage to Lisbon

121 *Dedication*: probably contributed by Fielding's first biographer, Arthur Murphy.

122 *fragment . . . Bolingbroke*: not included in this edition.

123 *Preface*: like the *Introduction*, composed by Fielding during his residence in Lisbon.

124 *Gray . . . Mead*: Grey's scholarly edition of Butler's satirical poem *Hudibras* was published in 1744. Dr Richard Mead died in 1754, leaving a library of 10,000 volumes, including many learned, rare, and esoteric items.

125 *Burnet and Addison*: Gilbert Burnet and Joseph Addison wrote memoirs of European travels in the late seventeenth and early eighteenth centuries, when travel-writing was coming into vogue.

Longinus: refers to a first- or second-century AD Greek work of literary criticism by an unknown author who rated the *Iliad* above the *Odyssey*. It is always known as *Longinus on the Sublime*.

the Telemachus: Fénélon's prose romance *Les Aventures de Télémaque* (1699). The first four books of Homer's *Odyssey* tell of Telemachus' roving quest for his father Odysseus.

Hesiod: early post-Homeric Greek poet. Fielding is probably thinking of the narrative poem *The Shield of Heracles*, not now thought to be by Hesiod.

126 *Ut . . . promant*: adapted from Horace, *Ars Poetica*, 144: 'In order that they might thence present astonishing wonders'.

127 *Mrs Behn's . . . Mrs Centlivre's*: Fielding is probably conflating *The Feign'd Curtezans* by Aphra Behn and *Mar-Plot; or, the Second Part of the Busie-Body* (1711) by Susannah Centlivre.

128 *my lord Anson*: Anson's *Voyage Round the World* (1748) was commended by the *Gentleman's Magazine* for its 'regard to truth'.

Horace: the recommendation of Horace, the first-century BC Latin poet, to writers to combine profit and delight (*utile dulci*) was a touchstone of eighteenth-century aesthetics.

129 *If . . . first*: Fielding is mocking the preface Richardson wrote commending his own highly moralizing novel *Pamela* (1740). Addison's *Spectator*, 85, describes finding a page of a distinguished book wrapping up 'a Christmas pie'.

the rehearsal: *The Rehearsal*, popular comedy (1672) by George Villiers, Duke of Buckingham.

130 *The Duke of Portland's medicine . . . Mr Ranby*: the medicine was a compound of powdered roots. Mr Ranby was a well-known practitioner; there is a reference to him in *Tom Jones*, viii. 13.

the Duke of Newcastle: Thomas Pelham Holles, first Duke of Newcastle, held various high offices of state in the ministries of Walpole and of his younger brother Henry Pelham.

132 *dropsy*: Battestin, *Henry Fielding: A Life* (1989), 577, attributes Fielding's 'dropsy' (oedema) to cirrhosis of the liver, normally caused by heavy drinking.

134 *duke of Marlborough*: the enormous and extravagant Blenheim Palace was constructed (1705–25) at the nation's expense for John Churchill, Duke of Marlborough, in recognition of his victory over the French at Blenheim in 1704.

135 *Dr Ward*: although Joshua Ward was recognized as a quack his 'pill and drop' had nevertheless either effected some remarkable cures or coincided with some unexpected recoveries. See also *Journey*, note to p. 18.

Mr Pelham: the Prime Minister Henry Pelham died on 6 March 1754.

136 *bishop . . . tar-water*: Bishop Berkeley's *Siris* (1744) commended the medicinal properties of tar-water, an infusion of tar in water.

the Female Quixote: the abilities of Charlotte Lennox (1720–1804), whose *The Female Quixote; or, The Adventures of Arabella* (1752) Fielding greatly admired, were in fact widely recognized. Dr Johnson wrote dedications for her.

Sydenham: Thomas Sydenham, author of *Treatise of the Gout and Dropsy* (1683).

137 *trochar*: properly spelt *trocar*. Combining a perforator and a tube, it was used for draining excess fluids from the body.

138 *so immense a trade*: the extensive trade with Portugal, and the subsequent popularity of port drinking, was established by the Treaty of Methuen, 1703.

the captain: identified as 'Richd. Veal' by Fielding in the heading of a letter of 12 July 1754 to his brother John. See Martin C. Battestin and Clive T. Probyn, *The Correspondence of Henry and Sarah Fielding* (Oxford: Clarendon Press, 1993), 104. There is a full account of Veal(e) in *The Journal of a Voyage to Lisbon*, ed. Keymer, app. II.

140 *my eldest daughter*: Eleanor Harriet, Fielding's daughter by his first wife, Charlotte Craddock.

Redriffe: now known as Rotherhithe.

contra bonum publicum: against the public good.

141 *Archimedes . . . footing*: Archimedes, explaining the principle of leverage, says 'Give me somewhere to stand [a fulcrum], and I will move the earth.'

wherries: not large sailing barges as now, but small rowing-boats or skiffs for goods and passengers.

gauntlope: gauntlope or gantlope was the original form of 'gauntlet', for the military punishment for running between two rows of men armed with sticks or cords.

142 *bashaw*: early form of 'pasha', a high-ranking Turkish official, but generalized to apply to any functionary exercising despotic authority.

Thursday, June 27 . . . pleasure: in this paragraph 'Humphrys' (see Note on the Texts) substitutes a bland and truncated account of the delay.

Hogarth: the engraving 'The Enraged Musician' (1741) by Fielding's friend, the painter and engraver William Hogarth (1697–1764), whose satirical and moral imagination had much in common with Fielding's own.

143 *Don Quixotte*: Fielding greatly admired Cervantes's satirical romance about Don Quixote's self-appointed mission to re-enact the histories of chivalric adventure, and was much influenced by its manner and spirit.

honourable societies . . . members: Fielding's derisive attitude to the Society of Antiquaries of London, formally established in 1751, is a manifestation of a long-running mockery in eighteenth-century literature of antiquarians, connoisseurs, and virtuosi who amassed collections of inconsequential curiosities.

144 *King of Prussia*: this reference may be designed to reflect unfavourably on the Hanoverian George II.

145 *Mr Montesquieu*: Montesquieu's *De l'Esprit des Lois* (1748) analysed various kinds of political constitution and advocated liberal, benevolent monarchy.

146 *English wife . . . them*: married Englishwomen had, in essence, no legal existence or rights independent of their husbands throughout the eighteenth century.

147 *prisoners and captives*: refers to the Church of England Litany in the Book of Common Prayer: 'That it may please thee to preserve all those that travel by land or by water, all women labouring of child, all sick persons, and young children; and to shew thy pity upon all prisoners and captives'.

privateer: a privately owned vessel with a government commission authorizing the owners to use it against an enemy, and especially against merchant shipping. There was felt to be only a very fine line between privateering and piracy.

Sir Courtly Nice . . . Surly: characters in John Crowne's comedy *Sir Courtly Nice, or It Cannot Be* (1685). The 'Humphrys' version of this paragraph (see Note on the Texts) removes all reflections on the captain's pretensions to be a gentleman.

148 *the play*: George Farquhar's popular comedy *The Beaux' Stratagem* (1707).

149 *the Downs*: the area of sea between the east coast of Kent and the Goodwin Sands.

Royal Anne . . . a first rate: the *Royal Anne* was built in 1704 and, though very large, was not in fact the largest ship ever built. The *Royal Sovereign* (1701) was over 150 tons larger and carried more men and guns.

150 *Battle of La Val . . . glory*: after defeat at the Battle of Lafeldt (La Val) in 1747 the Duke of Cumberland conducted the retreat to Maastricht that Fielding refers to flatteringly here.

151 *Royal Hospital*: designed by Sir Christopher Wren. Building began in 1694.

152 *Nocet . . . voluptas*: Horace, *Epistles*, I. ii. 55: 'Pleasure bought by pain is harmful.'

153 *beautiful holders . . . heart*: 'Oh! There's nothing so charming as admirable teeth. If a lady fastens upon my heart it must be with her teeth.' Crowne, *Sir Courtly Nice*, IV.

154 *Robin Hood society*: a free-thinking debating society in London which comprised lower professionals and tradesmen in its membership. There is a snobbish element in Fielding's mockery.

a young lady: Jane Collier, whose sister Margaret sailed with the Fieldings.

156 *Plato, de Leg. . . .* : the *Laws* was the last work of the Greek philosopher Plato (*c.*427–348 BC). There is a wide range of references to Plato's thought and work in Fielding.

alma mater: the title 'bounteous mother' was originally applied by the Romans to the generative and natural goddesses Ceres and Cybele. Fielding's application of the title to trade reflects a deep and widespread feeling about its human and social value in the eighteenth century.

157 *the Nore*: near Sheerness on the northern Kent coast.

an island: no longer.

160 *a great lady*: Lady Anson, the First Lord's wife, was the daughter of the Lord Chancellor, to whom Fielding had dedicated *An Enquiry into the Causes of the Late Increase of Robbers* (1751), and so there was in fact a very slight connection for him to try to exploit.

162 *Mr Addison's observation*: Addison's allusion to *King Lear*, IV. vi occurs in *Tatler*, 117.

beat the sea: to 'beat the sea', or simply 'to beat', in a sailing vessel is to attempt to make progress against the wind with a series of diagonal movements. Early sailing vessels were square-rigged and much less effective at this than modern ones, which is why so much time is spent on this voyage waiting for favourable winds.

163 *island*: 'Humphrys' continues this paragraph with a flattering reference to the captain's seamanship.

bear it like one: an allusion to *Macbeth*, IV. iii. 219–21:

MALCOLM. Dispute it like a man.
MACDUFF. I shall do so
But I must also feel it as a man.

threshing: common early spelling of 'thrashing'. It implies wildness, but not necessarily that the captain is the victor.

165 *a large hoy*: small sailing vessel used for the coastwise transport of passengers and goods.

Omnia . . . Ponto: Ovid, *Metamorphoses*, i. 292: 'Everywhere there were waters, and there were no shores to the waters.'

a bubble: a dupe.

166 *Mrs Francis*: see 'Note on the Text'. Her real name was Ann Francis. For biographical information see Battestin, *Henry Fielding: A Life*, 589 n. 382.

169 *White's*: an early eighteenth-century chocolate house which had by mid-century turned into a club famous for gastronomy.

charde . . . perigord-pye . . . ortolan: charde: a dish prepared with artichokes. Perigord-pye: made of meat and truffles, originating in Périgord in France. Ortolan: a small delicate-flavoured bird, now the garden- or ortolan-bunting.

Hern: Thomas Hearne (1678–1735), author and editor of works of antiquarian history.

170 *five people, and two servants*: in fact four 'people' (Fielding and his wife and daughter and his wife's companion) and two servants (the manservant William and the lady's maid Isabella Ash). Cf. numbers and phrasing at p. 206.

171 *This wind . . . any other*: these facetious paragraphs about the vulgar confusion of 'wine' and 'wind' comprise several strands, but include allusion to the oratorical 'wind' generated at parliamentary elections, which by the Septennial Act of 1716 had to occur at least every seven years.

172 *grand climacteric*: commonly taken as the age of 63. Years that were multiples of seven, and sometimes of nine as well, were considered climacteric. The grand climacteric is thus 7 × 9 years. Fielding does not here exploit the ambiguity mentioned in the note to *Journey*, p. 63.

Cornaro: Luigi Cornaro, Italian author whose sixteenth-century work on temperance, written in extreme old age, had recently appeared in an English translation by T. Smith as *A Treatise on the Benefits of a Sober Life* (1742).

173 *Cheney, Arbuthnot . . . Dictionary*: Dr George Cheyne and Dr John Arbuthnot were well-known medical practitioners and authors. Dr Robert James was the author of a *Medicinal Dictionary*, 3 vols., 1743–5.

attorney: the Attorney-General, Sir Dudley Ryder.

Diodorus Siculus: Sicilian compiler of a 40-book history of the world. Written in Greek in the first century BC, it assembled very diverse material from mythological times up to Julius Caesar's conquest of Gaul.

174 *Quin . . . hand*: alludes to the keen rivalry between the contemporary actors James Quin and Charles Macklin.

Mr Derham . . . industrious: the Revd William Derham, eighteenth-century naturalist, had a long note on the stings of wasps or bees in his then well-known *Physico-Theology* (1713).

176 *the light . . . own estate*: a duty on windows was levied from 1695 until 1851.

Lucian: second-century AD satirical author. Fielding found his wit and his distaste for hypocrisy and pretence highly congenial.

177 *one of the comedies of Plautus*: *Poenulus*, a minor comedy of the Roman comic dramatist Plautus, features some speeches apparently in the Carthaginian (Punic) language.

178 *serjeant at arms*: an official of the House of Commons charged with enforcing its commands.

179 *vagrant act*: the Vagrancy Laws were revised several times in the eighteenth century. Fielding refers to the revision of 1744, which established the law for the next 78 years.

spunges and raps: extorts and snatches.

180 *Sir William Petyt . . . Political Arithmetic*: Austen Dobson (Fielding, *Complete Works*, ed. Henley, iii. 298) identifies this as a reference to the last chapter of the posthumous edition (1691) of Sir William Petty's *Political Arithmetic*, which commends England's potential 'to drive the Trade of the whole Commercial World'.

182 *Superanda . . . est*: Virgil, *Aeneid*, v. 70: 'every fortune is to be overcome by bearing it'.

183 *mundungus*: foul-smelling tobacco.

Tajo: the river Tagus.

185 *Denham . . . Pope*: Sir John Denham's topographical poem *Cooper's Hill* (1642) and Pope's *Windsor-Forest* (1713) both contain passages celebrating the Thames.

187 *extents*: seizure of property in the execution of a writ, normally for debt.

188 *Gibraltar and Minorca*: both ceded to Britain by Spain in the Treaty of Utrecht (1713). From this point on, for the first four paragraphs of this day's journal 'Humphrys' substitutes a brief and innocuous account of the nephew's visit, together with some remarks about the present contentedness of British troops stationed in Gibraltar and Minorca.

191 *a perfect hurricane*: before the devising of the Beaufort Scale for the measurement of wind strengths in 1805, terms like 'gale' and 'hurricane' were approximate and descriptive rather than exact.

194 *Circe*: in *Odyssey*, x, the sensual enchantress Circe laces Odysseus' shipmates' wine with a memory-obliterating drug and turns them into swine.

Ars Cauponaria . . . Metabletic . . . Chrematistic: respectively, the innkeeper's trade; concerning exchange or barter; money-making.

195 *Calipash and Calipee*: these were the upper and lower shells of the turtle, containing delicious meat. See *Tom Jones*, I. i: 'The tortoise . . . besides the delicious calibash and calipee, contains many different kinds of food.'

Dr South . . . wash: refers to a sermon on 'The ways of wisdom are the ways of pleasantness' (Proverbs, 3: 7) by the Revd Robert South (1634–1711).

196 *Mark Anthony in Dryden . . . aut modus*: Fielding's memory seems to be conflating 'As if increase of appetite had grown | By what it fed on' (*Hamlet*, I. ii. 145–6), 'Other women cloy | The appetite they feed, but she makes hungry | Where most she satisfies;' (*Antony and Cleopatra*, II. ii. 241–3), and the passage in Dryden's *All For Love*, III. i beginning 'There's no satiety of love in thee; | Enjoyed, thou art still new'. The Latin is an adaptation from Horace, *Odes*, I. xxiv. 1, and means 'as if there should be neither shame nor measure in such a desire'.

198 *Bear key*: a quay on the Thames in London.

199 *an alehouse in Drury-lane*: alehouses in Drury Lane were notorious as resorts for prostitution.

200 *Axylus*: a very minor character in *Iliad*, vi, notable only for being hospitable. He is killed by Diomedes.

Cibber . . . Dunciad: Colley Cibber, made Poet Laureate in 1730, is crowned King of Dulness in the final version of Pope's satirical poem *The Dunciad* (1743).

201 *Mammon . . . Quin . . . Epicureans*: Sir Epicure Mammon is a character in Jonson's *The Alchemist*; Quin is the eighteenth-century actor. The school of Epicurus (341–270 BC), who emphasized the importance of sense experience and of pleasure (though not the exclusive concentration on self-indulgence associated with Epicureanism), was in fact located in gardens; hence Fielding's remark.

Macklin: the proprietor of an eating-house opened in the Grand Piazza, Covent Garden, in March 1754.

203 *bills of mortality*: a metonym for London, referring to the publication of periodical returns of numbers of deaths in individual parishes and districts.

Cuncta . . . cuncta . . . Westminster market: *Cuncta prius tentanda*: all means are to be tried first; *cuncta prius tentata*: all means having been tried. Westminster market: an unsuccessful project designed to circumvent the fish-trade monopoly.

204 *cabin*: the whole of the following spirited episode, including the reflections on the captain's use of the word 'pitiful', and right down to the beginning of the next day's journal, is omitted in 'Humphrys'.

Peter Taylor . . . honest port: a Peter Taylor, a silversmith, was a long-standing friend of Fielding's; *led captain*: a hanger-on or parasite; *postpone*: treat as inferior to. If Taylor is associated with the port-wine trade, as the context implies, this complex sentence refers to a sales ploy of Taylor's to induce the susceptible to reject, by distinguishing it by the name of champagne, another kind of wine in favour of port.

206 *six persons, (two of them servants)*: cf. p. 170 and note.

207 *kennel*: surface drain down the middle of a street, for all kinds of waste material.

211 *Sir Matthew Hale . . . witchcraft*: Lord Chief Justice Hale had two women executed for witchcraft in 1665.

213 *Nautica fides . . . Punica fides*: 'sailors' faith'; 'Punic faith'. The Romans used the concept of 'Punic faith' ironically to describe the untrustworthiness of the Carthaginians. The phrase was used by the first-century BC historian Sallust, but became proverbial.

214 *melioribus avibus*: with more favourable omens (literally, 'with better birds').

216 *Lat. 47°4'*: about level with the southern coast of Brittany.

217 *Virgil's . . . storm*: see next note.

218 *that very wind*: in Virgil's *Aeneid*, i, Juno, knowing that a Trojan race will later threaten her beloved Carthage, incites Aeolus to let loose a storm on Aeneas's ships; some are wrecked, and the fleet is scattered.

219 *snow*: small two-masted ship.

Porte: Porto, in northern Portugal, about 170 miles north of Lisbon.

the Burlings: the Berlenga Islands, about 50 miles north of Lisbon.

223 *Palmyra*: ancient Syrian city, of which only its famous ruins remained following its destruction after the defeat of Queen Zenobia.

providore: presumably from Portuguese *provedor*, 'purveyor'. He evidently acted as harbour-master and/or customs officer; cf. Portuguese *providenciar*, 'to make arrangements'.

224 *their defection*: Portuguese independence of Spain, attained in the seventeenth century.

Virgil tells us: *Aeneid*, ii. 15.

Egressi . . . aerena: Virgil, *Aeneid*, i. 172: 'Having disembarked the Trojans took possession of the longed-for sands.'

hic . . . viaeq;: Horace, *Satires*, I. v. 104: 'this is the end of the story and of the journey'.